A Name Unknown

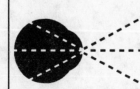

This Large Print Book carries the
Seal of Approval of N.A.V.H.

SHADOWS OVER ENGLAND, BOOK 1

A NAME UNKNOWN

ROSEANNA M. WHITE

THORNDIKE PRESS
A part of Gale, a Cengage Company

Farmington Hills, Mich • San Francisco • New York • Waterville, Maine
Meriden, Conn • Mason, Ohio • Chicago

Copyright © 2017 by Roseanna M. White.
Thorndike Press, a part of Gale, a Cengage Company.

ALL RIGHTS RESERVED
This is a work of fiction. Names, characters, places, and incidents are products of the author's imagination or are used fictitiously. Any resemblance to actual events or persons, living or dead, is entirely coincidental.
Thorndike Press® Large Print Christian Historical Fiction.
The text of this Large Print edition is unabridged.
Other aspects of the book may vary from the original edition.
Set in 16 pt. Plantin.

LIBRARY OF CONGRESS CATALOGING-IN-PUBLICATION DATA

Names: White, Roseanna M., 1982— author.
Title: A name unknown / by Roseanna M. White.
Description: Large print editon. | Waterville, Maine : Thorndike Press, a part of Gale, a Cengage Company 2017. | Series: Shadows over England ; #1 | Series: Thorndike Press large print Christian historical fiction
Identifiers: LCCN 2017029030| ISBN 9781432842123 (hardcover) | ISBN 1432842129 (hardcover)
Subjects: LCSH: Man-woman relationships—Fiction. | Women spies—Fiction. | Large type books. | BISAC: FICTION / Christian / Romance. | GSAFD: Christian fiction. | Love stories.
Classification: LCC PS3623.H578785 N36 2017b | DDC 813/.6—dc23
LC record available at https://lccn.loc.gov/2017029030

Published in 2017 by arrangement with Bethany House Publishers, a division of Baker Publishing Group

Printed in the United States of America
1 2 3 4 5 6 7 21 20 19 18 17

To Mom and Dad,
who named me Roseanna
To Nanny, who named me Banana Boat
To Brittney, who named me Annie
To Jennifer, who named me Pooky
To David, who named me Hunny
To Xoë and Rowyn,
who named me Mommy
To Stephanie, who named me Ro
And to the Lord, who whispered
in my ear, "Mine."
The sweetest name of all.

ONE

London
May 1914

Rosemary Gresham may have been a thief, but she was a thief who preferred to work in broad daylight. Pulling her coat more tightly around her middle, she stopped in one circle of streetlight outside the park and looked toward the next. Perhaps it was that she knew all too well what could hide in the darkness. Perhaps it was because she had spent too many nights overwhelmed by it as a child, huddling in a dark alley and praying to a deaf God that her parents would live again.

She ought to have protested when Mr. V designated this meeting place at such an hour. Ought to have . . . but hadn't been quite that brave. She had completed two successful small jobs for the man before, but she still knew nothing about him. Nothing but that he paid promptly, in pounds sterling. That he was of average height, average build. That he spoke with the careful cadence of a man who had worked hard to obliterate his natural accent.

A hack drove by, the horse's hooves *clip-clopping.* One street over, an automobile rumbled along. From a flat somewhere nearby came the smell of cooking onions . . . and the sound of raised voices. Rosemary drew in a long breath and walked toward the next light. Not so quickly that she would look afraid. Not so slowly that she would look lost or without purpose.

"Miss Gresham."

She didn't like the dark, but she knew how to use it as well as the next thief. Without so much as a flinch or start, she stepped outside the circle of golden light, summoning a tight smile. "Mr. V."

He stood beside a darkened bench. As he had during their meetings, he wore a bowler on his head, a crisp tie under his coat. His clothes were of good quality but without the flair or ostentatiousness of those with more wealth than taste. The hair peeking out from under his hat was a silver-gold that spoke of age and . . . heritage?

Rosemary's stomach went tight. He could very well be a German. Not that she had any particular loyalty to her own country, which had ground her under its very heel — but she had more loyalty to it than to any other, she supposed.

Mr. V stretched out an arm to indicate the bench.

She approached it but declined the invitation to sit. He wouldn't, and she wasn't much for being hovered over. Were it any other client, she would have issued a sharp, quiet *Make this quick.*

Such words were unnecessary, she had learned, with Mr. V. He acknowledged her denial with a nod and reached into his inner pocket. A moment later he pulled out an envelope identical to the other two he'd given her in the last year.

Rosemary took it, extracted from her handbag the letter opener she'd brought for just this occasion, and slit the top of the envelope. The sheet of paper inside contained the name *Peter Holstein* and a direction in Cornwall. "This is where I'm to go?"

"Indeed." Mr. V had folded his hands in front of him now and looked carved from stone, yet somehow completely at ease. "I need you to gain access to his home and discover his loyalties."

She tucked the direction into her handbag, working hard not to let her puzzlement show. "Need I remind you of my expertise, sir? I am no mind-reader. I get *things.*"

"And the *thing* I need just now is information — are you telling me I've hired the wrong girl?"

Her shoulders edged back. He paid well, she reminded herself. And promptly. "It's simply not where my experience lies. I'm a thief, not a spy. You'll need to tell me what exactly I'm looking for."

With a nod, Mr. V slid a step closer, no doubt so he could speak in a whisper. "Mr. Holstein has the ear of the king. Certain parties are most eager to ascertain whether he is filling those ears with ideas for or against Germany."

Which parties were eager? English ones or German ones? But she didn't ask, just nodded. "So you need . . . documents?"

"Hard evidence proving him a traitor to England. We cannot move without hard evidence, you understand."

There, then, a physical thing. Papers. Letters. Telegrams, perhaps. *Things.* She could deal with things. "Right."

"They could be in German — you read it, I understand. That is why I've come to you."

The hair on the back of her neck stood up. How would he have known that? How *could* he have? She'd only learned it to complete that museum job three years ago.

Had he somehow been behind that one too, and she'd not known it?

If so, he hadn't paid as well as he had been lately.

And she couldn't afford to ask such questions. Certainly couldn't afford to mention the missing manuscript from the British Museum. If he *didn't* know, it would be a fool thing to tell him. It still ranked as the biggest job she had ever pulled off — well, she and Barclay.

She simply nodded in response to his question. "I apparently have a bit of a knack for languages. It won't be a problem. How long have I?"

Mr. V nodded as well. "You should plan on going to Cornwall within the fortnight. Take however long you need, but be aware that if war is declared, we must act quickly. When that eventuality comes to pass, you will have but days to get me the documents. Send them to the same direction you did last time." He held out a second envelope. "You will need appropriate clothing, no doubt. And perhaps other supplies. Contact me for anything you require."

She took the second envelope and opened it. Her eyes bulged. One hundred pounds — twice what most people made in a year. Twice what he'd paid her for the last job.

"You're paying me up front?"

"That, my dear, is just a down payment. Pull this off and there will be another nine hundred coming."

"Nine . . ." A thousand pounds. She'd never dealt with a number that large, with so many zeroes. The things the family could do with that much! She swallowed, nodded.

Mr. V took a step back, where the shadows cloaked him again. "A good-faith deposit, Miss Gresham. Assuring us both of continued partnership in the future. I have many more tasks for you after this one, if you can pull this off."

More coming? Tamping down a smile, Rosemary turned. No farewell, no more questions. She knew better. When someone hired her, it was because they needed her particular set of skills, which meant they lacked them on their own. He wasn't the one to help her think of how to accomplish the task. But she knew who would.

Though she listened for them, she didn't hear his footsteps move away. The heels of her pumps clicked on the bricks of the walk, though, as she left the park and strode down the familiar London streets. The nearest tube stop was just ahead, around the corner. She hurried toward it, mind whirring.

She couldn't think of those unnamed

future jobs, not yet. She must focus on this one. How was she to gain entrance to the house of a wealthy gent? Apply for a position, perhaps? But no, then she would answer to a housekeeper. She needed a way in that would leave her independent. And yet gain her access to all his private papers — a tall order indeed.

She bought a ticket at the counter, turned away from the booth, and headed for the platform. Shadows lurked there too, but she ignored them and let this newest puzzle crease her brow. She needed to learn more about Holstein. About his house in Cornwall. The answers usually came with enough research.

A jerk jarred her shoulder as someone caught her handbag, yanking it off. Perhaps most women would have cried out in alarm. Rosemary instead caught the strap with reflexes born of necessity, spun, and prepared to deliver a punch to the would-be mugger's jugular.

Until she caught his outline in the bit of lamplight that reached them. "Georgie! What the devil are you about?"

The young man — not a day over seventeen by her estimation, though he hadn't a clue as to his actual birth date — gave a sheepish laugh. "Oh, Rosie, I didn't realize . . . is that a new hat you're wearing? It changes your look."

She jerked her bag out of his hand and scowled at him as she fancied a mother would. Her voice pitched low. "And what are you doing out here, haunting the tube station this time of night? We've talked about this. You'll get nothing worth getting at this hour."

Georgie shrugged and looked away, hands in his faded pockets. "I had no luck earlier, so . . ."

"So if you're determined to change that luck, you —"

"Miss, are you all right?" A stranger jogged her way, the glow of the streetlight casting his frown in gold. He wore a frayed jacket, had worn spots on the knees of his trousers. If he carried anything in his pockets, it wouldn't be more than a few shillings. Not worth the effort of picking them — which she had *told* Georgie repeatedly. Apparently this bloke had an inclination to be a hero, though. "I thought I saw this lad attack you."

Rosemary smiled and tucked her hand through the crook of Georgie's arm. "Just my brother joking with me, sir. Though I do thank you for your concern."

The stranger paused a few steps away, still

frowning. Glanced from Rosemary to Georgie and back again as if searching for a confirming resemblance in the low light. Apparently he decided he had no reason to doubt her word. With a nod, he moved off.

"Hmm. I could pick him easy enough. Do you think he —"

"No." She took her arm from Georgie's and then gripped his elbow to steer him away from the station. "We don't prey on the poor; they're in worse shape than we are. How many times must I tell you that? If you want to change your luck, Georgie, you have to know where to focus your efforts." She paused at the edge of the walk and nodded across the street, to where a hired cab was parked. And had been since she got *off* the tube to meet with Mr. V. "I've seen a gent go inside that building before. He stays for about an hour and then leaves. Always uses a cab, but he's well dressed."

Georgie breathed a laugh. "And I bet a pretty miss has a flat there, eh?"

"No doubt. You want a worthwhile mark tonight, little brother, you wait for him to come out. I bet his wallet is fair to bursting."

With an enthusiastic nod, Georgie said, "I can do that. Thank you, Rosie. And, ah . . . are you heading to meet the family, then?"

Rosemary loosed his elbow and folded her arms, well able to imagine what would come next. "Let me guess — if I would just not mention this little mishap to Barclay . . ."

"He'll be cross and put me on division duty again, and you *know* how I hate numbers."

She rolled her eyes upward, to where stars probably shone somewhere beyond the foul air and glowing lights, though she couldn't recall seeing more than a stray twinkle here and there. It would serve Barclay right if she let slip how much *he* hated divvying up the week's take, after the way he lorded his elected position of head of the family over the rest of them.

But no. They were careful about keeping the balance of authority right. It worked well enough to have the young ones hold their older brother in awe. "All right. This time. But learn the lessons you're taught, Georgie."

"You're the best, Rosie." He leaned down with all the enthusiasm of youth to smack a loud kiss on her cheek and then scurried off into the shadows.

Rosemary sighed and turned with a shake of her head to wait for the train. Georgie always made her feel so blasted old, though she had only seven or eight years on him.

But the really young ones . . . she and Willa were old enough to be their mums. How had that happened? Where had their own youth gone?

The wooden platform rumbled, a fair warning that the train approached. Rosemary queued up with the other few passengers still out and about, Mr. Would-Be Hero among them.

Perhaps the better question would be whether she'd even had a childhood, not where it had gone. Only the most shadowed of memories remained to tell her about her parents, about what it had felt like to wake every morning in the same bed and know that someone who loved her was just down the hall. Then came that confusion of waking one morning, feeling sick and confused, and realizing she was all alone.

She shook away the memory before it could take her stumbling down the hall to discover her parents. Shook it away and took a seat on the familiar train, smoothing down the tweed of her skirt. She'd sewn it herself, carefully following the guidance of the pattern in *Mode Pratique* until she had a garment that looked professionally tailored. That made her look, to the eye of those arrogant marks milling about London, like one of them.

As if she would ever be one of them. As if she would ever *want* to be.

Mr. Hero nodded her way, but his gaze didn't linger. Married, she would bet, and happily so. He'd have been out late for legitimate reasons. Working, most likely, to put meager food on his meager table, determined to live the honest life and provide for his family. He'd have a babe, given that white stain on his shoulder. Perhaps an older child too, if that was a jam stain on the side of his trousers.

Holstein — whoever he was — probably looked far different. If he had the ear of the king, then he sure wasn't scrounging around the factories for work, with barely two pence to rub together. No doubt he was of the ilk that she and the others had learned to mingle with ever so briefly at the galas they sneaked into. So rich he'd never notice the absence of a few pieces of jewelry or pounds sterling. His nose so high in the air that he couldn't be bothered to look down it long enough to see the people all but starving in the streets.

"Hello there, Jonesy." Another bloke sat beside Mr. Hero, nodding toward the newspaper he — Jonesy, apparently — had pulled out. "Anything good today?"

Jonesy sighed. "More about the tensions

in Europe."

The newcomer sighed. "Blighted Germans. If that Kaiser Wilhelm ever showed his snout around here, I'd —"

Jonesy snorted. "If he did, it would probably be to pay a visit to his cousin the king. Certainly not to see *you,* Percy."

Percy echoed the snort. "Cousins . . . why is it that every blamed monarch in Europe is the cousin of every other blamed monarch? 'Tain't right, if you ask me. All this intermarrying. And making it so we have a German on our own throne."

"Now . . ." Jonesy's face somehow softened in one respect and hardened in another. Though to be sure, Rosemary studied it only in the reflection of her window as the train chugged off, not outright. "I reckon he's as English as you or me, Perc, excepting that he's traveled more'n either of us ever could. Just his name is German is all."

"You know, I heard tell there was talk of him changing his name from Saxe-Coburg. Can you believe that? To something more English-sounding. That'll be the day."

Jonesy chuckled. "I remember Granny talking about how old Queen Victoria had to have a team of researchers just to figure out what her surname *was*. How do you suppose he'd go about changing it? To another family name, do you think?"

"Maybe. Who's to say? Surely there's an Englishman in his lineage *somewhere.*"

Lineage. Rosemary pursed her lips. Was that something this Holstein might be concerned about too? Quite possibly, in a day when his very name shouted an allegiance that he no doubt didn't want it proclaiming, wherever his loyalties lay. Perhaps that was her angle.

Her lips twitched up. Wouldn't Barclay and Willa think it amusing if she could steal a bloke's very name? Retta would laugh until her sides hurt. And Lucy would get that look on her face, the one where her mouth was a perfect O.

Jonesy folded his paper as the train slowed again for the next stop — her stop. She could have walked, and would have had it not been dark. But this time of night, it was worth the two pence to ride.

The other man leaned his head back. "You read where that author fellow — Wells? H. G. Wells, that's it. He accused King George of being uninspiring and foreign."

"Did he really? What did the king have to say?"

Rosemary stood, handbag clutched in her hand, knees bent to steady her as the train screeched to a halt. The doors opened, and she stepped off, barely catching Jonesy's reply.

"Said he may well be uninspiring, but he sure as blazes wasn't foreign."

Rosemary's lips curled up as she stepped off onto the tube platform and hurried away. The king had certainly been born and bred in England, there was no disputing that — but what of this Holstein? She'd have to figure it out. Barclay could tell her where to go looking for such information. Probably — unfortunately — some library somewhere with newspapers archived.

She screwed up her face at the very thought of that. Give her a ballroom glittering with gems ready to be swiped any day. A museum full of the latest security. She'd even learn to drive one of those rumble-throated automobiles if stealing it paid well enough.

But nothing paid so well as Mr. V. So she'd likely have to suffer days in the library. It wasn't that she disliked reading, it was just that she preferred reading certain things. Old newspapers not among them.

Light spilled from the windows of the pub, making her hasten her step. Pauly would have a kettle on and a cup waiting to steep for her. And, today being Tuesday, meat pies. Her mouth watered at the very thought. She'd skipped tea. And luncheon. Breakfast had been a boiled egg. She and Willa had given most of their food to a couple of urchins the night before — after feeding the little ones they claimed as their own, of course — and they both agreed they would rather not dip into their savings to buy more just yet. Willa had need of a new evening gown — some stumbling drunk had ripped hers beyond repair last week — and the silk and beads would cost all they'd put back and then some. Though with this advance payment from Mr. V, that wouldn't be an issue. Tomorrow they could go shopping.

But tonight would be meat pies, laughter, a steaming cup, and perhaps even . . . yes. She smiled as she pushed open the door and heard the lively strains of a violin. Willa was playing. With gusto tonight — an energetic tune that sounded Irish to Rosemary's ears. Her best friend — her sister for more than a decade — grinned at her as she slid through the crowded room but didn't interrupt her playing.

Rosemary grinned back and nodded to let her know she'd taken the job from Mr. V. An occasion deserving of an energetic tune and savory pie if ever there was one.

"Rosie!"

She headed to their usual corner, where the older members of the family were crowded around two tables shoved together. Her quick glance showed only Retta missing, and Georgie. Retta must have taken the little ones back to her flat after their early meal.

It was the youngest of this older group who had shouted for her. Elinor, with her rosy cheeks and shining golden hair — she was getting far too pretty, their little Ellie. Pretty was notable, and notable was bad in their line of work. But Barclay was aware of that and had begun using her merely as a distraction.

Much as it sometimes annoyed her to admit it, he knew what he was about, Barclay did. Even if he was a pain in her posterior. She waved her hello to Ellie and moved to the empty chair beside the oldest of her brothers, greeting him with a punch in the arm and a kiss on the cheek. "I got the job."

"Of course you did." He raised his nearly empty pint. "To a successful day for Rosie!"

"Cheers!" the group called out, raising their mugs too. A few even stood. Shakily. They must be celebrating something more than her success.

She motioned them all back down and took her seat. "Good day?"

"Oh. Oh, Rosie. The best day." Barclay laughed and drained his cup. Then raised it again. "Another round, Pauly."

"You'll regret that in the morning." But she smiled. It had been too long since Barclay had grinned quite like that. "Let me guess . . . you stole the Crown Jewels."

"Ha!" But he laughed — at least until Pauly poured coffee into his mug rather than ale. Rosemary wrinkled her nose at how those flavors might mix, but after glaring at it for a moment, Barclay shrugged and took a sip. "Not bad, actually."

Rosemary shook her head and glanced over her shoulder to watch Willa play. She should have been wearing some overly fine gown while she did so, and be standing up on a stage at a conservatory. Not in a pub in a run-down neighborhood of London, with pipe smoke and curses clouding the air. "If not the Crown Jewels, then what?"

Barclay chuckled again. "I'll tell you what — I *did* it, that's what. I stole the wedding ring right from the duchess's finger and slipped it onto the duke's mistress."

"No!" That got her full attention, and she spun back to face her brother with wide eyes. When she'd issued that challenge a month ago . . . "How did you manage it?"

Barclay wiggled his fingers. "Magic hands, Rosie. Magic hands."

"I helped!" Ellie bounced on her seat across the table, blue eyes glittering like stolen gems. "I came up to the duke like I knew him, which of course made Her Grace wonder how . . . as if I'd ever know him like *that* — he's so *old*! He's fifty if he's a day."

And a known philanderer, which was why it'd seemed like such an amusing challenge when she'd made it — though apparently she ought to have come up with something more difficult. Rosemary narrowed her eyes at Barclay. "Enlisting help is against the rules."

"Is not. You're just a sore loser, little sister." When he grinned, Barclay was very nearly too handsome, just as Ellie was too pretty. Luckily, he rarely found cause to grin in public. He took another sip of the tainted coffee and nodded toward Ellie. "And a fine job she did too. After I'd done the switch, she went up to the mistress all innocent-like and complimented her on the ring. Loudly. Loud enough to get the attention of the duchess."

Ellie's cheeks flushed to an even rosier shade. "I can't believe they were all there together, at the same ball. When I have a

25

husband, you can bet he won't be getting away with having another gal, and certainly not under my very nose."

Sweet, optimistic Elinor. Rosie reached across the table to chuck her under the chin. "No man would ever need another but you, little luv. Though I ought to be cross with you for helping this oaf." She elbowed Barclay in the side.

He gave her an easy shove away.

Ellie grinned. "Well, I got to wear Lucy's new gown — how was I to say no to that?"

Rosemary laughed, despite the fact that she knew well what was coming.

"Meat pie for you, Rosie." Pauly put a plate in front of her and a warm, burly hand on her shoulder. "You been a good girl?"

She grinned up at the closest thing any of them had had to a father in recent years. "Only on the bad days."

Pauly smiled down at her with that easy warmth that meant acceptance, no matter what. The exact same smile he'd given her when she was a mite of nine, rooting through his rubbish. Perhaps there *was* a God, to lead her to this particular pub's back alley.

The music came to a rousing end, earning hearty applause and shouts for more from the pub's patrons. "Later!" Willa shouted, stepping down from the tiny little stage Pauly had built for her.

Rosemary scooted her chair closer to Barclay's so Willa, her straight hair slipping from its knot as it always did when she played, could squeeze into her seat on Rosemary's other side. "Irish?"

Willa rolled her blue eyes. "You've no ear for music, Rosie. You're lucky I continue to speak to you."

"Speaking of speaking to her." That impish grin back in place, Barclay drummed his fingers on the scuffed edge of the table, drawing hooting, shouting attention from the rest of their group. "Your turn, Rosie!"

"No." With an exaggerated groan, she made a show of resting her head in her hand. Which put her face right over the plate of fragrant food. Her stomach's growl was covered by the family's laughter at least. "It was just my turn two months ago!"

Never one for mercy, Barclay pointed a finger at her. "You should have chosen a harder challenge for me then, shouldn't you have?"

It had seemed hard at the time. Everyone in England knew the duchess was paranoid about theft, crying out over every bump and casual brush. More staff had been fired from their house than could be counted —

and the out-of-work maids and footmen always had plenty to say about it. Loudly. No one could steal from the duke's house; it was battened down tighter than the British Museum.

No one.

Except, apparently, Barclay.

"All right." She straightened, drew in a large breath, squared her shoulders. "I'll face it like a man. What's the challenge?"

Willa's laugh burst with cruel glee. "You'll never do it. Never."

"Never. And I shall reign as king supreme." And would never stop gloating, as evidenced by the way Barclay leaned back in his chair, stretched his arms before him, and cracked his knuckles. "Here it is. I hereby challenge you, Rosemary Gresham, to steal . . ."

She closed her eyes, grimaced, and waited through the drumming of every set of fingers upon the tables. Only when they stopped did she open her eyes again.

Barclay was smirking, a single eyebrow lifted. "A manor house."

Rosemary just stared at him. "A *house*? You want me to steal a whole *house*?"

He laughed and reached for the mug again. "And don't try to get clever with me. I'm talking about an honest-to-goodness house, complete with grounds and outbuildings and whatnot. The whole estate. Which you will never manage. Then there will be no more doubt of who among us is the best. I am, hands down. No question. Because never in a lifetime will you pull off this one."

Rosemary picked up her fork, pointing it at him rather than her plate. "Don't be so sure, Mr. Pearce."

"Oh, come on, Rosie. Admit defeat." Willa bumped their shoulders together. "Even you can't steal an estate."

Probably not. But she'd be willing to bet that this Holstein fellow had a manor house. And if he were a traitor and were stripped of his estates . . . well, she didn't know how that would help her. But who knew? Maybe she could fake her way into his family and have herself named an heir.

She would tackle this challenge along with her new job. She grinned and forked a bite of pie. "Don't count me out so soon, luvs. You've yet to learn what Rosemary Gresham can do when she sets her mind to a thing."

Two

Southwest Cornwall
Late May 1914

Well, he was home. Though for the first time in his memory, Peter Holstein wasn't entirely happy to walk through the doors of Kensey Manor. The box was heavy in his arms as he trudged down the familiar hall to his study, bringing a measure of comfort.

It did little to calm the nerves still frayed from London, though. He only had meant to pass a quiet spring there, as he had done in years past. How had it devolved so quickly into accusations and suspicion? As if he were anyone other than who he'd always been.

But never mind the gossips of London. It was good to be home. No, better than good. It was a blessing.

He pushed open his study door with his shoulder and paused just inside to breathe in the scent of inspiration — old books, ink, and always a lingering hint of the pipe tobacco Father had favored. Mrs. Teague had scrubbed and polished the room, trying to get rid of that last smell, but Peter was rather glad she had failed.

Not that he'd ever tell his housekeeper that.

His desk, old and scarred, was neat as a pin — which likely wouldn't last till morning — and beckoned him to come nearer. He set down the heavy box upon the waiting surface, but rather than unlatching it, he turned to the window. There was no view in the world quite like this one — looking out at the bald-of-trees bluff that tumbled down into the sea. If he were lucky, a gale would blow in soon. Nothing like nature's savagery to soothe the beast within.

And the beast within needed a bit of soothing after this last fortnight in London. Otherwise it would take him a week to set it all aside and focus on his work. A week he really didn't have.

"There you are, Pete. I was a bit worried when I got your wire. Was it as bad as all that?"

Peter turned from the window to see his closest friend striding through the study door with all the ease and confidence Peter had never been able to muster. "G-Gryff.

W-Worse."

Gryffyn Penrose lifted his brows, that worry of which he spoke darkening his eyes. "Must have been. Anything I can do?"

Peter shook his head and shoved his hands into the pockets of his trousers, pulling in a long breath. He let it out again slowly, willing his tongue to cooperate. Reminding himself that he was with Gryff, no one else. "I'll be, ah . . . fine." Better. Not exactly eloquent, but not outright stuttering either.

Nothing betrayed his inner turmoil to his old friend like his stuttering.

Gryff sank into his usual chair beside the unlit hearth, his brows not smoothing out. "Well, Jenny was glad to hear you were coming home. You're to join us for dinner tomorrow, of course."

Where his friend's wife would no doubt go on about how thin he'd grown in London and ply him with every sweet he'd ever expressed a fancy toward. He grinned. "Shame."

Gryff, well aware of his wife's methods of welcoming Peter, smiled too. "And Elowyn asks if you'll marry her, now that she's older."

A chuckle rumbled its way up Peter's throat. The young Penrose had had a birthday while he was gone, it was true . . . which put her at five. He'd have to remember to bring her the dolly he'd found for her in London. "Not until she . . . she can read."

Gryff's laughter hadn't yet faded when a quick knock on the door signaled Mrs. Teague's arrival. She poked her head in, her ample girth following. "The boys have everything unloaded, Mr. Holstein." He always missed hearing the Cornish say his name when he was in London. The way they dropped the *H* and made it *'olstein.* "And I'll tell Treeve to bring Cadan with him tomorrow. Will you want your supper in the dining room or in here? Or did Mr. Penrose convince you to go with him tonight?"

Peter cleared his throat and looked to Gryff.

His friend folded his hands over the stomach that had once been flat. Before he married the best cook in Cornwall seven years ago. Now . . . not so much. "We've claimed him tomorrow," Gryff said.

Peter nodded his agreement and patted his jacket pocket. Which hadn't the letters he'd slid in it that morning. Where had he put them? He must have moved them into his bag, which Benny had already set there, by his desk chair. He headed to it and found the missives, sorting through them until he located the one with *Mrs. Teague* scrawled across the outside.

She waited with a smile, holding out her hand for the note as he neared. Wasting no time before flipping it open, she nodded as she read. "I suspected as much — though you be well aware, young man, that you'll not be holing yourself up in here every evening. Do you understand?"

He gave an overly serious nod.

She grinned and reached up to pat his cheek, as if he were still a boy of seven. "It's good to have you home, Master Peter. Now, back to work I go. I'll leave you boys to yourselves."

After the door clicked shut behind her, Peter took up his spot by the window again. The sky was an unfortunate blue, the wind barely gusting. Why did it always rain when he wanted a walk and remain clear and cloudless when he needed a good storm? "I k-keep making en . . . enemies."

"You?" Gryff's scoffing laugh soothed one of those rough places inside him. "Don't be silly, Pete — you haven't any enemies. You're the single nicest man in England, which is why I would absolutely hate you if you weren't like a brother to me. Which, hmm . . . perhaps doesn't prove my point."

The comment brought laughter to Peter's throat and soothed him a bit more. He leaned into the white-painted window frame and turned to watch his friend. "It's not m-me. Not really. Just . . . they all . . . they c-call me *that German.* As if . . . as if I . . ." Giving up, he shook his head.

Gryff looked genuinely baffled — an odd state for such a quick-witted man. "Where do they — whoever they are — get their information? You are as English as the king himself."

Peter snorted. "Their point. They've actually . . . they've accused me of . . . of . . ." It was unthinkable. Unsayable. "Espionage."

"Nonsense." Gryff rested his chin on his palm, elbow on the arm of the chair. "Well, listen, old boy, don't let them bother you. Your grandfather may have hailed from Germany, but that shouldn't matter. You've spent all your life in England, aside from a few holidays."

But it *did* matter, apparently. "But they've . . . been talking . . . a-b-bout Mother."

At that, Gryff rose to his feet. "What sort of talk? A more saintly woman has never set foot in — ah." For a moment, he clenched his teeth together, making the muscle in his jaw tic. But he was never one to be silent long — it was perhaps why they made a good pair. "Yes, *they* would be using the fact that your father went back to Germany to find his bride to prove — what, exactly? That he wasn't fully loyal to England? That *you* aren't?"

Jerking his head in a nod, Peter drew in a long breath through his nose. "And what . . . what am I to say? I don't . . . that is, I . . . I don't know why he did, Gryff. But Mother, she . . . she loved England."

"Well, of course she did." Gryff stomped to the hearth and scowled at the mantel. Their photograph rested there, Mother and Father's. Somehow looking as peaceful and loving in the serious, unsmiling pose as they had been in life. Gryff's face relaxed as he studied it, no doubt as he remembered how they had always welcomed him as another son. "And everyone always loved your mother. It will surely pass, Pete. There may be a bit of a panic right now with Germany threatening war, but it will calm down. Then everyone will remember who you *really* are."

A stupid assertion that didn't even deserve a response. Gryff would be hearing in his own head as clearly as Peter did in his that loving remonstrance Mother had always made: *No one will know your heart if you refuse to speak, Peter. I know it is difficult for you. But you must try. For your own good, you must try.*

As usual, she had been right. He turned from the window and those mocking blue skies, back to his desk. He could never speak up in his own defense, and now — if war came, if he were accused of this crime . . . he could lose everything. Be arrested. And though in peaceful times such a ridiculous accusation couldn't stick, who knew what a judge might decide in the panic of war?

And he couldn't have people digging into his secrets. Even if they *weren't* treasonous. Crouching down, he began to unload the bag from which he'd taken the letters. He'd done his best to make himself understood in spite of the stammering. He'd learned to excel at writing where he failed in speech, but that apparently wasn't enough.

Well, it had been enough to earn him friends, to be sure. Ironic, really, that those very friendships were what now made him trouble. He slid out the books he'd been reading on the train and put them on the desk.

Gryff picked up one and flipped it open. "Surely the king or Prince Edward can hush the rumors — what is the point, after all, of having friends in those highest of places if they cannot offer you a bit of protection now and then?"

"I don't want to . . . to put them in that . . . position." Peter made a face but directed it at the last notebook he withdrew rather than at his friend. "And no one would . . . would care about me if I . . . if I hadn't such friends."

Snapping the book closed, Gryff set it down. "Perfectly unfair. And unjust. If you want me to file a suit against someone, just name the culprit. Surely we can trump up some charges of malice or slander or maligning or . . ."

"Brilliant, counselor." Peter stood again and put his notebooks to the right, beside the box still front and center. "That will . . . that will surely solve everything."

"You never let me have any fun at all, old boy. Nothing but paperwork and real estate — though perhaps that could help. Mr. Arnold could be right about that, you know, if you let it be known." Gryff rapped a knuckle on the book. "Or the king could knight you. Perhaps that would hush a few of your detractors."

Peter reached for the copy of Sir Arthur Conan Doyle's *The Poison Belt* and set it on the shelf behind his desk. "Why would he? I've done . . . done nothing."

Gryff folded his arms over his chest, leaned against the desk, and arrowed a look into him. "You've done as much as Conan Doyle."

He shot the look right back at his friend and turned to the box, though he wasn't quite sure if it was dread or appreciation that coursed through him as he unlatched it. "I can . . . can hardly claim *that*."

"Not can't — *won't*."

"Semantics."

"Precision — something I know well you appreciate, so don't try to argue with me. And pray tell, what *is* your plan for dealing with it, if not appealing to the Crown for aid? Do you intend to hide yourself away here in Cornwall until your detractors forget you exist or Germany ceases threatening Europe?"

The thought had crossed Peter's mind, though he'd no intention of confessing that to the man who liked nothing more than donning his white wig and black robe and arguing before the courts. "I intend to . . . to find answers."

Gryff blinked at him. "Answers to *what*?"

"To the qu— questions they are raising. If I can . . . if I can prove to those loud f-few that I . . . that my *family* is loyal, then . . ."

"And how will you do that?"

Peter sighed and turned toward the door. The one he was rarely brave enough to open, though the room behind it bore a name he loved above most others — *library.*

Gryffyn snorted again. "Then I bid you good luck. I interviewed no fewer than four chaps for the job while you were away, and they all ran for the hills when they got a look at the place. If you want to tackle the cave, you're on your own."

Feeling a bit like the stalwart adventurer Locryn James, whose fictional escapades had captured countless hearts, he flung open the door. And then just stood there staring at the mess. "Even Locryn would . . . would tremble."

Gryff laughed and came to his side but made no move to enter either. "Your family may be loyal, but it must be said, Pete. You are all a bunch of hoarders."

Only of books. And magazines. And newspapers and journals and diaries and missives and . . . He scrubbed a hand over his face. "It is enough to . . . to make a man go grey. But then I would . . . would look like *you.*"

"I beg your pardon." Gryff passed a hand over the hair more silver than brown, though he was only thirty. "You should be so lucky as to gain such a dignified look at such a tender age."

Peter grinned, though it faded fast. "They

never should have . . . have forbidden Mrs. Teague from . . . cleaning in there."

"Ah, but zere is a mezod to zee madness!" Gryff held out a hand, doing a fair, if exaggerated, imitation of Peter's grandfather.

"If only Opa had . . . shared it."

"Hmm. My friend, here is my wisdom." He clapped a hand to Peter's shoulder and leaned close, saying in a mock whisper, "You really need to find that help, even if it's someone untrained in history or libraries."

And well he knew it. He pasted on a smile as exaggerated as Gryff's German accent. "Gryffyn, old friend, old . . . chum."

"I don't like you that much." Laughing, Gryff retreated to the desk and took the liberty of lifting the lid from the box.

Peter followed and then stood for a moment staring at the machine within. Usually seeing the typewriter made his fingers itch to strike the familiar keys. Just now, he had half a mind to toss it over the cliffs and into the sea — the blighted thing had been resisting him at every turn since the trouble started in London.

Ah well, there was nothing for it. He lifted the heavy base, letting Gryff slide the bottom of its box out of the way. Then Peter set it in its place before his chair.

His friend peeked at the stack of pages bound with brown paper and rubber bands that Peter had unloaded from his bag. And frowned. "Is this it?"

Peter squeezed his eyes shut, but reopening them didn't make the stack grow. "Yes."

"And you have only until August?"

"Yes."

Gryff winced. "Perhaps I should leave you so you can get to work."

"It won't help." Perhaps a walk along the cliffs would, though, even if God hadn't sent him a storm today.

There was always tomorrow. And maybe he needed sunshine just now — the Lord, after all, had far more wisdom than Peter could ever boast. He motioned with his head toward the window. "Join me?"

"For a bit, then I should get home."

They headed out of the study, down the hall, and to the nearest exit, which took them into the gardens. Mr. Teague's pride and joy, they were a riot of color just now, long-stemmed flowers bowing in the breeze and sending their sweet perfume into the air. Peter had to pause, as he always did, to take in the splendor for a moment. Rather than the careful, cultivated look of neighboring houses, Teague had gone for a wild arrangement, a profusion of mixed blooms mingling in beds crowding the paths.

Peter had dreamed it was a jungle when he was a boy, what with the tropical flowers Teague had imported. He'd spent many hours on the benches situated here and there, a book in his hand and adventure in his heart.

Were he a different man, one who could command a presence and charm people wherever he went, perhaps he would have struck off to see more of the world than this imitation jungle. Perhaps he would have made his own way, cut his own path with machete and pistol.

As it was, even the jungle of London sent him running for cover.

"You're brooding. You know how I detest it when you brood." Gryff strode ahead through the garden, his aim the path that would take them, after a five-minute walk, to the cliffs.

"I'm not . . . brooding. Just wonder . . . wondering what else is out there." Hands in his pockets, Peter kept pace with his friend, letting his eyes soak up every familiar hedge and then the equally familiar scrub that adorned the cliff tops. His ears strained for that first sound of wave crashing on rock.

Birdsong serenaded them, and the wind whispered a harmony to it. They were the only sounds for that quick walk, along with the scuff of their feet over the granite stones placed here and there along the path. In the other direction, between the house and the main road, was the wood, of which Peter was equally fond — but not in a mood like this. Nothing could soothe him like the wind whipping salt air into his face and a gull crying out a greeting. Peter dragged in a long breath, the release of which was always Gryff's cue.

Gryff never missed his cue. "What will you do, then? If rumors get worse, and if you can't find anything in that dreadful room to prove the Holsteins above reproach? What will you do if war comes and your loyalties are called into question? What if even selling off the last of it doesn't help?"

Peter's nostrils flared. What *could* he do, really? Hopefully here, in the village where he'd grown up, where everyone knew him — more or less, though perhaps less, given his habitual silence — he'd still be welcome. Still be trusted. People would speak up for him.

But, just as likely, that snarling Mr. Jasper would trump up charges. If war were declared, he could be arrested, just because of his last name. Because of his father falling in love with a German woman. He could lose everything. *Everything.* And even if it didn't come to that, he would never shake the suspicion. Not in this climate. "The k-king is . . . he is considering . . . changing his name."

Not that His Majesty was ready to make such a monumental decision soon — a monarch didn't just toss aside a family name because of shifting politics.

But the politics were dire enough that King George was considering it. Seriously considering it and already had hired a historian to revisit all the research that Queen Victoria had sought out on their family history. Already he was trying to determine what name the house of Saxe-Coburg should take, if take a new one they did.

"Peter. You can't be thinking of doing the same. You can't. It would break your father's heart, and your grandfather's."

He swallowed, though his throat felt tight and his mouth dry. "I can't be sure it . . . that it would even help. But perhaps . . . it may make a statement. If I were to so visibly d-distance myself f-from my German roots."

Gryff stepped between him and the view of the rolling sea, his face a mask of concern again. "Listen to yourself. This is obviously as distressing to you as it would be to them, so why are you even considering it? How can you possibly think it would be worth it?"

Because Cornwall was the only home he'd ever known, and if he were all but forced out of Kensey Manor as he had been out of his little townhouse in London . . . well, what sacrifice wouldn't be worth keeping his home? This place he loved? "A rose by any other n-name, right?"

Gryff's face didn't soften any. "A lesson everyone else needs to learn about the name Holstein — not one you need to learn about changing it."

But it wasn't possible to change the world — only himself. Though perhaps by changing himself he could cause a greater change too. That had always been his hope, his prayer. That the Lord could somehow use both his shortcomings and his gifts to make others better. Stronger. More faithful. "It is only . . . only a notion."

"Well, dismiss it and focus your energies on digging through that cave of paper you so optimistically call a library. Surely there is ample proof in there that your family has always been the most loyal of English subjects — your father and grandfather were both always writing things and filing them away. Find it, present it to whomever in

Parliament or the Home Office is giving you trouble, and let that be that."

The journals, those were what he needed. Surely if anything could prove his family's innocence, it was those missing journals. "You would con — consign me to that mess alone? And here I . . . I thought you were my friend."

At least he smiled, finally. "Call me a coward if you must, but I'm not setting foot in there. And if you have any pity on future generations, you'll stop adding to the mess with those boxes of correspondence."

He'd move them up to the attic eventually. When he got around to it. Besides, future generations looked none too promising. No woman he'd ever met had any interest in a stammering fool. Especially one with a last name like Holstein.

Maybe he *did* understand why his father had gone back to Germany for his bride.

Gryff's smile had faded into a squint. He nodded toward the house. "Are you expecting company?"

"Hmm?" Peter spun around, squinting into the sun as well, until he caught the gleam of its light upon an automobile bouncing up his drive. "No."

They both started back without the need to discuss it, their pace quicker than it had been on the way up. It could be no one from the village, not in an unfamiliar car. Perhaps a tourist who had taken a wrong turn?

They hurried over the rocks, through the scrub. The rumble of the engine breaking the quiet of the day nearly made Peter wince. The machines were here to stay, it seemed, but he rather missed the days before their advent upon the countryside. Things would never be the same.

Once in the side garden, the contraption came into clear view . . . and brought Peter up short. There were two young women in its open cab. The driver had a somewhat round face with a flattish nose, middling brown hair, and stared at the front of Kensey.

The passenger's hair was a few shades darker, with a bit of curl, her face narrower, her sharp nose topped by a pair of spectacles. Pretty, both of them, with that kind of beauty that it took a few moments to notice. They rather put him in mind of the sisters Locryn James had met in *This Mad Caper,* in Spain. They had been on their way to a convent, determined to take their vows.

A resemblance Gryff didn't seem to pick up on. "Well now, that's interesting. Ladies. Here. Perhaps there is hope yet for those future generations." Chuckling, Gryff elbowed him in the side. "Come on, old boy. Let's go and say hello."

He would rather brave the library.

THREE

"You're never going to pull this one off. Never."

Rosemary reached behind her for the valise she had stowed behind the seat of the borrowed car. "Shut up, Willa."

"Ever. You're aware of that, right?" Willa leaned back against the seat, wrist braced against the steering wheel as if she were perfectly at home driving the borrowed automobile. Her gaze remained on the stone edifice before them. "It isn't even that big, as manors go. Probably employs no more than a dozen."

"And how would I afford the upkeep of a bigger place after I steal it?" Straightening, Rosemary gave her sister a cheeky grin.

Willa turned and made a face at her. "Are you really going to wear those things? You look ridiculous."

"I look the part." Rosemary touched a hand to the wire-rimmed spectacles whose glass did nothing to magnify. Her gaze strayed to the house. Grey stone blocks, nearly white in some places. Ivy growing up the corners. The garden, visible on the side, looked disorderly, wild . . . and yet somehow inviting. And, she noted, had two men striding through it. "We've been noticed. I'd better get out and you gone."

Willa nodded. "I can come back 'round in an hour."

"No — you'd better return the car before that sot stirs from his stupor and realizes it's gone. If I fail to gain entrance, I'll just walk back to the hotel."

Willa pursed her lips as Rosemary opened the door and slid out, valise in hand. "Are you certain about this, Rosie? The real part, I mean."

No more sure than she had been about the museum job or the designs she'd liberated for Mr. V six months ago, but she'd pulled those off, hadn't she? She closed the door behind her. "I'll be fine." She rounded the bonnet and paused on the other side to lean in and kiss Willa's cheek. "I appreciate you coming with me."

"Nothing better to do." Despite her grin, Willa's eyes shone with uncertainty. "Besides, you know how Barclay is about sending us off alone."

She had wriggled her way free of that "rule" plenty of times before — and would be happy to send Willa home once she was established here. But just now, it was rather nice to have a friend at hand. "Right, well. With the greatest risks —"

"— come the greatest rewards." Willa nodded and faced forward. "Good luck."

She was going to need it. Drawing in a deep breath, Rosemary clutched the valise in one hand, smoothed the linen of her new skirt, and drew in a breath to steady herself as the car puttered off down the other side of the drive's loop. *Rosemary Gresham, librarian.* A stretch, she would be the first to admit. Not a role that would come naturally. But she would bluster her way along as she always did, and it must begin now with a smile. She fixed one in place and turned just as the two gents touched foot to gravel.

They may have been about the same age, though it was hard to say, what with the one having grey hair. His face was smooth though, as smooth as the other's — that second man a blond. Testimony to his German side? Or did the bold step of the first signal *he* was master of the house?

Well, she wouldn't fumble the introduction by assuming. Instead, she strode forward with the smile in place. "Good day!

52

I'm seeking Mr. Holstein."

The gents stopped a few feet away, the grey one looking to the blonde. "You have found him. May I inquire as to your purpose, Miss . . . ?"

"Gresham." She had debated — and rejected — using an assumed name. Given how long a job this would likely be, she couldn't risk getting tripped up with such nonsense. She held out a hand to the blond. "Rosemary Gresham, librarian, at your service, sir."

She expected wariness. Confusion. Perhaps a dose of animosity. Instead, light sparked in Holstein's eyes as he stepped forward and shook her hand. "A li— librarian, you say? Have you . . . have you c-come to apply for the p-position?"

"You didn't make an appointment." The other man scowled. "I've yet to meet a librarian who isn't fond of making appointments. So do tell me, Miss Gresham, what brings you to Kensey."

Not a question. And she was rather glad she had taken a week in London to work out all the details and make acquaintances. Now she could beam as she reclaimed her hand. "Of course, sir. I have been working with a Mr. Hall in London, who is delving into the history of the royal family — upon

His Majesty's request, of course — and he mentioned that you have been looking for some assistance with your library, Mr. Holstein."

Not that the chap, even with his tongue loosened by gin, would have recommended *her* for the task. But hopefully the name itself would do the work.

It appeared to do so. Holstein rocked back on his heels and sent the other man a look that said . . . something. Rosemary couldn't quite decipher it.

The other gent sighed. "It's worth a conversation, I suppose. Though we both know she'll run for cover when you show her the cave, like everyone else has."

Cave? Rosemary adjusted the hat that the wind was trying to tug free. "I'm a resilient sort, Mr. . . . ?"

"Gryffyn Penrose. Barrister."

A lawyer? It took considerable effort to keep her smile in place. She'd never liked the blighters. Though they were better than bobbies. A bit. "How do you do, Mr. Penrose."

"Very well." He didn't return the greeting or reach to shake. Rather, he folded his arms over the slight paunch that his jacket did little to hide.

Holstein sent his lawyer — friend? —

another look, this one more easily interpreted. "D-Don't be r-rude, Gryff." He offered Rosemary a smile. A smile peaceful enough to seem odd, following that stuttered command. "W-We were j-just discuss . . . discussing . . ." He cleared his throat but looked neither embarrassed nor frustrated. He merely nodded to Penrose.

The lawyer sighed again. "We were just discussing Mr. Holstein's need for a librarian to organize, as well as to help locate certain family documents. I'm sure Mr. Hall mentioned why."

He had, at that, on his third pint. A rather slurring story about how the blasted Germans were littered through London society, thanks to the king's family. Including the mysterious Mr. Holstein, who had certain powerful sectors in an uproar. Apparently there was some question as to whether he was even an English subject.

What he hadn't mentioned was that the man couldn't even speak a sentence coherently. And yet people were worried that he had the ear of the king? Obviously there was more at work than she could see in a single glance. "He gave me the gist, sir, and let me know where I could find you if I wished to apply for the position, and perhaps help you with your family history as he is helping His

Majesty."

Never had she imagined she would utter a sentence that linked her, however distantly, to a monarch. What had Mr. V gotten her into?

But Holstein returned her smile, his shoulders even relaxing a degree. He nodded. His chin, she noted, had the slightest of clefts. Elinor would swoon. "You are an answer to p-prayer, Miss Gr— Gresham."

Well, that was a first. And made a strange little something wiggle around in her chest. "Am I?"

He turned toward the house. "C-Come. I'll show . . . show you the l-library."

Penrose fell in beside Holstein, leaving Rosemary to bring up the rear. What an odd pair they were. They were of the same height, give or take a smidgeon, though where Penrose looked settled and commanding, Holstein bordered on underweight and could have easily appeared timid. Yet he didn't, not really. He was the one who led the way, his step sure.

Of course, it *was* his house. No doubt that lent one a certain something when it came to authority. Rosemary followed with her valise still in hand.

Penrose cast another suspicious glance over his shoulder at her. And didn't bother

lowering his voice to ask, "Pete, are you sure
—"

"Yes."

"But there are —"

"No."

Penrose huffed. "You are impossible once you've made up your mind."

"Thank you."

"Mr. Holstein!"

They all stopped at the new voice, one that perfectly matched the aged but hardy fellow who rounded the far corner of the house, waving a hand. He had a ragged hat over white hair, dirt on his knees and hands.

Yet Holstein didn't hesitate to detour from his path to greet the old fellow, nor to grip the grubby hand. "Teague. Hello."

"The missus said you'd made it home — and good it is to see you, sir." Teague shook Holstein's hand, going so far as to clasp it in both of his, transferring more dirt. Rosemary glanced at Penrose to see if the lawyer would object — since that seemed to be his natural response to everything — but he was smiling. And ignoring her.

Suited her just fine. She looked back to the greeting in time to see Holstein pat the pocket of his jacket, frowning. He then rolled his eyes and held up a finger. "Study. On my . . . desk."

The old man grinned. "Aye, I'll get it. Did you see the gladioli?"

"Beautiful. Ab . . . absolutely beautiful."

The gardener, presumably. Which certainly explained the dirt. Rosemary set down her valise, her gaze snagging on Penrose's shoes. They were pricey-looking, more so than his clothes. But now that she was closer, she could see a gleam of gold from a watch fob — and his cufflinks were certainly silver. He must do well for himself. Holstein's were of even better quality, though the styles were understated. Obviously a man who didn't care to call attention to himself.

Even the gardener looked well cared for. Though the clothes were filthy, they didn't look over-mended. And he certainly didn't look like he ever missed a meal.

Not that she intended to help herself to anything while she was here, to be sure. She had a far bigger payday coming than any of their pockets would give her. Though a week or two of steady meals wouldn't go amiss.

Holstein came toward them again — and now he looked embarrassed. "F-Forgive me, Miss Gresham. L-Let me h-help you with . . . with that." He reached for her valise.

It took her a moment to get over her shock

— he, a gentleman, master of the house, reaching for her bag? — and object. "Oh! No, sir, that isn't necessary. I can handle it, I assure you."

"N-Non . . . sense." His mind made up, he turned back for the stone steps looming before them.

Penrose sighed. "I see you plan to stay for a while, Miss Gresham. And who was that who drove you here?"

"My sister." She had claimed it so often, it felt more truth than lie to her tongue, and she put a bounce in her step. "She's always wanted to see Cornwall so came along for a bit of a holiday while I'm here. We've a room in the village — I only brought that with me now because it has my notebooks in it."

The door opened before them. Holstein, already up the stairs, looked over his shoulder at her as he crossed the threshold. "If . . . if you d-decide to st-stay and help, there's a . . . a c-cottage. You may . . . it's empty."

Willa would never agree — she wanted to be in the village where she could find what opportunities were to be found. But a cottage on the grounds would certainly give Rosemary better access to everything. "That sounds absolutely perfect, Mr. Holstein. If, of course, you decide to hire me. I do understand that a female is hardly the usual person for such a job, but . . ." Her breath caught as she stepped inside.

Perhaps, as Willa had said, it wasn't so grand as other manor houses. They had passed bigger ones on the journey here, to be sure, visible from the train's windows. And they had blustered their way into balls in London hosted in some rather impressive venues.

But this was different. This was a house, a home, and yet like nothing she'd ever seen. The words she used to describe the things in her own flat — walls, floor, chairs, tables — didn't seem to do justice to the features here. Such rich colors, from the woods to the fabrics. Gleaming metals. Fresh flowers in perfect vases.

The men stopped to look at her, leaving her little choice but to exaggerate her response. She pressed a hand to her chest. "What a lovely home you have, Mr. Holstein. I don't believe I've seen lovelier anywhere in London. Is that tapestry French?" Did the French even specialize in tapestries? She was as bad at naming decor as she was composers.

Holstein, thankfully, didn't appear any better at it. He shrugged, his lips curling up in a hint of a smile. "All I . . . all I can tell you is th— that it's r-red."

Her smile went genuine. "What a keen eye you have."

He chuckled and headed toward a hallway to the right. She followed, forcing herself to focus on the important things — that none of the windows or doors had electro-magnetic alarms affixed to them. So unless he had a vault somewhere, the place was largely unsecured.

Penrose, scowling, held up to walk beside her. Not, she suspected, a friendly gesture. "I trust you come with references, Miss Gresham, even if not an appointment?"

"Of course, sir. They're in my valise there." All provided just yesterday by Mr. V, after she'd sent him a note telling him what she needed. They looked genuine to her eye, and she was an expert at spotting a fraud. But it hadn't occurred to her to make an appointment. It should have.

Penrose grunted. "We'll take a look once we're in the cave, if you dare to venture that far inside."

Rosemary lifted her brows and adjusted the spectacles. They were making her ears hurt. Perhaps they hadn't been such a smart addition after all. "Are you not fond of libraries, Mr. Penrose?"

"Libraries are delightful. This particular room is more the site of an avalanche of books."

"Now, Gryff. They are . . . they are not in p-piles. Just st— stacks."

At the end of the hall, Holstein paused before the final door and drew a breath that looked, oddly, as though it were meant to bolster him. He set his gaze on her — his eyes were a deep blue-green — and inclined his head. "D-Don't be . . . alarmed, Miss Gresham. There is . . . there is an — an order."

Penrose grunted again. "No living creature has ever determined it, but certainly. An order."

Oh gracious. She pasted a smile in place and drew up an image of all those crisp pound notes. All those lovely zeroes to follow, promising her enough income to support the whole family for the rest of the year. They'd be able to get new coats before winter — nice ones. Shoes nearly as sturdy as the ones Mr. Penrose wore. She could make a real Christmas for the little ones. Books for Barclay — new ones, not used. A new bow for Willa's violin. Paints for Retta.

How bad could a library really be?

She had her answer when Holstein swung the double doors open, inward. Perhaps, once, the room had been majestic. The ceiling soared high overhead, a magnificent mural painted on it. The chamber stretched the whole width of the house. Shelves lined the walls, floor to towering ceiling. Lined with books, all of them. Then with books stacked in front of them. Books stacked on the floor. Books stacked on the chairs, the tables, lining the windowsills. Boxes of them. Random cases of them at odd places.

She couldn't help the gasp. But surely Rosemary Gresham, librarian, would be in love with the sight. Right? She stepped inside. "Oh, it's heaven."

A place she'd long known the Almighty would never let her enter — now He'd plunged her into its opposite, right here on earth. Perhaps it served her right in the eyes of His ultimate justice, but really. She was only trying to survive, to feed the mouths He'd placed in her care. What had she really done to deserve *this*?

She took another brave step inside and turned to look at the men again. Who hadn't, she noted, ventured beyond the threshold. Still, she smiled. "What would you like done with the place, Mr. Holstein? A general organizing? Or, as Mr. Hall indicated as a possibility, are you looking for family documents?"

"Ah." He set down her valise, straightened again. His eyes flitted over the room. "Both. I am n-not . . . not sure wh-where their . . . journals are. They m-must be found. But books. Could be r-relevant. There are . . . some there. And there. And h-here. Some perhaps . . . perhaps there." His hand started at the left and moved to encompass everything. Absolutely everything. "Plus g-general . . . organizing."

She spun back to face her certain destruction. Never mind her estimation of a week or two. It would take her months to go through it all. Years. She might never get done. And librarian or not, she figured that would daunt anyone. Her fingers tugged at the lace of her collar. "Oh dear."

"And much of it's in German," Penrose declared with far too much amusement. He was leaning into the doorway, looking downright jolly. "Will that be a problem for you?"

She wondered again how Mr. V had known. He knew, it seemed, everything. Which couldn't be good. But it had gotten her hired for this job, so she wouldn't question it. Her lips returned to their smile. "No problem at all, Mr. Penrose. I'm afraid I speak it atrociously, but I read it passably well."

Holstein sent Penrose one of those looks, this one bright and cheerful.

Penrose pushed off the frame. "Those references, if you please."

"Certainly." They would pass muster. They must. Which meant she'd be stuck for the foreseeable future here in this shaking tower of tomes ready to suffocate her. Praying to that irony-loving, ever-unhearing God that war would hold off until she had made significant headway. She picked up the valise from the floor and prepared to seal her fate.

Maybe he didn't need a storm — for beginning so dismally, this day had taken the best of turns. Peter whistled a happy tune and edged another step into the room while Gryff claimed the two square feet of empty table space to flip through the papers Miss Gresham had withdrawn from her case. It didn't look *so* daunting. Not now that he had a trained librarian who hadn't run for the hills, as Gryff said, the moment she glanced at the room. And if she'd been working with Hall, then she was the best. Capable of bringing actual order into the place.

He smiled and toed one of the boxes he'd dropped inside the door on his last trip home, full of letters from Wells, Doyle, Joyce, Baum, London . . . all of whom he owed letters back. And with this weight off him, he'd be in a better frame of mind to write them.

His glance went back to Gryff and Miss Gresham. True, her shoulders looked rather narrow to carry this burden . . . but the Lord had clearly sent her. Clearly. Within minutes of saying how desperately he needed a person of her profession, here she was, without even stopping at Gryff's office first. And if he understood the Lord at all, then he must trust she was the perfect personage for the task, however unsuited she might look.

Nothing but prejudice on his part, he knew. A woman was perfectly capable of finding her way around a library, and Mother would have boxed his ears for even thinking otherwise.

Gryff straightened with a grumble ill-humored enough to signify he'd found nothing amiss in the references. "Looks to be in order. Of course I shall have to —"

"Gryff." Really, sometimes he took the whole barrister thing too far. Peter widened his eyes and shook his head, needing no words to ask his friend why he was trying so hard to spoil such a good thing.

Gryff rolled his eyes. "Fine, have it your way. What think you, Miss Gresham? Do you dare to tackle such a monstrous room?"

"Well, of course!" She declared it cheerfully and stepped over a stack of periodicals, her sights set on something over by the window. Or maybe *on* the window, if she needed a reminder that there was still a world outside this overwhelming room. "I'll just poke around a bit to familiarize myself, if you don't mind, Mr. Holstein."

"P-Please." He waited for Gryff to join him by the door and leaned close. "See? She . . . she seems to actually . . . to *like* it."

"Evidence of insanity. We ought to have her examined by a —"

"Gryffyn."

"Well, other trained men didn't last two seconds, so one must ask why she is so eager. She could be about something foul."

Peter rolled his eyes. "Or . . . or need the . . . money." Positions in her chosen field probably weren't easy to come by for a woman.

"You are too quick to trust, Pete." Pursing his lips, Gryff watched her as if she might try to pocket the miniature globe that sat atop a stack of biographies. "She doesn't look like a librarian," he said under his breath.

Mother would have boxed *his* ears too. Peter sighed. "And what . . . what, pray tell . . . does a librarian look like?"

"Like something other than she does." He waved a hand, encompassing the brown curls twisted into some sort of a bun under her hat, the pale linen suit, the graceful gloved hands.

Really, she wasn't bad to look at. No great beauty, perhaps, and he couldn't even tell her eye color behind those spectacles. But if he were going to have someone underfoot for the summer, he could think of worse options.

So long as she was quiet. Though surely a librarian would know the value of silence.

"Hmph." Gryff angled himself toward the door. "Bring her with you tomorrow, if she lasts that long. We'll let Jenny get a look at her. No one can tell people at a glance like Jenny can."

"Except . . . except her obvious breach in judgment when . . . when she married *you.*"

Chuckling, Gryff stepped out of the room. "I'll see you tomorrow. Cheerio."

Peter waved his farewell and then looked around the room. There really were twice as many books in here as there should be. Perhaps three times, if one factored in the newspapers and magazines and correspondence. He really ought to take his boxes of letters up to the attic. Perhaps if he did, it would begin to look more like a library and less like a cave.

It would be as dark as one in another hour too — though the rest of the house had electricity, the man had taken one look at this room and declared it impossible to wire. It had been years since he'd peeked in here in the dark, but he well remembered how the towering stacks had loomed like trees, dense and thick. Primordial.

A cave. He straightened, his mind's eye supplying those shadows where nature hadn't yet. That was what he needed. Cold and stony and dark . . . and a perfect symbol. A cave like Plato's, where truth lay just outside, but its light was too blinding for mortal eyes at first. A perfect analogy. A perfect device. Locryn would —

"Did you hear me, Mr. Holstein?"

He started, then took a step back when he realized Miss Gresham was only a few feet away. "S-Sorry. I was . . . was th . . . think-ing of a novel."

She smiled. Brown — her eyes were a brown as clear as the tourmaline Mother had once worn. "And whereabouts are *those* kept in this place?"

He motioned toward the door to his study,

still open. His walls there were lined with books too, but they were ordered. More or less. With only a few stacked before the orderly lines, when his collection had outpaced his shelves.

She lifted her dark brows. "May I?"

"Of c-course." He led the way into his study and motioned her toward the bookcases. "You are wel . . . welcome to b-borrow any. If you . . . if you stay."

"How very kind, Mr. Holstein. And of course I'm interested in staying, if you'll have me. Though, to be sure, I can make no estimation just yet on how long it will take me to catalog those books. And if you *do* intend me to read them to determine any family history, I will need instruction on what it is I'm looking for. That will, of course, add to the time needed."

Twilight sunshine shafted through the window and landed on his typewriter. Beckoning. "I under . . . understand. It i-is a daunting t-task. But I c-can pay you f-fifty pounds for . . . for the job. And b-board in the . . . the c-cottage. M-Meals too."

"Quite generous, sir. I happily accept the terms — though I daresay your Mr. Penrose will insist upon some sort of contract." She pulled out a copy of *The New Machiavelli.* "A bit different from *The Time Machine,* I've heard. My brother said — why, it's auto-graphed!" She put it back, pulled out another, opened it, spun. "As is this one, by Sir Arthur Conan Doyle."

He slid over to his desk, noting that the other letters he'd left there were gone. No doubt the Teagues had spread the word on where he'd left them and the rest of the staff had slipped in to fetch theirs. They all knew he'd have one for them, right down to young Benny.

There came a series of sliding and thunk-ing as she apparently withdrew and then replaced a whole line of books. His lips twitched up. On that particular shelf, she'd find the same thing, mostly. His favorites, all signed.

"Ah ha! This one isn't. *This Mad Caper* by Branok Hollow."

His favorite of the five Locryn James books, to be sure. Thus far. He pulled out his chair and darted a glance at the banded bundle of papers, to make sure they were still wrapped in that masking brown paper. "Mr. H-Hollow is . . . is a r-recluse, you know. N-No one knows w-where to r-reach him." No one but his lawyer.

Miss Gresham stepped into view and leaned onto the edge of his desk, as comfort-able as if it were her own. Which made his brows pull in. Certainly he wanted the assistance of someone capable, someone undaunted by the library — but that someone must also recognize boundaries.

And his desk was off-limits. "M-Miss —"

"It can't be that hard to find him." She was examining the book, flipping through a few pages. "With a name like *Branok Hollow* he is surely Cornish. Probably one of your neighbors."

"Excel . . . lent deduction. You should . . . you should g-go back into the l-library and see . . . and see if you can find c-clues as to his . . . identity in there." And give his poor exhausted tongue a break from trying to speak. And his fingers the chance to find their home on his typewriter keys.

"Here twenty minutes, and already you're trying to be rid of me? Should I be offended, Mr. Holstein?" She fiddled with the earpieces of her spectacles and sent him what she probably thought was a charming smile.

Peter sighed. Gryff had no doubt alerted Mrs. Teague of their guest — she would be in soon to rescue him, to show Miss Gresham to the cottage. He could grant her a few more minutes now. Even if half of his mind *was* wandering up the Amazon, searching for that cave. Legend would no doubt say it had treasure within. But it would have to be a trap, of course. The true treasure would have to be without.

Treasure was never where one sought it.

Miss Gresham flipped another page. "I'm not the reader my brother is — novel reader, I mean. Of course."

"Of c-course." Where had Benny put his fresh paper? He needed it always at hand . . . there. Some of it, anyway, on the floor at the corner of his desk. He leaned over to pull up a stack of it. And his books. He needed his books on the Amazon.

"Don't get me wrong, I enjoy a good Austen or Brontë. But I don't devour all these modern stories like Barclay does. Full of machines and science and whatnot. I'm of the mind that a book should have a bit of a love story in it. Don't you think so, Mr. Holstein?"

His box of research books was there too. He flipped off the lid and drew out a few. Amazon. Andes. Alps — hmm. Perhaps next, Locryn should go to the Alps. Peter had at least seen them on one of his family's holidays to Germany. Though he'd be wise to avoid the German side of things in his stories, unless he were making a point of it. Switzerland, perhaps.

Or perhaps he should make a point of it.

Hollow could get away with saying what Holstein never could.

"Barclay always scoffs when I say such things. He says romance is not the point of literature. Though to my mind, it rather begs the question of what its point *is*. What think you, sir?"

He looked up even as he set his books on the desk. She seemed to actually be awaiting a response this time, her eyes wide and brows lifted behind her spectacles. "F-Fiction can . . . can . . ." It was no good. His mouth wouldn't wrap around the words that came so easily to his mind.

He shook his head and positioned his chair better. He'd write her a note with his thoughts, that was all. After dinner, perhaps. Once he'd gotten this cave image down on the page.

Miss Gresham closed the book. "Well, you certainly seem to have a great appreciation for it — these shelves are nearly as bursting as the ones next door. Have you any Melville? Barclay has been after me to read Melville, insisting he's one of America's most brilliant writers of the centuries past, but I've yet to —"

"M-Miss Gresham." He rested his fingers on the edge of the desk rather than the keys. He never wrote with another in the room.

Never. And even if her voice was of a pleasant enough tone, this would never do. "Do . . . do you always t-talk so much?"

"I beg your pardon." Though it wasn't apology in her tone as she straightened. It was offense. "I am only trying —"

The shattering of glass silenced her. Peter leapt to his feet and rounded the desk, trying to pinpoint where the sound had come from. Down the passage somewhere. He hurried that way even as Mrs. Teague rushed from the opposite direction, both of them charging into the drawing room. The one with the wide, welcoming windows that looked out over the open expanse of the lawn.

Dusk was falling. The room was dark, though in here he could simply switch on the light. It showed him a hole spilling in night where the window should have been, a figure nearly out of sight on the lawn . . . and a stone wrapped in paper resting in the pieces of glass on the floor.

The shards crunched under his shoes as he stepped over to it and picked it up. His hands didn't shake. His breath didn't catch. But there was a matching stone in the pit of his stomach as he freed the paper from the one in his hands.

Mrs. Teague appeared on one side of

him . . . and Miss Gresham on the other, both looking over his shoulder as he smoothed out the paper and read the words shouting up at him.

Go back to Germany.

Still his hands didn't shake. His breath didn't catch. But his jaw felt so tight he could barely stammer around it as he looked over at the wide-eyed librarian. "You . . . you start f-first thing in the m-morning."

He spun on his heel and strode from the room, the rock still in his hand.

FOUR

Tea sloshed from her cup as she poured it, but that was only to be expected. Dawn had barely streaked the horizon when the blasted birds had started tweeting right outside Rosemary's window. And it had taken her two hours to get to sleep last night, what with that ridiculously soft mattress, free of lumps. The pleasant smell of flowers from the bedside table. And the unending, bizarre, utterly baffling *silence* of the night.

Sirens might warn of approaching monsters in the dark, but silence surely cloaked them.

"How does anyone live like this?" Willa poked a finger at the tea service. Serviceable and plain, but still beautiful. Free of chips. Elegant. Just like the birds, Willa had come with the first streaks of dawn, having apparently heard via the village gossip that a librarian had taken up residence in the cottage at Kensey Manor.

"Happily, I should think." Rosemary opened the little bowl by the teapot and let out an involuntary squeak. Sugar! And it wasn't even Christmas. She scooped a heaping spoonful into her not-quite-steaming cup. "Have some toast."

Willa had already taken a bite out of a slice slathered in marmalade and closed her eyes in bliss. "For a day or two, certainly. But don't you think it would get boring? Never wondering what comes next? Never needing to work for anything?"

Rosemary's gaze drifted to the middle of the small table in the cottage's kitchen, where a shard of glass still sat. It had been stuck in the laces of her half-boots last night, and she hadn't noticed until she'd had the lights on in here. "Oh, I daresay everyone wonders what comes next, now and then."

Willa followed her gaze, and her brows knit. "I saw the window covered over with card paper when I walked up the drive. What happened?"

"Someone threw a stone through it."

Her sister paused with the toast halfway back to her mouth. "Rosie, maybe this isn't such a good idea. If you get hurt . . ."

As if she were afraid of random stones or the cowards who would throw them. No

Cornish vandal could possibly intimidate someone from the roughest streets of London. Rosemary took a sip of tea and leaned forward. "A thousand pounds, Willa. One. Thousand. Pounds."

Willa ran her tongue over her teeth. "It's a fortune. More than we've ever brought in, combined. Even factoring in that diamond necklace Barclay lifted."

"I know." But that was the problem with stolen goods — they had to be fenced, and fences never paid full price. It was better when they had clients requesting specific things, but there were never enough of those. "We could find a place in a better neighborhood. Perhaps even all together. We've never all been together. We could send the little ones to school."

Willa sat back, her eyes unfocused. "They could have a chance. A different life, if they wanted it."

The words hung in the air like fog. How many times had they cheered for their life, their success in it, the fact that they were no worse off than the honest blokes in the factories and hadn't had to work so hard to achieve it?

But they'd never really had other options — not really. If Jory could, though, and little Olivia . . . if they didn't have to go through life ducking every time they heard a bobby's whistle . . ."

Willa reached for Rosemary's cup, having not poured her own. "And with the greatest risks, right? Just be careful, Rosie. Even carefuller than careful."

"I know. I will." She picked up a slice of toast but then put it back down. Mrs. Teague had fed her last night, scowling the whole while, and had obviously slipped in this morning with the tray of food and tea. Rosemary hadn't even heard her, which wouldn't do at all. She must stay alert, on her guard. *Rosemary Gresham, librarian.* She couldn't afford to slip, even for a moment. "I'd better head to the house. Get started. I've no idea what to do with that library, Will."

Smirking, Willa polished off the last bite. "Maybe you should have sent Barclay here in your place."

She snatched back her teacup and took a swig as she stood. "I am every bit the thief he is, and more. *I* read German."

"Whoever would have thought it would prove useful a second time?" Willa stood too and grabbed a second piece of toast. "I'll spend the day in the village, then come back here tonight to see you. Is there anything you need me to do?"

Give me a quick course on how books ought to be organized in a proper library? Rosemary downed the last of the tea from the dainty china cup and set it upon the table. "Nothing I can think of yet. I'll let you know if there is."

Willa paused with her hand on the door, surveying the kitchen much as she had twenty minutes earlier, when she first came in. "We could fit the whole family in this place — and they call it a *cottage.*"

Rather close to the thought Rosemary had entertained the night before when she'd followed Mrs. Teague over the darkened lawn and to the stone house set against the woods. It had five bedrooms — five! And electric lights. Hot water actually came from the tap when she turned it on in the bath . . . and the tub. The tub deserved to have sonnets written about it. In London, they shared a lavatory with the whole floor and counted themselves lucky if they managed to find time for a ten-minute bath — and that after hauling up their own hot water.

This had been pure bliss . . . and accounted for her lateness in retiring. Before the terrible quiet and too-comfortable mattress had kept her awake.

Willa narrowed her eyes and leveled a finger at Rosemary's nose. "Don't get spoiled. Even with a thousand pounds, we'll not be *that* well off."

"I know." But she smiled as she grabbed up the linen jacket that matched her new dress. It was somber, beige, even had a border of the most boring brown plaid. But it was similar to what she'd seen other women wearing when she'd gone in search of Mr. Hall. "But it makes for a nice little holiday, doesn't it?"

Willa grinned and opened the door.

The morning air was cool and damp — nothing unusual. But there were no traffic sounds. No crowds pushing their way toward the factories. And it smelled of . . . of . . . Rosemary sniffed. "What *is* that?"

Willa sniffed too. "Grass? Flowers?"

Bizarre. Rosemary enjoyed walking through a park, of course, but to be hit in the face with the scent of green life the moment she stepped out her door would take some getting used to. "It's so *quiet.*"

"Even the village is — though not compared to this."

They walked a few steps together before Willa turned toward the driveway. Rosemary lifted a hand to wave good-bye. "Have a good day, Will."

Striking out along the brick path that led toward the kitchen, Rosemary adjusted the bothersome spectacles she'd nearly forgotten to put on and wished for the sound of the tube chugging by.

The kitchen door stuck, but she employed a hip to get it open and then collided with the rock-solid glare of Mrs. Teague, who stood beside a woman she'd been introduced to last night only as Grammy. The cook.

Rosemary produced a smile. "Good morning. Looks as if it's going to be a beautiful day out there. To whom do I owe the thanks for the lovely breakfast tray?"

"Mr. Holstein for ordering it sent out, that's who." Mrs. Teague sniffed and spun away.

Grammy — who looked an awful lot like Mrs. Teague, now that Rosemary saw them both in morning's light — offered a small smile but turned back to her pot.

Well then. She didn't really want to linger here anyway. "Thank you. Now don't mind me, I'll just slip through to the library."

No one stopped her, though she did hear the housekeeper mutter something about watching her. Rosemary aimed a departing smile at the older woman and wiggled her fingers in farewell. Let her watch. She didn't intend to lift the silver, and the woman certainly wouldn't be hovering over her shoulder in the library to notice anything she *was* interested in.

The manor house wasn't so big that she could really get lost, especially having been shown this ground floor last night. She easily found the hallway with the library and Holstein's study, the drawing room with the broken window, and a few other anonymous rooms. She headed for those terrifying double doors at the end of the hall.

Then paused outside Holstein's closed study door. An unmistakable *click-clacking* came from within. The typewriter. Whatever he was writing, he was going about it quickly. *Click, clack, ding, slide.* And then again.

Rosemary shook her head and continued to the library. Much as he had done yesterday, she paused outside for a fortifying breath, then pushed open one door. A search of the wall showed her no convenient switch for producing light, and the lamps had no cords. But they were filled with oil, and matches lay nearby.

She took a few minutes to light each and every one she found sitting on tables or stands, that *click-clack-ding* echoing, muffled, through the room. Then she turned to the wide table that someone had cleared off for her. Though that only meant moving the stacks of periodicals from its top to the floor beside it.

Really, what did one family need with all this?

She picked up the valise she'd left in here last night, set it on the smooth tabletop, and paused.

A folded piece of paper rested in front of the single chair, *Miss Gresham* scrawled across it in an elegant but decidedly masculine hand. Warily, she reached out. A summons from the barrister? Or perhaps instructions from the master of the house?

She flipped it open, sinking down into the chair when she saw that the page was more than half filled with the neat, looping hand. Her gaze returned to the beginning.

Confession: I have trouble expressing myself in speech. A deduction I daresay you have made already on your own. But you raised an interesting question tonight about the point of literature, and I did want to discuss it.

I am by no means an expert, of course, but love of the written word runs deep in my family — also no great mystery to you, having seen the library. But I do hold fiction in especial esteem. Fiction is a way to express mankind's deepest heart. His fears. His hopes. His failings. His successes. Fiction is truth . . . in a pretty wrapping.

Rosemary leaned back in the chair as she read the rest of it, as he spoke of *The New Machiavelli,* which she had picked up last night, and Wells's way of speaking of Parliament. Of *Moby Dick* and the soul's quest for God — adding that, yes, he had the complete works of Melville, and she was welcome to borrow them.

Her lips tugged up at that, especially when he went on to inquire about the brother she'd mentioned.

Barclay would have an apoplexy over the fact that she'd mentioned him at all. But she had already claimed Willa as her sister, and how was she to be around all Barclay's favorite novels and *not* bring him up?

At the end of the letter were a few quick lines of instruction that reiterated what he'd mentioned yesterday — that in addition to organizing the room, her focus should be on finding a set of journals that his father and grandfather had written. And that if she could look through any books that might mention his family history, he would appreciate finding some solid information as to why the Holsteins had left Germany and that expounded on their ties to England rather than the Fatherland.

He knew, then, of the suspicions. And wanted to be able to meet them head-on.

Well, she was far more likely to find what *she* needed — evidence to the contrary.

All of which promised to make her eyes ache, and she was happy to ignore the daunting stacks a few minutes longer. She drew out a sheet of fresh paper from her valise, along with the fountain pen she'd purchased in London before she'd left but hadn't yet had cause to use.

Her hand hovered above the page. Her writing wasn't so neat, so tidy, so elegant. She'd learned her letters, after all, behind Pauly's bar, on a stray piece of slate he'd dug up for her somewhere. No fancy tutors or expensive schools.

Would he expect something more from a librarian? Would she be giving herself away with her very hand?

"Drat it all." She put down the pen and stood again. She would do better to focus on slaying this many-paged dragon.

Should she begin in the corner and work her way around? Or from right here at the table and work her way to the outsides of the room? Or maybe take a sampling from each section and see if there were any classification within it at all?

Or perhaps she'd start at the door. There was a certain logic to that. Then she might not have to fend off claustrophobia just by stepping inside.

Notebook in hand, she headed that way and knelt on the floor to trail a finger down the spines of the first stack. The two on top were religious works. She made a note, jotting down the authors — one English, one German.

The book beneath those, on the other hand, appeared to be . . . mathematics? She slid it out of the stack. *Essay on the Theory of Numbers.* For a moment, she could only stare. Who in the world could spend a hundred pages theorizing about *numbers*? Now, if they were attached to a pound sign and one was discussing what to do with them — but plain, simple numbers?

Copernicus lay beneath that one by Dedekind. But beneath him was a book on floral arrangements.

Floral arrangements.

She shook her head and wrote that down too. Perhaps these by the door had been looked through more recently and put back in here helter-skelter. Perhaps in other parts of the room, there would be more order.

She turned to the other side of the doorway. Boxes were stacked upon boxes there, all of them closed up. Rosemary took the lid from the topmost one and peeked inside. Unbound papers filled it to bursting, all of them unfolded but bearing creases. Setting lid and her notebook down, she pulled one out.

A letter. Addressed to Peter from . . . her eyes went wide. The signature merely said *George.* But there was a crest under it, one everyone in England knew. She held in her hands a letter from the king himself. Only inviting Holstein for a game of cricket on some Thursday long since past, but still. And there, a reference to Peter's last letter to him. *I have been pondering your words.*

What words? That was the question, wasn't it? But how was she to know only from the letters he received? She would have to try to piece together from the responses what he'd written in his. Leaning against the wall, she read that last line again.

The wall shifted — or rather, the stack of boxes she'd mistaken for the wall shifted. Swayed. Teetered. "No!" Tossing down the letter, she reached to steady the stack.

She only made it worse. The two top boxes came crashing down. They were so densely packed, their contents didn't even spill, but they did send a stack of books tumbling, which created such a din that it would surely bring the whole house down upon her.

"What a start to a new job, Rosemary," she muttered under her breath.

The door to the library opened, and Holstein surged in, brows up. "Miss Gresham, are . . . are you all right?"

She shoved back a curl that had slipped free and knew her smile was more frustrated than reassuring. "Sorry. Clumsy me — I won't knock over everything, I promise. Just not quite used to how close everything is."

"No n-need to a . . . apologize." He wove his way through the room, frowning at the boxes now on their sides on the floor. "You n-needn't worry with . . . with those. They are m-mine. Just . . . letters."

Letters *from the king.* She smoothed down the linen of her jacket over her hips, reminding herself not to overstep. "Excellent. I'll just move them to a corner, then, shall I? So they'll be out of the way and I won't knock them over again."

"I can h-help you."

"No need, sir, I assure you. I can manage a box of papers well enough."

But he had already arrived at her side and crouched down to retrieve the lid to the formerly topmost box. And her notebook, which he glanced at.

So much for keeping her handwriting from him. Her cheeks went warm when he squinted at her scrawl, and she snatched the book from his hand. Then backed up a step — she was well used to using close proximity to strangers to her advantage, but it seemed different in an otherwise unoccupied room. Far too . . . friendly. "Forgive my script, Mr. Holstein. I was by nature left-handed, you see, but forced to learn with my right, and . . ."

It was Pauly's excuse for *his* poor penmanship, and it seemed to appease her employer. He slung his hands in his pockets and made no move to get any closer. "Are y-you sure you . . . you d-don't need any help?"

"Quite. Though I do appreciate the offer, I don't want to keep you from your business." She darted a glance toward his study.

"Ah." He edged back in that direction, gaze latched on the open door. "Right. Then . . . if you need any . . . anything, j-just let m-me know."

"Certainly, sir. Have a pleasant morning — oh, and thank you for having breakfast sent out."

He disappeared into his study with a wave over his shoulder, shutting the door firmly behind him.

Rosemary pursed her lips. She ought to be paying attention to *him* as much as to the documents in this room. And to be sure, he had some odd quirks. But then, how many of them stemmed from his unfortunate inability to speak properly? That would be enough to make anyone a bit of a hermit.

So then . . . how had he come to be such chums with the king — a man at least a decade his senior? She'd have to go through those letters. And she'd have to be discreet about it, since Holstein could burst back through that door at any moment.

For now, she did as she'd said she'd do. Moved the boxes into a corner — which required first scooting out the stacks of books that had already been there. Books that ranged from French poetry by some chap named Baudelaire, to a Latin something or another that went well beyond her comprehension, to an English tome two inches thick on how to cultivate cotton. Cotton!

Within half an hour, she'd shed her jacket. After another hour of shoving, pulling, stacking, and sorting, she flung open the windows. She couldn't be sure she was organizing things as anyone else would, but it at least made sense to her — she was making stacks for each subject. Shoving into the corners the ones she couldn't see having any bearing on his family history, and putting in the middle of the room the ones that might.

By noon, she couldn't tell by looking at the room that she'd done a thing, but there was a line of perspiration trickling down her back, and curls that had slipped free of her chignon were sticking to her neck. She'd tossed the spectacles onto the table after they'd all but rubbed her raw behind the ears. And her growling stomach was reminding her that she hadn't tried any of that lovely-looking marmalade on toast.

She needed a rest. Some water wouldn't be ill-placed either, but she was a bit too tired to venture into the kitchen just now. The table looked inviting though, so she took a seat again. She ought to pull forward one of those volumes she had set aside that seemed as though it might deal with Holstein family history.

But the letter was already out, before her. She looked at it again instead. Never in her life had she gotten a proper letter. Willa had left her a note here and there, when she'd slipped out before Rosemary awoke, but those had always been scrawled with chalk on that same slate — they hadn't funds enough to waste on spare paper.

She picked up her pen. Her first proper letter deserved a response.

Are we confessing our insecurities? Then I shan't be left out. I have always been afraid of the dark, and I noticed that the library is the one room in this lovely house of yours without electric lights. Cruel irony, sir. Though I shall further confess that my flat in London doesn't have them either.

What it does have, however, is family, about whom you asked.

My family? Positively huge. And we always, always encourage one another. I can't imagine life without them. My eldest brother is the one I mentioned last night, Barclay, who seems to share your taste in fiction. My sister Willa is a year younger than I — she is the one who drove me out here yesterday. And there are scads of younger ones.

I do see your point about the power of fiction. That is, perhaps, why Willa and I both like stories with a bit of romance to them. They remind us that there's always hope for happiness tomorrow, no matter how bleak today might be.

Her new pen was perhaps too smoothly

flowing, too easily used. Why else would she have written so much, and all of it true? Screwing the cap back on, she folded the letter. She wouldn't give it to him. He certainly didn't really want to know about her family. Or why she would take Jane Eyre and Mr. Rochester over *The War of the Worlds* any day.

Except . . . he had asked, hadn't he? And why would he have done so if he didn't want to know? He was under no obligation. If it were nothing more than polite interest, then this was nothing more than a polite response.

She opened the page again, and the pen. Glanced at the letter from him. He'd signed it *Peter,* which seemed rather familiar, but what did she really know of letter-writing? Perhaps that was how one *always* signed a letter, with one's first name.

So be it, then. She had practiced her name more than anything else and could write it with a fair imitation of beauty, she thought. A looping *R,* careful middle letters, and a long, curling tail on her *Y.*

She stood, grabbed up the paper. He obviously received a mountain of correspondence. This would mean nothing to him — just an answer to his question. That would be that.

95

A breeze came through the open window, ruffling the pages of a magazine and soothing the heat trapped under her collar. She enjoyed it for a moment and then moved to the door joining the library to his office.

No *click-clacking.* No *dings.* She rapped on the door.

Nothing.

Well, he *did* say she could borrow a novel, didn't he? She opened the door slowly, peeking in. Empty. Good. Breathing more easily, she strode over to his desk. And gaped.

Last night it had been so neat. Now there wasn't a spare inch of space on it anywhere. The entire top was covered with papers and books and half-filled teacups, a plate with crumbs, and miscellaneous rubber bands and paper clips.

The rock that had made such an ignominious acquaintance with the window anchored down a pile of papers.

The typewriter sat empty. And none of the papers strewn about had anything typewritten upon them.

"Hmm." That twitch in her stomach told her she'd have to find out what he was typing at some point — but not without knowing his schedule and routine. If he would be happening back into this room in a matter of minutes, she didn't want to be caught with her hand in a desk drawer. Wouldn't do to be dismissed her first day here.

She put the note on top of the typewriter — that being the only space not already littered — and then turned to the shelves. He didn't seem to employ any better order to his books here than he did in the library, but there were at least fewer of them. It took her only five minutes to find *Moby Dick*.

He still hadn't returned, but that twitchy place inside told her he'd been gone long enough to be due back any second, so she slipped into the library. And jumped, squealing, when she saw a figure straightening from the table.

Mrs. Teague scowled at her. "And what are you doing in Mr. Holstein's study, young miss?"

Her instincts had certainly been right on not wanting to arrive as a domestic. She could only imagine how unpleasant it must be to live under this woman's thumb. If ever she *were* mistress of a house like this, she wouldn't let her housekeeper lord over the rest of the staff. Holding up the book, she breathed, "He said I might borrow a novel."

"And you were quick to take advantage, I see." The housekeeper lumbered a few steps her way. "I brought you your meal — you will of course want to take it in here so you can keep working as you eat and get done all the faster."

Rosemary fought the sudden urge to insist on eating it somewhere else — anywhere else. She dredged up a smile. "How thoughtful. Thank you."

"You're not fooling me, you know."

Her pulse might have increased, but she had long ago trained herself not to show it. She had slithered right between two bobbies last autumn, hadn't she, with a liberated bracelet on her wrist? And they hadn't suspected a thing. She lifted her brows. "I'm not *trying* to fool you, Mrs. Teague."

The woman pointed a chubby finger at her. "I know what you're doing here, and I'll not have it."

Rosemary blinked. She may have *thought* she knew something, but she certainly didn't know Rosemary's real purposes. "You don't want me to help Mr. Holstein with the library?"

"Oh, by all means. Help him with this heap of nonsense. And let that be the end of it, do you hear me?"

"All right." Sidestepping the wide woman, she slid the book onto the table and tried not to ogle the tray of food. Sandwiches, fruit, even fresh greens.

"The Penroses may have invited you to join Mr. Holstein for dinner at their home tonight, but don't think it's for any purpose but to keep an eye on you."

Strawberries. There were strawberries, and they smelled like heaven. "I'm not — pardon?" She snapped back around. "Penroses? Dinner?"

"Mr. Holstein asked me to inform you. You'll leave promptly at seven, and don't think Mr. Teague or I will so much as blink until you're back again."

Dinner with the lawyer? She had to stifle a groan. "How lovely. I look forward to meeting Mrs. Penrose."

Given the housekeeper's satisfied *hmph,* she had to wonder at what kind of beast she'd find in the lawyer's wife. "And she's looking forward to meeting you too, I'm sure. Now I'll be off. Don't want to distract you — and you'll do well to extend the same courtesy to Mr. Holstein and keep that door *shut.*"

Unable to resist any longer, Rosemary swiped a strawberry from the plate. "What does he work on in there all day?" It was, she thought, a reasonable question for anyone to ask. And if she could get an answer with a simple inquiry . . .

Mrs. Teague pulled the door closed with a

solid *thunk,* apparently not trusting Rosemary to do so. "I don't know, nor do you need to. Mr. Holstein's business is his own. You'll do well to remember that — he's our employer. Nothing more."

Funny — she could have sworn the Teagues both greeted him with far more warmth than they would a mere employer. But she wouldn't detain the woman any longer. She put the strawberry to her lips and took a bite, letting the juice trickle over her tongue.

Her eyes slid shut until the teetering stacks of books simply ceased to exist and it was just her and the fresh red fruit. There would be time enough to worry about overbearing housekeepers, foul-tempered barristers, and stuttering employers with clefts in their chins. Just now, Rosemary Gresham, librarian, was going to enjoy this life she'd borrowed.

FIVE

Peter finished the last bite of his sandwich, his gaze out on the churning waves, his free hand finding a stone beside him. Clouds gathered, out where sky kissed water, and the ever-present wind whipped past him with furious gusts. The storm he'd wanted yesterday would probably be here by morning, if not by dark tonight.

He lifted the rock, flung it out. Somewhere between cliff and waves it vanished from his view. Rarely could he ever see the *plunk* into the water. But still he tossed a few stones. And he remembered his grandfather's voice in his young ears, as Opa threw a stone of his own. As he said, *"They are like our prayers, ja? We send them out, and we cannot see, always, what they do. Once in a while we see their ripples. But more often we cannot. Still we pray. Because just like our logic tells us these rocks fall and gather and join the other rocks below, so our faith tells us our prayers whisper into God's ears and gather and join the prayers of the other faithful. And His Word says the prayers of the faithful avail much."*

Peter's lips curved up into a smile. All the prayers in the world probably wouldn't stop war from coming — not so long as men were set in their courses and gave little heed to the Lord. And if war came, life would get complicated for any man in England with a German surname — especially one who had somehow managed to make enemies of a few vital politicians.

Jealousy, that was all it could be. He'd done nothing other than become a friend to the king. More of a friend than some other parties who had been trying for years to flatter their way into the monarch's inner circles. It was just bad luck that Mr. Jasper was in a position to make trouble for him.

When he closed his eyes, he could still see the man's sneer. The way he turned his ring around on his finger, flaunting it — the symbol emblazoned on it was supposed to be a threat, he supposed. As if Peter feared the man simply because he was a member of one of those ridiculous fraternal orders that claimed ancient roots.

Insurance cooperatives, that's all most of them were. No more than a few decades old, no power to accomplish anything aside from negotiating medical costs. No matter how important-sounding their Latin names, Peter had no desire to be one of them — someone had approached him a year ago, offering membership — and he had no fear of them. Jasper could twirl his ring about all he wanted.

But "secret" societies aside . . . would jealousy really lead the man to make accusations of espionage? That wasn't a small thing, a silly thing. That was a life-or-death thing. He could be imprisoned or even *killed* over such an accusation.

His chest went tight, and he gripped another stone without throwing it. He would keep praying. And God would hear. He would see Peter through it. Somehow.

He stood and dusted the cliffside soil from his trousers. Locryn was not a man of faith. He had suffered as a child, had turned from his mother's teachings. He ran all around the world searching for what was always waiting within his own heart. But the quest itself could teach the reader. The quest, and Locryn's aging friend.

He would have to work Thomas into the cave scene. At the end of the last book he had headed back to London, leaving Locryn alone within a day of arriving in South

America from Africa. Necessary, at the time. But Thomas definitely needed to be there now. How, though, to bring him back without it feeling contrived?

Peter turned back toward the path that would lead home. In this direction, the sky was cloudless and blue and stretching on forever, the sun smiling down on Kensey Manor. Thomas had gone home because his father was dying. He wouldn't have had time to get there yet, tend to matters, and come back.

A bird cried overhead and flapped its way to a slab of granite. The father had passed away — the readers didn't even know him, they would not mourn the loss. But it would leave Thomas with an inheritance that would make him no longer reliant upon Locryn James — definitely necessary. The critics were all beginning to complain about that, and they had a point. Locryn didn't need a lackey, he needed a friend.

He could have gotten a telegram on the ship. Saying his father was gone, everything left to him. He wouldn't then have to hurry home, if the estates were neat and tidy. He could change ships at a port in the Caribbean and turn back around. Be there outside the cave when Locryn stumbled his way out again.

He would symbolize the truth, then. That blinding, Socratic truth. There could be beauty in that.

Peter meandered his way around a granite boulder, eyes on the path through the scrub to keep his feet from stumbling over any wily stones. Or to give his legs a message to pause, even when it took him a moment to sort through his brainstorm and realize what he was seeing.

Cigarette butts. And not just one that would indicate a stray wanderer who had happened over his property or a hired hand slipping away for a few minutes' break — though Peter knew of no one on his staff who smoked much. There were at least a dozen butts snuffed out amid the stones, half-kicked beneath the bell heather. Someone had stood here for quite a while. Or came here frequently.

He hadn't noticed the collection yesterday. Of course, he'd been talking to Gryff when he'd walked this path yesterday. Even so. They stood out, being white and human among the green and brown and natural.

Well could he imagine someone standing here, crouching down behind another huge slab of coastal granite. Looking . . . Peter drew in a breath. From right here, someone would have a fine view of Kensey. Or the back of Kensey, anyway. One could see the kitchen, the back garden. The cottage.

He may not have thought anything of it. Except that last night someone had tossed a rock through his drawing room window.

Withdrawing his handkerchief from his pocket, he gathered up the refuse. He would check this spot each day. And if more appeared, he would know if it was one at a time, or in a mass like this looked. And if the latter . . . then it meant someone had stood out here for quite a while, watching his home.

Or . . . or watching the cottage. Though he couldn't imagine why anyone would have followed Miss Gresham here to spy on her while she cleared out his library.

He pocketed the rubbish and kept on the trail. There could be no knowing. Not yet. But he would keep an eye on it. His fingers still itched to do something when he considered that shattered window, the rock sitting on his desk. But what? He could storm into the village and demand to know who had done it.

That would go well. He knew the words he'd want to say — *"I am as English as any of you. I have lived here all my life."* — but he could hear himself now, stumbling and stuttering and getting out no more than an

"I — I — I . . ." amid the laughter of his neighbors.

And even if he got it out, their rebuttals would be quick. His father may have been raised in England, may have *become* English when Opa had appealed to become a subject. But his mother . . . She had never relinquished her German citizenship, and she and Father had in fact taken steps to preserve it. To give Peter options, she had said. So that he would be both German and English until such a time as he could decide for himself which he preferred.

He sighed and sidestepped a jutting rock when his feet took him too close to the side of the path. He had decided when he was eighteen — but apparently the world didn't care about *that*. Or at the very least, Mr. Jasper didn't. He was determined to make Peter out to be a villain.

Villain. Maybe Thomas shouldn't be there right when Locryn came out of the cave. That may be too on-the-nose. Perhaps . . . perhaps it should be the villain instead. Peter clapped a hand to his hat to keep a particularly ambitious gust of wind from snatching it away and let that idea simmer. He didn't quite know who the villain was yet — should he revive Masters from *This Mad Caper*? Masters had been a villain the readers had truly loved to hate. Or Williams from *The Final Journey*? Come up with someone new altogether?

His eyes strayed to the cottage again. Perhaps a woman this time. That could get interesting. A bit of a love interest — not that Miss Gresham was a love interest. And not that it would please any female readers seeking romance if she ended up the villain. Still. He certainly hadn't done that before.

Yes, yes, that was it. Thomas could be waiting in town, but it could be a young woman who was there outside the cave. This could work. And if it did, he would owe Miss Gresham a very vague thank-you. A bonus, perhaps, when she finished the library.

If she finished the library. He ought to go and check on her. Make sure none of the stacks had collapsed on her while he was out-of-doors. She could be gasping for her last breath under a hundred tomes on medical science and no one would ever know it.

He picked up his pace a bit as he trod the rest of the litter-free path through the heather and gorse and granite, emerging into Teague's Italian garden with a smile. Though he highly doubted Miss Gresham had really been buried alive in books, his fingers were ready to find their home on his typewriter keys again.

He chose a side door to enter through — one not quite in sight of the broken window, which would just irritate him and distract him from caves and adventurers and South America — but near enough that he wouldn't have to sidestep Kerensa, who would be busy cleaning the main floor. He slipped inside, mind conjuring up ideas of what kind of flora might be found at the cave entrance.

"Oh!" Mrs. Teague leapt out of his way, a luncheon tray in her hands. *"Gav dhýmm."*

Peter quickly closed the door that had nearly struck her, offering a sheepish smile. "No, no, ex . . . excuse *me,* Mrs. Teague."

Her reply was a smile all warmth and fondness. "Think nothing of it, Mr. Holstein. Did you have enough to eat? We've berries in the kitchen. And you really ought to have some greens. Or the shortcake Grammy made last night, perhaps."

He started with a nod and changed it to a shake of his head as the list began. "I am . . . I am fine. Really." Though his gaze took in the many dishes on the tray she carried, and the empty state of them all. Miss Gresham had apparently quite enjoyed Grammy's cooking. Though how she managed to tuck away so very much, he couldn't fathom. She was as thin as a whisper. Jenny, if she didn't scare Miss Gresham all the way back to London tonight, would have quite a bit to say about his guest's figure, which went beyond fashionable in its slenderness.

Not that he had particularly noticed her figure. Beyond what was expected of a man who made his living observing people and putting words to them.

Mrs. Teague was no slouch in the observation department either. She too looked at the cleaned-up tray. And sniffed in that way she did. "She apparently has no qualms about taking full advantage of your hospitality. I don't think she left so much as a crumb."

Peter chuckled and angled toward his study. "Grammy will be p-pleased."

Unable to argue with that, Mrs. Teague sighed. "If you ask me, Mr. Holstein — not that anyone has, mind you — a young woman who shows up to a house uninvited is no lady, and not meant to be trusted."

"You sound like . . . like Gryff." He waved it off — it had been no secret that he'd been looking for a librarian, after all — and headed for his study door, which stood shut and inviting. He decided the empty luncheon tray was proof enough that Miss Gresham still lived among the stacks of

110

books and followed the siren song of his typewriter.

Until he stood before his desk and saw that folded piece of paper on it, anyway. Then his muscles coiled. His neck went so tight a headache blossomed at the base of his skull.

It wasn't that no one was allowed in his study — they were. It was just that no one ever entered without getting his permission first. No one. Even Mrs. Teague would leave the becrumbed plate and cup with the dregs of his morning coffee until he either left the door open for her or she tapped upon it and had express leave to enter.

True, he always put his manuscript away before he left the room. Or opened the door. Or, really, as he wrote it — the drawer remained open by his side while he was at the desk, and each sheet he pulled from the typewriter went directly into it. That way he never needed to do more than remove the one he was typing upon and slide the drawer shut to give someone leave to enter. And he always locked it before he left the room.

But still. Someone had been in here. Without permission. To leave him a . . . note?

He reached for it much like Locryn would soon be reaching for the pit viper guarding the entrance to the cave. Flipped it open, sent his eyes to the signature.

And frowned. *Rosemary.* Rosemary? His gaze darted to the door, shut, between him and the library. What kind of young lady signed just her first name on a note to a gentleman she didn't know? It was forward and familiar and not at all what was done.

And she had *come into his study* to leave it here. *On his typewriter.*

Gryff and Mrs. Teague might be right about her after all.

He loosed a *huff* that sounded, in his own ears, like Father always had when something went wrong. A chuff of breath, quick and hard. Which, in turn, made him remember Mother's chuckle in the face of it, and how she would say, *"Are you a locomotive, Aksel? Will you whistle next?"*

A bit of his mood seeped out as he recalled how Father would smile. And whistle, just to make Mother laugh.

Four years had done nothing to dispel their echoes. It had been heartbreaking enough to lose Father to that cancer, but then when Mother succumbed to fever within five months of him . . .

Peter eased down into his chair and smoothed out the crease in the paper so he could set it back on his typewriter keys and

112

read while he unlocked his manuscript drawer. His brows drew together.

A response to his note, that was all. But that was so very *odd.* She was right there, beyond the door. If she wanted to tell him about her family, she could just *tell* him. Like everyone else always did at Kensey. That was the way it had always worked — stymied by his tongue, he would write everyone his thoughts. But they knew they didn't need to write back to him, not when they could simply seek him out to give him the answers to his questions far more quickly.

But then, Miss Gresham had no way of knowing that was how things were always done here.

He leaned back in his creaking wood-and-leather chair and read it again, more slowly. Actually paying attention to what she said this time, rather than just noticing she said it.

Her hand was atrocious — he had thought it appalling in school that the teachers would bind the left arm of students to their sides and make them learn with their right, whether they were predisposed to that or not. He thought it no less ridiculous now.

But terrible handwriting aside, there was a certain charm to her words. Light, informal, but by no means too familiar, aside from that signature. He touched a finger to *afraid of the dark* and then folded the missive back up and slid it into the top-right drawer, opposite the one that held his manuscript. His lips twitched. Perhaps in London, fear of the dark could be mitigated by streetlamps and electric lights everywhere one went. Miss Gresham may be in for a surprise out here in the country, where the night seemed endless and untouched as soon as one stepped outside the house. The library would be the least of her concerns.

But it couldn't be too terrible a fear if she admitted it so readily to him. She would get along all right.

Better than Locryn would in that cave, and he'd had no phobia going in.

He chose a fresh sheet of paper from the stack and fed it into the typewriter, scrolling it up until he had a perfect inch margin at the top.

Within minutes — hours? — he'd put words to the scene. Darkness and snakes and a torch that wouldn't stay lit. Air so heavy that it nearly suffocated Locryn James as surely as it did his flame. The search, the quest burning him with its intensity, that need to *know* pulling him onward. Deeper into the darkness until his skin began to crawl with it.

Peter brushed an imaginary cobweb from his shoulder, reached for the cup that he forgot was empty until he lifted it to his mouth and got nothing out of it but a whimper. Not taking his eyes off his paper, he stretched behind him for the bell cord that would ring the kitchen. He needed more coffee. Or tea. Or something. Grammy would know what he needed, she always did.

Knock, knock, knock.

Locryn, however, had spilled his canteen some indeterminate amount of time ago — what did time really matter when one was in a primordial cave? — and his thirst was growing uncomfortable. He may be feeling a bit of claustrophobia too. Especially when his torch gave one last sputter and then died.

Knock, knock, knock.

Darkness. Thick, sour darkness. Heavy with humidity. Light on oxygen. Locryn was getting dizzy. He —

Knock, knock, knock.

Peter blinked, then blinked again to clear the darkness from his eyes. The door. Mrs. Teague with his coffee. Or tea. Or whatever Grammy had concocted. He pulled the unfinished page from the machine and put it in the drawer, then closed and locked it. Hurried his way toward the door to the hall.

No Mrs. Teague stood there, tray in hand. Nor Kerensa the housemaid. Nor even Grammy, who occasionally brought him something out herself, if the others were busy. No one at all. But he had heard a knock, he was sure of it.

There it came again — from the door to the library. Of course. "Idiot." He closed the hall's door and spun to the library's, pasting on a smile that still felt a bit cluttered by cobwebs and darkness.

Miss Gresham scarcely glanced up to notice. She surged into the room, a book in her hands, open. To this was glued her gaze.

"Do pardon the intrusion, Mr. Holstein. I don't mean to bother you and will be out of your hair again in a flash. Only this was too interesting to pass by. This, here. Do you see this photo?"

She had stopped just a few steps inside and stood right where she was, pointing at a glossy photograph page in some enormous tome. Her hair was slipping from its chignon and sticking to her neck. The jacket of her suit had vanished . . . as had her glasses, though there remained red marks on her nose to show where they had been.

He had to step closer to be able to see at what she was pointing.

Not that she had stopped talking while he

realized this. She tapped the photograph. "The caption says *Wilhelm Holstein.* I have no way of knowing, of course, if it's someone in your family, except that this page was marked. Which is, of course, what drew my attention to it as I was moving the book. I can see a bit of a resemblance to you too, I think. Or perhaps I'm convincing myself of it."

And had she stopped talking at *Wilhelm Holstein,* he could have answered that with a single nod. He offered said nod now, but it only made her brows draw together.

"I'm convincing myself?"

Peter sighed and shook his head. "Wilhelm is . . . was m-my . . . my opa." Though to be sure, he'd never known him when he was as young as he appeared in that photo, as he stood beside . . . Queen Victoria? Now *Peter's* brows drew together. Opa had never mentioned an acquaintance with the queen.

"Excellent! I hoped it was, perhaps, your grandfather. I read a bit of the pages surrounding this photo and didn't see any mention of him . . . but then, with the photographs all lumped into the middle like this, it's unlikely the mention, if there is one, would be right beside it. I'll have to read more of it, I suppose."

The scent of lemon teased his nose as she

shifted. Coming, he supposed, from her hair. Peter eased away a step, back to where he'd been. Focused again on the question at hand.

To be sure, Father had known King Edward and sometimes even called him *Bertie* — a relic from the days before the king had changed his name upon taking the crown and was still Albert. So Father must have known him when he was a young man, which meant he had likely met said young man's mother, Victoria. It ought not to be surprising, then, that Opa had as well.

Though it was likely an oddity that had captured him with her in a photograph. And that it had ended up in a book. Knowing Opa, he had taken great delight in that. No wonder the page was marked. Peter nodded again.

Miss Gresham was flipping through the pages. "I'm making a stack of the books I ought to read once I've brought a bit of order to the place. It seems the most efficient way to go about it, though that *does* mean I'll have no answers for you for quite some time as to what brought your family to England. It may take weeks just to sort through them. If that's acceptable?"

Another nod. Peter's gaze drifted back to his desk. Family connections . . . they could be quite long-stretching. Reaching out into unexpected places. What if . . . what if Locryn weren't the first James to make his way to this village? It had been, after all, a drawing he'd found at the end of the last book that had spurred him to South America. Peter hadn't paused to think where the drawing had come from. But what if it was a relic of the father Locryn could scarcely remember?

". . . if you prefer." Miss Gresham stepped into his line of sight again, brows lifted into a facial question mark.

He had missed something. And hardly cared. A connection to his father deep in the Amazon — that was pure gold. Peter had been wanting to work in more about the James family, and this was a perfect way to do it. He stepped around Miss Gresham and reached for paper and his favorite fountain pen. He must record this thought before he lost a few of the strands blowing about in his mind like those cobwebs in a sudden draft.

LJ's vat–30 y bf? 40? 1860/7

". . . if you think *that* would work better. Or I could . . ."

Should it have been before Locryn's birth or after? He scribbled down that question too, in his abbreviated shorthand that

119

combined English and German and what Gryff always called "Petese." No one else ever understood it — which was rather the point.

"Which would you prefer, Mr. Holstein?"

Peter glanced up solely because she had stepped into his space and now looked at him with a clear demand for an answer. The elder Mr. James could have . . .

"Mr. Holstein?"

"Would you s-stop . . . stop talking? P-Please." He closed his eyes to shut her out and latch hold of the idea floating around. He had dropped a hint about Mr. James in the last book, *The Final Journey.* That was what the final journey alluded to — that of Locryn's father. He had thought it was to Africa, that was why he had gone there in *Journey.* But what if it hadn't been? What if he had come here, to the Amazon? The new adventure that had taken Locryn and Thomas to South America at the end of the book had seemed to have nothing to do with the late Mr. James. But it could have.

He could even be here still. Alive.

No. That might be too heavy-handed. Bringing characters back from the dead was quickly becoming cliché. But Locryn could think it. Hope it.

Fear it.

Fear it? He jotted that down too. Why would Locryn fear finding his father? A question to ponder. It could add depth.

He followed a few more random trails of thought, wrote them down, and then rubbed a finger over his neck when it itched. With half a start he realized Miss Gresham was standing exactly where she had been a minute — five minutes? — ago, staring at him.

No, not *staring.* Drilling her gaze into him as if to prepare a hole in which to put the dynamite that would remove him from her path.

Or perhaps he had been reading too many American railroading stories.

He cleared his throat and shuffled to the side a step. "F-Forgive me, Miss . . . Miss Gresham. You w-were say . . . saying?"

She pasted on a smile so sweet it made his teeth hurt. And so false he had to wonder if she had a trunk of them in her mind's closet, just ready to be pulled out and put on like a costume. "No need to apologize to *me,* sir. I will refrain from bothering you with questions in the future. I shall simply do as I see fit."

She spun on the heel of her pump and marched back toward the door to the library, which still stood open.

Peter chuffed out another locomotive-Father breath and took a step to block her path. "I d-did not . . . did not m-mean to . . . to . . ." He clenched his teeth together and held up a finger, strode back to his desk and the never-ending pile of blank paper. It took him only a minute to put down his explanation in neat, precise English that his tongue refused to grasp.

But when he turned again, she was gone and the library door closed.

Of all the . . . she *was* his employee, if only for a few weeks or months. She could have a *bit* of respect, could she not? Was that so much to ask?

He yanked open the library door and felt a bit like Locryn as he stormed in. Fearless. Strong. In the right. Or thinking he was in the right, anyway, even when he was quite clearly wrong. And as Peter's vision was slammed with those eternal stacks of books, he could hardly help but think that he may indeed be in the wrong just now.

It was too much for one person on her own, without even the right to come in and ask questions of her employer. Too much to expect that she would have no need for guidance.

Blast. Rather than approach her where she was picking up books from a stack and slapping them into new stacks in rapid succession, he headed for the table and her pen. He scratched out the quick missive he had just written at his own desk and replaced it with a better one. Or what he hoped was a better one.

For half a second he considered just leaving it there for her to look at when she was finished steaming. But that was the coward's way out. Instead, he wove through the teetering towers and held it out.

She ignored him.

He gave it a wave.

She turned to a new stack, presenting her back to him.

Another chuff very nearly slipped out. But she had a point. Had someone ignored him as fully as he had ignored her, he would be offended too. So instead of a huff, he loosed a breath heavy with apology, if she had the ears to hear it. "Miss G-Gresham. P-Please."

At least she stopped, even if her shoulders remained in a line so rigid he couldn't help but notice the sharp angles and planes of them. She really was too thin. Even the ladies in London who had waists so small he wondered if they starved themselves had softer curves at shoulder and jaw than she did — and not to be a snob, but a working woman had no reason to aspire to such ridiculous fashions.

But perhaps it wasn't a choice she made for fashion. Perhaps it ran in her family, as it did in his. *He,* after all, wasn't exactly one to judge a person for being overly thin.

And what in the world was he doing staring at her bony shoulder when he had an apology to bumble through? He drew in the breath that he'd leaked out a moment before. "I d-did not . . . did not m-mean to be r . . . rude. I'm . . . I'm s-sorry."

She spun to face him so fast he nearly backed up a step. Though, really, he had no reason to think she was about to punch him. Sharp as her shoulders may be, she was still a woman of education, which meant some breeding. She wasn't going to haul off and strike him just for daring to offer an apology.

Probably. And even if she did, it wouldn't be the first time he'd had a fist come at him. There were always boys who wanted to pick fights with those they perceived to be weaker. And stuttering made him appear weaker. Hence why Father had taught him to box — not that he would use such skills against a woman, even if she *did* throw a punch.

She didn't. Of course. Though he swore

he felt the heat of it when she swiped the letter from his outstretched fingers and read it. Her sharp edges didn't soften any, and she didn't even look up at him as she said, "Fine."

"F-Fine?" She certainly didn't *sound* as though she thought it fine.

"That's what I said, isn't it?" She presented her back again.

"Then . . . fine." Prickly woman. Shoulders like a knife edge and the personality of a pincushion. Peter shook his head and wove his way back to the door. Which he closed not-so-silently, but without the gusto he had a mind to employ.

The smell hit him when he stepped back into his study. Books and pipe smoke and Father. Funny how, just now, the comfort of it condemned him. Funny how all those words written upon paper in here sounded like Father's voice in his ears. *Above all, Peter, we must be gentle. Self-controlled. This is how others see the love of Christ in us.*

Peter closed his eyes and breathed in the smell of wisdom. Breathed out a prayer.

He'd never considered himself a man of unbridled temper. He dealt with people all the time, after all, in London. He had no reason to get upset at having to do so here at home, in his haven. Not when he was the one who had invited her to stay.

He headed back to his desk and the page full of Petese. It took him a few minutes to focus his mind on his story again, but it helped to draw out his page from the drawer, to reposition it in the machine, to line it up just so, so that the new letters would be exactly aligned with the old.

His fingers found the keys and picked up his thought from where it dangled upon the page. A few more minutes of struggle through the blackest of caverns. Then, finally, a sliver of silver light shafting down. Not the entrance he had come into the cave through. But he groped his way toward it. Pushed his way up, halfway out.

And there, in the soft strokes of silver moonlight, she stood.

Peter paused, debating how to introduce this woman he'd decided to use. He needed a name too. Should she be South American? Or another ex-patriot like Locryn?

Born there, certainly. It would make Locryn trust her as a guide, and also dismiss her as being beneath him socially — which would prove a mistake on his part. Dorothea? Isabella?

No. His lips twitched up. Something with "Rose" in it. *Rosita.* He hunched over his typewriter and let the description flow. *She stood there with a hand outstretched. He saw Spanish in her face's angles and planes, and in the long, deepest brown hair that hinted at curl. A few tendrils stuck to her neck where the humidity of the night lured them. He grasped her hand and let her pull him over the lip of the vooga's opening. Her fingers were thin. Her shoulders, he noted as they bunched up to tug on him, were sharp and bony.*

Peter chuckled and kept tapping away.

It served her right.

Six

The words from Mr. Holstein's ridiculous note wouldn't leave Rosemary's mind's eye.

~~Forgive me for ignoring you. But I need quiet when I am in my study.~~
Forgive me if I come off as oafish from time to time. I don't mean to be. It is just that I'm unaccustomed to sharing my space.

That is no excuse, I know. And I didn't mean to ignore you so fully. Perhaps we can reach an agreement. If you will honor my need for quiet privacy during most of the day, or when I specifically request it, I will be happy to answer all your questions at set times. Luncheon and dinner are a logical time to plan for these conversations.

Again, please forgive my behavior.

He had the right of it. "He's an utter oaf.

A ridiculous, self-righteous oaf, and I may just lose my mind if this stretches out as long as it looks like it may." She gripped the bedpost, not because Willa was pulling her corset tight — she wasn't — nor because she really *had* to hold on while her gown's buttons were being done up. But just because she needed to dig her fingers into *something,* and Peter Holstein's flesh wasn't available.

"Well, what do you expect, Rosie? A bloke born and raised in this place — he no doubt thinks the very sun revolves around him." Willa's voice contained a bit of calm, a bit of consolation. A bit more amusement than was really called for.

Rosemary stared at the print of the wallpaper until it blurred. "I'm going to enjoy proving him a traitor. I'm going to take his money, destroy his name, and find a way to take his blighted house from him too, whether I keep it or not. Four dashed minutes and thirty-nine seconds! Have you any idea how long four minutes thirty-nine seconds really is? When you're just standing there like a — like a piece of *furniture*?"

Willa snorted what sounded suspiciously like a laugh. "Sounds as though *you* do."

"It's an eternity, that's how long. While he wrote a bunch of gibberish as if it contained the keys to eternal youth."

Gibberish that had made her stomach go tight once she'd calmed enough to think of it. The bits she'd glimpsed made no sense whatsoever. What was it? Some sort of shorthand? Or . . . or some sort of coded language?

To whom had *that* note been written?

Willa must have finished the last button marching up Rosemary's back, given that she reached for the sash to tie it. "Maybe he's some great philosopher. Or mathematician. Maybe . . . maybe he's designing a new automobile."

Rosemary gave an answering snort. "Or maybe he's coming up with some secret code for the Germans."

Willa's fingers stilled. "But that one isn't funny."

"I wasn't sent here to find a joke, was I?" She let go of the bedpost and turned to the mirror. It was full-length, in a pretty wooden frame that attached at two points to a structure that would let her flip it all the way around, if she wanted. She'd never had a mirror bigger than a sheet of paper before, and those were always cloudy and scratched and made her look like a carnival show.

This one showed her a woman with rage in her eyes but a very nice evening dress draping her just as it should. She smoothed a hand down one of the tiers. They'd bought this silk with what they'd fenced from a pair of diamond earrings last year. Found a bargain on it, but still. It had pained her to spend the money on silk instead of food.

But the silk had aided her in a job six months ago at a ball, at which she'd lifted a necklace that had fetched four times the cost of the silk. Now she was rather senti-mental about the deep blue fabric.

Willa stepped into the frame too. Her lips were pursed. "What are we going to do with your hair, Rosie?"

Rosemary reached for the beaded head-band she'd picked up for a song a few months before. "Just a chignon and this." No need to get too excited about a dinner with the Penroses. She gripped the band until the beads dug into her palm. The meal would no doubt be a chore. Worse would be the drive to and from . . . and every meal hereafter, according to that note. "You don't think he really means we should take *every* luncheon and dinner together, do you?"

Willa chuckled. "He was trying to be nice, and you well know it. Provide you a set time to ask him questions. Twice a day. Gener-ous of him."

Yes, *generous.* To give his hired help two

hours a day in his esteemed company —
and otherwise insist that if he requested
quiet, she give it without argument. What
nerve he had, to actually write down that
demand. And then have the gall to *grant*
her two meals a day!

It was going to be torture for them both.
And no doubt he knew it as well as she did.

"And when the annoyance is high, just
think about this." Willa clapped hands to
Rosemary's shoulders and turned her
around. Her eyes were wide. "One. Thousand. Pounds."

Rosemary grinned. "And strawberries."

"Strawberries." Willa slid those eyes shut
now and loosed a blissful sigh. "If there are
more tomorrow, save me one. I saw some in
the village, but they were too dear."

"I'll bring you the whole bowl, if there
are. Well, perhaps minus one. Or two."

Willa laughed and gave her a helpful push
toward the dressing table's bench. "Sit. I'll
do your hair tonight."

Rosemary sat, and they spoke of the usual
nothing while Willa brushed and gathered
and tugged and coiled and pinned. Which
left her mind free to wander — just now
toward the wardrobe that stood, formidable
and closed, in the corner. She had brought
two evening dresses with her, not knowing

132

what occasions she might be expected to attend . . . and rather expecting never to use them. But if she had dinner with Holstein every night, she would have to dress for it, wouldn't she? Wasn't that what these families did, donning their best every night?

An utter waste. What if she spilled something on one of her only two gowns? She didn't know who here was in charge of laundry, but she highly doubted Mrs. Teague would take kindly to her adding her own to the mix.

And would two be enough? But it wasn't as though anyone would expect a woman in her profession to have a bursting wardrobe.

"There." Willa stepped back and nodded at their reflections in the smaller mirror attached to the table. "You look the part. Are you going to wear those ridiculous glasses?"

She should . . . but the very idea made her ears and nose hurt. "No. If asked, I'll claim I only need them when dealing with books."

"Well. I can't do any more damage here, so I'm going to head back to the village for my own dinner." To prove it, Willa reached for the hat she'd tossed onto Rosemary's bed an hour earlier. "I'm thinking I'll stay a week and we'll see how you're doing. If you need me longer . . ."

"I'm sure I'll be all right." Tortured, but all right. She could hardly expect Willa to stay here forever. And it would take *forever* to go through those books. She'd taken to looking in any of them that had pages marked, and a fair number mentioned the Holstein family.

A world she could scarcely fathom. Who really had their name in a book? Really? And photographs of themselves with monarchs? The Holsteins moved in high circles, to be sure.

The question was, did those circles revolve around England or Germany?

"Well then. 'Night." Willa smiled, wiggled her fingers, and disappeared out the bedroom door.

Rosemary glanced at the clock on the mantel. She still had half an hour before the time when Mrs. Teague had informed her, with narrowed eyes and pursed lips, that she ought to be at the front of the house to await the carriage. Spotting the collection of Melville on her bedside table where she'd put it earlier, she headed that way and took a seat in the plush armchair in the corner of the room.

An armchair — in her bedroom!

Her eyes very nearly crossed within five minutes. Barclay surely didn't really *like* this, did he? He'd probably recommended it solely so he could laugh at the look on her face as she read it. So he could lord his supposedly superior intelligence over her.

"Well." She slapped the cover closed and tossed the book toward her bed. "I'm not stupid just because I don't want to read about a bunch of smelly fishermen out hunting whales."

The *tick-tocking* clock agreed with her, practically nodding its head.

She pushed to her feet and decided to wander through the cottage again. It had been dark last night when she got here, and though she'd glanced into every room, she hadn't really explored them.

Her expedition began in the next bed-chamber, appointed with blue and white linens and light-colored furniture. Its window had much the same view of the wild-looking garden as hers did. She crossed the hall to the rooms opposite — these looked into the wood. For a long moment she stood at one of the panes, gazing out.

There were trees, of course, in London. But no proper woods. Perhaps tomorrow she would find the time to explore them a bit. Or follow that path through the heather that ended, she suspected, at the famous Cornish cliffs.

The next room was a bedroom only in the loosest sense — it had a bed, of sorts. But instead of bureau or chair, it had shelves. Filled, of course, with books.

Were she in the mood, she might have found it amusing. Today, it made her scowl. Whoever the Holsteins were, they had a serious problem with book collection.

Her scowl didn't lessen when she stepped close enough to the shelves to see the titles. Many of them were the same as she had looked over in Holstein's study earlier. Novels, some with familiar authors and titles, some she had never heard of. Some in German, most in English. All looked utterly pristine, their spines uncreased and pages, when she pulled one tome out, without the slightest wear.

Whenever Barclay got a new book, "new" didn't mean *new*. Ever. One couldn't eat a book. Couldn't wear it. Couldn't use it to keep warm on a bitter winter night. And so, they only ever picked up the cheapest ones in used-book shops.

But Holstein obviously had multiple copies of most of these. Just think of it — multiple copies of the *same book*.

She replaced the perfect example and perused another shelf. Let her gaze fall to the table, where an electric lamp sat beside yet another story in an untouched binding. *This Mad Caper* by Branock Hollow. Hollow's fourth book, wasn't it? Barclay had gone on and on about it. Which didn't, apparently, say much if he liked Melville.

Rosemary reached for it, flipped it open. The first paragraph was promising. And since Barclay need never even know that she had tried ol' Herman and given him up after a page . . . She headed back to the chair by her bed in her room and wasted the next fifteen minutes happily enough. This Hollow chap was no Austen, but he was a far cry easier to read than the whaler-loving American.

He wasn't, however, distracting enough to make her lose track of time. At precisely the minute she had deemed right for walking out of the cottage, out she went. Along the path, through the garden, toward the front of the house.

Halfway through the profusion of blooms, her step hitched. An odd smell drifted on the breeze, one that didn't fit with the fragrance of flowers and earth. But it gave her pause only for a moment, until she realized it was nothing but cigarette smoke. A common enough smell in London, just not one she had been expecting out here. She wasted no time looking around for the groundsman or stable hand responsible, just hurried along the path.

The carriage with its four matching brown horses was pulling up into the circle that Willa had driven their borrowed car around yesterday. She had rather expected Holstein to have an automobile too. Wasn't that the latest thing for well-to-do blokes? Heaven knew he could probably trade in just a portion of his book collection and be able to afford to buy one. Though she doubted finances were much of a concern for him anyway.

She couldn't imagine such a reality. To rise every day with no question of how to put food on the table. Of whether one should invest in a new pair of shoes or put back the coin for a winter coat. If one could afford to splurge on a hot cross bun on Good Friday.

The carriage drew to a halt, leaving Rosemary with the question of where in the world she was to wait for Mr. Holstein. Did she go ahead and climb in? Or stand on the stairs until he emerged?

Luckily she needn't wonder for long — the door opened, and Holstein emerged in evening dress, and with a wrapped package tucked under his arm.

Rosemary took a moment to absorb the

image, so she could regale Elinor with it when she got back to London. Her insufferable employer, looking dapper and polished and so very cleft-chinned as he came down the steps. To look at him, one would never know that he could be such an inconsiderate oaf. He *looked* nice, kind, thoughtful as he shifted the package — probably a gift for someone in the Penrose house — and looked up to spot her, sending her a polite smile. And no doubt the blighted lawyer thought his good friend all things noble and admirable.

But if she were to hazard a guess, she'd say neither Peter Holstein nor Gryffyn Penrose had ever gone, gift in hand, to a poorhouse or orphanage. She had her doubts whether they had so much as tossed a two-pence to a beggar on the street. Their kind always seemed to think anyone who was poor deserved to be. Or were crooks.

A funny little discomfort wormed its way through her veins. But she wasn't a *crook*. She didn't do what she did because she found pleasure in hurting anyone, like some of those sleazy back-alley moneylenders. She wasn't a swindler. When she stole, it was from those who could well afford to lose a bit, and to feed those who couldn't well afford to miss another meal. Not that she was a modern-day Robin Hood exactly, but . . . but more a Robin Hood than a crook.

And really, what choice had she had? What was a girl to do when she found herself in the gutter at the age of eight? There'd been no option but to steal, if she wanted to survive. And now she had no other skills to keep her and the dozen children in her charge out of that gutter.

"You look . . . look n-nice, Miss . . . Gresham."

He managed to say it in a way at once warm and dismissive — in that manner that indicated he would have said the same had she emerged in a gunnysack, simply because it was the thing he *ought* to say.

She pasted on a smile that went more genuine than she meant it to when she recalled the way Mrs. Teague had lectured her on proper dinner attire as she was ready to slip back out to the cottage. As if the housekeeper had thought her so utterly devoid of sense that she *meant* to emerge in a gunnysack. "Thank you, Mr. Holstein. And for inviting me to join you in the first place. I do hate to intrude." *On your precious* space, *you oaf.*

He didn't seem to hear her silent addition. Just motioned toward the carriage and the servant waiting to help her into it.

The groom, or driver, or whatever he was, greeted her with an outstretched hand and a smile considerably more attentive than Holstein's. He was a handsome chap, aside from the unfortunate arrangement of his yellow teeth. Not that she was one to judge such things. It was pure luck that her own teeth hadn't rotted and fallen out from poor nutrition long ago.

"Evening, miss." Maybe he was a footman? No, she thought those were reserved for inside the house. Maybe. He grinned as her fingers landed in his palm. "Hope you're enjoying Cornwall." He said it with the thick accent of a Cornish native. No *h* at the start of *hope,* the rolling *r* at the end of *you're.* So very opposite the clipped tones of London.

"Thank you, yes. It's lovely." She rewarded the fellow with a warm grin.

Holstein was there behind her as she used the man's hand to vault up into the carriage. "K-Kenver. How is . . . how is y-your new . . . wife?"

Rosemary settled on the cushion, lips twitching. Genuine interest on Holstein's part? Polite inquiry? Or a warning to her not to flirt with Kenver?

The cushion received her like a friend,

soft and gentle. She ran a hand over the smooth upholstery, better by far than any to be found in her flat.

Mr. Holstein ducked through the doorway. "You want me to take that package up with me, Mr. Holstein?"

But he continued his entrance, pausing for just a moment inside as he regarded Rosemary. Having the sudden certainty that she'd taken his usual spot, she had to stifle an exasperated sigh.

Then he sat on the seat opposite and directed his oh-so-polite smile toward Kenver. "B-Better . . . not." He nodded toward the out-of-doors at large.

Rosemary bent her head to look out the window. How had she failed to notice the black clouds hunching their shoulders over the horizon? There would be rain tonight, and likely tomorrow. She hoped poor Kenver had a mackintosh up there with him. And that Willa got back to the village before it let loose.

Rosemary would have done well to bring a wrap too. She'd not grabbed it though — nor had she remembered her handbag. Drat, she *never* forgot her handbag — far too convenient for hiding small valuables, not that she'd need it for such tonight. And she kept her picks in it. One never knew when one might need those.

Perhaps that novel had been more distracting than she'd thought.

Kenver closed the door, and silence pounced with a *whoosh*. Rosemary hoped against hope that the Penrose place was nearby. What in the world was she to talk about for who-knew-how-long, with a man who likely wouldn't even attempt to reply to half of her comments?

The carriage rocked as Kenver climbed up onto the front, and a moment later the horses tugged them forward. Rosemary kept her gaze directed out the window, fully prepared to pretend the awkward silence didn't bother her in the slightest. To pretend that she was accustomed to quiet rather than always having younger "siblings" around her, clamoring for this or for that or just *clamoring*. To pretend that it didn't faze her in the slightest to be out on a road with practically no traffic or noise or sirens or bobbies' whistles.

Holstein cleared his throat. "I f-feel I . . . I should ap—pologize again."

So then she would pretend instead that she had already forgotten how right he'd been to call himself an oaf in that letter he'd waved at her. Pretend conversation wasn't even more awkward than silence. She brought out a smile that said *I am but your humble servant.* "Think nothing of it, Mr. Holstein. You are entitled to act however you wish in your own home."

In her experience with the so-called *gentle* class, it was exactly what they thought, what they based their every action upon. Why, then, did his brows draw together? Why did he shake his head?

"N-No one has the . . . r-right to be . . . to be rude."

The corner of her mouth quirked up before she could stop it. "No? Your counterparts in London seem to disagree."

He sighed — a heavy, quick *chuff* — and looked to the window. "Trust m-me. I know."

He most assuredly did *not* know. He'd never been a ragamuffin hiding in an alley, praying for a pence or two to fall from a wealthy gent's pockets. He'd never been spat upon by some dandy just for having the audacity to exist. He'd never had the police called on him just for being poor and orphaned and confused by it all.

He had enemies though. Her presence here was proof of that. And the upper-crust bullies likely plied their skills on their own, not just the lower classes.

Blast it all, she didn't want to be fair. It

was more comfortable to simmer about it. And besides, he likely *deserved* the scorn of those upper-class bullies, given his presumed allegiances.

They reached the end of his long, winding drive, but rather than turn toward the village, Kenver directed them to the right. She and Willa hadn't ventured this far, so her gaze took it all in through the window. Here, away from the cliffs, trees stood sentinel. The expected elms and moorland trees bending into the wind, and a few that looked suspiciously tropical. "Is that a palm tree?"

He smiled and shook his head. "C-Cabbage tree. We . . . we call them C-Cornish palms though. From . . . from New Z-Zealand."

"Well." They were more of the tropics than *she'd* ever see. She'd tell the family they were palms. Make the place seem foreign and romantic. "It's beautiful country."

"H-Have you s . . . seen St. M-Michael's Mount?"

She'd never even heard of it. So a shake of her head, a lifted brow.

He smiled. It made the cleft in his chin all the more charming and lit warmth in his blue-green eyes. Not that Rosemary cared for such things, but Ellie would. She was only noting it so she could spin a compelling tale.

"The St. Au . . . Aubyn f-family castle. There is a p-painting . . . a painting of it. In the p-parlor."

She waited a moment, but he said no more about it. Because, she supposed, there was no point. Apparently it was a lovely enough place, if someone painted it, and if his family admired said painting enough to hang it prominently in their home. But she could hardly comment on it until she had seen it. And he would hardly waste words trying to explain it to her when a picture could say it more clearly.

As to why he'd brought it up, then . . . She nodded. "I'll have a look at it tomorrow. Is it near here? The place, I mean, not the painting."

He set the package in his lap. "Ab . . . about fif . . . fifteen miles."

Accessible, then. Perhaps, if it were truly spectacular, she'd make an attempt to see it while she was in the area. Though she hadn't the foggiest notion when she'd do such a thing. "Mr. Holstein, it occurs to me that we haven't discussed my hours. I am familiar enough with manor houses to know that most employees get a half-day off sometime during the week." Though that had always struck her as unfair — even factory workers got a full day, on Sundays. What made these dandies think they could demand more? If she were mistress of a place like Kensey, she wouldn't be so stingy with her staff's free time.

"You are . . . you are not h-household st . . . staff." For all his stuttering, his tone was mild. "I am . . . well aware of th— that. You will h-have the s-same schedule you . . . you would have had. In London."

Her heart jumped up into her throat. In all her plying of Mr. Hall in the pub, she hadn't thought to ask him what his usual schedule was.

But Holstein was only pausing for a long breath. "Half days on . . . on Saturdays. S-Sundays off."

That would leave plenty of time for sightseeing, then. She nodded, careful to keep her countenance clear. As if she had expected nothing less. "Excellent. Thank you, sir."

He returned the nod, and she thought for sure he'd let silence fall. Instead, he said, "And y-you may . . . you may b-borrow one of . . . of the carriages. Any t-time I am . . . I am not using them."

She had a suspicion that was most times. Surely a man who so hated having anyone interrupt him wasn't the type to go out to the local pub every night for a pint and a pie or to catch a moving picture — if they even had such things in the village. So it wasn't exactly a sacrifice to offer the use of his vehicles. Still, it was more than she would have thought a gentleman would feel obligated to offer an employee.

She shifted on her plush, overly comfortable seat. Having been so busy getting her story ready to come here, she hadn't paused to wonder what kind of man this new "employer" of hers would be. And she was far from ready to accept that he was really all generosity and kindness — it was too directly opposed to all she'd ever known of his type.

Gentlemen never gave freely.

But if this one tried to get anything from her other than a tidy library, she'd teach him a few lessons about how tough a Cockney girl could be.

He was frowning at her. "Are you all . . . all right, M-Miss Gresham?"

Her face must have fallen into hard lines. She smoothed it out and put that smile back on. "Of course. And thank you, sir, for the offer. No doubt I'll take you up on that."

The carriage slowed and turned, though they couldn't have come more than a mile on the main road. "Does Mr. Penrose live nearby?"

Holstein nodded. "V-Very. I often . . . walk. When not in . . . in evening dr—dress."

She made a mental note to head in the opposite direction if ever she went out on foot for a bit of exercise. And covered it with a grin. "A concession I rather appreciate, given these shoes."

After the expected returning smile, Holstein repositioned the package again and turned toward the door, obviously anticipating a quick arrival at their destination. Having nothing to reposition, Rosemary settled for watching said destination approach out the window.

They turned onto a drive of crushed rock. The grounds were well-tended but decidedly lacking the extravagance of Kensey Manor. No exotic blooms rioting for dominance, other than a few of those cabbage trees lining the drive, and otherwise just the usual trimmed shrubbery and careful flowers. An expanse of lawn before a modest house of grey stone blocks that had become a haven for climbing ivy. Pretty. Prettier than she would have expected of Gryffyn Penrose. She rather thought he'd live in some grand, imposing structure that was all hard lines and ancestral paintings of barristers of generations past. Perhaps with those electro-magnets on the windows to shrill if someone dared open the pane without permission.

This was . . . charming. Irritatingly charming. What business had a glowering blighter like Penrose to live in such a lovely, cozy place?

She could imagine the family in a house like this. They'd all have to share bedrooms, but they wouldn't know what to do with themselves otherwise. The little ones could tumble about in the yard, chasing one another. And a cat. They needed a cat to scramble up that elm there.

The halting of the carriage jolted her from that dream — which was just as well. She'd never have a place like this. Her family would just have to settle for Kensey Manor, even if it were too large.

Pressing her lips against the grin, Rosemary nodded when Holstein motioned for her to precede him out the door. Kenver was there again to help her down, though she paid little attention to whether or not he graced her with a smile. Her gaze pulled to the wooden slab of a door with ancient-looking iron fittings as it flew open.

A girl ran out. She looked to be about four

or five, with dark curls whipping around her head that made Rosemary miss little Olivia. Though to be sure, this girl was soft and round where Olivia was all bones and angles. The joy on her face was the same though.

The little one charged directly toward the carriage, even as a call of "Elowyn!" came from the house's door.

The girl ignored the command heavy in the name. She didn't seem to notice Rosemary or Kenver at all, so intent was her gaze upon Peter Holstein as he stepped down. "Uncle Peter!"

He laughed. It was a good laugh, without any of the hesitation that filled his words. Warm and comfortable and . . . and *good.* Rosemary turned a bit, just in time to see Elowyn hurtle herself at him and him stoop down and scoop her up, the package abandoned on the ground.

Being the favorite of his friend's child didn't make him a good man. Didn't make him loyal to England. But Rosemary couldn't help but draw in a deep breath as she watched him swing the girl around and settle her on his hip. And when she let said breath out again, she couldn't help that some of her irritation with him leaked out with it.

Her attention was snagged by other foot-steps. These came at a more reasonable pace, but they belonged to a woman obvi-ously Elowyn's mother. She had the same black curls, and her dress was too fine for her to be a nursemaid.

Silk, and with an intriguing design. The top was in a kimono style, a pale green with bold pink insets. It looked like two rectangu-lar panels sewn together, leaving a bateau neckline and wide sleeves. Rosemary could make something like that easily, if she could find the right silk. Though she would have to see what the under-dress looked like. A simple sheath, probably. Easy enough to replicate. She would sketch it when she got home and show it to Willa. One of the fam-ily was bound to need a new dress soon, and this had the look of the height of fashion. It would, she thought, suit Retta best.

This woman wore no necklace — it would have interfered with the neckline of the dress. But the bracelet embracing her wrist was studded with diamonds, and they looked real. As real as the gem on her finger set in ornate gold. And they weren't so distinctive that a fence would have a hard time moving them. Not to mention that the bracelet had a sliding clasp that was so, *so* easy to slip without the wearer noticing.

Not that Rosemary planned on slipping it. But really, didn't people think of these things?

Mr. Penrose was exiting the house as well. In self-defense, Rosemary turned away from his bludgeoning scowl and back to Holstein and the little one.

The little one had a scowl every bit as bludgeoning as her father's and aimed just as squarely at Rosemary's head. "Who are *you*?"

She may have felt a bit of affront — children usually loved her — had the arm Elowyn slung around Holstein's neck not gone tight and telling. Rosemary smiled and held out a hand, gentleman style. "Rosemary Gresham, Miss Penrose. At your service."

Green eyes remained wary, but Elowyn reached out and shook. "You came with Uncle Peter?"

She really was an adorable child. She had dimples, and a fan of impossibly long lashes framing those pretty green eyes. Rosemary nodded. "I did. He's just hired me on to clean out his library. Have you seen it?" She leaned closer and pitched her voice down. "He should have hired someone ages ago. Not that I'm complaining that he didn't."

Elowyn's lips hinted at a smile, then the frown won the battle. "Papa says no one was mad enough to take the job. But they don't let me in there. They say a pile of books might squash me."

Rosemary chuckled. "They have the right of it."

The scowl only deepened, and the arm around Holstein's neck tightened. His face went a bit red, but he made no complaint.

Elowyn lifted her chin. "I'm going to marry him someday, you know."

And so she disliked any woman who showed up with him — an astute young lady. Rosemary widened her eyes. "Congratulations! Have you set a date yet?"

The frown lessened. "Christmas Day in 1927. I'll be eighteen then."

Rosemary's wide eyes went genuine. "You are quite good at mathematics, Miss Penrose. I'm impressed. Do remember to send me an invite closer to the time, won't you?"

There, the smile won. And lit her eyes as well as her lips. "I will. Do you want to see my room?" She squirmed to be put down.

Holstein shook his head. "Forgotten . . . already. And I came with . . . with a gift."

Elowyn was either too politely bred to clamor over such a thing or too spoiled with gifts to be excited about another. She didn't even glance at the package, just reached up and took Rosemary's hand. "You can bring it up after you've talked with Papa, Uncle Peter. I want to show Miss . . . Miss my new book. I'm going to learn to *read* it."

The girl had a tug every bit as forceful as her scowl had been, and she used it to pull Rosemary forward. She had little choice but to follow. "An excellent thing to do with a book. Far better than just stacking them about a room until the walls vanish."

Elowyn giggled. So did her mother.

Penrose did not. And Rosemary didn't turn to see Mr. Holstein's response.

The missus stepped close, her smile natural and welcoming — at least until a raindrop had the audacity to spatter on her face, at which point she frowned up at the sky. "Better hurry in. I'm so glad you could join us, Miss Gresham."

"Likewise, ma'am."

The lady of the house led the way up the three stone steps and through the door that still stood open, a black-clad young man holding it so for them. And shutting it directly behind as the wind kicked up and new raindrops raced to keep up with their friends.

Elowyn didn't give her time to pause, just kept on tugging. "My room is upstairs. It's still the nursery, even though I'm not a baby. I'll get a different one, Mama says, when I'm just a bit older."

Mrs. Penrose stilled her daughter with a hand atop her head. "Ellie, where are your manners? Do we pull and tug upon new acquaintances?"

Elowyn paused, apparently having to consider that, given the scrunching of her face.

Rosemary tamped down a smile. "Do you know, I have a sister who goes by Ellie sometimes."

The little one's eyes went round. "Is she called Elowyn too?"

"No." Unable to resist, she reached out and smoothed down one of the plump curls springing from Elowyn's head. "She's called Elinor."

Elowyn didn't seem to mind the attention. "But will that not get confusing? Having two of us who are Ellie?"

Her mother sighed, no doubt ready to point out that it was something people dealt with all the time, with the abundance of Georges and Jacks and Marys running about England.

Rosemary grinned before Mrs. Penrose could speak. "You're right. Perhaps instead I'll call you . . . Wyn. Or Winnie."

"Oh!" The little one's eyes went wider still, and twinkling. "Oh, I should like that very much. Wyn. It sounds terribly grown-up. Yes, you should call me Wyn. *Everyone* should call me Wyn!"

The chuckle that came from behind them was far too warm to be Penrose's. "Here all of a . . . a m-minute and renaming their d-daughter."

Rosemary's gaze flew over to Mrs. Penrose's. "Sorry! I didn't mean —"

"Think nothing of it, Miss Gresham." The lady was wearing a smile that looked like laughter. "Last week she insisted we all call her Rufus for some reason I could never discern."

"Because it's the neighbors' dog's name, and he's the noblest dog in the whole world." Her voice a singsong, Elowyn gave another tug on Rosemary's hand. Discreetly, so her mother wouldn't see.

Rosemary followed the urging. "Makes perfect sense. And while we're still on the subject of names, you needn't call me Miss Gresham, ma'am. Rosemary will do quite nicely."

"A lovely name. Thank you. And you're welcome to call me Jenifer. Or Jenny."

Tension that she hadn't known she'd carried seeped right out of her shoulders. She didn't know what she'd been worried about. Mr. Penrose might be a scowling blighter, but his wife was an absolute delight.

SEVEN

Peter followed Gryff into the parlor, not bothering to hide his smile as his friend's expression went from frown to one of bemusement. It finally settled on resignation, and Gryff lowered himself into his favorite chair with a grunt.

Peter slid the package for Elowyn onto an end table and took his usual seat on the twin to Gryff's chair. "Ready to admit you . . . you were wrong?"

Another grunt. "I can't remember the last time she invited someone to use her first name within five minutes of meeting."

"Well, as you say . . . Jenny is an excellent judge . . . judge of character." Which made a bit of guilt prick for having turned Miss Gresham — or someone who borrowed her physical description anyway — into a villain. But she would never know, and one had to take one's inspiration wherever one could find it when one was struggling to finish a book by one's deadline.

A third grunt from the chair. Which was really quite redundant. Gryff rubbed a hand along the back of his neck, and one corner of his mouth pulled up. "Can't blame a fellow for being protective of his closest friend, can you?"

"Never." Inhaling deeply, Peter tried to put a name to the particular scents wafting through the house. Whortleberry pie, perhaps? Hard to tell, what with the heavy aroma of roasting meat covering it. But blueberries were his favorite, so he'd be willing to bet Jenny had made a pie for him with what she'd preserved last summer.

She was the only woman he knew who could afford a cook but still chose to prepare all the meals herself. She took joy in it, she said — and everyone else took joy in her taking of it too.

Maybe he shouldn't have gone to London this year. Never mind that it had been at the invitation of King George himself. He should have stayed here, where he belonged. Where friends defended him and made his favorite dishes. Where children ran to greet him and declared him their favorite.

Where neighbors threw rocks through his windows.

"How goes the writing today?" Gryff sent

his gaze upward as he asked it, to where the floorboards overhead squeaked enough to assure them that Miss Gresham was well out of earshot.

Peter nodded. "I'm getting . . . getting back into my rhythm."

"That didn't take you long." A bit of relief entered his friend's eyes at that. No doubt he hadn't wanted to be the one to contact the publisher and beg for more time. "I've a box of correspondence for you too, that just came today. Probably all six months out of date, of course. If you wouldn't insist upon such a circuitous route from the publisher . . ."

Peter saw no reason to dignify that with a response. Gryff knew well that his privacy was of the utmost importance to him. Even his publisher didn't know who he really was. Just that all correspondence should go to a solicitor in London, who sent it to one in Bristol, who sent it to another in Devon, who sent it to Gryff here.

It wouldn't do for his readers to find out who he really was. If anyone knew that Branok Hollow was really a stammering German, he'd fall out of favor so quickly the impact would likely break a few bones. His career — the one thing he'd earned for himself rather than inheriting, the one thing

161

that wasn't rooted in generations of German heritage — would be gone.

Silence tapped an impatient foot on the rug. One beat, two, punctuated by Gryff's raised brow. And chased off by his, "Well? Haven't you anything you mean to tell me? About rocks coming through your windows, perhaps?"

There were definite drawbacks to making one's home near a small village. He could only guess as to how word had reached Gryff within a day — someone from Kensey could have said something to a brother or cousin or neighbor.

Or the perpetrator could have been boasting of it in the pub, for all he knew.

Peter shook his head. "Your gossip source has . . . has failed you. It was only *one* rock. One . . . window."

Gryff didn't look amused. "Did you report it to the constable?"

Peter glared at him. And rolled his eyes for good measure. Locryn James may think himself smarter than the law and so never engage them, but they all knew Peter Holstein was no renegade swashbuckler.

Gryff sighed. "Of course you did, as it was the reasonable thing to do. Have they any idea who did it?"

"If they . . . did, I would have . . . would

have told you sooner."

Laughter echoed down through the floor-boards. Two lower notes, and one high, making a chord of happiness. Laughter always followed Elowyn about. Though, much like her mother, she was a bit choosy about whom she let partake of it with her.

He would admit it — he felt better about having Miss Gresham in his house, knowing Jenny and Elowyn liked her. Their reaction was confirmation of what he'd felt certain the Lord had done. And just now he could use all the confirming he could get.

"Mr. Arnold came by to tell me about it, when he heard it at the post office this morning. He was, of course, concerned for you, so you may want to pay him a visit soon to relieve his worry." Gryff reached for the pipe sitting on the table at his elbow, though he didn't light it. He wouldn't until later, after Elowyn was abed. She detested the smell. "I bet it was Jack Foote. He's been rather loud about his opinions of Germans. Or Pomeroy. He's been all but walking around with his nose in a news-paper, shouting out all the anti-German sentiments to anyone who will pause two seconds to listen."

Peter cleared his throat.

Gryff didn't wait to see if he had anything

to add. Gaze distant, he tapped the pipe to his palm. "Or . . . or Michael FitzSimmons. He —"

"Right." Peter had to fight the urge to borrow one of Gryff's abundant sighs. Or bring Father's chuff to life again. But he forced his lips up. "So what you're . . . what you're telling me is that it could have been . . . anyone. Anyone at all in the village. They all . . . distrust me."

"It isn't *you.* Those men would turn on their own grandmothers if it suited their panic." Another tap of the pipe and Gryff leaned forward, sudden humor blazing in his eyes. "You know what you need to do to put it all to rest?"

Given his recent conversation with the elderly Mr. Arnold, Peter could well guess as to the advice. "I still feel . . . uneasy. About selling. My cousin said . . . he said someone has been buying up . . . stock. Trying to gain majority holds. If I sell . . ."

But Gryff shook his head. "That isn't actually what I meant, though I do think that ridding yourself of those German holdings will be wise in the long run. But immediately — be seen. Be seen as one of them, one of us. Come to church on Sunday. Have dinner at the pub with me and Santo on Tuesday."

Peter could only pray his face didn't *really* twist in distaste as badly as it felt like it did. He got along well enough with the younger Penrose brother, but they weren't exactly friends. And Gryff knew well that he had a hard time worshiping among so many *people* — and the vicar understood too, which was why he came over for dinner every Monday, if Peter didn't make it to church. They had conversations on whatever Mr. Trenholm had studied for his homily the week prior.

Of course, he'd just promised Miss Gresham they would take dinners together, and luncheons too, to discuss whatever she found in the library that day, any questions she had. He would have to make Mondays the exception to that.

Gryff's eyes grew still brighter. "And you know what would make it even better? Go out with Miss Gresham on your arm. She's obviously of fine common stock — the villagers would love her. She'd make you seem . . . rooted."

Peter folded his arms over his chest. "You are, as always . . . hilarious."

"Aren't I?" Chuckling at his own joke, Gryff leaned back again. "Though listen, old boy, it's not as bad an idea as all that. Go out. Be seen. Remind everyone of my excellent taste in friends."

A quick laugh tickled his throat, insisting on being heard.

Gryff waved his pipe in the air. "If I know Jenny, she's already making plans with Miss Gresham to go to the millinery or whatnot this week, so people will soon be seeing *her*. And if Jenny likes her, everyone else will too. And they'll all know she's working at Kensey. So then if you're seen with her now and then . . ."

"Gryff. I will *not* . . . not put on a . . . a *show.*"

The amusement in his friend's eyes snapped away, quick and sure. "I'm not talking about a show. I'm talking simply about convincing *her* of what an upstanding character you are, and then letting her chatter about it. Heaven knows you've ridden into town now and again with your staff. Do the same with her. I'm not saying to pretend there is some romance there, simply to let it be seen there is respect. Good feeling, even though she hasn't known you forever as I have. That will suffice."

Peter's fine mood seeped out onto the fading Turkish rug beneath his feet. Always good to know that his dearest friend had so little faith in him that he knew nothing Peter did would convince anyone to hold him in esteem — but that if Miss Gresham just chattered for a few minutes to the baker, all would be well.

He was right, but that was hardly the point.

The floorboards squeaked again, and within moments the distant feminine laughter grew louder. More distinct. He could pick out Elowyn's easily, and then Jenny's. Which in turn identified Miss Gresham's.

The little girl skipped ahead of the women into the parlor and headed straight for Peter with that dimpled smile that always reminded him how blessed he was to be counted an uncle to her. He helped her clamber up onto his lap and chuckled as her gaze now darted to the wrapped package and was held there as if by glue. "Would you like your . . . your birthday gift now, Ellie?"

She twisted her neck around to send him a scowl. "You mean *Wyn.*"

That would take some getting used to, if she held to it for more than a week. But he smiled. "Right. Wyn."

Giving another grin, she nodded and reached for the box.

"Careful." He steadied the package with a hand beneath it. "It's . . . it's breakable."

Her eyes went wide, visible as she positioned herself sideways on his lap. "What is it?" Her fingertip traced the ribbon.

"I believe . . . the idea is to . . . to open it and see."

First she smiled up at him, eyes filled with that pure, unquestioning love. "Thank you, Uncle Peter. I'm sure it's lovely. Whatever it is."

He smiled back. "Even if it's a . . . a warty toad? Or . . . or a slimy worm?"

Her giggle was joy as she pulled the ribbon from its bow. "You wouldn't give me those! And they're not breakable."

He may have teased a bit more had he not made the mistake of glancing up and spotting Miss Gresham ambling in beside Jenny, thereby rendering his tongue utterly useless. Not that the ladies were paying any mind to him. Jenny was leaning close to examine Miss Gresham's . . . shoulder? As if it contained all the secrets of Locryn James's past.

"But it's perfect! I can mend a tear or sew on a button, but skill like that . . ." Jenny straightened, eyes as wide as Elowyn's could get. "You have real talent, Rosemary. If ever you tire of books, you could open up shop as a seamstress and I could send you dozens of customers."

"Oh." The hand Miss Gresham pressed to

her waist was less self-conscious than absent. Her expression less flattered than baffled. "I had never even considered it. It isn't something I enjoy so much as something I must do if I mean to look as I should. I cannot afford to hire anyone else." But her eyes stayed thoughtful. Almost confused, it seemed to him. As if she had never once considered doing something other than what she did.

Which was odd indeed. Surely no young woman grew up with such single-minded determination to be a librarian.

"If your position does not support you so well, why choose it?" This shot came from Gryff, who apparently forgot that he had given up his dislike of her. "It was hardly an easy path for a woman, I should think."

Miss Gresham arched a brow that reeked of challenge. "Indeed it wasn't. Especially, sir, since a woman does not garner pay equal to a man for the exact same job. But that's the way of things, isn't it? And as I have a dozen siblings to support, I count myself lucky to find *anything* not in a factory, and I make our clothes so that I can look the part I need to play. Aiming at a better-paying position is hardly an option for someone born absent a silver spoon already in her mouth."

Peter lifted the box for Elowyn so she could rid herself of the paper she had folded away from it. And he tried not to be so impressed by a too-thin woman with a manner as inviting as a steel trap.

But there it was. Had he not been born to a life of privilege, he was none too sure he would have had gumption enough to rise above his birth and fight for something better. To make his own way. Especially in a world that labeled one *less* simply because of one's gender.

Or last name.

He lowered the box again for Elowyn and held the bottom while she lifted off the lid. His chest felt a couple sizes too tight. He wasn't sure he had the gumption to fight for fair treatment now, either, when his silver spoon did nothing to protect him. When the friendships he had made put him at risk — and put those friends at risk too.

Not that King George or Prince Edward had anything to fear because of him. But if Gryff defended him in the village, it could well turn opinion against him too. And he hated to even think about how old Mr. Arnold could suffer — would his Austrian heritage put him in any danger? If so, Gryff would have said something.

But the very thought of a rock coming

through one of these windows, frightening Jenny and Elowyn . . . and what if Mr. Jasper really did accuse him of espionage? Could Gryff be arrested too, being his barrister and friend?

"Oh, she's *beautiful.*" Elowyn drew out the doll, hands gentle and reverent, eyes wide as she took in the dark curls and the perfect face painted upon the porcelain. "Look, Mama! Isn't she beautiful?"

Jenny stepped near them, making obliging *ooh*s and *ahh*s.

Miss Gresham kept to her post nearer the door. She was smiling, but he had the distinct impression that it was simply over Elowyn's reaction, not over the doll itself. Or his buying it for her. Which mattered not the slightest to him — he had gotten the thing to bring delight to the girl he thought of as a niece, not to impress anyone else. Certainly not a prickly librarian he hadn't even known when he saw the doll on display in a toy shop window in London.

But would it kill her to relax half a degree?

Elowyn fussed with the lace of the dress the doll wore, then toyed with the curls. "I shall name her Rosie after you, Miss Gresham! Doesn't she look like her, Mama?"

"That's perfect, Elowyn." Jenny smiled.

Miss Gresham's smile went warmer too. Though her shoulders didn't relax any. She may have curls of the same shade of brown as the doll, but any resemblance ended there — she certainly wasn't all soft stuffing from the neck down.

Jenny let Elowyn chatter on about her new Rosie for a few minutes more, but then she held out a hand, her smile that particularly unshakable one that meant argument was futile. "All right, *chiel.* Time for you to go back up to Janey."

"But Mama —"

"Now don't get teasy. You knew you'd have only ten minutes, just as you know well that Uncle Peter will come back to see you more on another day. For now, you must have your supper and get to bed."

Miss Gresham's brows puckered. "Pardon me — *teasy?*"

"Sorry, a bit of local dialect. Fussy." Jenny smiled again.

Elowyn didn't. With a long sigh too weary for a five-year-old, she wrapped an arm around his neck and gave him a mighty squeeze. "Thank you for Rosie, Uncle Peter. Will you come back soon?"

"Of . . . course."

She kissed his cheek and then scurried down, pausing to dip a wobbly curtsy to

Miss Gresham before putting her hand in her mother's. "Good to meet you, Miss Gresham."

Miss Gresham chuckled. "Likewise, Miss Penrose. Have a lovely evening."

Peter stood, now that his lap wasn't occupied and it became loudly obvious that he had neglected to do so when the ladies had entered the room.

Gryff did as well and motioned to a chair. "Please, Miss Gresham. Make yourself comfortable. Jenny will be back in just a minute."

She edged toward a chair, though the look she sent them was as baffled as the one she'd given Jenny over the thought of a different profession. "Thank you." Posture as careful as her tone, she eased to a seat on the very edge of the chair's cushion.

Peter sat back down too, as did Gryff. Which she seemed to find either confusing or amusing, given the twitch of her lips.

"So." Gryff toyed with his pipe again. "How went your first day in the cave?"

"Oh." Her fingers fluttered once against her dress. Went still. The smile she put on was confident . . . and inscrutable. Showing nothing of her thoughts. "A trifle overwhelming, but quite interesting overall."

"You weren't frightened, I hope, by the

rock's intrusion last night?" Gryff arched a silver brow. She would have had to be a fool to miss the veiled challenge in his tone, though why he was directing such a challenge at her, Peter couldn't determine.

She lifted a brow in return, a parry to Gryff's thrust. "Why would I be frightened by a rock? It is a coward's way of sending a coward's message."

Gryff's smile was far more easily deciphered than hers. It said he liked her attitude, despite himself. And because his wife's acceptance had told him he should. "Good. Well, I hope you like pasties, Miss Gresham. Jenny makes the best pasty in Cornwall. Which, of course, is the only place that knows how to make them at all."

A happy breath leaked from Peter's lips. It had been too long since he'd had one of Jenny's pasties.

Miss Gresham still wore that nothing-smile. "I look forward to it."

"You've never been to Cornwall, have you? I told her I didn't think you had. But she maintains that if you come to Cornwall and don't have a pasty, you might as well be in England still."

Now her brows drew in. "We *are* in England still."

Peter choked on a laugh. "Don't . . . don't

say that too l-loudly in these . . . these parts, M-Miss Gresham."

"Ah." She said no more. Just smoothed out her brow and kept her face in that pleasant, neutral smile.

Peter's brows puckered. Why would someone develop that particular expression? It had the look of a mask. No, more a cloak. Meant to render one invisible. Not to hide feeling so much as to hide oneself.

But she had thoughts ricocheting through her mind, he knew she had. They had snapped out at him plenty today, yelling from behind her polite lips. Keeping her shoulders as sharp as blades and her fingers utterly motionless now in her lap. She had thoughts and she had judgments and she had opinions well beyond the few she had voiced.

Perhaps, if shared meals ever wore away the unfamiliarity between them, he would learn to decipher some of her opinions. It could prove interesting — she obviously had grown up in circles far different from his. She would have different points of view on almost everything.

That was invaluable. He needed more perspectives than his own if he meant to write convincing characters.

"Now then." Gryff leaned forward, frowning, but in that way that said he was intrigued. "Have you really a dozen siblings?"

Her smile shifted. A slight change, but enough to turn it from a cloak to a ray of sunshine. "Well, counting me. Barclay is the eldest, and then me and Willa. Retta is next, and Lucy, then Elinor and George. Then we have the little ones — Jory and Olivia and Nigel and Cressida and Fergus. Not that Cressida and Fergus appreciate being called little ones, as they both are eleven."

Gryff blinked. "Twins?"

"Eleven months apart. Cress will be twelve in a month." A shadow whispered over her features. "I suppose I shan't be home for it."

"You'll have to send something, then. If Cressida is anything like Elowyn, the idea of getting mail will send her over the moon dreckly."

She didn't question the Cornish *dreckly* as she had *teasy* — perhaps it sounded enough like "directly" that she assumed that was what he'd said. Perhaps because she was too caught up in examining the idea. Her gaze went a bit distant, her lips turning in a curious way that was neither a proper smile nor belonging to any other category he knew. "What a good idea. She's never got a letter in the post. None of them have

— I ought to write to each of them while I'm away."

She would need paper, then, and he doubted she had brought any stationery with her, since it seemed to be an idea she'd never entertained. He would deliver some to the library for her — heaven knew he had no shortage.

Jenny soon returned, and a minute later she and Gryff led the way into the dining room. The maid stood sentinel, ready to unveil the food from the shining silver dome holding it captive. Peter went to his usual chair, on the far side, next to Gryff at the head.

Jenny touched a hand to Miss Gresham's elbow. "You'll sit by me. A bit unconventional, I know, but that way we can chat while the men devolve into their interminable discussions of books and politics. I cannot tell you how glad I am to have another level-headed female to keep me company."

Gryff laughed. "So you can talk of level-headed things like dress patterns and hats?"

Jenny's scowl was playful. "And children. Rosemary said her youngest sister is near Elowyn's age, so no doubt we can exchange many stories about their antics."

And of course, Peter oughtn't to have gone to his usual chair — he ought to help

Miss Gresham be seated. He rounded the table before anyone noticed his oversight — hopefully — and pulled out her chair for her as Gryff did the same for Jenny.

She sat in time with their hostess. Nothing awkward or uncertain in her movements. But her shoulders were blades again.

Peter rounded the table once more and took his own chair, across from Jenny. After Gryff spoke a blessing over the food, she gave the nod to the maid, who lifted the silver dome from the plate.

No doubt Miss Gresham, if she lived as modestly at home as it seemed, was unaccustomed to formal meals. She didn't *seem* to be watching any of the rest of them too closely, but her actions were still a half second behind everyone else's as she picked up her napkin, placed it in her lap, smiled her thanks as the maid served her, and then reached for her fork.

Peter frowned. She held it in her *right* hand — none of the left-handed people he had met, even if forced to write with their right hand, also *ate* with their right hand.

Perhaps her parents had insisted on binding her left arm even when at home.

Or perhaps . . . perhaps she had lied. Though for the life of him he couldn't imagine why she would have.

EIGHT

Rosemary stretched the kink out of her neck and moved toward the window open to the stiff, damp breeze. It made the room less stifling. Though it also made the whole place feel sticky.

The humidity probably wasn't good for the books. But knowing the window was open helped with the feeling of being penned in on all sides and suffocated. She leaned onto the frame to look out at the damp, misty world.

It wasn't exactly early morning anymore, but fog still clung to everything, rolling in off the sea in a great wave of almost-rain. The ground had been soaked this morning when she made her way over from the cottage, and the rain had only stopped pounding just as she was searching for a brolly to aid her in her short journey. It had kept Willa in the village.

And, apparently, had kept Mrs. Teague

from bringing her a breakfast tray this morning. When Rosemary had squished her way through the kitchen, wiping her feet, Grammy had promised that the housekeeper or a maid would bring her something "dreckly."

She was beginning to think that "dreckly" did *not* mean "directly," as she had assumed. Three hours had gone by, and the only sign of life she'd noticed was the *click-clacking* from behind Holstein's study door. What was it he typed every day?

Not that she wasn't used to going without a meal. But she'd told herself she could have a break from the books when breakfast arrived and look more closely at that stack of very fine, very beautiful paper that had been waiting on her table when she'd entered.

Well, she needed the break, be there a nice cup of tea to go with it or not. She'd just spent those three hours moving books into stacks and moving stacks as out-of-the-way as she could manage, and frankly, her arms hurt from stretching so unnaturally. And her neck from being always bent. And her back from the constant up and down.

She stretched again and let the magnetism of the stack of stationery pull her toward the table.

His note still lay atop it. She'd glanced at

it when she'd come in, just to make sure the paper beneath was really for her use, but that truth still felt wrong. He'd given it as if it were nothing. But she had looked at paper like this when she stocked up on supplies to come here. She knew how dear it was. This stack would have cost more than any of the gifts Lucy or Willa or Retta or Barclay had given her over the years. It was family policy to never give stolen goods as presents, which meant that gifts were rare. And modest.

She ran her fingers over the thick stock. It felt as decadent as cloth. And there were at least fifty sheets of it. *At least.*

Pulling out a chair, she picked up the note again. Sat. Read his few words.

I thought perhaps you would need this to write to your brothers and sisters. I always keep plenty on hand, so if you need more, do let me know.

P. H.

She touched a finger to the *P. H.* It wasn't exactly an abbreviation. The first period looked less like a proper period than it did the beginning of an abandoned letter. As if he had begun to write the *e* and then changed his mind. The *H* was natural enough, but the period following *it* looked far too deliberate.

He probably meant to deduct the cost of the paper from her salary.

Her fingers wandered toward yesterday's note, which she'd tossed to the table in a fit of pique solely because there was no fire handy to consume it and it had felt petulant to rip it to shreds when he left the library.

She flipped it open. Read it again.

It didn't seem quite so infuriating today, after her stomach was full of Jenny Penrose's amazing pasties and she'd had a good night's sleep, what with the rain creating a welcome din on the roof. She still wasn't sure that two meals a day with Peter Holstein was the best idea — really, what could they possibly talk about for that long? — but she could appreciate that he'd tried to think of a way to provide them both with what they needed.

Mostly.

Though why anyone would need so many hours of *quiet* . . . She shuddered at the very thought. This place hadn't enough noise as it was.

Her fingers itched to write to the children straightaway, but that could take more time than she really wanted to use up just now, when she was supposed to be working.

She'd do that later. Now, she granted herself only another two minutes.

Bypassing the fine paper — his notes to her were never on such stuff after all — she tore a sheet from her notebook and jotted a quick thank-you to him. Pursing her lips, she debated for a moment . . . and then tacked on a brief apology for being so angry yesterday.

He'd apologized — she sure as blazes wasn't going to look like the childish one, refusing to do so.

Folding the sheet of paper, she recapped her pen and stood. Stared at the closed door to his study. The interminable *click-clack-ding* was sounding, as it had been since nine o'clock on the nose. She certainly wasn't going to interrupt him. So she eased over to the door and, feeling a bit ridiculous, slipped the paper underneath it.

He could very well not see it. But she didn't much care. He'd find it eventually, and it would prove that she'd done the polite thing.

So then. Back to work.

She was amassing a considerable stack of tomes that had markers in them, and whose marked pages had names upon them that might be relevant to the Holstein family. Sometimes the Holstein name itself —

really, who had their name in *multiple* books? — sometimes other German-sounding names that seemed to have some link to the house of Saxe-Coburg. At the moment, she was operating on the assumption that if Wilhelm Holstein had marked the pages, they were important. And she was jotting down the names. At luncheon or dinner, she would run them by Mr. Holstein and see if he recognized any of them.

But for every book on historical or then-current events or politics or whatnot, there were twenty on subjects surely of no relevance to the family search. These occasionally had markers in them too, but she'd given up flipping to them. If they denoted pages of interest, she couldn't figure out why. Around the room she'd begun various stacks, and most of the next two hours she spent scurrying from one to another.

A glass of water would have been nice. She should ask about how to fetch such things for herself. Surely even the lowest of scullery maids was entitled to water now and again — it oughtn't to be too much for her to ask. And waiting on the staff to bring her something "dreckly" was apparently a mistake.

If ever she were mistress of such a place, one could be sure she'd make certain each and every person on the property had such basic needs met.

At noon, a throat clearing in the doorway brought her to a halt mid-stride, her arms full of books bound for the wall shared by the study. She looked up to see a maid, who dipped a quick curtsy. Rosemary's brows arched.

The girl smiled. "Luncheon is ready in the dining room, miss."

"Thank you. Though you needn't . . ." The girl was already gone, so Rosemary's "curtsy to me" was spoken only silently.

Rosemary continued to the stack against the wall. She could hear the muffled knocking from the next room, presumably of the maid upon the outer door. Three knocks, a moment of silence. Three more knocks. Wait. Thrice again.

Her lips twitched up. It took fifteen knocks before Mr. Holstein's distracted, "Just a moment!" put a halt to the summons. Worse even than when Rosemary had knocked yesterday.

No stammer or stutter on that either. And he could apparently converse well enough with Penrose to have established a friendship. What made it so much worse at other times?

She put the last of the books on the stack

in the corner and dusted her hands off on her skirt. Perhaps, if they really did take meals together twice daily, he would eventually relax around her. Perhaps his tongue would be more at ease.

Perhaps if she befriended him she could lure him somehow into revealing the information she needed to prove his loyalties lay with Germany.

She detoured to the table to fetch her list of names and the eyeglasses she'd tossed down at some point, positioning them as she headed for the door.

Holstein was even then opening his door into the hallway.

The maid curtsied. "Luncheon is ready in the dining room, Mr. Holstein."

"Th— thank you . . . Kerensa. I'll be . . . r-right there." But the door clicked shut again.

Not sure if his "right there" was perhaps synonymous with the Cornish "dreckly," Rosemary granted herself the time to head to the water closet and tidy herself up before hunting down the dining room. Though when she returned, the massive table had no occupants other than a pretty set of dishes and a covered platter.

There was no point in going in there and sitting alone. Instead, she headed toward an open set of double doors through which was a room she hoped was the parlor. She might as well look at the painting of St. Michael's Mount while she awaited her host.

Either she was in the right place or he had many landscape paintings, because the moment she stepped in she drew in a sharp breath at the oil-on-canvas across from her. It was huge, taking up almost all the space between couch and ceiling, between windows. And *stunning.*

Retta would love to see this — she was enthralled by all things artistic, and no doubt she'd go on for days about the light and the water and the brushstrokes and this and that. All Rosemary knew was that the result was utterly enchanting. It had the look of a magical world, this island out in the waters with the castle built so organically into it that it seemed the walls sprang directly from the trees and the earth had heaved its way with pure will out of the sea. And the pathway out to it . . . it looked even with the waters. As if it rose up to allow worthy feet to tread upon it, and then might just sink back down again to keep villains from the hallowed walls.

Fifteen miles away, he had said. It would take a whole day off to get there, see it, and get back. But it would be a day well spent.

"My f-father com . . . commissioned the painting. For my mother. It was . . . was her favorite p-place. She used to s-say . . . she would say she f-fell in love with Cornwall first. Father s-second."

Rosemary smiled, though she didn't turn to direct it toward Holstein. "The sort of thing one only says if one loves the other person so very much they can never question it."

"Indeed." His sigh was the soft kind. The kind that said, *I miss them.* And maybe, *If only they were here.*

She hadn't had the leisure to sigh so over her own parents, so busy had she been trying to survive after their deaths. But she knew the sigh. Perhaps everyone was born knowing that sigh. Born with the readiness to use it.

She looked his way now and found his gaze moving over the painting he had surely seen thousands of times. He likely saw things in it she never could — memories of the parents who had loved it first. "Where was your mother from, if not Cornwall?" she asked.

His smile was just a tight, small turning of his lips. "Rothenburg ob . . . ob der Tauber. In Germany."

Her skin prickled. "Did you father grow

188

up there too?"

He shook his head. "Opa . . . Opa and Oma moved here when F-Father was just a . . . a b-babe."

So his father hadn't been an English subject by birth. Nor, of course, his grandfather. And his father had married a German woman. So what, then, of *him*?

A question she suspected he would not answer here and now, when it was a veritable stranger asking. She settled for a bright smile. "Well, I can see why she fell in love with Cornwall so fast, if this is the kind of landscape to be seen." She motioned toward the painting, then pivoted, ready to see what kind of offerings were on that tray in the dining room. "I've a list of names to go over with you while we eat. They were all on marked pages, so perhaps they have something to do with your family."

He nodded his agreement and turned as well, leading the way into the dining room. He did that thing again — indicating where she should sit and then pulling out her chair for her, scooting it in as she sat. She had seen other men helping other women sit, of course, and standing when they entered a room, as he and Penrose had last night. But not for *her*. She'd been born to a station more apt to scurry about in a maid's uniform than to sit at the table with the master of the house.

What was she doing here?

Stealing this man's good name, that's what. Now focus.

The same maid who had summoned them — Kerensa, was it? — appeared to ask them what they'd like on their plates and then fill them. As if they were incapable of reaching toward the platter themselves and selecting a sandwich. But Rosemary played along, and warned her empty stomach that they mustn't make a spectacle of themselves, even though she wanted to try one of everything. It growled its protest, though thankfully the sound was covered by Holstein's murmuring to the maid.

Then he looked up, met her gaze, and made her glad she hadn't already shoved a sandwich into her mouth. "Shall we . . . pray?"

They'd done so last night, but she'd rather thought it because of the formality. Her family only ever remembered to bless the food when they had a lot of it — a rare occasion indeed. Rosemary nodded, but she didn't bow her head as he did, nor close her eyes. It was more interesting to watch him as he did so. To try to find a word for the expression that settled on his face. Comfort?

Peacefulness? Satisfaction? None seemed quite right.

"Dear Father. We thank you . . . for this food." He looked perfectly at ease as he spoke, those slight hesitations between his words sounding natural. "We ask . . . ask that you bless it, and the hands that have . . . prepared it. Grammy and Kerensa and Mrs. Teague."

Did he always pray for the servants? Did he *mean* it as he did? Rosemary traced a finger along the edge of a button. He'd actually named them, each person who had participated in this meal. Had anyone ever prayed for *her* by name?

If so, she was unaware of it.

And really, she doubted it. Who would? Pauly, perhaps. But he wasn't a man given to religion. And his wife, if she prayed for them, would have prayed that they be removed from her life.

"Be in the midst of our conversation and . . . and show us your ways. In Jesus' name. Amen."

Rosemary murmured an echoing amen. It didn't matter if anyone had prayed for her. Perhaps God heard people like Peter Holstein — perhaps — but He certainly didn't show any indication of hearing people like *her.* So why should anyone waste their breath?

She gave her host a small, meaningless smile and followed his lead in whether to pick up the sandwiches with her hands or use a utensil. Not that she could think of *why* society marks would use a fork for a sandwich, but she had seen stranger things in their circles.

He didn't. Just picked up his roast beef, glanced at her once, briefly, and cleared his throat. "Before we b-begin. With your . . . with your questions. You're not r-really . . . really left-handed, are you?"

She paused mid-reach for her water. Mid-reach with her right hand, blast it all. She really should have thought that lie through better, or committed to it more fully. Hadn't she noted plenty of times how Pauly did *everything* backward, aside from writing? Her breath eased out. "Forgive me, Mr. Holstein. It's just that I know my script is atrocious, and that it oughtn't to be. I learned, you see, from a man who *is* left-handed but was forced to learn with his right. Pauly."

Holstein lifted a brow that asked, with no need of words, *And who in blazes is Pauly?*

She sighed. "He's my . . ." What? Technically speaking, he wasn't her anything. She

192

should never have mentioned him. But she had. She replenished the breath she'd sighed out. "He's my uncle." It seemed the safest answer. No one would believe that some random pub owner had taken in a bunch of street rats, as much as he was able. And she couldn't claim he was the father she tended to think of him as, not when she'd just called him by his first name.

Holstein nodded. "Anything . . . anything else y-you'd like to confess?"

She was already failing at her cover? No. He was just shaving off some of the unnecessary parts of it for her, that was all. With a hint of a grin, Rosemary took off her spectacles and tossed them to the table. "I don't really need those. Just thought they made me look the part."

Holstein's lips twitched too. "Is th— that all?"

All she had a mind to admit. Rosemary nodded. "Sorry to have lied about anything, sir. It's just . . . it's difficult enough to find a position in this field as it is, being a woman. And I've all those mouths to help feed."

He nodded again and narrowed his eyes with seeming consideration at her . . . shoulder? "What of . . . what of your parents?"

Turnabout, she supposed, given that she'd asked him about *his*. She could lie again. Make up a set of loving parents. But when she opened her mouth, out came, "They're both dead. Fever."

"I'm s-sorry." He set down his sandwich. "R-Recently? Your . . . your youngest sibling is . . . isn't v-very old."

She closed her eyes for a moment, when the darkness insisted on an echo of itself. Felt again that confusion of stumbling into the dingy hall. So thirsty, her skin crusted with sweat that had poured off her, had dried there. Hadn't been sponged away by a loving mother. That dread of leaning into the doorway of the main room in their flat, the one that doubled as her parents' room, and smelling something she couldn't name. And yet knew was death.

She'd been eight that day. And a week later, scrounging through rubbish bins, she'd been ancient. "It seems like yesterday. And a century ago." Always there, too clear. Always distant, beyond her reach.

His breath sounded half like a laugh, half like a sigh. "I know ex . . . exactly what you mean."

She took a drink of blessedly cool water and then a bite of fresh greens while the silence took its own seat at the table. It

194

couldn't last long, she knew — she had a friendship to create and questions to ask before he shut himself up with the incessant *click-clack-ding* again. But he was obviously a man who deemed quiet one of his closest friends. If she could appear to be on good terms with it too, perhaps it would recommend her to him.

A minute or two later, he set down his water goblet and cleared his throat. "You . . . you have a l-list, you say?"

"I have, yes." She drew it out of the pocket it had been nestled in and smoothed it. Drew out the stub of a pencil she'd put in her pocket too. "First from a German title." She read him the list of names that had been mentioned on the marked page, pausing after each one. To the first, he shook his head. To the second, he informed her he was a German politician fifty years earlier. But when she said, "Hans von Roth," his brow furrowed.

"Von Roth is . . . is my m-mother's maiden name. What kind of b-book was this?"

"A history of the Prussian kings before German unification, I believe. Given the *von* in the name, your mother's family must have been well positioned — no great surprise, I suppose, that they get a mention here or there." She made a star beside *Hans von Roth,* though, and circled the title of the book so she knew to keep it in the stack of books she must read.

Her German was sure to be greatly improved by the end of this assignment.

Holstein looked none too convinced by her logic. "She . . . she always said her f-family led a . . . a quiet l-life."

Rosemary snorted. "And I said I was left-handed. People lie, Mr. Holstein."

Silence screamed at her, and she looked up from her notes to see storm clouds swirling in his eyes. Apparently he could accept her falsehoods more easily than he could her truths — at least if it besmirched his vision of his mother.

But people *did* lie. Denying it didn't change it. It just made one guilty of lying to oneself.

She returned his silent storm with a lifted brow.

The muscle in Holstein's jaw bunched up, then released when he opened his mouth again. "It c-could be a different . . . a different von Roth."

On a page marked by his father or grandfather? Wouldn't it be infinitely more logical that they'd marked it because it was the name of his mother's family? She said nothing. If he liked silence so well, let him interpret it as he chose.

"Or . . . or as you say, j-just mention of a . . . a noble f-family."

"Mm-hmm." She drew a box around the name too and then added a few more stars.

"Or even . . . even if th— they *were* involved in . . . in politics. Mother m-may not have known."

Rosemary reached for the discarded eyeglasses and positioned them back on her nose. At his look of confusion, she gave him a sweet smile. "You obviously prefer not to have to change your understanding of people. Far be it from me to force you to do so."

She wasn't sure, for a moment, if he would yell or laugh or just seal his lips into stony silence. Frankly, she wasn't sure if *he* knew what he'd do either. But after a pulse, his face relaxed, and amusement kindled in his eyes. "You're . . . you're very c-clever, aren't you?"

It shouldn't have warmed her. But she couldn't quite help that her smile went genuine. "Not the word most often chosen, sir. But I'll take it."

He chuckled, ate a bite of his sandwich, and pointed back to her list.

She read off the names from the next book . . . and made a mental note that Peter Holstein appreciated wit. And was, in fact, willing to be open-minded when someone called him on being the opposite.

It was more than she could say for most people, she supposed.

NINE

Peter may have finished his food fifteen minutes before, but he was still chewing on the conversation as he and Miss Gresham meandered down the hall toward the study and library. She was still chattering about the sheer volume of books in there and his need for more shelves somewhere if he meant to keep them all.

He let her chatter. He'd send a note to Mr. Teague when he got back in his office, asking who, either at Kensey or in the village, could outfit one of the unused rooms into a secondary library. But until he had an answer on the matter, there was little point in wrapping his tongue around unnecessary words. At least not when she was capable of filling the silence all on her own.

Besides, it wasn't shelves he really cared about just now. It was the presence of the name *von Roth* in that book. They couldn't know, of course, until someone had read it what it really meant, if anything. It *could* be explained by any one of the reasons he had listed. It could. Heaven knew there were plenty of von Roths in the world, and Hans was by no means a unique name either . . . even if it was his own middle name, in honor of his maternal grandfather. It could still be entirely coincidental.

Or it could be that his mother had painted him an incomplete picture when she described her family as one that enjoyed a quiet country existence, never venturing into public life.

"I do have to wonder . . ." Miss Gresham paused, drawing his attention to the fact that they'd reached their respective doors. Her brows were lifted, implying a question he hadn't heard. Or perhaps one that was forthcoming, as she continued with, "What are you reading for entertainment these days, Mr. Holstein?"

"Ah." He rarely read when he was this close to a deadline — not fiction, anyway. It was too easy to get distracted with someone else's story. Or compare himself to them. Always dangerous. "I am . . . I am between b-books at the moment. But . . . but I promised you Mel . . . Melville. I c-can get it for you."

"Oh, no need. I borrowed it when I left

that note for you. Which . . ." Her frown pointed out the one tugging at *his* brows. "Apparently I should not have done — do forgive me, Mr. Holstein. I am accustomed to having many siblings running about borrowing from each other. It didn't occur to me that you would mind if I fetched it myself, having granted your permission."

And he shouldn't let it bother him.

But it bothered him. He cleared his throat and, hopefully, his face. "It's n-nothing. Did you . . . did you start it yet?"

He had to chuckle at the way she wrinkled up her nose. "Started and deemed it not to my liking. I abandoned it a page in and perused the shelves in the cottage instead. I got a few chapters into *This Mad Caper* last night. By that Hollow fellow who won't sign your copy for you."

"D-Did you?" His stomach went sick, his palms damp. He never really spoke of his stories with people who were currently reading them — there were so many books in the world to discuss, after all, why would those few titles come up when he was around? This was another reason he preferred a *nom de plume.* He could only imagine how much worse he would react if people knew they were talking about *his* book. He had no desire to know what anyone thought about it. Not when looking at them, instead of at a lovely sheet of paper and some flat ink that blunted their words. No, he would just as soon remain oblivious to Miss Gresham's opinions. "W-What do you think of it?"

Blast. Unruly tongue. Since when did it speak when he *didn't* want it to?

Miss Gresham laughed and eased another step toward the library door. "It's a far cry better than smelly whalers, that's for sure. I'll give you my full opinion after I've finished. Have you Hollow's other titles as well? I only spotted that one in the cottage, but there are so many books there. . . ."

Better than smelly whalers . . . what high praise. Though *better than Melville* was a happy — albeit untrue — way to interpret the statement. "They are . . . they are all there."

"Excellent. I shall get back to work then, and let you get back to . . . whatever it is you type all the day long."

If she was waiting for an explanation, she would be waiting for a long time. Peter smiled, nodded, and turned to his door. On the small table he kept beside it, the day's post had been piled. He gathered it all up — no fewer than a dozen letters to promise him company this evening — and slipped into his study.

A white rectangle of folded paper caught his gaze when he entered. It was just this side of the door to the library, as if she had slipped it underneath. She must have done, before lunch. He clicked his main door shut, dropped the pile of letters into an unruly heap upon his desk, and headed toward it. Bent, picked it up, flipped it open.

A thanks for the paper. And an apology for her anger yesterday. Again, things she could have just said over lunch. But if she wanted to write them instead, who was he to argue? And she'd signed it *Rosemary* again — he was to blame for that. He'd realized it when he'd scratched out the note to put with the stationery and had caught himself signing *Peter* to the bottom. He'd managed to stop himself at the start of that first *e,* but he knew well he hadn't on his first note. She was just following his lead. Had probably thought *him* forward.

Habit, that was all. But he'd try to watch himself.

He tossed the paper, folded again, into the cacophony that was his desktop and rounded the desk, eyes already on the typewriter. But when he'd sat down and put his fingers on those lovely circular keys, his mind refused to conjure up images of

Amazonian forests and James family secrets.

Holstein family secrets bludgeoned him instead. Or von Roth ones, perhaps. He had always thought he knew perfectly well who his family was — he had looked into their eyes and felt the love they gave so freely. He had learned how to live, how to trust in God, at their knees. He had been told, ever since he could remember, that they had been blessed indeed to find a home in a land that valued the sort of freedom the German emperors — and specifically Chancellor von Bismarck — sacrificed for the sake of a unified, imperial Germany.

Opa had moved here before von Bismarck was chancellor, when he was just minister president of Prussia, and the German states were a loose coalition rather than a nation. He had seen the direction the minister was taking the land, the power he was seizing. It had taken a decade before Opa's predictions happened, before von Bismarck curtailed religious freedom and launched the so-called *Kulturkampf* — the "culture war" against faith. The Catholic faith specifically, but it had made Protestants rally around their Catholic brethren in a way that probably hadn't been much done since Luther had led the Reformation in their land three hundred years before.

Because when a leader declared one faith an enemy, others wouldn't be far behind.

Peter leaned back in his chair and tilted his head until the ceiling swam before him. Who had his grandfather been in his youth? What had shaped him into a man who would leave his country as he had done? His early years were during the reign of King Frederick Wilhelm IV — years of art and culture and romanticism. Years of galleries and cathedrals and zoos.

Then came the revolution in 1848. Opa had still been a boy then. He would have remembered the uprisings more clearly than the arts.

Peter rubbed at his eyes and leaned forward again. He couldn't dwell now on the history of the Hapsburgs, on Germany and Prussia and Frankfurt Parliaments. He would leave those questions — or rather, the one of what in the world the Holsteins and von Roths had to do with any of it — for another day. A day when his library was in order, his family history laid out in a row of neat journals to be read, and answers could actually be found.

For now, he must concentrate on Locryn James and the mysterious Rosita currently leading him through the jungles. He unlocked and opened his manuscript drawer, pulling out the last few pages so he could remind himself of where he'd been before family history derailed him.

Rosita, with her bony shoulders and pretty smile — she needed something to charm Locryn, after all, if she was going to be an effective false-romance — had just led Locryn back to the safety of the village, after a close call with angry natives who had not taken kindly to their intrusion upon the sacred caves. Peter's lips twitched up. He may wish he had ventured out into the world more than he had done, but all things considered, he didn't regret never having poisoned darts aimed at his chest. Rocks through windows were, frankly, preferable. If one were going to have enemies.

So Locryn and Rosita had just slipped into the tavern that her uncle owned — the one Locryn had first inquired at early that day as to where he might find this series of caves. Peter hadn't realized when he wrote that earlier scene that the barkeep's niece was listening, of course. Nor that she had taken it upon herself to follow him. But he did like where it was going.

Especially now. His characters had just stepped back into the bustling room, filled with Spanish and smoke and the spice of the food being served. And Locryn had spotted Thomas. Who . . . what? What had Peter meant him to do? He'd had a perfect line of dialogue in mind before that incessant rapping had sounded upon his door, knocking it straight out of his head.

It would come back. He inserted his last sheet of paper back into his typewriter. Lined it up. Drew in a deep breath.

Stared.

He couldn't remember. And blast it, but they were perfect words, and he didn't want to use something else now and then just have to retype the whole page later when they came back to him.

He grabbed his pen and a blank sheet of paper — sometimes those old friends were all he needed to get the words flowing again. But when he put nib to sheet, only shapes came out, no words. Random geometrical . . .

No, not random. Blast it all, he was drawing that silly symbol, the one on Mr. Jasper's ring. With an impatient growl, he balled up the page and pushed to his feet.

Grabbing the stack of post, he flipped through the envelopes while he paced. A walk outside would probably be better, but rain kissed his windows again. It hardly mattered. A few minutes to let his brain work out the question would suffice. He had only to let it turn it over while he did something else.

His hands paused when the royal seal caught his eye. It was awfully soon after leaving London for him to be getting a letter from the king or Prince Edward. They must have written it while he was packing his bags. Curiosity — no, dread — curled up in his stomach. He tossed the rest of the stack back down and tore open the envelope.

The king. And that curled-up dread unfurled into full-fledged anxiety as he read the words.

I should not be writing this to you — I do so only because I know your heart is loyal and detest the underhanded workings of Jasper. You know, surely, that the Home Office is already making plans for the eventuality of war with Germany — what they shall do here if that comes to pass. I have just been informed of this particular portion of their plan, and while I do not like it, I cannot argue with the general wisdom.

Any German or Austrian male between 18 and 50 living in Britain will be relocated for the duration of a war against their homeland. You are a British subject, so this ought not to apply to you — but that duplicitous Jasper was making noise this morning, when he heard you were leaving Town, that you are not, in fact, a British subject. Something about being born in Germany? That your father maintained a dual citizenship, as did you? This does not align with what I know of your family, but I highly suggest you request the records of your family's naturalization from the National Archives, Peter. In this current political climate, you may be called upon to prove you are English and not German. I suggest you have your evidence ready to do so — from the Archives, or perhaps find the copies they surely had there at Kensey Manor. Even the deed may suffice, as they could not have bought the place had they still been German citizens, not in those days. It should be easy for you to prove — and I pray you can do so. I will do what I can for you, but we both know the danger just now of me taking sides with anything the public would deem German.

God keep you, my friend, better than I can do.

Peter swallowed. Or tried to. His throat was too dry, too tight, just as his fingers were too tightly curled around the paper.

George should *not* have written such

things to him, to be sure. But he was in the king's debt for it.

Except that there was just enough truth to the accusation to mean trouble, if he couldn't prove everything with neatly printed forms and documents. His parents had only wanted options to be available, if Germany were to change her direction. But she hadn't, and they had all — every last one of them — chosen England as the better homeland. Had chosen it legally and officially, just as Peter himself had done.

So there were records. Here. Somewhere. Naturalization documents. Or as the king had mentioned, the deed to Kensey. Their family's tenure here had begun as a lease, to be sure, but Father had purchased it at some point. Peter knew he had, for otherwise he wouldn't have been able to will the property to Peter, just the lease. So the deed must be about too.

Blast it all. *Where?* In the library somewhere? Or with the other important family documents filed in the attic? He would have to check. And he would also write a request to the Archives for a copy of *their* copy of the records.

Later. Tossing the crumpled paper onto his desk, he rubbed at his temples. He must put this all aside for now. He would write that letter and look for the documents later, when his poking around the library or attic wouldn't stir up any questions with the staff.

Right now he must concentrate on his story.

Thomas. He must put himself back into the mind of Thomas, and he paced again to do so. Thomas had just been on that voyage home. He had received a telegram en route, saying his father had died and the estate, now his, was in fine condition. Thomas, feeling the urging of the Lord, had immediately debarked when his ship put in for coal and had found another ship back to his friend.

Thomas had finally found the village where Locryn had gone, only to discover that his friend had headed out into the jungle. Alone. Armed but with a machete and one sidearm.

Thomas was furious. Thomas was concerned. Thomas, when he saw Locryn with Rosita, was suspicious. Thomas was — *ouch*.

Peter's arms flew out when his foot collided with the box. But windmill as he might, he still tipped forward. Struck his knee on the side table beside which he'd foolishly dropped said box. Knocked off the old oil lamp sitting on said side table. Winced at its crash.

Three . . . two . . . one . . .

"Mr. Holstein! Are you all right?"

The voice hammered at the door to the library, but at least the door stayed shut. He cleared his throat. "F-Fine. Thank . . . you."

A moment's pause. "Can I help you with anything?"

His gaze tracked to the typewriter, its paper still positioned under the type guide, the drawer still opened to the stack of finished pages. "No n-need." He would just have to call for Mrs. Teague, that was all. For now he would pick up all the broken glass and be thankful it had landed on the wood floor and not the rug. Surely he had something in here somewhere with which he could sop up the oil.

He did, in fact, find an old towel stored in a cabinet — Mrs. Teague would probably scold him for using it on lamp oil, but it seemed a good idea to get the stuff up as quickly as possible. He took care of the mess as best he could, wiped his hands on the part of the towel still relatively clean, and went to put his manuscript page — and the crumpled letter from the king — in their respective drawers with their friends.

As he turned from his desk toward the bell, his gaze locked on the blamed box. The mail from Branok Hollow's readers. He had thought it perfectly safe to leave the thing there, sealed as it was, until he had the time to go through it. But apparently he had underestimated his own clumsiness. Best to put it now with the others in the . . .

"No. No, no, no." He charged to the library door and flung it open.

Miss Gresham spun, gripping the book in her hands like a weapon. Then chuffed out a breath to make Father proud. "Mr. Holstein!"

He had the feeling he had narrowly avoided having that tome of Latin verbs fly at his head. "C-Could you . . . could you please fetch Mrs. Teague? Or Kerensa? I've a . . . a b-bit of a mess."

If he could just get Miss Gresham out of here long enough to make sure the boxes of other reader mail were secure . . . He should have moved them before. Should have remembered that they were the bottom two of the stack he'd told her yesterday not to bother with. Already she had touched them, had moved them to the corner. What if one had come open? What if she had seen all of those missives addressed to Mr. Hollow?

She hadn't. If she had, she would have sounded something other than off-handed as she mentioned *This Mad Caper.* She had just moved the boxes. As he'd instructed. She had done her job and left it at that.

And he would make dashed sure that was all she had the chance to do too. If she found him out, if she blabbed it, if the press got hold of it — if Mr. Jasper did — he would be ruined. Aspersions would be cast from every direction, words he had written in innocence years ago would be said to be rooted in German ideals. Branok Hollow would never sell another manuscript.

Miss Gresham nodded, set down the book, and hurried toward the door to the hall. No doubt she expected him to spin back around and try to minimize the mess he'd mentioned. Instead, he waited for her to clear the threshold and then scurried to the corner where she'd moved his correspondence.

Really, he ought to move it all. He disliked the idea of anyone nosing through his letters from friends as much as he did the one of them discovering his *nom de plume*. He lifted the first two boxes from the stack and wove his way back to his door. For now, they would just have to sit in his study. He would move them to the attic later, after Miss Gresham had retired for the night. Heaven knew he needed to rummage about up there anyway.

He thumped them down in the hall-side corner of his study, where no one was likely to spot them from either open door. Hurried back in for the others. He had just put the newest one into place on the top of the stack when he heard feminine voices coming down the hall.

"I am so deeply sorry, Mrs. Teague." Miss Gresham sounded about as sorry as Locryn James when he bested a villain. "Next time our employer asks a favor of me, I shall first drill him with a thousand questions so that I can answer them for you, rather than simply doing as I'm told."

Mrs. Teague's voice was a low Cornish murmur. Peter didn't catch it all, but the few words he *did* hear made him wince on Miss Gresham's behalf.

They came into view as they rounded the corner. Miss Gresham was wearing that sickeningly sweet grin again. "You know who you remind me of? I've just figured it out — my uncle Pauly's wife."

Mrs. Teague's face reddened. "I am *not* your aunt, missy."

"Neither is she." Head high, as if she had just delivered the most abusive of insults, Miss Gresham sailed into the library. And took the liberty, a moment later, of slamming shut the door to his study.

Peter greeted the housekeeper with a steady look.

215

She pressed her lips together. "Don't you be looking at me like that, Master Peter. That girl is trouble. Mark my words."

He just shook his head and indicated the mess he'd made. "I b-bumped the table. Broke the . . . the lamp."

Her lips pressed tight again when she spotted the oil-soaked towel, but she assured him she'd have it taken care of in just a minute and vanished again to retrieve a dustbin.

Peter was left to rub a hand over his face. To look out his window at the foggy, dreary day. And to wonder if his life would ever be put to rights again.

Rosemary slipped into the cottage and reached for the light switch, breathing a sigh of relief as golden light spilled into the room. Dinner with Holstein hadn't been as bad as she had feared, but she hadn't much relished walking back here in the dark again. And it was a darkness she'd never experienced in the city, with all its streetlights and lamps in windows. This dark was thick and corporeal, so whole she knew no lantern could possibly dispel it.

Who knew what monsters lurked in it? She had heard snapping twigs from the woods. A thrashing sound. And an otherworldly hooting too.

A bird. An owl. Her logic told her so.

She shut the door and leaned against it, wishing her logic were a little stronger in the face of darkness. Because at the moment, she was pretty certain that owl was ten feet tall and capable of snatching *her* up like a field mouse.

"Rosie, *there* you are!"

She jumped, squealed, splayed a hand over her chest. And then threw her handbag at Willa's head, where she sat at the table. "You *know* better."

Willa didn't smile. She just dodged the handbag and stood. She wore her overcoat, the one they'd rescued from a rubbish bin last year and painstakingly cleaned up. And she had her valise. "I've been waiting ages. What took you so long?"

"They have ridiculous numbers of courses at dinner." Rosemary pointed to the luggage. "You're leaving. I thought you were staying the week. Has something happened?"

Willa's nostrils flared. "I had a telegram when I got back to my room. Barclay."

Rosemary shrugged out of her wrap and dropped it onto the table so she could reach for Willa's hands. Barclay didn't send telegrams. Telegrams were expensive. And

217

they were easily intercepted, easily traced. "What's happened?"

"It's Olivia. She's sick."

"Sick." It must be more than just a normal sick if it had Barclay sending telegrams. Rosemary squeezed Willa's hands tighter, her stomach threatening to make some sick of her own. "What is it?"

Willa shook her head, but her eyes were a swarm of worries. "Didn't say. You know you have to pay per letter. The wire just said, *Liv in hospital. Come.*"

"Hospital?" The word emerged as a tremor. They never — *never* — went to the doctor, much less the hospital. The cost was too great. The best they could ever do was a trip to the apothecary. When she blinked, she saw little Olivia, only six, lying on a colorless bed. Colorless herself. Nothing but skin and bones and misery. She dropped Willa's hands and spun toward the kitchen's exit. "Give me two minutes. I'll be packed and —"

"You can't." Willa grabbed at her shoulder. "If you leave this job, there's no way we'll be able to pay for whatever she needs. You're her best hope right now, Rosie, but only if you stay here. This money from Mr. V — it has to be the only way they could take her to a doctor. But what will that man do if you leave here? If you fail to complete the assignment?"

Her throat was too tight to swallow. Her eyes too blurry to see. "I don't know. I don't know what he'll do."

"Exactly. What kind of man is this you're working for? What if he takes his displeasure out on the family or has you arrested?" Willa shook her head and wiped at her cheeks. "You stay. I'll go. I'll send you word just as soon as I know anything, cost-per-letter be hanged."

"But —"

"I know, Rosie. I do. But I've been sitting here two hours turning it over and over, and this is the only way."

The blurry Willa gripped her hands again, then pulled her in for a tight embrace.

Rosemary sniffed, squeezed her back, and then stepped away. "Is there a train or something this late?"

"No, but there was a family at the inn going to London tonight. They were there in the dining room when the telegram was delivered and offered to let me ride with them."

Good people. Rosemary nodded. "Don't lift anything from their pockets."

Willa rolled her eyes. "I only bite the hand that *refuses* to feed me." She leaned down and picked up her valise. "They'll be waiting for me at the crossroads in ten minutes. I almost thought I'd have to leave you a note."

Glad she'd turned down the pudding, Rosemary reached for the door latch and tugged it open for her sister. "Hurry, then. And send me word the *minute* you know something."

"I will. You know I will." Willa hurried to the threshold but paused on it. "You're doing your part, Rosie. More than the rest of us can do right now."

Then why did it feel like she was abandoning the precious little girl she'd rocked and sung to for the past four years? Olivia had been just a baby when they'd found her crying in an alley. A baby, toddling around on unsteady feet, crying for a mama who lay there covered with blood. The woman had been barely coherent enough to beg them to see her baby to safety. She had no family.

But she had one now, did Olivia. Brothers and sisters who doubled as mothers and fathers. Who would do anything in their power to keep her safe.

Even if it meant staying too far away, sorting through stupid books so she could prove a man a German spy.

Ridiculous. What could it possibly matter

whether Holstein was loyal to England or not, when Olivia was in hospital?

Willa stepped into the night, clicking the door shut behind her.

Rosemary stared at the darkness, waiting for it to pound its way through the windows. To seep in under the door and slurp her up. She listened for Willa's footsteps, but after a few seconds there was nothing. Just monster owls hooting and the hum of the lights and the lingering whiff of cigarette smoke that the door had caught and had pushed inside, which faded again in half a moment.

She stood there. One minute, two, perhaps a hundred, she didn't know. She just stood there until her pumps started to hurt her feet and she was sure Willa wouldn't be coming back. Though *of course* Willa wouldn't be coming back. Willa was needed in London.

"And you're needed right here." The words, whispered into the room, fogged up the window in the door but had no other effect. They may be true — but they meant nothing.

Eventually she turned away from the door. Standing there would do no good, would do nothing to help Olivia. Rosemary sniffed back the tears that wanted to fall and pulled off her shoes, let them clatter to the floor by the table. She turned lights on as she went toward her bedroom, until most of the cottage was aglow.

The room still looked as it had a few hours before, as she'd dressed for dinner and told Willa about her day — the luncheon with Holstein, the impossible attitude of the housekeeper, the breakfast that never appeared. But none of the same things mattered now.

What if Olivia died? Rosemary sank down onto the mattress that fluffed out around her. Her little sister would be on a hard hospital cot even now. No soft mattress filled with feathers. No blankets so smooth they made one aware of the roughness of one's own skin. She was probably being sneered at by nurses and doctors who knew, just by looking at her, that she was an urchin. A nobody.

But she wasn't a nobody. She was Olivia. So what if they'd never known her last name? She would take one of theirs, when she needed one. Gresham or Forsythe or Pearce. Sayers or Archer. Plenty of names to choose from — it was just a matter of picking which sibling she wanted to claim in such a way, once she was old enough to care.

Rosemary sniffed again, but this time it

didn't keep tears from trickling down her cheeks. They should have given her a last name — voted on it years ago. She deserved a last name. Olivia, with her beautiful curls in fair brown. Her big eyes in sapphire blue.

What if she died without a last name?

Arms wrapped around her middle, Rosemary stood again, moving to the window just because it was there. The pane was as cool as the night. And though her bare arms were cool too, still she leaned her forehead against the glass. *Olivia, I'm here. I love you.*

God, do you see that little girl? Do you care?

He didn't. She knew He didn't. When had any of their prayers ever been answered? Maybe God was blind or deaf. Or maybe . . . maybe He was a gentleman. Only caring for His own. The people born with bursting bank accounts and fine things. The ones who didn't ask Him for much because they already had it all.

Maybe it was anger that swelled in her veins. Or desperation. Maybe her ears were still ringing with the easy, confident words of prayer Mr. Holstein had spoken over their dinner. He knew God, that was what His words said. He knew Him, and the Lord listened when Peter Holstein prayed.

So be it. If God would only hear men like Peter Holstein, then Rosemary Gresham

223

would play that game. She could humble herself — for Olivia's sake.

Nearly tripping over the hem of the gown that was too long with no shoes on, she scurried out of the bedchamber again, to the stack of paper at the little secretary in the other room. She'd managed to write one letter this afternoon between coming from the library and preparing for dinner. Now she'd write another. For Olivia's sake.

You seem to be on good terms with the Almighty. I need you to pray to Him for me — for my little sister's sake.

She told him what she knew — which was precious little. About Olivia being in hospital. About Willa cutting her holiday short to go home to London. Of how dire it must be.

And then . . . then she just wrote, not quite sure what words were coming out. Her eyes were too blurry, and her hand probably went from bad to nearly illegible, but she didn't care. God wouldn't hear her, but perhaps Peter Holstein would. Enough to say one of those non-stammering prayers for Liv anyway. Surely, even though Rosemary was nothing to him but a new acquaintance, he would spare a few minutes for her sister.

He knew what it meant to love a child.

He had little Elowyn. If *she* were in a hospital, he would be on his knees for her, she knew he would be. So if perhaps he would give Olivia just a portion of that time, of that effort. Perhaps that would be enough to make God take note.

Were the darkness not so very deep, she may have run the note to the big house now. But he was probably not in his study anymore, and she knew no other place to leave it. He wouldn't see it until morning anyway.

Still, she went to the window, the folded sheet in hand. Which room was his? Was it visible from here? Would she even know it if she saw light shining from it to tell her he had retired? She hadn't paid any attention last night.

No second-floor windows were alight though. A faint glow came from the kitchen on the ground floor, but that was it. Nothing to indicate he was in some parlor or drawing room or other chamber with an important name. Just that light in the kitchen. And one on the topmost floor, coming from a tiny little window she hadn't even noticed was there until it was lit.

Servants' quarters, no doubt. Probably the Teagues or Kerensa or . . .

A figure passed in front of the window. A strangely shaped one, part slender man and part square box. Her brows knit. It could be anyone. And surely was nothing. Someone moving a box about — no matter to her.

Except that it looked distinctly like Peter Holstein's form. Not that a man didn't have a right to move things about in his own house — attic, probably. But wasn't that what he had servants for? To do such heavy lifting?

As she watched, he leaned just out of sight with the box, looking to be putting it on top of a stack of something, or on a shelf perhaps. Something that required sliding, pushing, but no bending. Then he fiddled with something in the same place and a moment later passed fully by the window again with something in his hands.

He vanished, but the light didn't move off, even though it had the distinct color and slight flicker of a lamp's flame. She watched for another minute, two, and was rewarded with the sight of him coming back into view, pivoting, retreating again. Pacing.

With a letter in his hands — well, some sort of document. The light half-shone through the paper.

It could be just his personal correspondence. But why hide it away in the attic? Why *read* it in the attic?

Something with the weight and tang of disappointment settled on her shoulders. She turned from the window, went to put the note for him on the kitchen table. Then just stood there with her fingers holding the folded paper shut. Hoping with all that was in her that God didn't care if Peter Holstein was a spy for Germany. Because she really needed Him to hear his prayers.

TEN

Dawn was barely a kiss on the horizon when Rosemary tramped across the path to the big house. In her satchel, tucked under one arm, she had the note for Holstein, the letter to Cressida, and *This Mad Caper* — just in case she decided she'd rather spend the hours before her work officially began doing something other than working. But she had to get out of the cottage, away from the questions it screamed at her every time she saw something Willa had touched or a chair she had sat in.

In her hands she carried her plan for survival. A pitcher, filled with cool water from her kitchen sink, and a glass. It wouldn't help if breakfast never appeared again, but she hardly cared about that. She was none too sure her stomach would accept food anyway, until she knew what had happened to Olivia.

Smoke puffed from the kitchen chimney,

and a warm light glowed already from the windows. Grammy would be up, whether the rest of the staff was or not, preparing Mr. Holstein's breakfast. Letting bread rise. All those other things cooks did in the early-morning hours that were more mystery and myth to Rosemary than things she'd observed. But she'd seen the products of their wee-hour labor in bakery windows.

Cliché torture for a street rat.

The door, when she reached it, was locked, despite the light coming from its panes. Rosemary clenched her jaw. She could knock. Or go back for the tools from her handbag and pick the lock — which would be far more entertaining. But no, she wasn't about to tip her hand to these people. They already disliked her. Best not to show them her true colors or they'd do far worse than withhold meals.

But blast it, she didn't want to deal with contempt today. Not today. Today she just needed some quiet and some pretense that everything was all right. In privacy, so that if tears surged unexpectedly, as they'd been doing all night, no one would see.

The door opened, and a flush-faced Grammy stood before her. "Miss Gresham. You're up and about early." The woman's plump cheeks sagged in a frown. "Those are some kind of circles you have under your eyes. Didn't you sleep, girl?"

Those blighted tears surged. When Grammy stepped aside, she sidled past, careful to keep her face averted. "I won't be a bother to you, ma'am, don't worry. Just passing through on my way to the library."

It ought to suit the cook just fine. So why did she put a warm hand on Rosemary's shoulder and say, "Now, hold you hard. I know the look of a girl with something weighing on her heart. Tell Grammy what's wrong?" There was something melodic about the way it sounded in the Cornish accent. The way the *r* rolled through *heart.* Or *'eart,* rather.

Melodic or not, she didn't mean to show any vulnerability to this woman.

Though Olivia could use all the prayers she could get. And perhaps God listened to gentlemen's staff members — how was she to know? Maybe it was just urchins He ignored. Still refusing to look at the woman, she swallowed. "My littlest sister is in hospital. I don't know yet what's wrong. But if you're the praying kind, I'd appreciate a word or two on her behalf. She's called Olivia. She's just six."

"Oh, dearover!" The way Grammy said it, Rosemary wasn't certain if the *dear* was

Olivia or *her.* And hadn't a clue what the *over* was for. The Cornish way of saying *of her* perhaps? "Of course I'll pray. Do you need to go to her?"

A sob tried to rise, but she let it do no more than shake her shoulders. Once. Then she wrestled it back and drew a long, steady breath through her nostrils. "I can't. If I leave this job, they'll never be able to afford the bills for it. The others will take care of her, I know that. Barclay and Retta and Willa. She's not alone." *But I am.*

Grammy made a *tsk* sound that was, somehow, comforting. And slid an arm around her waist. Rosemary had never had such a plump arm around her, such an ample waist pressed to her side. It felt . . . lovely. "Poor dear," she said, and this time Rosemary knew well she meant her. "You sit down at the table here and let Grammy get you a nice cup of tea. Or coffee, which-ever you've a mind to have."

She'd never win the battle against the tears if she did that. Rosemary shook her head. "Thank you, Grammy. But no. I . . . I just need to get to work. Keep my hands and mind busy. Willa will send a wire just as soon as she can, and then I'll know more. Until then . . ."

"All right, then." But rather than let her

231

go, Grammy just urged her forward, toward the door, that soft but muscled arm still around her. She took the satchel from under Rosemary's arm and put it under her own instead. "I'll help you get all those lamps lit in the library. It'll still be as dark as a vooga in there — a cavern, I mean."

A shiver flew up the path the sob had made, quaking her before she could dampen it. She hadn't thought of that, to be sure. "Thank you."

The woman made no mention of the pitcher of water in her hand, of the glass. She had to have noticed them, but if she took it as an indictment of her hospitality, no apology came for it. She just chattered about when the son of some bloke Rosemary had never heard of had gone to hospital. He'd apparently emerged whole and well. Rosemary was apparently to take that as encouragement.

Rosemary had no idea how to accept such encouragement.

Grammy led the way into the dark-as-fear library, still talking about good doctors and medical advancements, and had she heard about the new gas they're using for surgeries? Then she released Rosemary's waist and turned to look for the lamps, finding one just inside the door. With hands steady and confident, she removed the glass chimney, struck a match, and had the wick flaming in half a second.

Its light was feeble indeed among all the towering shadows, but just enough to give Rosemary courage to advance a few feet. To put down her water and glass on the table and hurry to another of the lamps.

Between them, she and Grammy had a dozen chimneys glowing within a few minutes, and the room looked nearly cozy in the golden light. Nearly.

Rosemary offered the cook a tight smile. "Thank you, ma'am. I appreciate the help."

Grammy returned the smile, nodded, and patted Rosemary's arm on her way by. Then left without another word. That was, apparently, all the goodwill Rosemary had earned.

So be it. She would choose to believe that the woman would indeed say a prayer for Olivia, which was all she needed from her.

Time to get to work. After sliding the note for Holstein under his door again, she decided to tackle first some of the heavy lifting she'd not had the energy for by the end of the day yesterday. She'd amassed stacks and stacks of books that needed to be moved out of the way, but at the moment they were still a haphazard jumble by the shelves, begging to be bumped and knocked over. Well, not today, thank you. Though the room still had a predawn spring chill, she shrugged out of her jacket, rolled up the sleeves of her shirtwaist, and prepared herself for some exertion.

Since the stacks were a mess anyway, she needn't worry with what order the tomes were in within them. She could load up her arms with those on the top, wind her way through the maze to the spot she'd designated for this subject, and just dump them on the top of a different stack. And when she forced herself to move at a quick pace, it soon resulted in a pleasant burn in her muscles and heat from within chasing away the cool of the room.

"Here we are, dear."

She jumped at the voice but managed to keep from dropping her armload of books as Grammy bustled back in, a tray in hand. From it emanated the smell of tea. And something hot and sweet and yeasty. Rosemary deposited the books on top of their comrades. "Oh, you needn't have, ma'am." But the smell . . . it was a siren song.

"Nonsense." Grammy slid the tray onto the table without so much as a clatter of china. When she turned, her cheeks were flushed again. "I completely forgot your breakfast yesterday — I'm so sorry for that.

My memory, sometimes . . . I didn't realize it until I went back to get this for you." Her smile was wavering, yet warm. She massaged the fingers of one hand with those of the other. "I hope you didn't think it a slight. And in the future, should I forget anything, please just pop into the kitchen and tell me. You're welcome in there any time, Miss Gresham. Any time."

"Thank you," Rosemary whispered. The kindness nearly undid her. She couldn't move, couldn't even smile while Grammy stood there watching her, or she'd shatter.

Perhaps the old woman knew that. With a nod and a sweet little smile, she showed herself out.

Rosemary drew in a breath that bumped its way into her lungs and then moved over to the tray. Tea. Milk. Sugar. Some little bun thing gooey with icing and cinnamon that looked even more delectable than a hot cross bun. And a whole bowl of strawberries.

She sank into a chair and let the tears come.

The napkin tucked under the saucer on the tray volunteered itself as a handkerchief, which she put to use as she stirred delectable milk and precious sugar into the cup of steaming tea she poured from the small pot.

She sipped, and she eyed the sugary bun. And she wished she could send one to little Liv at the hospital. And she sighed and looked to the corner of the room . . . and frowned.

The boxes — they were missing. The ones she'd hauled into that corner first thing on her first day. Gone.

Cup in hand, she got up to investigate, though they certainly hadn't just gone on a promenade and left a trail of breadcrumbs in their wake. There was nothing there but a loudly empty spot where they'd been.

Holstein must have gotten them out. He'd every right to do so — they were his correspondence after all. Maybe he'd decided they didn't belong in the library.

She stared at the wall, seeing that light aglow in the attic last night. Peter Holstein pacing the floor, a sheet of paper in hand.

Blast it all. She was going to have to figure out a way to get up there and see what those letters contained, if he so wanted to hide them.

Preferably during daylight hours.

Peter finally stumbled from bed when morning was just about to give way to noon. He'd been up in the attic until nearly midnight, searching for his family's naturalization documents or his father's will. When that failed, he'd taken to reading through most of the letters from his readers. They represented the usual fare — much praise, ample criticism, and a few people who invited him to weddings and christenings and balls.

Those always made him smile. He would never go, even if the world knew him as Branok Hollow. Such scenes always made him uneasy to a ridiculous degree. But it was nice to think that somewhere out there, beyond all the political adversaries and naysayers and villagers ready to destroy his home, there were people who considered him a friend.

He'd stood up there in the sloping attic and thought too long about whether this was his answer. Whether, after proving to the world that he really was a British subject, he ought to legally change his name to Hollow and embrace the identity he'd already created for himself. Father and Opa would understand, wouldn't they? After all, Opa had given up his homeland. Had moved here. He'd *wanted* to be an Englishman. Why would he mind if Peter made their name reflect it?

But then all he could hear in his ears were Father's words, spoken out of the blue one day after a trip to London. *"All a man has is his name, son. The reputation we make with it. Whether it brings a smile or a frown, love or fear to those who hear it. All a man has is his name — that's who he is before the Almighty."*

Peter had come down to bed, wondering if he was his name. And which name. Wondering if, when he knelt before God, the Lord saw the stuttering fool or the novelist. The man who couldn't make his neighbors like him, or the one who inspired adoring letters from complete strangers. Whether he was Peter or Branok, Holstein or Hollow, or some combination of the two.

Whether he would ever be the man he'd created for himself.

His ceiling had thrown his questions back at him. And the sheets had twisted them into new questions — less important but more easily answered ones. Questions of Locryn James's past, his family, *his* questions of identity.

He'd ended up down at his typewriter again, until the words had run dry and his eyes had been too heavy to hold open any longer at four o'clock.

Peter shrugged into his clothes and glanced out the window, glad he employed no valet who would have tried to wake him at his normal hour. There was no way three hours of sleep would have been enough.

Though to be sure, he'd regret his late night and later morning. He was in danger of missing his luncheon with Miss Gresham. And wouldn't be anywhere near ready for bed again by his usual time to retire. These late-night writing sessions, when they struck, always fouled up his routine for days.

But they were worth it. The pages had stacked up and up, and he was rather pleased with where the story was going.

The sun was out today, more or less. The clouds were just white scuttling things passing before it and then running away. He could take a walk later. Through the heather toward the cliff, where he would see if there was a new collection of cigarette butts. Or through the wood. Perhaps to the Penroses for a visit.

For now, to his study.

He passed Kerensa on his way down, greeting her with a nod. He heard Grammy and Mrs. Teague's voices as he turned down the hall but paid them no heed. Perhaps he'd ring for some coffee in a few minutes to fill the forty minutes until lunch. Or perhaps he'd just wait.

His door opened with a greeting, and the light came on when he asked it to. His desk was more cluttered than ever after his frantic search for the answer to a research question at three in the morning. Peter grinned now to see it. He'd done good work last night. He hoped. He'd have to read through it again to be sure, of course.

A white rectangle on the floor by the library door caught his eye. It was in nearly the exact same place as the note yesterday had been, though turned about thirty degrees. He scooped it up on his way to his desk and flipped it open as he sat, leaned back.

He didn't stay leaned back for long. Instead, he leaned forward, elbows on his desk and brows knit more and more as he read. Her script degraded as it went down the page, but he could make out every heartrending word she'd written.

He leapt from his chair, sped to the door, pulled it open. "M-Miss Gresham?"

The library was a tomb. Silent books, a dozen unlit lamps. No librarian tromping from shelf to shelf. His gaze scanned the room, wondering if she'd stepped out.

He spotted her at the table. Head on folded arms, eyes shut, shadows circling them, evident even through sleep. She looked terrible.

The library, on the other hand, showed

significant progress. He didn't know when she'd arrived this morning, but it had to have been long before the nine o'clock they'd agreed on. And she must have been working with a proper fury.

Understandable.

Edging out of the room again, he closed the door with a soft *click*. Returned to his desk. Got out paper and a pen instead of his manuscript.

The pen in his hand hovered over the paper without making a mark. What did one say to a woman in such obvious distress? He had limited experience with females. His mother had always been of a calm disposition, generous with her smiles but blessedly stingy with any display of negative emotion. The female staff certainly never came to him with tears or dismay. And Jenny . . . Gryff had told a few tales, of course. But Peter was never sure where reality stopped in them and exaggeration began.

Well. The Lord was no respecter of gender, so Peter wouldn't be either. He'd respond to her exactly as he would had this letter come from Gryff or King George or any other acquaintance. He whispered a prayer, as was his custom, for wisdom. And touched the pen to the page.

First he prayed, there with iron gall and

241

paper, for little Olivia. Gryff always thought it strange when he put a prayer down in a letter, but Peter thought better with a pen in his hand than with spoken words anyway. And when he wrote a prayer meant to be shared with someone else, then they could have no doubt he was actually praying as he'd said he would. To his mind, that meant something.

He prayed for Olivia . . . and then he paused, looking at Miss Gresham's words to him again. There was more there than desperation for her sister. There was a desperation to be heard. There, where she'd said, *Perhaps God will listen to you.* Silent but clear was the invisible *because He never listens to me* after it. She didn't write those words — she didn't have to. He saw them beneath the blur where a tear must have fallen, in the shaking, too-fast hand into which she had lapsed.

And he ached. It wasn't a fear that had ever possessed him, though heaven knew he had plenty of others. He had never doubted God heard him. The rest of the world — they were the ones who couldn't make out his intent through his stammering tongue. But what must it feel like to doubt that basic truth? That God heard. God answered. God could be trusted.

He drew in a long breath and bent over the page again. *God will hear. He does not always answer in the way we want, but He always hears — and not just me. He hears anyone who comes to Him in humility. Anyone who is willing to let go the idea that they can fix it all on their own and instead submit to His will. That is when people see Him work. That is when miracles can happen. That is when lives are forever changed by His touch.*

More words poured out, until he'd filled the page. She probably had no desire to read all this. Gryff, if he saw it, would be ready yet again with that familiar quip: *"If you want to deliver sermons, Pete, you should have joined the church."*

As if he could ever stand behind a pulpit. No, he knew his path. And though he certainly never poured a whole sermon into his novels — that would hardly be right in an adventure story — the ideas still snuck in. Through the people Locryn met. The friends he made. In the wisdom he too-often ignored.

But the readers got the message. Those letters in the attic assured him they did.

Hopefully Miss Gresham would too, both through *This Mad Caper* and, perhaps, like this. After testing to make sure the ink had dried, he folded the page . . . and then sat there with his hand resting on it. *Give her your peace, Lord. Your assurance. Awaken her heart to the truth of your love.*

He'd read that ache in her words too — she knew God was there. But she didn't know He loved her.

A knock came on the door to the hall. "Y-Yes?"

Mrs. Teague peeked in. "Luncheon is ready, Mr. Holstein. But that girl is asleep on the job. Shall I wake her?"

Peter sighed. "She has al— already put in . . . put in most of a d-day's work. By the l-looks of it. Her sister is i-ill. She . . . she's worried."

Mrs. Teague's face didn't soften much. "A ploy for affection, I'd wager. Grammy said she came in at the first crack of dawn. And now there are telegrams being delivered for her as if —"

"T-Telegrams?" He shot to his feet. "Where? Did you . . . did you give it to her yet?"

Lips pursed, the housekeeper pulled the familiar yellow paper from her pocket. "I *would* have, had she not been sleeping at the helm, as it were."

He had no words to convince Mrs. Teague to relax in her opinions of their guest. So he just held out his hand. "I . . . I'll take it t-to her. I daresay . . . I daresay she'll b-be happy to wake up . . . for this."

Mrs. Teague snorted. But handed over the sheet of paper.

Perhaps if he ignored the attitude and continued to model a better one, she would relinquish her mysterious prejudice. With a nod, he turned back to the door to the library, knocking as he opened it solely so that it might rouse Miss Gresham.

It apparently worked, or else their voices had done the job. She was even then pushing herself up, rubbing at the neck no doubt protesting her makeshift pillow. Her eyes, a clear brown with no spectacles to mask them, were fogged with disorientation. Until they latched upon that yellow paper in his hand. Then she sprang to her feet, gaze instantly alert.

He held out the telegram, and she snatched it without a word of thanks. But with a little squeak that somehow sounded like one anyway.

Had it been someone he knew better, he would have read the message over her shoulder. That hardly seemed appropriate now though, so he instead slipped back into his study to fetch the note he'd written.

She didn't even glance down at it as he set it on the table, but he could hardly blame her for that. She was reaching the end of the message — it must have been a rather long one or she'd read it twice — and she drew in a slow breath. Her nostrils flared.

She didn't look to be in danger of crying. She looked to be more in danger of throwing something. And there were far too many missiles handy.

Peter cleared his throat. "Is she all . . . all right?"

"No. She's not all right. She has a broken leg, broken ribs, a concussion."

Injury, not illness. Her letter had assumed the opposite. Peter rested a hand on the back of the chair. "D-Did she . . . did she fall?"

"With help, into the street. In front of a carriage." Miss Gresham tossed the paper to the table and shoved away a few locks of hair that had slipped out during her nap. "A horse trampled her. She's lucky to be alive."

Peter's stomach went tight. "With h-help?"

She picked up the book that had been beside her on the table, gripping it so tightly her knuckles went white. "Liv stumbled in front of a rich bloke. He kicked her out of his way. Into the street."

He would never understand some people, these everyday villains who saw only their own concerns. "Was he . . . was he held a-accountable?"

Her snort said *hardly*. Her lips said nothing. She stomped to the corner of the room and slapped the book onto a stack.

He had to wonder if it was the right stack or if she was just doing something to have something to do. "If you . . . if you need to go . . . your j-job here will . . . will be waiting when y-you . . . when you return."

She didn't turn to face him again. Indeed, she turned more fully away. Her shoulders were still two blades against the crisp white of her shirtwaist. Her hair was a wreck, looking about to tumble down altogether. And the breath she drew in sounded about as steady as the last leaf of autumn clinging to a branch as a gale blew in. "Thank you, sir. But it's best I stay."

He nodded, even though she couldn't see it, and relaxed his fingers on the chair. No doubt her sister had a long convalescence ahead of her, and there would be bills from it all. They would need the income.

But it wasn't right. The man who'd kicked her ought to be responsible for these costs. Someone ought to find him and force him to do the right thing. To take responsibility for his actions. Someone ought to ram justice down his haughty throat.

A sentiment more native to Locryn James than Peter Holstein . . . because Locryn wouldn't hesitate to do the ramming.

Peter would never. But there were quieter ways to see to things. He cleared his throat. "I believe it is . . . it is t-time for luncheon."

"I'm sorry, Mr. Holstein. I'm not really feeling up to it just now, and my questions will hold until later. Could we skip lunch?"

He'd been hoping she would suggest it. "Of course. Later, then. And I . . . I will k-keep praying. For Olivia."

He turned and slipped back through the door connecting their spaces, closing it behind him. But he didn't head to his desk and typewriter. He exited the room again into the hallway and hailed Mrs. Teague, who had quite obviously been listening at the library's main doors.

She didn't look ashamed to be caught at it either. More put out at what she'd overheard. "I'll have Kerensa put the second setting away then, shall I?"

Guilt prickled at inconveniencing his staff — not that putting one place setting away was a terrible thing, but he'd been about to say he wouldn't be taking luncheon either. Though really, he did need to eat. He might as well do so before he headed outside. With a nod, he put his greater plans on hold and went into the dining room.

At least when he was alone, the meal was quick. He ate without paying much attention to what he put into his mouth, asked that his thanks and compliments be given to Grammy, and then beat a hasty retreat toward the front doors.

The entryway table and stack of outgoing post gave him pause. He could run the mail to the village himself — be seen, as Gryff had suggested. Smile. Greet the neighbors. Remind people he was a good chap, all things considered. Stop in to see Gryff, who would know how to help him put into action this nebulous plan forming in his mind. He hoped. Then, once home, a jaunt to the cliffs to check on the cigarette-butt situation.

The out-of-doors embraced him with warm air, assuring him he needed no overcoat atop his jacket. He put on the hat he'd grabbed on his way out and flipped through the letters in his hand as he started down the steps. Had he put in the one he'd finished yesterday to Conan Doyle?

Ah, yes. There it was. He'd finished it just before he left his study to dress for dinner but then had inspiration for one more line in his manuscript, so it would have been no great surprise to find he'd forgotten to carry the letter out with him.

He flipped through the rest of the stack, halting when he spotted Miss Gresham's increasingly familiar hand. The letter was addressed to *Miss Cressida Parker.*

Parker? She hadn't mentioned the younger children being *half* siblings. But they must be, if her sister had a different surname.

Shuffling all the letters back into a neat stack, he tucked them into the inner pocket of his jacket and set out down the drive with a long stride.

"Mr. Holstein!"

He halted at Kenver's voice, turned to see the groom jogging from the stable. "If you're headed to the village, sir, you'll want a horse. The road is a ruin."

Peter sighed. He *didn't* want a horse. He didn't want to wait for one to be saddled, and he wanted the chance to stretch his legs. Still, he knew wisdom when he heard it and relented with a nod. He would ride to the village and back. Save the walk for the woods.

Within a few minutes, Kenver had delivered his favorite mare along with a nod and smile, and Peter mounted with a stuttered thanks. It didn't take him long to be glad he'd taken the advice — the rain had turned the road to sludge, pocked with puddles.

Sheep bleated their greetings to him from the roadside fields, no doubt laughing at the mud that splattered him with every step of his horse.

He tried to set his mind on his story. But every time he conjured up the image of Locryn and Rosita, he saw instead Miss Gresham. Shoulders hunched in angry pain. The fury of injustice in her eyes. Worry whitening her knuckles. And so he prayed his way into the village, scarcely noting when others passed on the narrow roads, but to nod.

Until he dismounted and turned to the post office. Something caught his eye then — the glint of meager sunshine on metal.

His gaze followed the shine of its own will. And then his blood went cold. He knew the man leaning against the exterior of the hotel a few doors down, though he couldn't have said what his name was. He knew him because he'd seen him all too often in London. Dogging his steps. Following him. And then appearing at the side of Mr. Jasper.

Blast it all. Whoever he was, Jasper's lackey stood now, grey hair peeking from a bowler that matched the crisp lines of his suit. A mean little smile curved his lips as he flipped a florin into the air, caught it, flipped it again. Watching him. Just *watching* him.

Well, Peter would give him nothing to see but a man going about his normal business. He delivered the stack of outgoing mail to the post office, keeping a smile in place even as the postmaster barely acknowledged him. Mr. Dell, who had always been a friend of Father's, didn't even return Peter's smile, much less his short greeting. Were his tongue as witty as his pen, he could perhaps have said something to cajole a smile or laugh from the aging man. As it was, he could only bring himself to say, "G-Good day," and beat a retreat.

Jasper's man still stood there. Watching.

"Mr. Holstein!"

Peter spun upon hearing his name called out in a wavering voice and pronounced in the German way rather than the Cornish. He paused on the sidewalk and offered a warm smile to his grandfather's friend. "M-Mr. Arnold. How . . . how are you?"

His neighbor tottered his way down the walk, cane in one hand and little dog trotting along behind him, as always. His face was lined and smiling. "Well, quite well. Though worried for you — I heard there was an incident at Kensey the other day." His wispy brows drew down. "Are you quite all right?"

Peter nodded. "Honestly, I . . . I was a b-bit concerned for . . . for *you.*" Though the incident looked a little different now, with the man from London flipping coins on the street corners. Maybe it *hadn't* been a local at all. Maybe it had been *him.* Which would, at least, mean that Peter was his sole target, and no other people of German or Austrian descent would be targeted. The aged Mr. Arnold would then be safe. Still, he had to be sure. "Has any . . . anyone . . . ?"

"Threatened me?" Mr. Arnold waved that off. "*Nein, nein.* Everyone knows I came here in protest when Austria and Germany finally struck an alliance, ja? I daresay no one is more vocal against Germany than I."

He said it on a chuckle, and Peter smiled in reply. His family may well have come here out of protest as well — but it didn't seem to have bought them any favors. But then, his family had never shouted their reasons for leaving Germany for all to hear.

Or for *any* to hear. Including him.

But obviously Opa's opinions were not so dissimilar from the Austrian Mr. Arnold's or they wouldn't have been such friends. And at the very least, if this relocation plan went forward in the event of war, Mr.

Arnold should be safe from it, not forced from his home. Not if they stuck to the age restriction the king had mentioned.

"Well, I am . . . I am glad n-no one has . . . has troubled you. I was w-worried."

Mr. Arnold patted his arm. "No need, my boy. Now, tell me you've taken my advice. That you're distancing yourself from all those ties to Germany."

"I . . . I'm looking into it." Though he doubted it would even matter — how could it, unless he then shouted it from the rooftops? And even then, documents could provide facts, but facts could so easily be ignored or altered. Actually *being* a loyal British subject with all ties to Germany severed wouldn't *prove* him such in public opinion.

"*Gut.*" Another pat on his arm, and then Mr. Arnold stepped aside. "You have a good day, Mr. Holstein. And come and have tea with me soon, hmm?"

Peter agreed with a nod and moved to give Mr. Arnold and his cane more room. Then angled himself toward Gryff's office. A minute later, he was sitting with a frustrated *whoosh* upon a chair in front of his friend's desk, thankful no other client was there.

Gryff glanced up from whatever he was writing but murmured something that loosely resembled "one moment" and kept at his task.

Peter spun his hat around in his hands, letting the texture of the felted fabric calm him. Never mind the opinions of the townspeople. Never mind Jasper and his lackeys or proving his citizenship. There were other things he could do just now that didn't require digging through his attic or library. Things to do *good,* not just try to stop an ill from befalling him. Not exactly brandishing a machete and slicing his way through a jungle, but something active.

"There we are." Gryff tossed down his pen and looked up with a grin. "And what can I do for you today, old boy? Have we somebody to sue? Perhaps a plagiarist?"

Peter's lips turned up. "No. No one to . . . to sue. Just . . . just someone to find."

Gryff lifted his silver brows and leaned back in his chair. "Well, I've been thinking of expanding into detective work — I'd be a regular Holmes, don't you think?"

Peter snorted his opinion of that.

Gryff chuckled. "All right, perhaps not. Who are we finding?"

"Miss Gresham's . . . her sister. Olivia, the youngest. She was . . . she was injured yesterday." He told the tale as well as he knew it, watching as Gryff's face went smooth and tense with anger at the news that it was a wealthy man who had caused it all.

"So we want to find this chap and see he meets justice." Gryff sat forward again, tapping a finger against a blank page. "It'll be near to impossible. There are no shortage of selfish, cruel men in London."

"No. I know. I mean . . ." Peter sighed and set his hat on the corner of Gryff's desk. "I would *like* to, but . . . but I know better."

"So then? If that's not your goal, who is it we're going to find?"

"Olivia." He darted a glance toward the door. Not that Miss Gresham would be anywhere nearby to overhear. Even so, he pitched his voice low. "The . . . the bills. They're sure to be . . . to be too much. I'd like to help."

Gryff frowned, though surely not at the desire. "Why does that require a detective? Just ask Miss Gresham where to send some aid."

Peter shook his head. "Anonymously."

Gryff sighed. Grumbled. And then reached for his pen. "You must always complicate things, mustn't you? So I'll have someone ask at all the hospitals for an Olivia Gresham."

"Or Parker." If it was the twelve-year-old's

surname, it was likely the six-year-old's as well. He scooted closer and motioned for the pen. "I've her . . . her direction." Really, that should make it entirely easy. Virtually no detective work at all. Gryff could simply get in touch with one of his cohorts in London, have someone drop by the Gresham-Parker home, assure them an anonymous benefactor would be seeing to Olivia's recuperation, and then let Peter know what all they needed. Depending on the severity of the broken bones and — may God forbid it — any infection or complications that set in, it could be quite a bit.

"It's good of you, Pete. But then, you know that. Hence why you won't do it openly. Although . . ." Gryff flashed him that smile that said, *I know it's hopeless, but I'll say it anyway.* "If you *did* let it be known, it might win you some favor with the populace."

His answer was to stand and reach for his hat. "There's . . . there's a man in the village. From London. One of . . . of Mr. Jasper's men."

Gryff muttered a *blast* and ran a hand through his hair. "And you didn't tell me this *first*? We'll alert the constable. To be harassed in your own hometown by that jealous reprobate . . ."

Not that the constable would be able to do anything. Peter put his hat on his head. "Come by for . . . for tea on Saturday. Bring the girls."

Gryff blew out a breath, rubbed the frustration from his face, and nodded. "I was going to suggest the same — Jenny wants to steal Miss Gresham away for an hour or two to go shopping, and I told her you and I could manage Elowyn while they were out, since the nursemaid has the afternoon off."

A good plan. If anyone could distract Miss Gresham from her worries, it was Jenny. And on Sunday perhaps he'd see if she wanted to go and see St. Michael's Mount.

Or . . . or perhaps it would be better for her if he asked her to join him at church instead. Mr. Trenholm probably wouldn't be expecting Peter this week — it usually took him a couple weeks after returning from London to work up the will to sit in such a crowd for an hour — but it could do her good. Trenholm's sermons were always well reasoned and founded on the Word.

If she would go. He would invite her. If she accepted, good. If not, he would suggest the day trip instead.

"See you tomorrow, then."

Tomorrow was Saturday already? Peter

paused, examined the days in his mind. Good grief, he really needed to stop these late-night writing sessions. He didn't even know what day it was afterward, apparently. "Tomorrow."

He went back outside and looked about. Jasper's lackey had vanished. Perhaps into the hotel, perhaps into the pub. Perhaps he was off sniffing up any whiff of scandal to be found concerning the Holsteins.

Well, he would find nothing. Nothing but evidence that his parents were well loved.

And that *he* was not.

Peter strode to his horse — and then stopped. A silver coin glinted from his saddle.

Not a florin after all. Fighting back a growl, he picked it up. It boasted the same geometric shape that Jasper's ring had. The inverted triangle, the lines of light, the concentric circles.

He fought the urge to toss it to the ground and instead pivoted and strode back into Gryff's office.

His friend didn't even look up when he entered — not until Peter flipped the coin directly onto the sheet of paper Gryff held. Then he did, with a frown. "Afraid I charge more than a florin for my services these days, old boy."

"It's n-not a f-florin."

Gryff frowned. More, Peter suspected, over the stuttering than over the coin. But he picked it up, squinted at it. "Right then, I'll play along. What *is* it?"

"It . . . I d-don't know. Exactly. The . . . the s-symbol is . . ." Peter had to pause and take a breath to calm himself. "Jasper. He had a . . . a ring with that symbol. He belongs to . . . to some secret society."

"Hmm." Gryff flipped it over, then back over again. "I've never heard of this one. Are they one of the insurance groups?"

Though he couldn't quite say why, the question made Peter relax. Brought a hint of a smile to his lips. "I don't know."

"It seems they all are. Or are branches of the Masons. Or one of those odd magical groups. This is no doubt one or the other. Do you want me to look into it?"

Somehow it was better, just having a friend to help. "Depends. How much more . . . than a florin will it cost me?"

Gryff chuckled and put the coin — or token or whatever it was rightly called — on the corner of his desk. "You check with your sources, I'll check with mine. Between the two of us, we'll figure out who these chaps are."

Peter nodded in thanks. Left again. And

knew that he'd never be able to enter the village again without looking for a silver head with a bowler atop it.

ELEVEN

Rosemary stared at the gibberish, but it made no more sense than it had the first time she'd glimpsed it ten days ago. It was just letters and numbers, all a jumble. Leaning back in her chair before the library table, she squeezed shut her eyes and then opened them again, hoping to note something new. She saw a hint of German in it, she thought. A hint of English. It bore no resemblance to the style espoused in the book on shorthand she'd found yesterday.

Nothing but those random letters and numbers. On this sheet, all of it was in Mr. Holstein's hand, but on the one beneath . . . not his. Given that she had found that other sheet of paper stuffed in a book, it could have been his father's. Or his grandfather's.

Or from some unknown correspondent.

But this one on top, the one in Mr. Holstein's script, she'd found on the attic stairs when she'd been poking about trying to locate that room. Kerensa had come singing her way up to the servants' quarters before she'd dared explore — she'd instead made a run for the opposite staircase — but she'd already grabbed up this page of . . .

Secrets. Whatever it was, it must be that. Something he wanted no one else to be able to read. Something with a hint of German in it.

Something likely tied to whatever he typed all day, given that she'd seen him writing in this coded language that first day while in his study.

Her eyes moved to the closed door separating their spaces. He wasn't typing today, though he was in there. He was *always* in there, it seemed, during daylight hours. She had to get in, snoop her way through the room. But it would require coming over in the dark and praying he didn't decide to take another midnight trip down here as Mrs. Teague had been grumbling about him doing last week.

Footsteps sounded in the hall — quite a few of them, punctuated by the bright voice of Elowyn. Rosemary's gaze flew to the mantel clock. She hadn't even known the Penroses were coming today, though it was the same time they'd arrived *last* Saturday. Perhaps it was a weekly event. Regardless, she knew Jenny would seek her out.

Quickly, she folded all the pages of gibberish together, stuffed them inside a massive tome on the history of the Hapsburgs, and shut the pages over them.

"I've come to liberate you."

That was too close — she certainly didn't need to be found looking at Peter Holstein's private papers by his closest friend's wife. Rosemary pasted a cheerful smile into place and looked up as Jenny swept into the library with a *bang* of the doors she'd tossed open. She looked much as she had the week before when she'd done the exact same thing — all casual elegance and happy expressions, with an added light in her eyes at the prospect of an afternoon out of the house.

Rosemary had never felt so frazzled. She stood and swiped a hand over her wrinkled linen skirt. "I didn't know you were coming or I would have put all this away by now. And gone to tidy up."

"Oh, you look fresh as a daisy as it is." Jenny planted her hands on her hips and surveyed the room. "You've made a lot of progress. It looks far better than it did last week."

She had Mr. Holstein to thank for that — on Monday, Mr. Teague had come in and informed her that some blokes called Cadan and Treeve had built shelves to install in a room upstairs, and any books she wanted moved there she could just carry into the hall. Monday and Tuesday had been spent transferring all books on mathematics and science to the newly dubbed "upstairs library."

They had lined what was formerly a bedchamber with shelves — every single space on the wall aside from the windows. And they had filled those shelves. With books on *mathematics*. And *science*.

The result had been not only floor space in this main library, but shelf space too, allowing her to move more floor stacks onto shelves. What it hadn't accomplished, though both she and Mr. Holstein had hoped it would, was uncovering the missing journals. Still. Rosemary smoothed her skirt and looked around with Jenny. Compared to what it had been when she'd arrived ten days ago, it *was* rather impressive.

"Thank you. I'm earning my pay with this job, I can assure you."

Jenny's laugh was a lovely thing. More robust than pretty. Rosemary had decided last Saturday that it must have been Jenny's laugh, even more than her bright eyes and comely face, that had inspired Gryffyn Penrose to fall in love with her.

She still didn't know what had inspired Jenny to fall in love with *him*. Why, the other day when Rosemary had gone into the village with Mr. Holstein to choose some thick paper with which to cut down cards for the library catalog, she had seen Penrose in deep conversation with the constable. The constable!

It wasn't natural. She had rather thought distrust of the law something that existed from birth in one's bosom. But perhaps only if one was born below a certain financial threshold, so that the law viewed one as the cause of trouble rather than one to be protected from it.

"Well, I daresay you're desperate for fresh air. Come." Jenny linked their arms together and tugged Rosemary toward the door. "Let's escape while Elowyn is regaling them with her latest exploits, before she remembers that I'm here."

Rosemary smiled. She had learned last weekend that, as eager as Jenny was for an hour or two with only adults for company, she hurried home at the end of it to scoop her little girl into her arms again. "All right," Rosemary responded. "If we could just stop at the cottage on our way out, I'll get my handbag and hat."

"Perfect."

It took only a few minutes to navigate the halls, step out into the sunny day, and fetch Rosemary's things. Granted, she stole a minute while at the cottage to smooth her hair, even though she knew it was a lost cause — the wind always seemed to be gusting in these parts, and it would be all the worse in the Penroses' open-topped automobile. But a girl had to try, didn't she? She was soon back out and climbing into the auto beside Jenny, who took the wheel.

Rosemary, as she had a week ago, ran a hand over the wood paneling on the door. "I rather enjoy the ride in this. Why do you suppose Mr. Holstein hasn't got one?"

Jenny snorted and waved to Kenver, who had cranked the car for them, then started down the drive. "I would have thought you'd noticed by now, having been here more than an hour — Peter is, let us say, a bit old-fashioned. Honestly, I think he would have resisted electric lights had his mother not insisted. They had them installed just after his grandfather passed away."

Rosemary hadn't yet pieced together much about the late mistress of Kensey Manor. While the name *Holstein* appeared in a shocking number of history texts, she hadn't found *von Roth* in any but that first.

Figuring out why the previous Mr. Holstein had returned to Germany for his bride — and if it had any bearing on to whom this current Mr. Holstein was loyal — was going to be far harder than organizing the library. "Did you know them? Mr. Holstein's parents, I mean."

"Oh, of course. All of Cornwall knew them, I think. They were so very *good.*" Jenny eased to a halt at the end of the drive, let a carriage and four trot past, and then turned onto the road that led to the village. "If anyone needed help, they were the first there to lend a hand. Everyone adored them. Honestly. I can't think of a single person who spoke ill of them."

Rosemary knew her brow was creased but couldn't manage to smooth it. Had it been a deliberate attempt on their parts to ingratiate themselves with the locals? A long-reaching, sinister plan to deeply root themselves so no one would suspect their treason? "Why, then, is everyone so suspicious of their son?"

It wouldn't sound like an odd question, not after Sunday. Rosemary had agreed to attend church with Mr. Holstein and had decided in short order never to subject herself to that particular torture again. Oh, Mr. Trenholm's homily had been rather interesting, but the *people.* They had actually snubbed Holstein. Literally turned away when he approached, noses in the air like a bunch of hounds sniffing the wind.

And why? They hadn't seen his notes in that odd gibberish. They weren't wading through all those books where his family name was mentioned.

But still she'd heard whispers when she'd stepped outside the church, whispers wondering if he was a British subject or a German national.

Mr. Holstein's mouth had gone white. He felt the accusation keenly, clearly. But why — because he *was* a subject and resented the question, or because he wasn't and didn't want to face any consequences that could come of it?

He'd said nothing, not all the drive home. Just kept glancing over his shoulder as they left town as if he expected someone to be following him.

There hadn't been. She could have assured him of that, but it might have seemed a bit strange for her to offer the information out of the blue. So instead she'd just chattered about his neighbors. It had earned her a few hints at a grin. A stride, or so she told herself, toward him trusting her.

Jenny sighed. "They wouldn't be suspicious, not if they knew him as we do. He's every bit as good as his parents. Every bit. He just can't express it so well."

Well, if he could just write to everyone in the village . . .

Rosemary pressed her lips together. He seemed to write to everybody the world over. She'd seen the post arrive the other day, and there had been a pile of letters for him that made her eyes go wide. How did he even have time to read them, much less respond? She'd managed to thumb through half the stack before Mrs. Teague had come by. There had been return addresses from the Americas, from all over Great Britain, from the colonies.

And one from the king.

High company she was keeping, given that he'd been writing to *her* as well. Every morning when Rosemary came down, she found a new note from him on her table, folded and impeccably elegant in its script. And every evening, she slid one under his door.

They meant nothing to him, surely. Just another missive for his stack, from a nobody living in his cottage.

She wasn't quite sure *what* they meant to her.

Jenny glanced over at her. "How is your

sister? Have you heard more?"

Rosemary tried to offer a smile, but it wouldn't stick. "I had a letter yesterday. Her spirits are good. They have her at home now, of course, but . . . but a telegram came this morning." It had consisted of one word — one terrifying word. "Infection has set in."

She knew what her note to Holstein would say tonight. *Why? Why, when we have begged everyone we know for prayers, is sweet little Olivia going through this? Why is God not healing her?*

He had said God was not deaf to her cries. He had said that the Lord loved the poor, the downtrodden, the outcast especially.

He could claim it all he wanted. Quote Scripture to back it up. But it didn't change facts — and the facts were that the rich waltzed through life pretty as you please, while the poor were hated by everyone from God on down the line.

Jenny made a sympathetic noise. "How terrible. Is there anything we can do? We can inquire about good doctors for you, make introductions."

And pay for them how? That sum from Mr. V was quickly shrinking — Rosemary had spent too much of it to outfit herself for this job. She oughtn't to have bought

271

that tweed. Nor the cotton for the shirt-waists — really, what did she need with so many? One would have sufficed. She could have just washed it in the sink at night and worn it again in the morning. And the shoes — she could have worn her old pumps. Perhaps they wouldn't have looked so tidy, but they would have done the job.

Then there was that splurge on sweets. The children would have gotten along just fine without the pound of chocolate.

Apparently her silence was too loud. Jenny sighed. "Let us help, Rosemary, please. I realize things are tight for your family — with so many to support, they *have* to be. But we could help a bit with the bills. It would be our honor."

And be beholden to Gryffyn Penrose? Rosemary would never put a price on Olivia's life — but she knew better than to welcome a gift horse without looking deep into its proverbial mouth. "I appreciate the offer, but we're managing right now." Things would simply have to get better, that was all. Liv would improve. The others would get back to work. Just before she'd left, Barclay had accepted a job from some nameless chap on the Continent with more silver than sense, so that would help. He only had to steal a Monet from a museum in order to get paid. The others would help him, and he had their experience with the British Museum to draw on for it. They would succeed. They must.

And she'd have more coming from Mr. V once she completed this task. It would be enough, surely, to cover any medical bills and then some.

She needed to find time to get into the attic and Holstein's study.

Jenny sighed. "If ever you *can't* manage, please come to us. I know we've only just met, but I consider you a friend, Rosemary. And I'm an excellent judge of character, ask anyone."

Was that guilt that made her chest go tight? Or perhaps confusion? Why, really, did Jenny like her? Rosemary could only smile and hold back a curl that the wind was blowing straight. "Thank you, Jenny. I shall certainly keep that in mind."

Jenny navigated the car around a tight bend, after which the village came into sight. "Shall we talk of happier things, then? I could use your help. If you're not opposed."

"So long as it doesn't involve organizing your bookshelves."

Her companion laughed. "Not at all. Another of your talents, rather. Would you help me with a gown? My seamstress is traveling to visit family in Derbyshire, but I need something new to wear to old Mr. Arnold's Midsummer Ball."

Had anyone but Jenny said it, with anything but that imploring smile, Rosemary may have called into question that "need." But she wouldn't scoff at this woman who claimed they were friends. "Of course. How can I help?"

"Oh, with everything. I haven't even chosen fabric yet, because I couldn't settle on a pattern. Have you any ideas? And you should find something for yourself too — Gryff's primary goal of the day is to convince Peter he cannot skip the ball again, not this year, and he has no one else to take with him, so you'll have to go."

It was a good thing Rosemary wasn't the one driving or she would have slammed a foot to the brake pedal so she could better stare. "Have you gone mad? I am hardly a proper choice for him to escort to a neighborhood ball."

"Rubbish." Slowing as the first buildings of town came up beside them, Jenny waved at a passerby and scanned the street. "By the time the ball rolls around in another three weeks, he'll be far more comfortable with you than with anyone else he could consider taking, what with working together every day."

That tightness in her chest multiplied. She didn't mean to make him comfortable with her. Or maybe she did, if she intended to gain his trust, his secrets. Blast it all, confidence schemes had never been her game. "We aren't exactly working *together* though."

"Close enough. Please, Rosemary." Slowing to a near-crawl when they came upon a wagon, Jenny angled a look her way. Begging. "You have to help convince him to come out. He needs to be more a part of the neighborhood."

And this fell to her *why*? She knew she looked every bit as uncomfortable with the plea as she felt and couldn't think of a single thing she could do to change that. "I don't know how I can if Mr. Penrose fails to do so — I've scarcely known the man ten days." And already she had thrice had him look up at her in complete exasperation and ask her if she would *please* stop talking. Thrice. That first time was bad enough, but he'd said it even during her so-called allotted times with him, as he worked through a question she'd put out.

Peter Holstein obviously needed to learn how to think when someone was speaking.

Or one of these days she was going to throw something at him. Which of course would make him fire her. And then what would she do?

Jenny laughed. "He'll say no to Gryff far more quickly than he would anyone else." She eased the car to a halt in front of a row of shops and set the parking brake.

"Oh, I don't know. He seems properly expert at saying it to me as well." Checking her hat with a quick flutter of her hand, Rosemary let herself out of the vehicle.

"Good day, Mrs. Penrose."

Rosemary looked over to find a matronly woman approaching with a wide smile aimed at Jenny. The woman's clothes were of moderate quality. Her shoes atrocious. No jewelry, easy to lift or otherwise. The only thing of promise she could spot on the woman was a bulging handbag — though it could well be bulging with yarn and knitting needles rather than pound notes. Not worth the risk, even had they been on the streets of London, where risks were worth taking.

And she'd called Jenny *Mrs. Penrose.* During their outing last week Rosemary had learned that if someone didn't address the lawyer's wife by her first name, it was because said lawyer's wife didn't like said person enough to invite them to do so. Even if it *was* highly unusual for a lady to be so familiar with so many.

Not that anyone would know Jenny's feelings now to see her bright smile. "Good afternoon, Mrs. Gladstone. How are you today?"

"Oh, I won't complain, though my back has been bothering me something awful and my rheumatism is so bad I can scarcely straighten my fingers," she said, straightening her fingers perfectly well in demonstration.

Jenny blinked, her smile holding fast. "I'm sorry to hear that. We'll be praying for you."

"Thank you, dear." Mrs. Gladstone's gaze wandered in Rosemary's direction. "Is this a friend of yours? I heard you were out last Saturday with a young lady no one knew. A cousin, perhaps? Your mother's people weren't from Cornwall, I know."

And from the way she said it, it was a sin for which Jenny would never be forgiven in this woman's eyes. Rosemary decided then and there that *she* didn't like Mrs. Gladstone much either. And that it was definitely knitting in her bag, given the way it moved as the woman gestured with her hands. Probably didn't have but a shilling or two on her.

Jenny, of course, didn't miss a beat. "Mother *was* from Cornwall, ma'am — Kilkhampton. Though Miss Gresham hails from London. She's working for a while at Kensey Manor, helping Mr. Holstein to organize his library. She's a librarian, you know."

Mrs. Gladstone obviously didn't know. And didn't seem much impressed by the lofty false title. Her lips had pursed at *Kilkhampton* — it was northern Cornwall, wasn't it? Near the border with Devonshire. Which apparently meant not Cornish enough. She narrowed her eyes the moment Jenny said *London.* Because if Kilkhampton wasn't Cornish enough for approval, she probably thought London all but next door to Hades. And she actually huffed — a full-fledged *harrumph* — at the mention of Mr. Holstein.

She now looked at Rosemary as if she had something catching. "My condolences on that, miss. Were there not positions enough in Town, that you came all the way down here to work for *him*?"

"And pass up the chance to see Cornwall and all its . . . *lovely* people?" Rosemary made an effort to look demur, though it didn't come nearly as naturally to her as it did to, say, Elinor. "I seized the chance to come down here when I heard Mr. Holstein might need help cataloging his impressive book collection."

Another *harrumph.* "Bet you regretted that in quick order. Never in all my days have I met a man so rude as young Mr. Holstein. His parents must have been properly ashamed of him."

"I hardly think so." Rosemary didn't know why the defense sprang so quickly to her tongue. Except, perhaps, that it was true. Not that such things usually inspired her to speak them. "Just because a man has trouble speaking doesn't mean he's rude." Though, granted, he *had* ignored her for four whole minutes that first full day. Yet she couldn't chalk it up to *rudeness,* not having spent a bit more time with him. He was, if nothing else, considerate. Just . . . distracted sometimes. Many times. All right, *most* times.

What in blazes did he think about so intently? That was the real question.

Mrs. Gladstone's face mottled. "I beg your pardon. Even if he stutters, it's no reason to avoid people completely."

"When people treat *him* so rudely because of it?" Rosemary snorted. "I daresay it is."

When the woman's nostrils flared like that, she bore a certain resemblance to a horse. "As if he has anything to say worth listening to anyway — likely just a bunch of rot and German ideals."

Rosemary lifted her brows. She had ten letters from him now, tucked away in her room in the cottage. He'd shared his thoughts on fiction, on family, and quite a bit on faith. But not a single word that intimated any loyalty to Germany or her current politics. Even if he *had* them — on which she was banking — he certainly didn't go around spouting them. "Do you think that's what his parents taught him? I rather thought everyone agreed that the late Holsteins were beyond reproach."

"Children are known to deviate from the path their parents put them on, you know."

Rosemary cocked her head to the side. "Did you ignore your parents' teachings, then? Or perhaps your children have ignored yours?"

Mrs. Gladstone just sputtered at that one. Jenny hid a smirk behind her gloved hand, trying — and failing — to cover it with a cough. The elder at length managed a "How dare you!"

"Look." Planting a hand on her hip, Rosemary pointed at the woman's heaving chest. "You want to judge him, I can't stop you. And I got nothing invested here anyway. But the way I see it is this — better to hold your tongue and risk having people think ill of you than to go 'round blabbing lies and *earn* their distrust. So maybe you should take a cue from him and be quiet once in a while, hmm?"

"Well, I never." Her nose tilted into the air — she was likely one of those hounds sniffing at church last week, though Rosemary couldn't say with certainty — Mrs. Gladstone spun on her heel. "Good day to you, Mrs. Penrose. Miss Gristle."

"Gresham." She pasted on a smile, even if the woman couldn't see it. "And good day to you too, Mrs. Sadstone. Very good to meet you!"

Jenny gave up on the cough and laughed outright, tucking her arm around Rosemary's and tugging her forward. "Oh heavens."

Rosemary smoothed her free hand down her hip . . . and winced at the echo of her own words. Oh, not at what she'd said. At how she'd said them. Had she really said *noffing* instead of *nothing*? She'd thought she'd obliterated that from her speech eons ago. "Is my Cockney showing?"

That made Jenny laugh all the more. "Delightfully. I've been waiting a decade for someone to put that woman in her place, and there's no better way than with an accent not Cornish."

Still. Rosemary had worked hard to make her speech more polished than it was by rights. They all had, and they were teaching the little ones the so-called proper inflections from the get-go, always speaking "correctly" at home. They couldn't blend in with the high crowd at a gala glistening with gems if a working-class accent clung to their lips.

Jenny pulled her into the closest shop, a bell tinkling over the door as they entered. The shopkeeper greeted them, obviously well familiar with Jenny Penrose. And apparently also knowing why they'd come in today, as she immediately proclaimed that some new patterns and silk had arrived just yesterday.

Though she followed her new friend and the tidily dressed shopgirl away from the door, Rosemary's mind didn't leave the street quite so easily. That self-righteous horse could rub anyone the wrong way. Surely it was that, and only that, that had made defense of Peter Holstein spring to her tongue. Because, really, she didn't like the bloke. And she certainly didn't think him innocent of the charges anyone could lob against him. But the more his neighbors accused him, the more defensive and careful he'd be, making it all the harder for Rosemary to discover his true loyalties.

By which logic, she *ought* to help get the town to like him. It *was* logical, right? Perhaps?

Or, she granted as she smiled at Jenny and accepted the new book of patterns handed to her . . . perhaps she was just doing as Barclay always accused her of and rationalizing a bad decision.

Blast it all. She should have let the horsehound go on sniffing and flaring her nostrils. What was it to her?

TWELVE

"Right . . . right here." Peter came to a halt between two massive trees where the undergrowth provided a good screen for anyone hiding. Whoever had been here last week would have had yet another unhindered view of the manor — this time the side opposite where he'd been before, of stables rather than the cottage. Of the drawing room rather than the parlor. Of Peter's study rather than the kitchen.

His fingers curled into a fist inside his pocket. There were no new cigarette butts here today, of course. But he suspected they'd find some elsewhere, if they searched.

Gryff hummed and craned his head around to check on Elowyn, who was behind them on the path, picking wildflowers. "But you've not seen the actual person anywhere on your property?"

"No." And a collection of cigarette butts wasn't enough to say for sure that it was an intruder. He knew that.

"A collection of cigarette butts isn't enough to prove it an intruder."

Peter chuffed.

"Which you know. And we're not trying someone in court, we're investigating. I know. I alerted Constable Newth to the presence of Mr. Jasper's man, of course, so he's keeping an eye out for anything suspicious." Gryff rubbed a hand along the back of his head, knocking his hat askew but not seeming to notice. "Look, old boy, I trust your instincts most of the time, and I do question that man's sudden presence in our neighborhood, but this . . . It could quite easily be one of the staff."

Peter shook his head. "The only . . . the only smoker is Cadan. But he doesn't . . . not that much. One a day, he says. Because . . . because of the expense."

Gryff pursed his lips. "Perhaps Benny's sneaking off. Boys have done such things before."

He'd have to be sneaking off for hours at a time and lighting one cigarette directly from the previous one to accumulate such a mass of refuse. Peter shook his head. "He's been . . . been accounted for."

"Someone from the neighborhood, then — and likely still a boy trying to hide from his mother."

Perhaps. His family had always made it known that anyone was welcome to use the paths through their wood or along their cliff. But there was no shortage of paths. Why would absolutely *all* of the places he'd spotted with this smoking rubbish be in places offering good views of the house? When his property was far fuller of places that didn't?

It didn't add up. Not unless it was someone watching them. Watching *him.*

Which inevitably brought him back to the grey-haired man in the bowler who was always there whenever Peter ventured into the village.

Which in turn took his mind back to the letter that had kept him up all last night for worrying.

We regret to inform you, Mr. Holstein, that the documents in question could not be located in the National Archives. . . .

Did Jasper have ties to the Archives? Could he have had the Holstein papers moved — or destroyed? Stolen? Would the man stoop so low as to hire a . . . a street thug to do him such damage?

With that perpetual shadow in the village, it was hard to convince himself of the absurdity of the idea.

286

Well, he'd just have to find his own copies of the records. That was all. Surely not as daunting a task as it seemed.

Gryff turned away from the view, back toward his daughter. She'd sat down on the path to weave together the flowers she'd picked, no doubt turning her white dress brown. Which would have made Jenny object heartily and loudly. Gryff didn't seem to notice. "Well, there have been no more rocks through windows. No other trouble. So try to relax."

Peter heard the words, but he also saw that his friend's shoulders were tight, his spine rigid, and that line chiseled into his brow that bespoke worry far more loudly than his lips spoke ease. "Did you find anything . . . about the coin? My search proved . . . proved futile."

Gryff's shoulders didn't relax. "I translated the Latin, anyway. Their name means 'Ancient Order of the Realm' — as vague as any other ridiculous society's name. But everyone I asked about them had never heard of them — but for one. And he thought they were one of the insurance groups. But I don't know that they are, or they wouldn't be so secretive. Those things only work with many members."

So then, nothing. Nothing but a veiled

threat from a sneering man in London. And his lackey here, watching Peter.

"The best thing I can tell you is to tread carefully but not be too alarmed, old boy. They can't be too terrifying if no one's ever heard of them. We'll keep our eye on the fellow in the village and our ears open for any other muttering against you. Though of course no one says anything negative about you in my hearing. Everyone knows you're my closest friend." Turning his face back toward Peter, Gryff drew in a breath. "And it's high time they all understand why. You need to get out more, Pete."

He seemed to be holding his breath, waiting for an answer — Peter let his own out in compensation. "Gryff, you *know* that would be . . . that would be disastrous."

"It would not. How do you think you've made the friends you have? You're a blighted genius with brilliant ideas that people can't help but find intriguing and a gracious heart that presents them in a way that makes you endearing rather than off-putting. You are a picture-perfect friend. Let people see that."

It was all he could do to keep from rolling his eyes. "I am . . . am hardly a genius." He had a way with words, was all. So long as he didn't have to speak them aloud. That hardly qualified.

"Oh trust me. I know more people than you, I'm the better judge of comparative intelligence."

Though he breathed a laugh, Peter also shook his head. "And no one finds me . . . gracious."

"Their perception that you aren't is solely because you're such a recluse, as well you know. Come out. Visit your neighbors. Eat a meal in the dashed pub now and then. *Something.*"

He'd come to church, hadn't he? And that had been a mistake. Aside from the Penroses and Mr. Trenholm himself, no one had received them warmly. What impression must that have made on Miss Gresham? No doubt she now thought church — and by extension Christianity — utter rot. And she had a point. Well, not about the extension, but about that particular church. Paul may have instructed them not to forsake the gathering together of believers, but when the church first forsook you because of your last name, what else were you to do?

He would worship at home, as he had always done. The vicar would come on Mondays. God understood, even if Peter's neighbors refused to.

"What you need to do is come to the Midsummer Ball." With a glance to the north, away from the coast and past the wood, where Holstein property eventually butted up against Mr. Arnold's, Gryff made the pronouncement in his barrister voice. The one that was all certainty. More command than request. And filled with nothing but wishful thinking.

It didn't even deserve a response, so Peter brushed by him and headed back toward Elowyn along the path. No point in hovering here where someone had hovered before. They'd left no clues but the butts he'd already picked up and discarded. But one of the butts had been smoldering still last week when he'd found that second collection. He'd nearly caught the person, whoever it was. Maybe next time he would manage it.

And then what? How did he mean to hold the culprit? And with what could he really charge him?

Gryff kept pace beside him. "It's still three weeks away. Plenty of time to prepare yourself, and I know well Mr. Arnold invited you, as he always does. You ought to do him the honor of accepting his invitations now and again, don't you think?"

One sideways look at his friend ought to have sufficed to silence him. Not that anything ever silenced Gryffyn Penrose.

"He did especially mention you to me the other day when I saw him."

"Well, I had . . . had tea with him on Wednesday."

"And no doubt he had some sound advice. No one is looking askance at *him.* But then, he's out and about all the time. As you should be."

Not to mention that his surname happily sounded English enough. Had he a name that ended with *stein,* it may well be another matter. Well, not that anyone was likely to pour their hatred upon an eighty-year-old man who hated Germany even more than they ever could. And who couldn't even walk without a cane. And whose miniature dog inspired coos from everything female.

Peter's lips twitched. Even so. "I'll not . . . not go to the ball."

Gryff clapped a hand to Peter's shoulder. "He'll convince you, I bet, when next you see him. You wouldn't have to go alone this year, you know. You could take Miss Gresham."

A ridiculous notion. Though it could prove entertaining. Her discourse on his neighbors as they drove home from church last week had been diverting, to say the least. But he *wasn't* going to the ball.

Interesting, though, that Gryff had suggested it. "Have you . . . have you accepted Jenny's opinion of her, then?"

Gryff sidestepped a root and stopped a step away from his daughter, who looked nowhere near ready to proceed on their walk. She had dozens of daisies scattered about her waiting to be woven into a crown. Or, given her current progress, tied into knots that refused to stay together. "It still seems highly unusual that she didn't bother making an appointment before just showing up. But her references all seem to be in order. And were rather glowing, at that."

"Good." Peter probably should have followed up on that sooner. But he'd only to look into the library to see that she was competent — he could actually see the floor now. Another week or two and the shelves would have order as well. She'd even promised to create a card catalog for him. Opa had purchased the cabinet itself but had never gone to the trouble of filling it.

If only she could locate those journals . . . and he really ought to tell her to keep an eye out for their naturalization documents as well. And the deed to Kensey. But it would sound so suspicious to ask that of her.

No, those he ought to find himself. Somehow. Somewhere. Unless she just *happened* across them in the library, in which case she'd surely ask him where to file them, right?

He watched Elowyn carefully select another daisy and happily mangle its stem as she tied it to the previous one. "What about . . . about the investigator? Has he found her family?" Every day as he prayed for little Olivia, he prayed for that as well.

Gryff's brows drew together. "I had a note from him this morning. It's a curious thing, he says. There's a Parker family at that address, but it's only four sisters, the youngest being eight. No Greshams at all."

"Hmm." Did they perhaps have more than one flat, there being so many of them? But that didn't seem right — that would cost more. Slinging his hands in his pockets, Peter tilted up his head to watch a lazy white cloud meander by. "What of . . . of the hospitals?"

"No Parker or Gresham had been admitted to any of them last week. He's still trying to sort it out based on description, but that's a considerable haystack."

Indeed it would be. But he'd find her eventually, because Peter had no doubt of the truth of the story. Not after watching the shadows in Miss Gresham's eyes these last ten days, deepening and darkening with each new sliver of news that reached her. One couldn't fake such concern for a family member, no matter what Mrs. Teague muttered about ploys for attention.

"Tell him . . . tell him to go back to that Parker address. See if one is . . . Cressida. If so, it's her sister. We can . . . we can send money there." Even if it wasn't where Olivia was, they were obviously connected. Sending to one would see it got to the other.

But it was curious. And his mind, so fond of unraveling mysteries and composing stories, kept turning it over. Why the different surnames? And why did they not all live together if they all supported one another?

Something didn't add up. Or perhaps he was just missing a few vital parts of the equation — but how to get them? He wasn't one to press a person for information. That required conversation. And while Miss Gresham seemed happy enough to chat incessantly, even about her family, when one sat down to examine the content of her words, one quickly realized she talked a lot about the people but never about anything that could help a body *find* those people. No mention of the names of places they visited. Of schools attended. Or churches. Nothing to indicate a neighborhood of residence, beyond vague references to the tube and "Pauly's."

It was curious indeed.

He looked up at the sky. Still blue and inviting, and if it held tomorrow, he would suggest that trip to Marazion and St. Michael's Mount. That would give him ample time in her company to try to figure it all out.

Rosemary waited in her cottage, watching. After nearly a solid week of rain that had started last Saturday night after she got home from shopping for cloth with Jenny, the sun was shining. Or, rather, promising to do so properly once it finished burning off the fog. She ran a finger along the edge of the book in her hands, though she'd finished it an hour ago. It had taken her forever to get through it, but it was no fault of the story. Branok Hollow knew how to weave an intriguing tale. But most of her evenings this past week had been spent on the silk Jenny Penrose had bought.

Measuring. Measuring again. Marking with white chalk. Measuring again. Cutting, breath held and praying she had measured aright. Pinning it together in the pattern they had decided on. Exhausting eyes already tired from reading half the day and sewing into the night.

Not something she wanted to turn into a profession, much as Jenny might praise her for her skill. Making clothes was something she did because she had to, and something she did well because the effort was useless if not done properly. Constructing a garment wasn't unlike picking a lock — one had to have the right tools, but more, one had to apply them in just the right way.

Perhaps she *could* become a seamstress, if it came down to it. Maybe. Though she would hate it after a week.

She slid the book onto the table when movement from the kitchen door of the manor house caught her attention. Finally, the staff was leaving for church, just as they had done last Sunday even when Mr. Holstein had stayed at home. Rosemary had followed the master of the house's lead, though Grammy had invited her to ride along with them.

Not a torture she cared to repeat, thank you very much.

She counted them as they left. One, two, three . . . the Teagues and Grammy, looking deep in conversation, given the sweep of Mr. Teague's hands. Four — Kerensa. Tugging on the hand of . . . five. The adolescent boy named Benny, who looked none too pleased to be going to church either.

Rosemary's lips tugged up. The boy obviously had more sense than the rest of them.

There was another housemaid, but she didn't live on-premises, as she was only needed three days a week. And the stable staff would already be outside. Cadan, Kenver, Treeve — those three were all brothers, apparently — and a few groundsmen whose names she hadn't learned in her time here, given that she had no cause to venture into their domain.

That was all the staff, then. They had no doubt left Mr. Holstein with a nice breakfast and a hot pot of coffee, which he would, if he followed last week's pattern, be enjoying in his study with his newspaper and a book of some kind. There had been no *click-clack-ding* last Sunday, but he'd stayed in his study most of the day still. She had hovered in the library through much of it, not working — on his insistence — but claiming she enjoyed the room and *wanted* to read in there.

Really, she just wanted to know what his pattern was when the staff was all gone and he wasn't at his infernal typewriter.

The answer had suited her well enough. She hadn't ventured about her tasks last week, to be sure — observation was key before action — but this week she would.

And be done and back down before she was to meet him at ten for their trip to St. Michael's Mount.

The staff would take the old carriage to church — she watched them head toward it now. A curricle was also out already, its matching pair of horses tied to a post. Waiting for Mr. Holstein and her, no doubt, though they had an hour yet. But better for the horses to wait, she supposed, than for a gentleman to sully his own hands with tack and harnesses. She was somewhat surprised to realize he would have to drive the thing himself — there was certainly no room for a driver otherwise.

But then, many a gent found it to be great fun, tearing down the streets in their over-priced vehicles, heedless of whom they might nearly run over.

If she were mistress at a place like this, she'd sell off the carriages and have an auto, to be sure. One she could crank herself, so she didn't have to bother the staff about it every time she had a whim to head to the village. So they wouldn't have to plan so far in advance on days *they* were out.

The carriage, filled with laughing servants, headed down the drive.

Rosemary pushed the book farther onto the table and stood. She was already dressed for their outing — a walking dress, sturdy shoes, hat in place. Her presence in the house wouldn't be questioned — Grammy had instructed her to come and get her breakfast from the sideboard in the dining room on Sunday mornings, as Mr. Holstein did, at her leisure.

Holstein had already gotten his — she'd watched him through the window. So she ran little risk of running into him. He'd be buried in newsprint, in another world.

He was always, it seemed, in another world. A German one? Was it full of secrets and lies and treason?

She slid out of her door, shutting it more quietly behind her than she really needed to do. Her handbag was looped over her wrist, her essential tools resting, as always, in the bottom. Just in case the attic door was locked.

The fog took on a glow as she hurried along the path, determined sunshine turning it golden and beautiful. She paused for just a moment beside the wilds of the garden to take it in. To just breathe. To wonder a bit at such beauty, full of growing things and rocks and clear skies rather than glistening gold and jewels and other valuables easily lifted.

It was another world here. One far enough

removed from London that sometimes she wondered how they could both exist a mere few hours apart by train.

But they did. And while Cornwall seemed to inch along through time at its own pace, it didn't stop things from hurtling forward in London. Rosemary had just yesterday gotten a note from Retta letting her know that she, Lucy, Cressida, and Jory had had to move again — some investigator had been nosing around, and as Retta had just fenced a rather distinctive box inset with gold, it had seemed wise. She'd sent along their new direction.

Rosemary frowned to think of it as she started moving again toward the kitchen door. They'd gone farther from Pauly's than usual this time. What they could find, Retta had said. But none of them liked it. They always kept three cheap flats — two for the girls and one for the boys — so that they could be nimble and move when necessary, and so as not to gain undue notice from any of the neighbors, who would surely note a family of twelve who looked nothing like each other. But they tried to keep those three flats within a street or two of each other, so they could pool their resources.

Blast it all, but it felt wrong to be here, safe and well fed and in a giant "cottage" all by herself, when her family was struggling as usual in what hovels they could find in the city.

But Olivia seemed a bit better, Retta had said. That was something. They'd had to take her back to the hospital, but only for a day, so they were doing all right in terms of funds. Thanks to that advance from Mr. V.

From whom she'd also gotten a letter this week, which had made her palms go damp. Oh, the name on the envelope had been a private library in London — one of the ones for whom she had supposedly worked previously — but she'd known the moment she saw it that it was Mr. V.

He'd only asked her if she needed anything else. And, if so, to write to him.

But it had felt like someone looking over her shoulder. Breathing down her neck.

She slipped into the kitchen and barely spared a sniff for the scents of breakfast. She hadn't time for that. Easing the door silently shut behind her, she toed off her shoes and carried them as she tiptoed out into the hall, heading away from the master's part of the house. Toward the back stairs, up them as silently as the old boards would allow. There was an occasional squeak, but they wouldn't be heard from

Holstein's study — she had verified that already.

Sunlight staked its claim on the window-panes she passed, making a bit of anxiety ease as she climbed ever upward. There were windows in the attic, so it wouldn't be too dark up there to see, even though there was obviously no electricity, given the lamp Holstein had had with him that night.

At the end of the hall, she opened the narrow door that revealed crude dark steps going up. This was as far as she'd gotten last time, when she'd found that page of gibberish. Today she eased the door shut behind her and padded her way up. A bit of sunlight beckoned her forward, out of the too-dark passage.

She'd explored a dusty old attic or two in her day. Once to find a valuable stored there that supposedly belonged rightfully to the bloke who'd hired her to poke around his cousin's house — she had her doubts about the "rightfully" part, but he'd paid up front, so who was she to judge? And then a few times to fetch things for landladies with aching knees . . . and abundant laziness. She'd seen her fair share of draped furniture, old steamer trunks, and boxes of things that could only be termed *rubbish*.

She ought to have known that the Holstein

attic would put them all to shame.

Standing at the top of the stairs, she set down her shoes and whimpered. It wasn't just the decades-old furniture one would expect, or the requisite trunks. It was the boxes. The boxes upon boxes upon boxes. And if the few little corners of yellowed-white sticking out of them here and there were an accurate indicator, they were all filled with papers.

Blast it to London and back again. Someone needed to teach these people how to burn a letter when they were done with it.

Well, she couldn't tackle the whole family's stored correspondence just now, though heaven knew it might be useful if she had endless days or an army to help her. She must focus on Peter Holstein. And Peter Holstein had put a box onto a shelf by the window.

One of the windows, anyway. There were eight of them, going the whole length of this extensive attic room, and shelves set up almost as false walls between them, cordoning off the room into eight near-chambers. At which had she seen him? She had to close her eyes, picture it again, flip the image to make it right.

Third from the right side, she thought. Though it had been the only window lit up

— no doubt thanks to those shelves blocking the light from the others — so she wasn't entirely sure of her count. It could have been the fourth. Or the second.

There were certainly boxes upon those shelves that looked like the ones that had been in the library. But then, there were boxes on *every* shelf that matched the description. She pulled out one at random and tipped up the lid, pulling out a handful of papers from the very front.

Letters, and they were addressed to Peter. Staying near the window for its light but out of view of the ground outside, she sat down on the floor and flipped the pages to see who they were from. Several of the addresses matched those on the letters she'd thumbed through last week. Most of the names were unfamiliar to her — though they all sounded English — but a few stood out. Namely because she'd spotted them on the bookshelves in the cottage and knew them from Barclay's conversations.

Authors. He apparently wrote to many of them, and they wrote back to him. But not in the way she would have expected — these letters, as she glanced through them, didn't seem to be the typical response to a fan who had asked for an autograph.

I cannot thank you enough for that timely prayer. It got me through a dark patch last month.

I need your advice, Peter, if you'll give it. What is a man to do when all he thought he believed seems like so much rubbish?

But faith can't be as simple as you say. If there is indeed a God in heaven, it is ridiculous to think Him involved so fully in the lives of man. If He were, our world would not be so in ruins.

Careful to keep them in their proper order, Rosemary read through the missives, her chest going tight. They all hinted at what Peter Holstein's words had been — and those words all aligned with the ones he'd been writing to *her* every day. Words about God, about Jesus, about faith. Prayers. Thoughts. Questions.

For the life of her, she couldn't reconcile those words with the thought that Peter Holstein was a traitor to England.

Unless . . . unless he thought it the right thing. Unless he thought Germany in the moral right.

Her fingers went still after flipping another page. The royal seal again. The same letter she'd seen in the library? No, this was longer. And not in the same hand, she didn't think. She turned it over, hunting for a signature.

Edward David

But that meant . . . that meant *Prince* Edward.

She had to force herself to read it. Because while it was arguably the most important correspondence for her to snoop through, it was from *the prince.* She was prying into the personal messages of *the prince.* It didn't seem right. *Wasn't* right. But necessary, wasn't it? Drawing in a deep breath, she skimmed over the opening paragraph with the usual greetings and dived into the meat of the letter.

Prince Edward, it seemed, struggled with his father's expectations of him. And had received, apparently, some advice from Mr. Holstein that was "sound enough in theory, but impossible to implement."

Her lips turned up as she read the prince's rather colorful explanation of why he couldn't be the same sort of heir that Victoria's children had been, and Edward's in turn. His script was elegant and tidy, yes. And his sentences as well put together as any in Hollow's novel. But somehow, in Prince Edward's words, she saw . . . a normal young man. It could have been Georgie complaining of Barclay's iron fist. Or Barclay himself, railing at the unfairness of something Pauly had insisted on. A strange thought indeed, that the heir apparent of the throne of England had anything at all in common with a thief in one of its streets.

She pulled out the cheap little watch she'd found in an alley three years ago and checked the time. Half-gone already. Muttering, she replaced those letters carefully and pulled out another box. She hadn't the time to read each and every letter — she must find the ones Holstein had come up here to read.

More of the same. But these, at least, bore more recent dates than the first box she'd pried into. Still, she didn't really mean to do more than glance at a few to see who they were from. But one grabbed her attention.

It was in German, unlike the rest. She flipped to the end, frowning at the signature. *Christof Holstein.*

He had family still in Germany.

Perhaps it shouldn't surprise her — what, after all, were the chances that he *didn't* have family still in Germany, when he was only the second generation to have lived his whole life in England? But still.

She flipped back to the beginning and read. Frowning most of the while. Most of the letter was just a chat, it seemed, about aunts and uncles and cousins. But there, at the bottom of the first page, was something different. She ran a finger under the German words, translating softly as she went.

" 'Oma asked me to thank you again for . . . *Verlängerung.*' What is that?" She skipped ahead a few words for context. And frowned all the more. *Miete* she had come across before. It meant *rent,* she was sure. But why would this Holstein's grandmother want to thank Peter Holstein about the rent?

Her chest went tight as she kept reading. There was no mistake. Mr. Holstein had apparently granted someone an extension — that must be what *Verlängerung* meant — on rents due to him.

He didn't just have family still in Germany. He had property.

Mr. V would be pleased.

Buoyed at what could only be termed progress, Rosemary put that letter back and kept flipping. More royal letterhead caught her eye next, this one signed *Geo.* The king. And his bold scrawl proclaimed, *God must have been smiling on me the day He led our paths to cross. I value your advice beyond measure, Peter.* If ever a letter she ought to spend some time on . . . but oh, how she wished she had the one Holstein had written first. Though this was intriguing enough.

My grandmother raised her children with a rigid set of ideals, of expectations. How, then, can it be that their children have ended up in such diverse places? Wilhelm is my cousin — my first cousin. Closer by rights to me than almost anyone here in England. But you're right. His focus is very different from my focus. His goals opposed to my goals. I don't want to wage war against my flesh and blood. But again, I fear you're right — that there are loyalties that run far deeper than blood.

Her eyes clung to that *you're right.* But that implied . . . that implied that Peter Holstein had warned King George *away* from Kaiser Wilhelm's policies.

Which made no sense at all, if he were a traitor. Unless he were the wiliest sort, speaking out of both sides of his mouth. Maintaining ties and property in Germany, then advising the king away from his own German ties. Working so subtly that it would take far more than a couple weeks of watching and reading his correspondence to catch him in it.

Was he that smart? That sneaky? That good at the covert?

Rosemary lowered the crisp, thick paper to her lap and stared at the dust motes gleaming in the morning sunlight. What did she really know of this man under whose roof she'd been living? That he detested changes in his routine. That he couldn't think well when others were talking. That he tended to cling to his preconceived notions. That he enjoyed wit. That he had mountains of correspondence. That he was overly fond of books. That he was a man of great faith. That he shared that faith with anyone willing to read a letter written by his hand.

That he had a coded language in which he wrote notes, perhaps learned from his father or grandfather. That he spent all the day at a typewriter behind closed doors, and no one but no one knew what he was up to as he filled the room with those *clicks* and *clacks* and *dings.*

If he was a spy, he was a master at it. And if he wasn't . . . then what in blazes was he?

THIRTEEN

Peter realized ten minutes into their drive to Marazion that the longest he'd been with Miss Gresham outside his own home was the seven-minute trip to the village and back that first Sunday he'd taken her to church. He realized it because he'd never before really seen her face lit by sunlight rather than electricity. And sunlight changed her look rather startlingly.

Were she Rosita instead of Rosemary, her skin would be a sun-kissed brown from tromping undaunted through the Argentinean wilds. Her hair would be in a constant state of being-put-back-up. Her clothing would be prim at first glance but quickly changeable into an outfit suitable for hiking a trail. But such obvious things were all Locryn had noted about her. He hadn't observed, because Peter hadn't observed, how she tilted up her face to the warmth of the sun and smiled. How she drew in the fresh air as if it tasted of honey. How her eyes went wide at each new sight.

But then, Rosita wouldn't react so — it was her home she led Locryn James through, not an unfamiliar countryside. These weren't observations he could put into his book, not for Rosita. These were simply Rosemary Gresham.

She pointed at a field full of sheep. "How do they keep them there without a fence?"

His lips twitched up. Anyone from the countryside would know that answer — but she had apparently not been joking when she said she'd never been out of London. "Th— there are . . . are ha-has."

The lift of her brows seemed to accuse him of making that up.

Peter chuckled. "D-Ditches. Dug around . . . around the edges of the p-pastures. The sheep s-stay away from them. But p-people occasionally fall . . . fall in. M-Making their companions say —"

"Ha-ha." Miss Gresham rolled her eyes but grinned. "A fitting name, then." She leaned back against the seat and craned her neck as they entered a wooded section of the journey and the road sank down.

The earthen walls rose up on either side, the tree branches stretching across the road above them and twining with their neighbors from the other side. He'd always loved the way they made a tunnel, sunlight filtering down through leaves and turning them emerald.

Miss Gresham's eyes darted from place to place, taking it all in. "Bet this road was a favorite of highwaymen, back in the day. Think how easy it would be to hide in those branches and drop down on the roof of an unsuspecting stagecoach."

No doubt. "Not un . . . unsuspecting. Th— those drivers were . . . were always w-well armed."

"Even so." As they emerged again from the tunnel, she lowered her head to a normal angle. But her smile didn't quite fade away, like a child awaiting a holiday. She was lighter out here, away from books and shelves and questions of Holstein and von Roth heritage.

He wasn't sure what he thought about that. So he just let her enjoy the day and didn't object when she kept ruining the bird-chirping silence with other exclamations about what she saw. Few of those exclamations required a response.

At thirty minutes into their drive, she sat up abruptly, eyes wide, and said, "Oh, I've finished it! I told you I'd give my opinion when I did, though I daresay you hardly care what I think about some random book. But all the same, I've finished. I would have done so much sooner had Jenny not had me working on her gown."

For a moment, Peter's brows stayed knit. What in the world was "some random book"? Then he realized she must mean *This Mad Caper,* and his throat went dry. "Ah. You m-mean . . . Hollow's n-novel?"

Her nod was energetic, her eyes bright. She turned a bit toward him, tucking back a strand of hair that the wind had whipped into her mouth. "It was great fun — far, far better than Melville."

He chuckled, because he couldn't help it. Even if it was far, far from true. "The c-critics would . . . would disagree."

She waved a hand in the air. Dismissive. And loosed a snort no lady would ever let pass her lips in company. "What do critics know? Talk all you want about Melville's subtextual treatment of the soul and his gaining popularity in recent years, but I'd rather have a nice adventure story any day. Well, any day I can't get one with a bit of romance."

It should make him smile. But it chafed instead. "Well, it isn't . . . it isn't *all* adventure. D-Don't you think he . . . that he introduced deeper thoughts as well?

Through T-Thomas?"

Another dismissive wave of her fingers that gave him the sudden urge to slap at them. "Who really cares about that when you've got a hero gallivanting over the globe to keep an ancient relic out of evil hands?"

Of all the . . . "*I* do."

She laughed. "You would."

"And what d-does that mean?"

Holding that strand of hair out of her mouth again, she grinned. "You know exactly what it means, Peter Holstein. It means you enjoy those deeper thoughts, which is obvious to anyone who has ever received a letter from you, I'm sure. You know, you should start writing letters to the newspaper, if you want to let your neighbors see who you really are."

He wasn't about to get distracted with that sort of suggestion. He glanced at her again and then back to the road, careful to keep his tension out of the reins or they'd either go galloping or come to a complete stop when he wasn't paying attention. "And you . . . you *don't*? Enjoy d-deep thoughts?"

"Well, not like you. I'm a simple girl, Mr. Holstein, from a simple world."

A simple world? One in which she'd worked so hard to achieve a position not usually given to her gender? Hardly. Though for the life of him, he couldn't quite figure how she'd managed the education required for such a job, given what he knew of her family. She must have had a benefactor. "You're a . . . a librarian. You are r-required to enjoy depth."

"Well, since you've put me so adeptly in a neat little box . . ." Rather than look offended, she let her lips twitch with amusement. Then her eyes went wide again. "Do you know what I absolutely hated in *This Mad Caper*? The villain. He was atrocious."

Peter's lips twitched to a mirror of hers. "He was . . . he was supposed to be."

"No, no, not like *that.*" Eyes laughing, she leaned an inch closer. "He was a pathetic excuse for a villain, don't you think?"

He lost all desire to smile, though he held its shadow in place. "How do you . . . how do you work that out?"

"He was an absolute dunce. It was no wonder at all that Locryn bested him, only that he didn't manage to best him sooner."

She was the dunce. "You're . . . you're out of your m-mind. Everyone l-loved Masters as a . . . as a villain." Mostly. Aside from those few letters he'd received saying much the same thing she was saying, but those were by far the minority.

She rolled her eyes and leaned back again.

"Only because everyone wants to think that the cleverest of thieves can be caught by even the stupidest of detectives."

Now such bristling overtook him it was a wonder invisible spines didn't slice through his shirt. "Locryn James is not . . . is not stupid."

"Well, of course not. Hence why he deserves a better villain than that ridiculous Masters. Moriarty was a decent example, in *The Adventure of the Final Problem.* Perhaps Hollow ought to take a page from Conan Doyle."

They were entirely different kinds of stories. Conan Doyle's Sherlock was an actual detective. Locryn James was a swashbuckling adventurer. Not solving crimes. What need had he of a criminal mastermind? "That would . . . would not have f-fit the story."

"I'm not suggesting he steal the exact personage, just the concept. Locryn is presented as being the best sort of hero. He needs the best sort of villain, then. And the best sort of villain is smart and subtle and so very tricky that you don't even *know* he's the villain, because *he* thinks himself the hero in his own story. Masters practically oozed darkness and acted as though even he thought himself in the wrong. It's just stupid."

The road ahead was clear and straight, so he turned his frown on her. "Well of c-course he knew it was . . . it was wrong. *Everyone* knows it's wrong to . . . to steal an invaluable art . . . artifact."

And why did she look so dashed exasperated? "Have you ever even *met* a thief? Hollow certainly hasn't, or he would know well that thieves have *reasons* beyond compulsion or selfishness for stealing, most of the time. But he made absolutely no attempt to dig deeper into Masters's motives. Into his psychology."

She said *psychology* so wrongly it took him a moment to realize what she meant — she pronounced the *P* at the beginning, and the *ch* as the usual *ch* rather than like a *k*. "Psy . . . psychology. It's pronounced psychology."

The correction made her spine go stiff and her cheeks flush. "My sincerest apologies. A word I've read but never heard. But don't think to deflect the conversation. I'm right, and you know it."

How had she managed to get through schooling and rub elbows with other librarians and scholars without hearing the word *psychology*? Shouldn't she have been able to trace its etymology back to the original Greek? Though granted, in the Greek one *would* pronounce the *p*. Perhaps that was the problem.

And perhaps he was fastening onto it to avoid her actual point. "Well, have . . . have *you*?" At her blank stare, he clarified, "Have you . . . have you m-met a thief?"

Her laugh was a grunt. "Try living in London for twenty-five years *without* meeting one."

She may have a point there. But . . . "And *known* it?"

"That's the point, isn't it?" Embarrassment apparently forgotten, she leaned closer again. "Masters all but shouts at Locryn in the beginning, 'I'm a bad guy, keep your eye on me!' But a real thief — a good one — wouldn't do that, right? The good thieves are the ones you've got no clue are thieves until you realize an hour after meeting them that something's gone missing. And even then, you think, 'But it couldn't have been *that* bloke. He was too nice.' "

He looked forward again, though he didn't see much of the road before him nor the houses they passed. She might have a point, at that. Masters's intentions *had* been known from the start. Mightn't it have been more effective if he'd been subtler?

He was suddenly glad he hadn't revived him in his current manuscript. Miss Gresham would probably much prefer the subtle methods of Rosita. And so would those other critics.

Her chuckle drew him back to the present, drew his gaze back to her. She was staring at him with the sort of smile that made him wonder if he'd forgotten to don some vital article of clothing that morning. "What . . . what is funny?" he asked.

"Oh, I was just thinking that *you,* Mr. Holstein, would make a most excellent thief, being so very unassuming."

He snorted a laugh and watched the road again. An automobile was coming their way, and he gripped the reins tightly just in case the thing backfired and scared his horses. "I stole some . . . some plums once. From M-Mr. Arnold's little orchard."

"You didn't! I bet you were all of seven."

"Six." And it had been Gryff's fault — Peter never would have done it without being goaded.

Miss Gresham dropped her voice to a stage whisper. "Did you get caught?"

"No. But they w-weren't ripe. Made me . . . made me so sick I swore never to st— steal again."

Her laugh blended with the engine sounds

of the motorcar that chugged past. "That's too funny. Usually stolen fruit tastes so very much sweeter than what you can pluck from your own garden."

Peter grinned. "Have you b-been reading Saint Augustine?" The theologian was certainly not the only one to talk of the sweet taste of stolen pears, but he was the most famous for it.

"Of course — but more to the point. What made you do it? The allure of that forbidden fruit?"

No, though that was the motivation he'd ascribed to Masters, that and the simple desire to possess something priceless. Had it been too weak? He shook his head. "Gryff."

"Smashing! The barrister introduced you to thievery. Do the courts know about this?"

He chuckled again. When had he last laughed this much, but with the Penroses? "An . . . an isolated incident f-for him too."

"Too bad. Handy thing to hold over his head were it not much too out-of-date to be valuable. Now — you know what would have made Masters better? He could have had something on Locryn."

Something like what? Locryn was an upstanding chap. Mostly. But there *were* skeletons in the James family closet — he was exploring that now, wasn't he? Yet again she may have a point. Not that he could change now how he'd written *This Mad Caper*. But maybe Masters *would* resurface in a later novel. Maybe Peter could deepen his character.

Another glance at his companion. "Like w-what, do you think?"

He had always rather assumed that if he'd asked someone to help him think up things for his story, no one would care to do so. That they'd wave him off, tell him it was ridiculous. Or perhaps that they wouldn't feel qualified to answer, having so much less information about Locryn James than he did. And he couldn't exactly share now, with Miss Gresham, the history he'd worked up for his adventurer as he wrote his first novel, pieces of which he sprinkled in here and there as he wrote. And, yes, pieces that he changed frequently as the character developed on the page.

But Rosemary Gresham leaned back in her seat and set her mouth in a look of contemplation. "Well now. He's a gent, so there's no lack of possibilities. The challenge to the writer would be, I think, making the reader understand how wretched certain things are, even if society turns a blind eye. Hollow could actually change some opinions on the culture, like Dickens did, don't you think? If he pointed out the unfairness of how the rich are treated, as opposed to the poor. Perhaps Locryn or his family hurt someone in Masters's family, if he were of humble origins. A sister who was used and discarded. A house of flats torn down, putting them out of a home."

"But M-Masters was not from a poor . . . a poor family." He regretted it the moment he said it — in part because Miss Gresham apparently *was* and in part because he oughtn't to have said it so clearly, as if he *knew*.

Her shrug said she thought nothing of his claim, anyway. "Who's to say, really? We know precious little about him. The reader may make assumptions based on the clothes he wears and his pattern of speech, but they're just assumptions. It would have been properly delicious to be proven wrong."

It would have been, at that. Could be still in the future. "Good . . . good point." He steered them around a rut in the road and adjusted his hat a bit to keep the sun out of his eyes but still allow it to warm his face. There was nothing like these first warm days of summer. "And many options."

"Far too many, if Hollow had gone that direction. Schools barred to him. A parent or someone who died because the doctor wouldn't see them, having no funds — though, granted, I don't know what those would have to do with Locryn in particular. But there could have been some decision-maker in the James family."

She went on. And on. And on, as the miles stretched out behind them. And for once, it wasn't the incessant talk that made something inside go tight. It was the fact that she never seemed to run out of injustices. And he hadn't an answer for a single one of them.

Perhaps Masters *had* come from this world of which she spoke. And perhaps Hollow *did* need to address it. After all, as she pointed out, Dickens had single-handedly rewritten the consciousness of a nation with his discussion of the situation of orphans in *Oliver Twist*. Maybe . . . maybe God meant for Peter to do the same. Maybe that was in part why *this* librarian had been the only one with gumption enough to tackle his library and not some stuffy chap as silent as he.

Marazion was in sight when Miss Gresham's list led her to pause for a second, look out at the approaching town, and then say, "I wonder what Locryn will do if war is declared."

A question he had asked himself already. "Sign up, I . . . I think. Locryn James can find ad . . . adventure in or out of uniform."

Her gaze was a skewer, sharp and hot. "And what would *you* do, Mr. Holstein?"

Another question he had asked himself already. But its answers weren't so easy. A sigh eased past his lips. "I don't . . . I don't know. If I were m-more like Locryn James, I . . . I would. If I c-could give orders." But what men would ever listen to him? And how would he even communicate? No army wanted a stammerer in any position of command, but he knew well that his skills lay more in the thinking positions than in the doing-with-his-hands ones.

And that was assuming he wasn't arrested or relocated for his German heritage and was even *allowed* to help his country.

"For now, I . . . I pray it c-can still be a . . . avoided. But if not . . ." He turned them down the street with the inn at which he'd park the curricle. From here, the old castle on the island was visible. Gleaming in the sunlight and promising a nation that she would survive through the centuries, no matter how feeble *his* efforts to keep her strong. "If not, then I shall . . . I shall do whatever England asks of me."

Simple words. But they echoed inside

him. What if England asked that he go quietly along to whatever internment camp they sent Germans? Would he do *that* for his country? Readily, happily? Leave the only place he'd ever called home without an argument?

And what if Jasper succeeded in achieving an end even worse than that and had Peter arrested for espionage? Would he sit quietly in a cell rather than make waves? Could that possibly be what God asked of him?

No. It didn't sit right. Not when it was so opposed to justice and truth. His duty, to God and country, was to prove who he was. An Englishman, born and bred. Loyal.

She watched him so long and so steadily that he thought for a moment she would question his resolve. Scoff. Perhaps even declare his efforts, whatever they may end up being, as laughable. Or to see through to his other thoughts, other questions. But she said nothing. Just eventually followed his gaze toward the castle, sucked in a breath so filled with awe that he couldn't help but smile, and stood even before he brought the horses to a halt. "Oh, it's stunning. And we can really walk over to it?"

"Tide is g-going out now. We can . . . we can take the causeway and have p-plenty of time to explore the c-castle before . . .

before we have to walk back."

She beamed down at him. And he realized with an uncomfortable start that she did in fact have the same charming smile he'd attributed to Rosita.

Good thing he was no Locryn James.

She would admit it — Rosemary hadn't expected to enjoy being out with Peter Holstein for a full day, away from all the books she could conveniently pull forward when conversation lagged. But as they turned back up the drive to Kensey Manor an hour before sunset, she smiled. It had been a lovelier day than she could have expected. St. Michael's Mount was even more beautiful than the painting had indicated. They'd toured the castle grounds along with other holiday-goers, and he'd purchased them a meal back in Marazion as the tide ate up the brick-and-stone causeway connecting the island fortress to the mainland. And the drive back had been more musing about the fictional worlds from books they'd both read.

She was used to Barclay, who thought it his sworn duty to mock all of her literary ideas, even if it was one she'd heard him espouse before. She'd rather expected Holstein to dismiss her just as fully, if not in so many words — likely without any words. Instead, he'd seemed to think about whatever she said, often adding to it.

It had been a good day. She'd have to write to Willa and Ellie and tell them . . . tell them what? That while they were at home worrying over Liv, she was out having a jolly good time with her employer, who was likely a German sympathizer?

"Are you all . . . all right, M-Miss Gresham?"

He'd stopped them outside the main house, gotten out, and now stood with a hand stretched up toward her while she sat there staring straight ahead like a ninny. Rosemary sighed, smiled, and accepted the help down. "Sorry. Just thinking about Olivia. And realizing I scarcely had all day, which . . ."

"Everyone needs a . . . a distraction from sad things. Es— especially when there is n-nothing they can do about them."

Was that why he'd asked her out today? Probably. And she was grateful for it, even as she rather wished it hadn't worked so well. It was a credit to him that he'd thought of it. Just not to her. "Well, I thank you, sir, for a beautiful day. I had a lovely time."

The sun, sinking toward the earth in a proper blaze of glory, painted his face in golds and roses. He smiled. "So did I. Good night, Miss . . . Miss Gresham."

"Good night, Mr. Holstein. See you to-morrow." At his nod, she gave one of her own and turned toward the path that would lead her to the cottage.

She halted in the wilds of the garden and sank onto the stone bench, still sun-warmed. What made people friends? In all honesty, she wasn't sure. Her friends were all the ones she'd claimed as family — people in like circumstances who had tossed their lots together in hopes that they'd find something better than what they could hope for on their own. If her parents had never died, she never would have met Willa or Retta or Elinor or Lucy. She would have gone to work in the factories, she would have guarded her handbag in the tube, she would have looked askance at every unsavory-seeming character in the streets. She would have been honest, and she would have been afraid, and she would have been every bit as poor as she was now. Perhaps more so.

She certainly never would have found herself in a place like this. Wondering why she wanted to count as a friend a man she intended to hand over to Mr. V. Wondering if she'd still get paid if he were wrong, if Peter Holstein *wasn't* loyal to Germany — or if she'd just be declared incompetent and sacked. Wondering if Mr. V would even ask back what he'd given thus far.

They'd never be able to repay him if he did that. It had already been sunk into the hospital bills. The clothing. The trip here.

Blast it all. She *had* to prove Holstein a traitor, and she'd do well to keep that in mind while they were chatting about books and castles and debating the merits of Cornish pasties as they'd done while eating them in Marazion — he'd been right that Jenny's were the best, but she'd seen it as her duty to defend Pauly's meat pies as every bit as delicious.

Besides, if the best thief was the one you'd never suspect of stealing, then the best spy was surely the one you'd never suspect of betraying his country. And Mr. Peter Holstein certainly filled that bill.

She had to increase her attempts to find the truth, that was all. Do less organizing and more reading in the library. Go back to that attic every chance she got. Find a way to get into his office.

Only a coward would have put that one off as long as she had. But every time she hoped to slip in unnoticed, he was there, regardless of the time of day. Or Mrs.

Teague would stride down the hallway, always ready with a disapproving, distrusting glare.

And how was she to sneak into the attic when it required passing the servants' quarters? Sunday mornings were the only time they were all out and guaranteed not to run back up to their rooms for a forgotten this or that. She'd have to be content with that hour or two.

The sun lit the clouds afire. Retta would love to see the colors — they looked somehow more like a painting than reality, like the strokes of a master's brush. Such beauty in a world that systematically destroyed it. Rosemary sighed out a breath, drew in another. And frowned. Smoke. It still seemed so out of place here.

She sniffed again. This wasn't cigarette smoke, actually. This was *smoke* smoke. Wood smoke. But it didn't smell like what came from the chimneys, it had something else in it.

A shout scorched the air.

She was up, on her feet, running back along the path to the front of the house.

Black smoke streamed from the stables.

FOURTEEN

Coughing, Rosemary flew into the house, letting the door bang upon the wall and not much caring what picture it might knock askew. "Mr. Holstein!" Her feet tore over the carpet in the hall, thankfully still covered in the sensible walking shoes she'd worn that day. "Mr. Holstein!" The telephone was in his study, though she'd never heard it ring. That was what Kenver had said as he took another bucket from young Benny's hand and told her to go and have the master call for help — *now.* And to send out any servant she saw to join the fire brigade.

"Mr. Holstein!" His door loomed before her — shut, of course. But there was no time to indulge his privacy. She pulled on the latch. Locked, blast it all. The blighted man. "Mr. Holstein!" She pounded on the door with a fist. With both of them.

Light snuck out from beneath it — he was obviously in there. She pounded more.

"Not . . . now! If you p-please. I need qu— quiet."

"You idiot man! Your stable is on fire and if you don't open this door *right now* you're putting the lives of everyone here in danger. Now open the blighted door!"

"What?" Footsteps, rushed, and then the wood *whooshed* open from under her hand. "Fire?" He didn't take the time to meet her gaze for confirmation, just brushed by and ran.

"The telephone! Mr. Holstein!" But he was already at the end of the hall, paying no mind to her. Growling, she went into his precious study and looked about until she saw the candlestick phone sitting on a table all alone, far out of the range of his mess.

She'd never used a telephone. Never even touched one, to be quite honest. They had them in London, of course, but not in any of the rooms she'd ever been able to afford. And whom would she call? But she headed toward it now and tried to remember seeing others use the contraptions while she was about in Town. Picked up the receiver. Held it to her ear. "Hello?"

"This is the operator. But you don't sound like Mrs. Teague, Kensey Manor."

Thank heavens someone was there. "No, it's not. But we have an emergency — the stable is on fire. Is there someone who can be dispatched with a fire engine?"

"Oh, of course!" The voice suddenly sounded young and panicked. "I'll get Tom to rouse the boys straightaway!"

"Thank you."

"Fire?"

Rosemary jumped and spun. Mrs. Teague stood in the doorway, her face frozen somewhere between disapproval and fear. She motioned toward the door. "Hurry, then. What are you doing standing about? They'll need all of us until the fire department can arrive."

Not until she was running back down the hall beside the housekeeper did she realize she should have found some excuse to stay there in that study, alone. She could have poked around. Looked into drawers. Seen, perhaps, evidence of what he typed all day. But she'd missed her chance, and when they stepped outside and the breeze slammed them with acrid smoke, she couldn't exactly regret it.

"Over there! The pump!"

She didn't know who shouted it, but she and Mrs. Teague obeyed the direction. Kerensa was already there, pumping with all her might into the line of buckets waiting. Black smoke billowed around them, turning sunset into night, making the maid erupt into coughing.

Rosemary elbowed the girl aside. "Run into the house and get towels that we can wet to wrap around our faces. Hurry now, luv."

Kerensa, arms hanging limply at her sides already, nodded and took off at a run. Rosemary took over the pump. Up, down, *gush.* Up, down, *gush.* It was an action she knew well — and one she had used once before to fill buckets for a fire brigade before the red engines could come whistling their way into the dank street with the old wooden buildings so easily set aflame. That had been her first flat, gone. She and Barclay and Willa hadn't yet been teenagers — Pauly had posed as their father so they could get the place. They'd stayed there two whole years, until the fire ate up everything they had.

That was when they'd decided never to keep everything in one place again. And when they'd met Retta and Lucy, orphaned that night thanks to the blaze.

She hated fire. Hated it nearly as much as she hated fever. Up, down, *gush.* It was like money — one needed a bit of it, for warmth and food. But too much and it charged out of control, taking over your whole life. Eating you up. Destroying everything it touched. Up, down, *gush.*

"I can take over and give your arms a break." Mrs. Teague set down more empty buckets, handed off the full ones to Cadan.

Up, down, *gush.* Rosemary shook her head. "I got me rhythm. You just keep on there."

A bell clanged in the distance, growing closer, as a weak siren whined. It gave her a sudden pang of homesickness — it was the first alarm she'd heard in Cornwall. Not like London, where every night there was some sort of clamor nearby. A fire or a robbery or a who-knew-what that sent police running or the fire department out.

Another two minutes and the long red wagon sped into the drive, pulled by galloping, heaving horses. Apparently their little village hadn't the funds yet to purchase one of the lorries she'd begun to see in London. But it had water hoses and ladders and a great tank no doubt ready to spout water onto the blaze.

Kerensa held up a small, wet towel in front of Rosemary's face. "Here. Shall I tie it around your neck for you?"

Rosemary couldn't bring her arms to stop. Not as long as Mrs. Teague kept replacing full buckets with empty ones, not so long as

Cadan and Mr. Teague kept taking those full ones and rushing toward the stable. She nodded, trying to hold her upper body still so that the maid could tie the thin towel around her and lift a portion of it up over her nose.

Only with the cool filter did she realize her lungs were burning with black. That she was tasting it as much as smelling it. Within a minute the terry cloth had gone hot from her breath, but it was still better than smoke. Up, down, *gush*.

Her arms burned, but she ignored the pain and kept pumping. She coughed, but she didn't let it interrupt her. She kept half an ear on the shouts from the men, on the sound of water streaming from a hose, of horses whinnying and thrashing against the hands leading them to safety. Someone shouted to someone else that all the animals were safe and accounted for. Another someone shouted that most all of the tack had been rescued, and the carriages were parked safely away. But the hay was quick tinder, and the blaze ate through the building, swallowing each stall in turn.

Greedy monster.

At some point, hands took her by the shoulders and pulled her away from the pump. Propelled her a few steps away, to a hot something-or-another that she sank to a seat on. Those hands then took her place at the pump, but it required a long minute of staring blankly to realize it was Gryffyn Penrose under the masking grey towel, no doubt summoned by the black cloud.

She couldn't lift her arms, they were so tired. And her stomach was trying to heave, her lungs to spasm. She untied her own towel and used it to mop at her face, which was streaming sweat and apparently gone black as midnight with soot.

She'd posed once as a chimney sweep, when she was just nine and had nothing to distinguish her from the boys who usually performed the task. Soot on her face, her hair under a cap, a gap-toothed grin as she knocked on the door of her mark. She'd climbed into an upper-floor window that day rather than onto the roof and made off with a handsome music box filled with jewelry. She'd seen the woman wearing the shiny jewelry and thought it would be easy enough to lift.

It was. Of course, it had also all been paste. But she'd been nine, she hadn't known real from fake back then.

She'd learned.

"Here." Kerensa pressed a cup into her hands. "Drink. You've worked as hard as

338

any of the men, you must be parched."

She gave her face one last swipe with the towel that was barely damp. There was scarcely any light left to tell her what the towel looked like after such a use, but she set it aside and raised the cool water to her mouth.

"They nearly got it under control." Kerensa took the discarded towel. "I'll wring this out for you."

"Thanks." Not that Rosemary was convinced she could ever stand again, having sat. Or raise her arms. Or breathe normally.

She hated fire.

What light remained died — it hadn't been the remains of the sun lighting their world, just the blazing stable. As the men staked their claim on the shell of a building and banished the flame, night pounced, cool and dark and complete.

She shivered. But didn't budge. No other monster would creep near, surely, with this one still fuming.

Unless it had been waiting for this chance.

She pushed to her feet, setting the empty cup in her place. With such little light, she could scarcely make out who was who. Penrose still manned the pump, and it was the mister of the Teagues, she thought, now replacing buckets. The missus had probably grown tired and had to take a respite as well. Rosemary counted a team of six shadow-figures that seemed to revolve around the fire engine. The more familiar silhouettes of Cadan and Benny and Kenver and then Treeve, cradling his arm. And Peter Holstein there, closest to the building, throwing a bucketful of water onto a smoking beam.

She didn't know what monsters she was looking for. Only that she didn't see any. Not here, not now. Aside from the smoke, and the darkness itself.

"Enough!" The shout came from one of the village men, who made a barely visible signal to one of his comrades. "It'll just smolder from here. No danger of it catching anything else."

A bit of silver light sliced through the smoke and illumined the ramshackle shell of the stable. The roof was gone. A few of the walls. Heavens but it was a miserable sight, even knowing the loss, aside from the building itself, was minimal.

With the urgency gone, the charge in the air changed. Led, of course, by Mrs. Teague, who physically tugged Holstein away. Even from where Rosemary stood, she could hear the woman's infernal fussing. "What a fool thing to do, Master Peter! Why did you pull

Benny back? He can throw a bucket of water as sure as you can, but what would we do if something happened to you? You with no heir, no one to see to the place if something happens to you." From there, the rant lapsed into gibberish. Or perhaps Cornish.

Holstein pulled away from Mrs. Teague's hands. "He's only a . . . a boy. He shouldn't have . . . been out here."

Rosemary's fingers curled into her palm. Benny was just a boy, it was true. Not yet come into his height at twelve, but strong. Capable. The few times she'd run across him, she'd rather liked him — he reminded her of Georgie in some ways, as he'd been when they'd first met him five years ago. Eager and willful and full of mischief that nothing could tame. Was her little brother still preying on blokes at the tube stops, even after she'd told him not to?

Probably. He never listened to anyone but Barclay, and seldom even him. Oh, how she missed him.

Benny likely wouldn't have stayed inside even had someone commanded it. He'd have wanted to be out here, helping. But it was good of Mr. Holstein to want to protect him from the most dangerous of the jobs. Even if Benny was probably better able to handle it than a pampered gent who spent all his days in front of a typewriter.

". . . do you think?"

It took her ears a moment to catch the low murmur, to distinguish it from crackling wood and the *whoosh* of smoke and the footsteps of all those people milling about, not sure what to do with themselves now.

Penrose's voice.

"I don't think. I *know*." Kenver, and it wasn't the scratchiness in his tone that brought Rosemary to attention, or the weariness. It was the anger, blazing as hot as the stable had done. "I saw someone running away, that's why I went in when I did. But they'd set it in the empty stall where we store the hay. It went up too fast."

Her fingernails bit, but she pressed them all the harder to her palm. It wasn't an accident.

Of course it wasn't an accident.

Penrose muttered something hot and low and fuming. "I'll go into the village. Get the constable."

"Aye, well, I'm going into the village too. And it ain't no constable I'm after."

"Don't do anything foolish, Kenver. If you know who it was, we'll give his name to the authorities. And if you don't, it won't do any good to make wild accusations."

"No, it won't do no good to sit around and let whoever it was gloat into his ale, that's what."

"Stop. This won't achieve anything. Go home to Tamsyn, get cleaned up —"

"Stow it, Penrose."

Rosemary hadn't realized how much she liked Kenver. Nor did she realize her intent to follow him until her feet started scurrying after him, with no input, it seemed, from her mind. A glance over her shoulder, though, told her that none of the night figures seemed to be concerned with her. No one called for her, no one was hovering near the place where she'd been sitting. They'd just assume she'd gone back to the cottage.

She followed instead the retreating footfalls of the stable master. He headed, of course, for the corral where all the whinnying had come from. He *would* take a horse. And she surely wouldn't — she hadn't the foggiest notion how to ride one of the beasts.

But the fire engine was preparing to leave, and all the blokes who'd arrived on it were climbing up near the front, hanging onto railings and talking in low murmurs. Once they were all in place, she simply slipped to the rear of the thing and stepped up onto it, wrapping her tired arms about the rails as the men were doing.

No one hailed her as the horses pulled the engine around the circle before the manor house and then down the drive. Glancing down at the shirtwaist that had once been white and was now black as the night, she guessed that they couldn't even see her, if anyone bothered to look.

The ride into town wasn't long, though the blasted thing seemed to hit every rut in the road, and her rubbery arms had a time of hanging on. But Kenver overtook them just as they reached the outer edge of the village, and she could more or less tell which direction he went. When the fire engine slowed to turn down an opposite street, she simply hopped off and, sticking to the shadows, headed in Kenver's direction.

The pub lay ahead, well-lit and loud. How many of the men currently in their cups inside had sat in a pew in that pious church twelve hours earlier? And how many had the foggiest notion what any of the words Mr. Trenholm had spoken actually meant? Not that she did either — but she at least knew not to pretend she did. She may be a liar and a thief and bordering on a spy just now, but Rosemary Gresham wasn't a hypocrite.

And if what the vicar had said was true, then Jesus had no trouble spending His time with liars and thieves and worse. It was the hypocrites He couldn't stand.

Kenver, his horse tied to a post, was even then striding through the door. He was still soot-covered and no doubt stank every bit as badly as Rosemary did. He hadn't even taken the time to wipe off his face, from what she could see as the pub's light caught him. Talk about making a striking entrance.

She ran on silent feet toward the building and found an open window facing the alley. Perfect. Keeping to the shadows, she stationed herself underneath it and listened as the usual hubbub died down to that particular quiet that bespoke discomfort and, perhaps, confusion.

"Who was it?" Fury weighed his words down so low that Rosemary could scarcely hear them. And had a feeling no one would dare stand up and stake a claim to the fire, especially not if it meant facing Kenver.

Heavy steps, a bit of scraping, like a stool or chair being dragged across the floor. Then, "I said, who — was — it?"

A throat cleared. "We heard the fire engine go by. Didn't know where it was headed. What happened, Kenny?"

Rosemary imagined Kenver turning toward whomever had spoken. She couldn't quite picture what look would be on his face. Was he glaring at someone he suspected or regarding someone he trusted?

"What *happened*?" The man could keep a rein on his anger, she gave him credit for that. His tone was taut, and there was no mistaking the undergirding of rage. But he didn't shout. Didn't snap. She had a feeling he stood with perfect calm, probably not even baring his unfortunate teeth.

She'd yet to meet his new wife, but whoever the girl was, she would be proud of him in that moment. Or should be, if she had a speck of affection for her man.

"I'll tell you what happened. Some coward set fire to the stable at Kensey, that's what."

Enough murmuring filled her ears that Rosemary nearly missed the scoffing laughter. But it came from near the window under which she stood. She turned toward it, though she didn't dare put her head within view. If she could see them, then they could see her.

Measured, stomping steps. "Something funny, Pomeroy?"

Perhaps this Pomeroy bloke was too drunk to catch the note of warning in Kenver's tone. Or too arrogant to care about it. Or perhaps too much of a fool to understand it. Because his next grunt of laughter was all the louder. "Aye, something's funny, all right. Tell me, Kenny — is it the damage to your darling boss's property what has you upset, or the thought of one of your darling horses being in danger?"

Shattering glass made her jump and apparently did the same for many others, because a chorus of startled shouts arose.

Kenver's voice outdid them all. So much for his calm control. "I could have been *killed,* you blighter! Or Benny or Cadan — Treeve's got a burn on his arm. How's he to work now, huh? How's he to help support our folks if my *darling boss* doesn't do the kind thing and keep him on even so? Did you think about that? *Did you?*"

"Take it easy, Kenny, it weren't me! I swear it! Must have been Foote. Or maybe FitzSimmons, he —"

"I don't care which of your cronies it was! You hear me now, all of you. You got a problem with Holstein, you face him like a man and tell him so. Scurrying around throwing rocks through windows and putting *our* lives in danger with fires does nothing but prove you a coward and villain. Do you hear me? You want a war, you wait for the king to declare one and sign up. Don't bring it here. Because if you declare war on

Kensey Manor, I'm telling you now, I'll take down every last cursed one of you with my own bare hands." He punctuated his rant with a few words in Cornish she'd never heard but whose sentiment she understood perfectly well.

Apparently set on making a grand exit, Kenver resumed stomping, heading toward the door. Rosemary didn't turn to see him go — better to keep listening.

What she heard was a soft, feminine voice calling from the back of the room. "Kenny — is everyone all right? Treeve?"

"You gave up your right to care about Treeve two years ago, Eseld." A door slammed, and the footsteps came from outside now.

Rosemary pressed a hand to the exterior wall. There was a world in there, just as there was at Pauly's. One full of old resentments, of loves that had flared and faded, of rivalries and friendships and courting. Were she to guess, she'd say Peter Holstein had never even set foot in this pub. But he was a part of it too. Did he know it?

Those inside did. The chatter sprang up in Kenver's wake. A few claims that he'd got what was coming to him, a few shouts that they were glad *someone* had delivered a message to the German.

Then that feminine voice again. Eseld's. "Shame on you all. Think what you will about Mr. Holstein, but it's *our* people working that manor, keeping it alive. You hurt it, you hurt *them*. You hurt Treeve!"

A swinging door sounded, followed by a hush that wasn't so easily broken. After a few minutes, glasses began to thud again, forks to scrape plates, murmurs to sound. But they spoke of nothing. Weather and the races and the latest cricket match. Nothing.

Rosemary eased away from the window. She'd met Treeve only in passing, had no idea what history he might share with this Eseld. And she had no doubt that Mr. Holstein would see to his care and would keep him on, no matter if he could work or not. What she didn't know was whether that would matter to anyone here. Because the loudest defense had been Eseld's, and it hadn't been for Peter Holstein — it had been for the Cornish people he employed.

His neighbors didn't trust him any more than she trusted Mr. V. Any of them. Because of his silence? Or did they know something she needed to?

Perhaps she'd find this Eseld sometime. If anyone had a fair opinion, it might be her.

Satisfied with that semblance of a plan, Rosemary eased away from the window.

Her nostrils flared. A chill clawed over her shoulders. Her head snapped to the right, to the back of the pub. Someone was there.

Someone who apparently hadn't expected *her* to be there. She caught only a low curse, the sound of a foot pivoting on loose gravel, and then footsteps pounding away.

Every street-born instinct within her told her to chase after whoever it was. But four fleet steps and then her body had other ideas. She had no reserves of energy left to go sprinting after anonymous shadows.

But her toe connected with something in the dark. Something soft and hollow-sounding. She bent, caught up the object, and frowned at the familiar feel of felted wool under her fingers. A man's hat — a bowler.

Mr. V? She couldn't tell, in the dark, if it looked like his. And didn't know why she should assume it would. Why would her employer, after all, be here? Many a man wore a bowler hat. And she couldn't picture Mr. V running from a confrontation with someone in an alley. No, that didn't fit him at all. His step was always measured, calm.

She tossed the hat back down to the earth, spun back toward the street and the road out of the village. And cursed. In her two seconds of brilliant planning, she hadn't bothered with one rather vital question.

How in the world was she going to get home?

FIFTEEN

Peter opened the pot of salve, inhaling the dual scents of honey and lavender. He mustered a smile for the young man sitting at the kitchen table with gritted teeth and wished he had the gift of conversation to put Treeve at ease. "R-Ready?"

It was hard to think of him as man rather than boy. Seven years his junior, Treeve had been a presence at Kensey Manor as long as Peter could remember, eventually taking over his father's job in the stables. But for most of Peter's memory, he'd been a child. Running about chasing butterflies and squirrels as often as he was helping in the stables or with errands.

His arm screamed, loud and red, when Peter unwound the bandage from it. The worst of the burn had healed — Mrs. Teague or Grammy could probably stomach dressing it now, though the first day they'd both fled the room to lose their breakfasts when they'd tried. Hence why it had fallen to Peter.

Oh, he could have found someone else. But the boy had been hurt saving *his* property. If anyone should tend him, it should be Peter.

"Does it s-still . . . hurt?"

Treeve's fingers curled, then went flat against the tabletop, worn smooth from years of service. "Not nearly as much. I should be able to get back to work soon."

Peter set aside the old bandage and dipped his fingers into the salve. Scooped up some, waited for it to drip. Applied it as gently as he could to the raised, bumpy skin. It wasn't hot to the touch anymore. Hadn't been for a while. "I am . . . I am less concerned with th— that than with . . . with your health."

"I know." Voice low, Treeve kept his gaze focused on the wall. In their daily meetings here in the kitchen, the young man had done his best to avoid looking at his arm altogether. "And I appreciate, sir, that you haven't replaced me during these weeks when my arm's been all but useless."

Peter focused on applying the honey to each bit of burned skin. If the scarring ever faded, it would take years. The doctor had declared it one of the more severe burns he had seen — though thankfully not large.

Had infection set in, it could have spelled disaster for the boy.

But they had been diligent. The honey had done its job.

"Re . . . replacing you was never . . . never a c-consideration." He wiped his sticky fingers on the damp rag he'd set on the table for that purpose. Then reached for the fresh bandage awaiting him. At least Treeve he could help. Miss Gresham reported that her little sister was still battling infection, but Gryff's man in London had failed totally in locating the family.

Which made precious little sense. He'd tried to find an address on her outgoing post again, but if she was writing to her family, he never saw the letters.

"It would have been for most. So I wanted to say it. Thanks, I mean. And for doing all this when it certainly ain't your job to do." Treeve lifted his arm six inches off the table, held it straight out.

Peter began the meticulous wrapping. They'd found a rhythm in the last fortnight. And usually performed it in silence. He wasn't quite sure why Treeve had gone chatty today. "A s-small enough way to . . . to say *my* thanks. For your . . . your f-family's loyalty."

"Mr. Holstein." Treeve shifted on his chair

and latched his gaze onto the table. "I . . . are you going to that big bash on Saturday? The one what Mr. Arnold throws?"

Peter's fingers paused. He looked up at the young man's face, not sure how he ought to react to such a question from such an unlikely source. "No."

Treeve's jaw went tight, making him look more like his older brother than he usually did. "You need to." He glanced up just long enough to meet Peter's gaze, showing his own to be as hard-set as his jaw.

Peter frowned. "Why?"

"Because everyone in the village says you won't. That you hate them all too much to go. You got to prove them wrong, Mr. Holstein."

Father's chuff sneaked out. He forced his hands to continue their task. "Is th— that even . . . even possible?" He ought to try. He knew that. Mr. Arnold had advised as much during their shared tea last week. And Gryff repeated it every time they met. But a *ball,* with all those people ready to sneer at him? "Maybe I'm . . . maybe I'm j-just a coward."

"A coward doesn't act like you did at that fire, sir. You would have taken that beam instead of me if you'd been half a second faster, and we both know it."

But he'd been too slow, hadn't had time to do anything but shout a warning when he saw it coming down. He could still see it all, playing out so slowly in his mind's eye, whenever he tried to sleep. He had lunged, ready to push Treeve out of the way. But the flaming beam had been faster, had fallen, caught the boy, forced him down. Trapped that arm.

He was lucky it hadn't caught his face or his chest. That Kenver had been there to help Peter lift the thing long enough for Treeve to roll away. All in all, God had preserved them that night.

Funny how it was easier to trust Him to do so in a flaming stable than in a crowd of gala-goers.

He pinned the bandage in place.

Treeve unrolled his sleeve to cover it. "Look, Mr. Holstein. We'll all stand with you — but in order to do so, you got to stand too. For yourself."

Peter rubbed at his temple. And realized he'd missed a bit of honey on his fingers, or gotten more on during the wrapping. "I don't . . . I don't know. A ball?"

The man-boy chuckled. "You sound like Kenny — though let it be noted he met his Tamsyn at the servants' ball last Midsummer's Eve."

"But K-Kenver isn't a . . . a stammering G-German."

Treeve grinned. "Nah. Just a talkative idiot as like to put his foot in his mouth as anything. You need to go. Sir."

Had Gryff put him up to this? He would have asked the question were the answer not pulsing from the young man's dark eyes. No one had put Treeve up to it. It was his own idea, of whose merits he was thoroughly convinced.

"I'll . . . consider it."

Treeve nodded and reached for the cap he'd taken off and set on the table. He pushed to his feet. "Take Miss Gresham, she'll help — she's been in the pub a good bit this fortnight past. Making . . . friends."

The way he said it left no question as to who her new friend was. Peter winced on Treeve's behalf. "I'm sure she . . . she didn't know."

"I don't mind if she likes Eseld. *Everyone* likes Eseld. What matters here is that everyone's also becoming quite fond of Miss Gresham. Take her with you and they'll all be kind, I think."

Or maybe Gryff *had* gotten to him. "I d-don't see why —"

"Just trust me, sir. Please. For your own good, and for all of ours. No one fancies

357

finding anything else set ablaze."

His chest went tight, his stomach turned. Treeve was right. He had a responsibility, not just to himself and his family's good name, but to every last person who had aligned themselves with Kensey Manor. They were all at risk so long as he was at odds with the neighbors — and were all convinced it was a local who had done it. Constable Newth had questioned the stranger, but it seemed the man was taking his dinner in the hotel's dining room at the time in question, seen by all.

Funny — he preferred thinking the danger from a stranger and a political adversary in London than that his own neighbors despised him so. Even if the man in the bowler had put someone up to it, it hadn't apparently taken much convincing.

Peter gave one short nod.

Treeve pulled his cap on with his good arm. "Good. I'll tell Kenny to have the carriage ready for you that night, then."

Peter stifled a groan and managed another nod. As he cleaned up his mess and prepared to get out of Grammy's kitchen before he could be in the way, he told himself it would be a good thing. It had to be. Perhaps it would be a few hours of discomfort, but what was that in the long run, if it could help his people?

He heard Treeve outside the door, informing someone — presumably Grammy — that she'd not need to prepare any supper on Saturday, as the master would be going to the ball. Grammy's excited — and relieved — exclamation chased Peter from the kitchen before she could come in and gush approval all over him. Best they all keep that in check until they saw whether he made a mess of it or not at the ball.

He stowed the salve and bandages in the linen closet that held all their medicinals and hurried to the main hall.

The library door stood open, as it generally did. His first glance made him think it empty, but Miss Gresham had an uncanny knack for hiding from him. Not that she *tried* to hide, but he had gone in search of her several times only to discover she'd been in the library all the while, hidden behind a piece of furniture or a shelf.

He stepped into the chamber. The visible progress of two weeks ago had reverted to new stacks of books on the floor last week as she set about reorganizing everything left in here. But it still wasn't as overwhelming as it had been before she arrived. And he now had a nicely organized secondary library upstairs. He wove around the maze of low shelves and books until, yes, he saw her. Sitting on the floor with her back to the wall, completely engrossed in whatever tome she had in her hands now. She chewed on a nail as she read, her lips silently forming the words. Must be a German book — those were the only ones with which she did that.

He knocked on the closest shelf to get her attention.

She didn't even look up. Which was, he knew without question, payback for the way he inevitably kept her waiting when she knocked at his study door. But unlike him, she actually heard him. She'd look up when she'd deemed the punishment long enough.

At some point in the weeks since her arrival, it had begun to amuse him. He reached for a small silver key on top of the low shelf, flipped it around in his hand, set it down again. Then picked up a slender booklet sitting beside it and frowned at the title. *How to Organize Your Library.* . . . What would a professional in the study of such things need with such a handbook?

But then, had he come across one called *How to Write an Adventure Novel,* he would have read it too. Just to see if it agreed with his own methods.

Still, when Miss Gresham stood and

walked to his side, he couldn't resist lifting the book, and his brows.

She grinned and took it from him. "Thought perhaps your grandfather had used its methods, since it was in here."

He kept his brows hiked.

She chuckled. "He didn't."

"Ah. That would have been . . . been t-too easy. W-What about the key?"

"I've no idea." She set the booklet back down and meandered over to the window that stood open to the fresh June breezes. "Your timing is perfect — I had a question. Does your mother's family, do you know, have any connections to Russia?"

She seemed to like the out-of-doors better than the in. Rather strange for a librarian, on the one hand. But he could understand it. He often preferred it himself. Just yesterday he'd happened upon her on the cliffs and had ended up sharing his luncheon with her.

It wouldn't be a chore to spend an evening with her. Though it would be less of one if it didn't involve the entire village. "Yes. My m-mother's . . . stepmother. She was Russian."

Miss Gresham turned her face back his way, though she kept her arms propped against the windowsill. "Did she know the

Duchess of Edinburgh, perhaps?"

King George's aunt? He didn't know how she would have. "I . . . don't know. But I have a . . . a question for you. I w-wanted to . . . to invite you to —"

"Dinner again with the vicar?" She turned fully from the window now, though the sunlight still clung to her. "As I told you last week, I appreciate the invitation, but I don't need to spend a whole evening talking religion."

An incredulous snort slipped out, halfway to laughter. "You don't . . . don't seem to mind it with me." Not that he really *spoke* of such things. Much. But every morning there was a new letter on his study floor, with more questions.

The kinds of questions that said she was looking at it all with fresh, unaccustomed eyes. As if she'd never heard any of it before. Another oddity he couldn't quite resolve with *this* Miss Gresham, who cut through a swath of books with speed and without hesitation. An oddity, but he rather enjoyed it. Sometimes that childlike perspective shed brilliant light on age-old questions.

Miss Gresham rolled her eyes and set the book she'd been reading on the top of a stack as high as her head. "It's different. It doesn't seem like talk of religion with you.

It's more . . ."

Warmth spread through him, even as she rolled her hand in a circle as if the right word would leap from the air into her mouth. He smiled. "Faith. But it's . . . it's the same with Mr. Trenholm."

The wrinkle of her nose said she wasn't inclined to find out.

An argument for another day. "That's not actually . . . that's not what I w-wanted to in . . . invite you to do. There's . . ." Blast. Even speaking about it made his tongue go knotted. He'd be an utter dunce when there. "A b-ball. On Saturday."

"Mr. Arnold's Midsummer Ball, I know. It's all anyone talks about in the village." Her brows drew together, and she planted her hands on her hips. "You can't mean to tell me you've decided to go. And that you expect *me* to go with you."

He put on his most pleading look, the one that he'd used to wheedle Grammy out of an extra biscuit. "Please?"

Panic flared in her eyes. For a moment he feared it was at the thought of going with *him,* but the way she dug her fingers into her skirt said otherwise. "Are you mad? I've nothing to wear beyond those two dresses I use for dinner every night — neither of which are suitable for a *ball* like this. Jenny has been talking incessantly of what every-one has worn in years past, and they're all . . . they're all . . ."

"But it . . . it doesn't matter. There are only a . . . a handful of women who . . . who can afford that."

She didn't calm. If anything, the opposite. "But *you,* Mr. Holstein, are the wealthiest man in the neighborhood! You can't show up there with raggedy *me.*"

He tried to keep his lips from twitching into a smile. He did. It was hardly his fault he failed when her hair, bent on proving her point, slipped from its pins. Or half of it, anyway, giving her a lopsided look that turned her expression from panic to exas-peration.

She pointed a finger at his chest. "Don't make fun or I'll throw a book at you."

"Wouldn't . . . dream of it."

Huffing out a breath that would have made Father proud, she twisted the disobe-dient hair back up and jabbed it into place with the pins. "At least you see my point. I am not an appropriate companion for this ball."

Peter leaned against the shelf at his back. "Nonsense. You are . . . are already better liked than . . . than I. Please, Miss Gresham. As a f-favor to me."

"Mr. Holstein . . ." Her tone became every bit as pleading as his had been. "It's not the same as driving me to Marazion or to church. I'm not a gentlewoman."

"And I'm not . . . proposing m-marriage. Just a ball."

The pleading hardened into what could only be termed stubbornness. "I can hardly dance."

He folded his arms across his chest to deflect that stubbornness back at her. "Nor c-can I. We'll be a . . . a matching pair."

"But —"

"I don't . . . don't want to go either. But I must, and . . . and it would mean a lot. To have a friend beside me." He straightened again, cleared his face of all exaggeration. Leaving nothing but the raw truth.

Her arms fell to her sides, and her latest exhalation sounded blessedly resigned. "I'm a friend?"

Should it have surprised her? Probably — it rather surprised him when the word came out so easily. But it was true, just as Gryff had predicted. They'd shared two meals a day for several weeks and had ended up speaking of many things beyond the books in this library and his family's history. They wrote to each other daily, sharing things neither ever spoke aloud.

If that didn't make them friends, then what would? He just lifted his brows in answer.

She had become adept at reading his expressions. Hers now went soft. "I suppose we are. Which is a very odd thought, don't you think?"

He granted it with half a smile.

She huffed again. "So be it. I'll go with you — on one condition."

Gratefulness pulsed through his veins. "Yes?"

He'd only seen that look on her face a few times, but he'd quickly identified it as a warning of mischief. And had borrowed it for Rosita, whenever she was about to do something slightly dangerous and utterly surprising to Locryn.

Miss Gresham leaned close. "Tell me what it is you do all day at that typewriter."

His lips pulled up. Crooking his finger to motion her closer, he bent over, hand cupped, mouth at her ear. And whispered, "I type."

She slapped him on the arm. But her laughter also wove through his as he turned and headed for his study.

Rosemary checked over her shoulder from habit more than the suspicion that anyone paid her any undue heed. But the townspeople bustled about as they always did. The only difference in the last few weeks was that they'd begun to greet her by name whenever she walked to the village, and everyone except Mrs. Gladstone seemed happy to do so.

She suspected it was in part because many of them found it amusing that she'd given Gladstone the what-for. No one she had found particularly *liked* the old biddy. Though she was one of theirs. So if it came down to an actual taking of sides, Rosemary wouldn't ever count on anyone coming over to hers.

The vicar's father was the only one out just now, and he'd already lifted his wizened hand in greeting. Rosemary had already called back her *good evening,* so now the old man was back to whatever book he had in his hand. And Rosemary was free to enter the post office without notice.

They'd be closing in a minute. Which was why she'd timed it this way, so that it was unlikely there would be a line of others behind her, ready to see the envelope she handed over. Not that she thought it her fault that someone had been snooping around Retta's flat those weeks ago — but she *had* just sent a letter there, and anyone either at Kensey or in the village could have seen the address. Best to be cautious — no one wanted to have to move again.

Especially with Olivia still doing so poorly. The postmaster greeted her with that distracted smile that shouted, *Hurry up, then, I want to go home.* Perfect. She rushed in, coin and letter at the ready, her smile as apologetic as ever. "Sorry, Mr. Dell! I tried to get here earlier today."

"No matter, Miss Gresham, no matter. You're always a quick one." But the man's rotund belly was no doubt growling for its tea, and he scarcely paid her any mind at all. Glanced only a moment at the direction upon her letter before affixing the proper postage to it. "There we are, ready to go. See you next week, then."

"Or Saturday, if you'll be at Mr. Arnold's ball. I've been convinced to attend." And if she were going to go, she might as well make it known. Announcing she'd be there with Mr. Holstein could well relieve a few tongues of their opinions of him.

Mr. Dell greeted her words with lifted brows and a warm-enough smile. "Are you, then? Very good. Going with Treeve?"

It shouldn't grate on her that he assumed she'd be attending the servants' ball held outside Mr. Arnold's home, rather than the

368

formal ball within. By rights, that was where she belonged. But he shouldn't have known it. "No. With Mr. Holstein."

"That so?" Rather than the disbelief she had expected, Mr. Dell's face looked . . . impressed. "Who convinced who?"

"He convinced me."

The postmaster smiled. "Didn't know he had it in him. And I hope you have a good time with him, Miss Gresham. Help him enjoy himself a bit. That boy's become so backward . . . his parents would be appalled."

"Would they?" She turned to go . . . but figured it would be a good idea to show some solidarity with him, if she were going to a public event on his arm in a few short days. "I rather think they'd be appalled with everyone in this village for treating him as they do. It's hardly *his* fault he cannot speak well."

"Does he with you?" Usually by now Mr. Dell would be all but pushing her out the door. Perhaps he'd sneaked a snack earlier in the afternoon and wasn't as famished as usual. "Speak, I mean."

"Of course he does." And really, he hardly ever stuttered anymore, unless the subject itself distressed him. Still fumbled for the right words, but it was more hesitation than stammering most of the time. Besides, if one were to watch his face, one could all but read his mind anyway.

She should really warn him about that — a good thief could exploit such things, if he or she were the confidence-scheme sort. And whoever had been listening in the alley beside the pub the night of the fire could well still be out there.

She'd taken to paying attention to every bowler hat she saw in town, but none of the men under the hats she saw looked particularly underhanded. And she knew underhanded. The only thing she was certain of in regard to Mr. Bowler was that he wasn't Mr. V. She'd had a wire from him the next morning, from London.

He may not be lurking about the village, but he was still looking over her shoulder — and she still didn't like it. She could do her job on her own.

Which made that funny little twitch wriggle around inside. Why was she thinking about warning Mr. Holstein about guarding his expressions, given that she couldn't very well issue it until she'd already stripped him of everything that mattered?

Blast it all. She sighed heavily. "He's really a very nice man, Mr. Dell. One of the nicest I've ever met." It *had* to be a front. Or just part of the story. Because, really, no one could be as good as he seemed. No one could really spend so much time dwelling on thoughts of God and Jesus and what faith really meant and then turn around and write notes in some secret code and spend all his time typing *something*.

Maybe he was writing a theological treatise on that contraption of his all day. It could explain why he insisted on those dinners every week with the vicar. She'd slipped into his study twice now to try to poke around, certain both times that no one would disturb her.

Kerensa had nearly caught her the first time. And the second, she'd managed to rummage through only a filing cabinet in the corner before Mr. Holstein had come back down for something. Last week she had even worked up the gumption to come over in the night — Teague had heard her at the kitchen door and come to open it for her before she could even pull out her lock picks. She'd had to make up some story about forgetting something in the library, and he'd hovered behind her the whole while, smiling indulgently, so he could lock back up behind her.

Blasted staff were better security than electro-magnets.

Mr. Dell gave a thoughtful little hum. "Perhaps you're right about him, Miss Gresham. In which case, perhaps you can help him show it."

She made her lips smile, made her eyes reflect it rather than the doubts clamoring about inside her head. She was the last person in the world to *help* him. But in another world, the world where she was Rosemary Gresham, librarian, instead of Rosemary Gresham, thief, that may be just what she'd do. "Let's hope so, Mr. Dell. Good day. Tell your wife I said hello and look forward to seeing her on Saturday."

She slipped out of the door as Mr. Dell assured he would do just that, and then she headed directly for the pub. Eseld, still an hour from the start of her shift, would be getting a bite beforehand. Rosemary's gaze found her the moment she stepped into the warm, fragrant building, and she slid over to their usual corner booth with a smile. "What's on the menu tonight, then?"

Eseld smiled and pushed a full bowl of some sort of stew toward her. Her own was half-empty already. "You're a full two minutes later than usual. I was beginning to think it wasn't really Monday and I'd asked the second bowl of Mam by mistake."

"Mr. Dell was chatty." Rosemary leaned

over the bowl to inhale. She'd done more talking than eating during the midday meal, and it was catching up to her, as she'd also skipped breakfast again. Her stomach just didn't know what to do with three meals a day. "Smells divine."

"I'll tell my mam you said so." Eseld smiled her charming smile and tucked back an escaped curl of the black hair Rosemary had found to be rather common — though no less pretty for it — here in Cornwall. It hadn't taken her long to figure out why Treeve had been courting Eseld three years ago. Though why the pub owner's daughter had tossed him over to marry the moody Colin Thorn, glowering now from behind the bar, she hadn't yet figured out.

But then, Rosemary was no expert on that kind of love. And she didn't rightly know what she'd do if and when her family members started thinking about romance and marriage. Ellie was the only one to ever talk of such things.

Eseld ate a bite of meat and carrots and then pointed her spoon at Rosemary. "Chatty, you say? At this time of day?"

Rosemary grinned and sampled her stew before going back to Mr. Dell. "When I mentioned that I was going to the ball on Saturday."

"Oh good! With Treeve?"

"No, not with Treeve." Rosemary expelled a breath. "Why is that the natural assumption?"

Eseld chuckled. "I suppose because he's the only unmarried man near your age at Kensey, and that's where you spend your days. And I want him to be happy — he deserves to be happy, so if you two —"

"There's no 'us two.' Nor will there ever be." She wasn't stupid enough to get involved with anyone here, not given that she was likely to have to leave in a hurry. Though let it be noted his teeth were superior to his brother's and his face every bit as pleasant. Hard to think she'd barely even known his name when the fire was set — now she saw him nearly every day, since he had to come to the house to have his dressing changed and usually stopped by her open window to exchange a tease on his way in. "He's just a baby. Three and twenty!"

Eseld rolled her eyes. "And I'm one and twenty. Am I a baby too?"

"Barely toddling." Rosemary reached for the mug that Eseld had waiting for her. "It's a wonder you're not still in nappies."

With a sweet little laugh, Eseld threw her balled-up napkin at Rosemary's head.

"You're terrible. And only two years his elder — Mam's two years older than Tas, you know. It's no great thing."

It became a great thing when one of them still believed the world was basically good and the other had known better for going on two decades. And when said idealistic one was still in love with a certain curly-haired Cornish girl. But she certainly wasn't going to point *that* out. "Much as I appreciate that you want him to find his true love, he'll not find her in me, Eseld Thorn."

Eseld's nearly black eyes danced as she took a leisurely sip of her steaming tea. "All right, then. Tell me who it is you're going with so I can weave you a romance with him instead."

A little snort of laughter escaped. "Hardly. It's Mr. Holstein. He's decided to go and wanted a friend beside him."

"Peter Holstein?" Spoon halfway to her mouth, Eseld froze. "Are you fooling me?"

She'd tried to tell him, hadn't she, that she wasn't a good choice? "I know. It doesn't make sense that he'd ask me —"

"Well, it does if he's sensible. But I rather thought he wasn't — that he fancied himself too far above the rest of us lowly villagers to want to spend any time with us." Eseld set down her spoon and traced a finger along the edge of her teacup. "You mean to tell me I've judged him wrong all these years? Next thing you'll be saying he's not the confirmed bachelor we all assumed."

"Haven't the foggiest idea about that."

A lack of insight that didn't seem to put Eseld off any. Eyes unfocused, she tilted her head. "Though I suppose you're not quite a common villager. You're educated."

Rosemary took a bite of stew. The School of Hard Knocks, as someone had put it in an old issue of *Cosmopolitan* she had found, was hardly the education Peter Holstein would value. But she was smart — one couldn't survive the streets without being smart, much less learn how to bypass all the newfangled alarms that were put to use in London. And when one had a few brains to spare, one didn't need a fancy college. Just a will to learn. "When it comes down to it, Eseld, I'm still nothing but a barkeep's ward."

"Well." Eseld shook herself. And grinned. "Good for him, seeing beyond it."

Rosemary just smiled and took another bite. And kept to herself the thought that bubbled up — that she didn't need a man willing to look beyond her past. If ever she found a man — which was hardly a priority — she wouldn't settle for less than one who

loved her *for* what she'd come from.
And that was a tall order indeed.

Sixteen

It could be that his mind was simply still in the ancient ruins deep within the heart of the rainforest, but Peter could have sworn there were eyes watching him with far more attention than his presence warranted. Perhaps they weren't the eyes of natives with poison darts in their hands. But they were the eyes of neighbors ready to judge. And honestly, he wouldn't have placed his bets on their kindheartedness had they been handed those darts.

Music drifted to him from the ballroom, where a string quartet reigned. Chatter crowded the drawing room, where he'd somehow ended up. All the windows were open, letting in not only the summer breeze, but also the sounds from the other ball outside, filled with hoots and laughter.

All of Penzance was here. They must be. Mr. Arnold's grounds throbbed with them — how long could it really hold out until it just burst at the seams?

"You're frowning." Miss Gresham, hand tucked in the crook of his arm, gave him a nudge. "And if you don't stop, they're all going to think it's because you find your companion displeasing, and then I shall never forgive you for forcing me to this thing just so you could ruin my reputation as charming."

"Sorry." He forced his face to relax. Even conjured up part of a smile — not hard to do for his friend. It was just the *crowd.* "Dis . . . distract me?"

She was good at it. She'd proven that innumerable times in the past month. And her eyes sparked now at the challenge.

She grinned. "All right. Let's see how honed your powers of observation are tonight." Shifting, she angled closer to him, the silk of her gown brushing his arm. From what he could glean, Jenny, in a rapture that they were coming, had foisted an entire trunk of outdated gowns upon Miss Gresham, which she was free to make over as she saw fit. He was no judge of fashion, but he thought she'd done a bang-up job of making her dress modern. And the color — a deep rose — suited her well. He made a mental note of it, so that Rosita could arrive sometime in the shade and render Locryn speechless.

Her eyes scanned the room as quickly as they did a book. "I spot a couple who just had an argument before they came."

His lips twitched. Were he to guess, he'd say more than one had. As for the particular couple she saw . . . he had to look around a bit before he realized that the Scaddens, though standing beside each other, were turned just a bit apart, and both had shoulders so rigid they could have held up a house. More, though no one else said much to them, they refused to look at each other.

Peter nodded in their direction. "Scaddens. Now . . . now my turn." His first glance around caught on Gryff and Jenny, who were laughing as they edged their way out of the ballroom, no doubt looking for him and Miss Gresham. But since they were so well-liked, it would probably take them another half hour to get here.

No matter. He smiled. "I spot . . . I spot someone with a flask . . . hidden on him."

"Hmm." Miss Gresham pursed her lips as she looked around. "No obvious bulges in pockets. Which means you're seeing something else. A stain, perhaps? Gin wouldn't stain. Those of rum or whiskey would be too faint to see on anyone but the nearest people, but . . . ah, there we are. Someone has snuck some sherry in, from the looks of it." She nodded toward the gentleman he'd noted. "I don't know his name. And would point out that he could have had it before he came, but it's still damp. Or that it could be from the wine Mr. Arnold is serving, but it's the wrong shade. You're quite right."

Someone hailed a couple walking past them, spurring the two in question to turn. Bringing them nearly to a collision with Peter. He pulled Miss Gresham back a step, until they were practically pressed against the floral-papered wall.

Why did people find this enjoyable?

"My turn." Miss Gresham smiled up at him. "I spot someone who just inherited a piece of jewelry."

His gaze toured the room even as he said, "How do you . . . how do you know it's inherited? Could it not . . . not have been a . . . a recent gift?"

"No."

That was part of the clue, then. If it were jewelry, chances were good the wearer was a woman. And if it had been inherited, it would have to be from a recently deceased relative — likely a close one.

He spotted two different women wearing something that could attest to mourning — Mrs. Tippet in black. And Mrs. Ellis in grey.

The Tippets hadn't lost anyone recently. But Mrs. Ellis . . . she had been a Gill before her marriage, hadn't she? And the matriarch of the family had just passed away a couple months ago.

It wouldn't suffice for Miss Gresham, he knew. Which of the pieces of jewelry that Mrs. Ellis wore was the inherited one?

Her necklace looked old. But did that necessitate an inheritance? The lady wasn't showing anything to anyone — that would hardly be couth. After a moment, he shook his head. "Mrs. Ellis. But . . . I don't know which . . . which piece."

Miss Gresham rewarded him with a grin — and chastised him with a *click* of her tongue. "Bracelet."

He hadn't even noticed that she had one on, what with the way the lady kept her arm over her middle . . . ah. She was favoring it. He would have thought it more cradling a sore limb if she didn't, as he watched, touch one finger to the wrist in question, and the gold encircling it. "Of course."

His turn. And he'd better make it a challenging one — she seemed able to notice an oddity on a fly's wing from ten paces.

Oh, but he had an idea. "I spot . . . someone who had . . . had strawberries with tea." She was quick to note things in other people — how quick was she to pay attention to herself? She'd be looking for telltale red stains on fingers or face, rather than simple knowledge.

Her eyes indeed worked methodically over the crowd. Back and forth, lingering, at a slow enough pace that it would seem she simply surveyed the crowd. No one, to look at her, would see calculation in her eyes. How did she do that? Keep her face perfectly pleasant, her expression perfectly at ease, her posture perfectly relaxed, while her senses were so alert?

Then, as he watched, her face went tight. "Ah, blast. I don't see strawberries. But I see a pickpocket."

"What?" He followed her gaze, knowing well that his voice had sounded as shocked to her as it did to himself.

Mr. Dell stood with his wife at the room's threshold, chatting with his uncle. She couldn't possibly mean any of them, could she? Why, none of them would ever . . .

There. Someone behind them, half in the hall. He couldn't tell who it was. But Mr. Dell's jacket moved just slightly, in a way the man couldn't have achieved on his own, given that his hands were busy gesturing as he spoke.

"What do we . . . do?"

"Make you a hero, that's what. Come on." She tugged on his arm, leaving him little choice but to keep pace with her — it was that or make a scene, and possibly bump into half a dozen people with punch glasses in the process.

He was tempted to let spill what may. "What are you . . . we can't . . . l-let's just fetch —"

"Oh, buck up, Mr. Holstein, it will be easy. All you have to do is hold the bloke while everyone swarms. Leave the rest to me."

Hold the bloke? That would be *easy*? He stuttered something apparently incomprehensible — or which she just completely ignored — as she tugged him toward the door and out into the hall.

He couldn't have said which of the men out here was the pickpocket — everyone looked largely the same in their dark jackets, and he hadn't seen hair nor face.

Perhaps she had, because she nodded toward a thin fellow weaving his way toward the ballroom. "You sneak up behind and grab his arms when I give you the cue."

"What . . . what *cue*?"

But she'd already let go and slipped away. She moved quickly, outflanking the man she'd indicated so that she'd reach the ballroom door first. Peter rushed to keep up, though he had no clue how he was to go about grabbing a fellow with nothing but her word to go on. What if it wasn't him? Or if he hadn't actually been stealing anything? The last thing in the world he needed was to have the whole of Cornwall saying he'd falsely accused a decent man of a crime.

Miss Gresham clearly hadn't considered that. She was going to enact whatever plan she'd come up with — he could either go along with her or leave her to whatever consequences came, on her own.

No. No, he couldn't do that to her. She was only here because he'd begged. What kind of gentleman would force a young lady to an event, lead her straight into potential trouble, then just abandon her to it?

He followed in the wake she made, summoning his inner Locryn as she maneuvered to the front of the chap in question. The closer he got, the more he noticed about the man. Not only did he look thin even from a distance, from here Peter could see that the evening jacket hung on him — and it was frayed at the seams. Not badly enough that one was likely to notice it at a glance, but when one looked closely . . . it would be expected, perhaps, of someone from the servants' ball outside.

Perhaps he had simply come in to convey a message to a guest within the house. Innocent. Peter wanted no part in accusing an innocent man of anything.

Miss Gresham reached down to her own wrist and did something. He frowned. She had on gloves, of course, and a bracelet he hadn't noticed — he apparently had a blind spot when it came to bracelets. But it was . . . wasn't that Jenny's diamond bracelet? He'd seen it before, he was sure. Jenny must have lent it to her.

Then, whatever she'd been doing apparently done, she eased into the wide, double-doored opening to the ballroom . . . and drifted to a halt, her back to the man. As if she'd not even noticed him and was simply surveying the room, looking for someone.

"Pete?" Gryff's voice came from but a few steps away.

Peter ignored him and moved toward Miss Gresham and their mark. He still wasn't sure what she was about, not until she fluttered the hand that wore the bracelet, as if greeting someone discreetly.

Drawing attention to the bracelet. And the man noticed. His head turned a bit to follow her movement, and his fingers flexed against his leg.

Blast — was she really toying with someone else's belongings like this? Now he had no choice but to catch the man in the act of stealing it. He certainly couldn't let anyone get away with nicking his friend's jewels.

The man reached forward, his fingers barely skimming the bracelet. But it was there, then gone. Her wrist bare. Peter had been watching the whole time and wasn't sure how the fellow had achieved it so simply — but he intended to tell Gryff to have that bracelet altered to have a more secure clasp, that was for sure.

Miss Gresham spun, raising her wrist — and her voice in a scream. "Thief! Thief!"

That, he supposed, was his cue. Peter lurched forward even as the man lunged to the side, in the direction of the doors that stood open to the midsummer breezes. Had he not been at the ready, the fellow may well have elbowed his way past the startled onlookers and out into the night.

But Peter grabbed his jacket in one hand, his arm in the other. "Stop!" And listen to that, his voice sounded firm and steady, at least on that one word. Energy coursed through his veins as it did in a rousing boxing match.

And just as in a boxing match, the man spun, fist raised. Peter ducked the punch and landed one in the other man's stomach on his way back up.

The man — boy? He looked young — doubled over, though it hadn't been *that* hard a blow. Was he faking the reaction?

Maybe so, but others had closed the space between the fellow and the door now. There was no chance he could get away. Not in that direction. Still he didn't rise.

Blast. He realized the man's intentions half a second too late to do anything about them as he rammed into Peter's midsection, plowing him out of the way. Or meaning to. But Peter had tussled with Gryff when they were boys, and his friend had never much liked playing by the rules of the boxing ring. He'd done this a time or two, and so Peter, rather than fall away or try to hit him, simply leaned over him until he could grab the man around the middle. It could do little but render them both immobile. But that was quite enough just now.

Shouts swirled around him, but he didn't notice their presence until they died down in the face of a steady *thump, thump, thump.* A cane against the hardwood floors. He recognized the unsteady gait of the legs that came into view. Mr. Arnold.

"Mr. Holstein. What is going on here?"

Deep rose silk swished into view as well.

"Oh, Mr. Holstein, thank you! This man stole the bracelet right off my arm, Mr. Arnold. If Mr. Holstein hadn't stopped him, I don't know what I would have done."

"What?" Mr. Arnold sounded horrified, not disbelieving. "Who is this man?"

Gryff was there now, gripping the arms of the chap. Peter eased off him, though he was ready to grab again if the fellow tried to make a break for it.

Apparently he realized the game was up. Face shuttered, jaw set, the stranger didn't struggle as another neighbor grabbed him from the other side and a third rushed up to reach into his pockets.

He came up with Jenny's bracelet. A wallet that earned a gasping claim from Mr. Dell. Two necklaces, and a roll of pound notes, bound by a silver clip.

Chaos naturally ensued. And given the hands that clapped his shoulders, Peter should have been glad of it. Glad that Miss Gresham's scheme had worked. Glad to have returned the goods to his neighbors and earned himself some respect in the process.

And he was. But he couldn't keep from watching the man. And so, couldn't help but see the shadows that chased each other through his eyes. He saw the way the fellow

glanced toward the parlor and gave a minis-
cule shake of his head.

Peter followed his gaze. A young woman
stood in the doorway, pale and obviously
horrified. A different shade of horror than
that worn by all the other ladies in at-
tendance. She gripped her dress's skirt with
bony white knuckles, but it didn't quite
camouflage the way her hands shook. She
pressed her lips together for a moment. But
only for a moment. A sob shook her, and
her lips parted. "No! Tim, *no*! Please don't
take him. *Please.*"

The thief muttered a curse. "Betty, I told
you —"

Mr. Dell grabbed the young woman by
the arm. "You're his accomplice, are you?"

"No!" The level of panic in Tim's eyes
shouted love. "No, she's not. She didn't
know what I was about, I swear it. It was
just a dare, it was. Me cousin outside came
up with the idea — I was going to return it
all, I —"

"Likely story. Which you can save for the
constable." Gryff spoke in his barrister
voice, which Tim and Betty both seemed to
recognize. They shrank, right before Peter's
eyes. Just curled up into themselves.

The shadows under the girl's eyes stood
out more clearly now than the ones in them.

And by the way her shoulders curved forward, he could see that they were sharper even than Miss Gresham's. That her cheekbones were far too pronounced. She was *gaunt*. The kind that came either of sickness or the most extreme poverty.

Tim wasn't that thin. Which made him suspect illness in the girl.

Made him *sure* of it — or something did. Maybe it was just the way she looked or the handkerchief he spotted balled in her fist — though it had nothing as obvious as bright bloodstains, it did have faded, rusty ones. Outlines of them, as if just the edges of the blotches wouldn't wash out.

Peter headed her way. "Mr. Dell, you're . . . you're hurting her." He must be — her arms had no meat to them, and the postmaster held on quite tightly.

"Well, she's a thief, Mr. Holstein. I bet if we search her, we'll find more of our valuables."

"No, you won't." Miss Gresham's voice came from beside Peter, though he didn't take his eyes off the girl to see why his friend spoke with such certainty. "Look at her, sir — she carries no bag, that dress has no pockets — where would she hide anything?"

Now Betty's whole self shook, not just her hands. "I didn't take nothing. I wouldn't."

Peter believed her, which probably made him a fool. Certainly Mr. Dell would have labeled him so — his grip didn't loosen. "Are you . . . are you ill, m-miss?"

The girl averted her face, which only managed to show off her too-severe jawbone. "It's not catching, sir."

"You need medicine." Miss Gresham said it on a sigh. The kind that wept with regret. "I'm sorry. I wouldn't —" She cut herself off, but Peter heard the completion of her sentence in his heart — she wouldn't have made a show of catching Tim had she known. She would have confronted him quietly. Or perhaps not at all. Perhaps she would have reckoned that Mr. Dell could afford the loss of the small amount he likely had in his wallet tonight, and it could mean life to this girl.

Peter reached into his own pocket before he quite knew his plan. "Here." He hadn't much on him either. Five pounds — paltry indeed. So he slipped his cufflinks off as well, they being the only other valuable he had with him, aside from the watch that had been Opa's. He pressed them into the girl's hands, though her fingers seemed to close around the offering by instinct more than desire, given the shocked circles of her eyes. He tried to reassure her with a smile.

"It's . . . it's all I have with me. B-But if you come to . . . to Kensey Manor — t-two miles out of town — my p-people will feed you. You can sleep . . . sleep there. And —"

"Mr. Holstein!" Mr. Arnold's voice sounded along with the thud of his cane. "You will not *encourage* thieves in our midst!"

He'd always appreciated the faded Austrian cadence of Mr. Arnold's voice, especially after Opa died. The man had always reminded him of his grandfather — the gentle demeanor, the white hair, the kindly smile. But just now their host was glowering and looking ready to bring his cane down across Peter's outstretched hand.

But he wasn't a recalcitrant child. He shook his head. And tucked his hands into his pockets. "As you d-do unto . . . unto the least of these, Mr. Arnold. Th— this girl needs help."

Another punctuating *thump* of his cane. "Three-quarters of England needs help. You cannot go offering cufflinks to all of them."

For once, he didn't savor the way *them* sounded like *zem* or the throaty vowels. He looked deep into the rheumy eyes of the old man everyone respected, whom *he* had always respected. And he shook his head. "No. J-Just . . . just the ones G-God puts . . .

before me." This girl. Little Olivia, if he could ever figure out how to find her.

Because he certainly wasn't going to make a show of it. He wished he'd have had the presence of mind to wait until later to make *this* offering.

But she could slip away. Disappear. He may never have had the chance to help her if he'd waited. And a clear conscience before the Lord was more important than the respect of his neighbors.

Which he repeated again to himself, and again, when the murmurs around him turned into a cacophony of opinions he had no desire to sort out.

Mr. Arnold, gaze disappointed, shook his head.

Peter looked over to Gryff, who sighed and then caught Jenny's gaze. Her hands were clutched to her middle, her eyes still wide. She nodded. "I've no desire to press charges. The bracelet was recovered. No harm done."

Mr. Dell sputtered. "Well, rest assured I *do* want to hold him accountable! Considerable harm has been done, to our sensibilities if not to our persons. We cannot suffer such crime in our midst or it will run rampant."

Tim's shoulders sagged. And when a

whimper came from Betty — his sister? wife? — he set his gaze on the floor and refused to lift it again. He had done wrong. Perhaps he knew it, or perhaps he only regretted getting caught, Peter couldn't know which. What he knew without question was that the man was now realizing that his gamble had cost him the comfort of caring for the girl.

Who else did they have? Was there someone else to see to her?

"Where *is* Constable Newth?" Mr. Dell stood on his toes to look over the heads of the crowd. "He was in the ballroom, was he not?"

And the magistrate too, no doubt. Peter sighed.

Mr. Arnold cleared his throat. "Mr. Holstein, you are obviously distressed. I will call on you on the morrow. After church."

The fingers still in his pockets curled at being dismissed. "We . . . we're taking the g-girl with us."

The prisoner's head snapped back up. Eyes dark with suspicion, he looked ready to say something. But bit his tongue when new commotion signaled the arrival of Mr. Newth, who didn't need his badge or a uniform — he wore his position for all to see.

Mr. Dell huffed. "You most certainly are not! The girl is a thief."

"Prove it." Miss Gresham planted her hands on her hips. "If she is, then take her in with him. But if you don't find anything on her person, you most certainly will *not* cart her off to spend a night in a damp, cold jail cell that could well be the death of her."

Mr. Dell's face went red. "Even if she hasn't stolen anything *yet,* it was obviously her intent. Otherwise, what's a girl like her doing here?"

Were the situation less dire, Peter would have smiled at the way Rosemary Gresham stood up tall. At the way her lips curled back from her teeth in a snarl worthy of the most ferocious beast. At the ease with which she stared down the town patriarchs.

For the life of him, Peter couldn't figure out how she managed to portray such perfect disgust with Mr. Dell just with a shake of her head. "Do you mean to tell me," she said in a voice of perfect condescension, "that you never once sneaked in somewhere you shouldn't have, just for the thrill of it? Then you *are* a paradigm of sainthood, Mr. Dell, for even little Elowyn Penrose has done that. Shall we cart *her* to the jail as well?"

Peter had to press his lips against what

was sure to be ill-timed laughter when Mr. Dell sputtered. Though a few people farther back in the crowd didn't bother with such restraint. Of course, they had the safety of many people between them and the object of their mirth.

Mr. Dell's nostrils flared. "It is hardly the same. Elowyn Penrose doesn't do such things in the company of a proven thief."

The point — a somewhat valid one, if Peter were being honest — didn't ruffle Miss Gresham in the slightest. "I suppose, then, you also haven't ever done anything without your sister's knowledge."

Given that his sister was the cantankerous Mrs. Gladstone, the question earned more laughter from those safely in the back. No one questioned her assumption of the strangers' relationship. Of course, the more Betty shrank back, the younger she looked. Too young, surely, to be Tim's wife.

Mr. Newth cleared his throat. "Look here, Dell. Miss Gresham is right that we're not going to charge a girl just for knowing a thief. Have your wife take her somewhere and search her. If she finds anything belonging to someone else, then in she goes. If not, we let her go, and Mr. Holstein can take her home to Kensey to feed her if he so desires. Heaven knows it looks like the chit could stand a good meal."

Mrs. Dell squealed. "I most certainly will *not*! The girl could club me over the head and make a run for it!"

Mrs. Dell had obviously been spending too much time with her sister-in-law.

Rosemary rolled her eyes. "Oh, for heaven's sake. I'll do it, then."

"You will not! You'd likely hide it if she *had* stolen anything!" This, obviously, from the mister of the Dells.

Jenny stepped forward. "I shall, then. Or will you accuse *me* of such dishonest intents as well, Mr. Dell?"

In short order, she left with Betty, who looked as slight as a reed beside her. Peter watched them go to the stairs and then looked back to Gryff and Tim. The boy — he couldn't be a day over seventeen, Peter noted now that he was looking closely — watched the females disappear up the staircase with an indrawn breath. Peter wished he could reassure him that he'd make sure she was seen to, but the commotion was swelling again, and Mr. Arnold was gripping his cane far too tightly.

He didn't want to cause the old man any more distress than he already had. Clearing his throat, Peter looked again at Rosemary. Held out a hand.

She didn't hesitate. Just took it and moved to his side. Aligning herself with him rather than the crowd.

Brave woman. Or foolish. Or perhaps a bit of both, but he was grateful. Gryff couldn't well leave, and Peter appreciated not having to walk this particular gauntlet by himself. He tucked her hand into the crook of his elbow — though a part of him preferred the feel of her lean fingers in his — and turned them toward the door.

The constable's nod to him looked . . . even. Newth had always been a fair-minded man. Gryff's look combined a bit of pride with a bit of why-can't-you-just-leave-things-alone.

Someone clapped a hand to his shoulder as he passed. He may have looked to see who, but then someone else sniffed and pivoted, giving him a literal cold shoulder.

Nothing new. Determined not to look at anyone else, he led Rosemary through the door and out into the sweet-scented night with its starlight above and music still spilling through the windows.

Rosemary. He'd done his best not to think of her as such, despite the fact that her every letter was still signed so. It was too forward to call her by a given name without her permission after such a short acquaintance.

But she'd proven herself a friend tonight, without question. He couldn't quite look at her and think *Miss Gresham* just now. Though he wouldn't let his lips forget their manners.

Kenver, his wife's hand in his, was there on the walkway to greet them. "We were on the lawn and heard through the window. Quite a stand you took, Mr. Holstein."

Peter sighed. Nodded. "I don't . . . I don't mean to p-pull you away." This was, after all, the anniversary of when Kenver and Tamsyn had met.

But Kenver just grinned. "No trouble at all. It's a fine night for a drive, isn't it, Tam?"

"The finest." She had a small voice, did Tamsyn, to match her small frame. "You did a good thing in there, sir."

He had done the right thing. He was sure of it. But it probably wouldn't make him many friends.

Kenver and Tamsyn moved off with a promise to fetch the carriage posthaste, leaving Peter with the night and the sounds from dozens of revelers inside and out, and a quiet Rosemary at his side.

His exhale was long and grey. "Now I've . . . done it."

Her fingers went tight on his arm. "You have indeed. You've shown them the true colors of Peter Holstein. And they're good colors."

But color, or rather whether it was good, was a matter of opinion. *He* might love yellow, but Gryff hated it. How much more divided would people be over *him*?

She shifted, moved more before him. And reached up to rest a gloved hand on his cheek. He hadn't quite got over the shock of that when she stretched up onto her toes and planted a kiss on his opposite cheek. Not softly or thoughtfully. The kind of bold, loud kiss that made a statement.

Hers said, *You're a good man.* And perhaps, *You're my friend.*

He covered with his right hand the fingers still resting on his left arm. And let his smile say, *Thanks.*

Then he made the mistake of looking past her, toward the road. Lanterns lit the expanse of lawn between Mr. Arnold's house and drive — he lived on the outmost edges of town, his property stretching back until it touched the far corner of Kensey land. And everyone in town was at one ball or the other.

His gaze shouldn't have been snagged so quickly by the island of unmoving man on the brink of darkness. But it was. And his breath caught.

Rosemary turned too, and her breath caught as well. "The man in the bowler."

She'd seen him too? Noted him? Where? In the village or at Kensey? Perhaps he ought to have said something about the fellow sooner. To her, or to the rest of the staff, so they could keep an eye out. "He's in . . . in the employ of a . . . a fellow in London. Who d-doesn't much . . . like me. I . . . thought he must've . . . left the area. Haven't seen him lately."

She shifted to fully face the stranger, planted a hand on her hip. Defiant. Confident. Daring the man to come closer, it seemed. "What does he want?"

Daring a confrontation for *his* sake. Peter let out a long breath. "His employer . . . is trying to accuse me of . . . of not being a British subject. And the records — they're not in . . . in the Archives. If I cannot . . . find copies at Kensey, or the deed that would . . . would prove we'd purchased it — we couldn't have if . . . if we weren't subjects. And if war is declared . . . I could be . . ."

She spun back to him, her eyes wide. "You mean to tell me that your entire social position rests on finding documents in your house and you haven't even *told* me so I could help you look for them?"

"I . . ." He hadn't wanted to draw anyone else into it. Not when he couldn't well explain how he even knew about the threat. Not when it would require looking not just through the shelves in his library but through the masses of personal letters and documents in his attic. "I thought I'd . . . be able to find them . . . easily."

Her brows arched. "And have you?"

His chuff, he figured, was answer enough.

She rolled her eyes and turned to tuck her hand through the crook of his elbow again. Then tugged him down the walk, toward where the carriage would pull around in another minute. "I'll help you look."

He needed the help. He would go up there when they got home and secure the reader mail, then let her have at it.

Still, it felt like an imposition to ask this of her, and he opened his mouth to say so.

"Don't argue with me — it's what friends do."

It was. So why that funny little catch in her voice as she said it?

SEVENTEEN

Rosemary wiped away the tear tickling her cheek and tilted up her face to let the warm summer breeze dry its track. To let the sun caress her face. To let the words sink in as the sheet of torn, raggedy paper fluttered around her fingers. Mr. Teague's prized flowers bobbed their heads as if assuring her of the truth on the page she held.

You'll never believe it, Willa had scrawled at the start of the letter, not even bothering with a greeting. And well she shouldn't have, not with news that good. That important.

Mr. V showed up at Pauly's last night. Said it was the only place he could find us, and find us he had to do. He'd heard, some-how, about Olivia. I don't know how, and that's concerning — how many ears does that man have pressed to how many walls? But he heard, and he came with money — not part of your payment. Said it had been delivered to one of his offices by an anonymous benefactor, meant for Liv. Though of course it must be from him. It's enough to pay off the bills, Rosie. And more besides. It's enough to make sure she has the good food she needs as she heals. And for the surgery to reset the bone.

I thought we were going to have to amputate. I really thought we would. But now . . . now little Liv may just walk again.

Another tear slipped out when Rosemary blinked. She didn't know who to thank. Mr. V? God? Peter and Grammy and Jenny for praying?

She didn't know whom to thank, but thankfulness swelled so great, so beautifully that it brought more tears to her eyes.

Maybe God *did* care. Or maybe, at least, He listened to the prayers of the rich, even when they prayed for the poor.

Refolding the letter, she sniffed and drew in a breath of fragrant air. If the others hadn't already left for church, she might just have gone with them this morning. Perhaps God preferred people thank Him in the walls of such a place. That surely made it more formal. And one should surely be more formal when offering gratitude to the Creator.

Except that Peter seemed to give his thanks right here, at home, and he and God were obviously on good terms. But then, maybe that was how he got away with informality.

She would ask him when she wrote to him tonight.

For now, she tucked the letter — which had obviously arrived yesterday, though Mrs. Teague hadn't seen fit to hand it over until this morning — into her pocket. And stared at those nodding flowers.

Last Sunday she hadn't gone up into the attic. She'd told herself it was because she was busy seeing to Betty, but that wasn't quite true. Betty had insisted on riding with the others into the village so she could visit her brother. And then Eseld had found her there and insisted the girl come to stay at her parents', behind the pub. Betty, grateful as she had been to Mr. Holstein for stepping in, hadn't felt comfortable at Kensey and had taken Eseld's parents up on their offer.

Rosemary, quite simply, hadn't gone up into that attic a week ago because she hadn't wanted to. She hadn't wanted to pry into Peter Holstein's life that day. She hadn't wanted to find anything that proved him a traitor. She had been quite content to enjoy a leisurely cup of coffee at the dining room table while he read his paper. And then to accept his offer to lounge about the drawing room, both of them reading.

She had the perfect excuse now to search his things — he would even thank her for it. She could look for evidence against him as she said she was looking for evidence *for* him. She could search and find and choose what to turn over to Mr. V and what to share with Peter Holstein.

She could betray him so very easily. And she didn't want to.

So what if he *were* secretly loyal to Germany? That was the thought that kept bothering her all last Sunday, and that hadn't quite left her mind since. What loyalty did she really have to this blighted country of hers, aside from what Mr. V had purchased with his stack of pound notes? And for all she knew, *he* was a German. Her loyalty was to the pounds, not the monarch upon them. Her loyalty was, and had always been, to those who gave a fig about her and hers.

Peter Holstein had proven himself the rarest sort of man — the kind who risked himself, his reputation, and gave what he had to help someone. Perhaps he hadn't come forward to offer any extra aid for Olivia, but he'd given her hours upon hours of his prayers, hadn't he? And apparently that had been enough.

But the money Mr. V had just delivered . . . She wasn't sure why he acted so generously, but she owed him. She owed him the answers he was paying her to find. Blast it all.

Guilt wasn't something she believed in. Guilt was just a name the rich gave to the stains of poverty that soiled street urchins who had no choice but to steal or to starve. *Guilty,* the judges were so eager to proclaim.

Poppycock. *Hungry.*

But what other name could she give to the snake of discomfort slithering through her as she let herself into the manor and climbed those back stairs? She knew which boards to avoid now, but she needn't bother. Not now that Peter *wanted* her to search his things.

Mr. Holstein. She had to get back into the habit of thinking of him as Mr. Holstein, despite the lapse in her thoughts this last week. Maybe that would help still the snake. Help her remember that she wasn't here to like him. She wasn't here to enjoy his company. She wasn't here to cheer him on in a crowd.

She was here to take his name from him — and his house besides. "And don't forget it, Rosie." It didn't matter to Mr. V if Peter Holstein was *good.* Only whether he was loyal.

The latch on the attic door gave under her hand without so much as a squeak, and she climbed the stairs into the heat that would be stifling in another hour or two. At the top, she surveyed the mountains of boxes and tried to recall where she'd left off.

The problem was that she'd gotten to know him. She wasn't used to having personalities to go along with her marks. To be able to finish their sentences. It was different, very different from simply picking a random face from a crowd based on how sparkly their accessories were. It was different from receiving a job from someone lusting for a particular piece and casing a house as a *house,* not as a home. It was different, and she hadn't realized it coming in. She hadn't known it would get so blasted *hard* once she knew him.

Or, no, she just hadn't ever considered that she might come to term a gentleman a *friend.*

She'd never stolen from a friend. Never.

So . . . so she couldn't be his friend. Because she had to steal from him. The end.

She should have left herself some marker as to which box she'd been on. Instead, she'd assumed she'd remember, and now all the boxes looked the same. Besides, during her previous searches, she hadn't dared to leave any evidence of herself up here. Peter — *Mr. Holstein* — obviously came up here, and he was too dratted observant not to notice something out of place.

Observant when he wasn't locked in his study behind that infernal typewriter, anyway. When he was typing away, Kerensa might have to keep knocking at his door for a solid five minutes to get him to acknowledge that it was time for luncheon.

Which she would *not* smile over. It was annoying, not amusing. Just as it had been from the start. She wouldn't change her mind about it now.

She stomped her way to the shelves instead of tiptoeing, which was far more cathartic. She stopped where she *thought* she'd been last time and studied the boxes for some clue as to which she'd already looked through. Not that the mountains of correspondence she'd read had shown her anything other than what she'd come to expect from him, aside from that one letter in German mentioning rents. If he shared disloyal thoughts with anyone, he either kept those telltale letters somewhere else, burned them, or they used a code.

Perhaps *God* was really *Germany*. Perhaps *faith* was really *treason.*

Her lips twitched. If so, then he was advising everyone to have treason, because Germany loved them.

Hmm. She bit her lip to keep from snorting a laugh and got down to business.

Which was all this was. Business. Not the betrayal of a friend.

And it was only the rising heat suffocating her as she worked through the next hour, not anything as ridiculous as guilt.

She paused as she lifted the lid of another box and saw a rather interesting word peeking up at her from the top of a large envelope. *Will.*

Did he really keep his will up here, in a random box? Perhaps. This was Peter Holstein, after all, who could make a mess of a perfectly organized desk in ten seconds. She pulled out the envelope and opened it, pulled out the papers.

A will, yes. But his father's, not his. Still. She read through it, not surprised to learn that Aksel Holstein, after stipulating that his wife be cared for should she outlive him, left everything to his only son, Peter Holstein. Kensey Manor and the four hundred acres surrounding it.

"Four hundred acres?" A few choice words came to her tongue at that, though she bit them back. But really, who could afford four *hundred* acres? When she could scarcely afford four hundred square feet a month in London?

Then came the question she knew Peter would ask — was this proof enough that his family owned the property? That his father had willed it to him? Would it suffice in place of a deed?

She knew nothing about that side of the legal system, but she suspected the answer was no. Still, she'd put the will aside for him. Unless, of course, it had something in it of interest to Mr. V.

She kept reading. It mentioned Kensey and its property, which was no surprise. All his funds, which were not enumerated, presumably because he wouldn't know, when he'd drawn up this will, exactly what his worth would total. But he had a few exceptions that gave her a clue. She counted no fewer than six chunks of thousand-plus pounds to be donated to various churches and charities.

She turned the page and sucked in a

breath. *To my son, Peter, I also bequeath the bulk of our remaining possessions in Germany, including . . .*

Her eyes bulged as she read. Peter Holstein owned considerable acreage in Germany. It wasn't just whatever his German cousin's grandmother apparently rented. He owned another house — no, *two* houses, one in the country and one in Berlin. He owned majority stock in a German steel mill she'd never heard of.

No wonder Kensey wasn't large, as manors went. The Holsteins had by no means relinquished their roots in Germany. They were still there. They were still earning them money. They were still . . .

Blast. Her eyes went blurry, though it was only because of the dust, nothing more.

Sniffling, she shoved the will back into the envelope and thumbed quickly through the rest of the documents with it. Nothing about naturalization. Nothing that she'd have to decide whether to hide or to present to him.

A decision she didn't want to make.

She had to get out of this stuffy, dusty, godforsaken attic before it suffocated her. She slapped the envelope onto the floor for easy finding next time and shoved the rest of the box back onto its shelf.

Perhaps she was quiet on her way down or perhaps she was loud. She couldn't rightly say. She only cared about getting *out*. Out into the fresh air and the warm sunshine. Out into the birdsong and the blue skies. She stomped through the gardens, over the lawn, onto the path that wound through the heather. Away from the wood, the Penroses' property, toward the cliffs.

The waves crashed on the shore as she reached the clifftops. The sun beat down, as furious as the waves. And the wind whipped her, ruining her hair but soothing her face.

Blast it all. Blighted man. She had . . . she must have begun to think him innocent of these charges. Hand in hand with the thoughts that it didn't matter if he *were* loyal to Germany was that deeper, more foundational thought — that Mr. V was simply wrong. Because loyalty to one's country was a virtue, and Peter Holstein was swimming in virtues. Therefore, Peter Holstein was loyal to his country. That he was a British subject as he insisted, that she'd find evidence of it eventually. He was a man who loved his country.

But he had two countries. What was that thing he himself had quoted to her in a letter two weeks ago? A Bible verse, though she couldn't have said from where in that intimidatingly large book it came. Somewhere in the new part, where Jesus spoke, she was fairly sure. Because it had been Jesus — who, Peter had pointed out, was just a poor carpenter by trade, friends with fishermen — who said it. *Where your treasure is, there your heart is also.*

Peter Holstein's treasure was still more in Germany than England. His heart was therefore, by his own admission, in Germany too.

She sank to the cliff top, the muscles in her legs soaking up the warmth of the rock on which she perched, her gaze traveling out to sea, past the gulls circling and shouting at one another. Somewhere on the other side of that sea, beyond the ocean that swallowed a quarter of the globe, was a whole other continent. Somewhere, beyond where those waters circled around to the other side of England, was *the* Continent, filled with countries people talked about on the tube as if they were neighbors.

She'd never go to any of them. That was all right. She'd never felt a need to travel, had never been away from London until this job. But people like Peter Holstein kept that world at their fingertips — he could go anywhere and travel in style. He could afford a leisurely tour of the Continent or a transatlantic crossing on some luxury ship to see the Colonies. He could go anywhere, he could do anything.

Her fingers flexed against the rock, found a pebble, and gripped it. She would find the evidence Mr. V wanted, she would give it to him . . . but he didn't really need to have Holstein arrested, did he? It would serve no purpose to imprison him or . . . what did they do to traitors?

What if they weren't just going to arrest him? What if they meant to kill him? The world would be a poorer place without Peter Holstein. She swallowed, or tried to, and blinked. She hadn't considered it when she accepted this job — that by doing it successfully, she could be sentencing a man to death.

She was a thief, not a killer. Why hadn't she thought more deeply about what she was signing up for?

Peter had admitted it was a man called Jasper in London who was out to prove him German. But it had to be Mr. V behind it all, didn't it? Or working with the culprit. If she found evidence that he was, in fact, an English subject, no doubt Mr. V would want that too. Perhaps he meant to destroy it, to destroy Peter no matter what.

But who said she had to let him? She

would just leave Peter with copies of anything she found. A letter when she left. A letter warning him to leave too.

The breath she dragged in tasted of sunshine and salt and a pervasive loneliness, and she tossed the pebble out as far as she could, until it fell to oblivion. Just like the thoughts she hadn't realized were hopes. The prayers that would amount to little more than vapor.

He could go back to Germany or into hiding somewhere else. She would go back to London. And that would be that. Her duty done. And this bizarre friendship relegated to the place it surely belonged.

Into nothingness.

Peter wandered into the dining room on Monday morning, his brain still working over the problem he'd realized existed in his plot yesterday evening, his tongue longing for his morning coffee. By rote, he looked around the room for Rosemary or for evidence that she'd been there. None. The cups were all still stacked on the sideboard, the toast and porridge obviously untouched.

She only ate breakfast one day out of three — and barely touched her luncheon those days she did. But he'd at least finally convinced her that when she did partake, she could do so in here. There was no point in Grammy making up a tray when Rosemary could just come in and help herself.

Mrs. Teague had pressed her lips against her displeasure when he'd informed everyone of that. But at least she'd not given voice to it.

He poured his coffee, selected his toast and some fruit. And wished Rosemary were in here now. Her perspective always helped him work through these dratted plot problems, even though she had no idea that was what they were discussing. He'd simply pose his questions as if they dealt with real issues — issues from the news, perhaps. And then just let her chatter.

Her chatter never failed to make him see things in whole new ways. Which meant Locryn was having his horizons expanded in unexpected ways too, thanks to Rosita.

Peter smiled, sipped his coffee, and reached for the newspaper waiting by his plate. The smile died the moment he opened it up. No smile could persist in the face of that headline. ARCHDUKE FERDINAND ASSASSINATED!

The words nearly blurred as he read through the article and then read it again. He flipped through the rest of the paper too, though precious few other articles dealt with this earthquake.

His world shook though, without question. He felt the tremors. And they brought him to his feet, breakfast forgotten.

He was running by the time he reached the library. Rosemary sat at her table, window open at her side and book open before her. Unperturbed.

Not for long. "It's the archduke." He had to pause for a breath. "Archduke Ferdinand of . . . of Austria-Hungary. He's been k-killed."

Her lips were moving through whatever German text she read. She held up a finger.

Peter chuffed. "Did you . . . not hear me?"

"Sorry." She looked over at him. Frowned. "Not really. The arch-what who of where has been what?"

At least she was listening now. He leaned onto the end of her table. "Ferdinand. Killed."

She blinked.

He chuffed again. "Heir to the . . . the Austro-Hungarian throne!"

"Oh." She slipped a marker into her page, but her face was all wrong. It showed simple, distant sorrow, not panic. Not urgency. "Well, that's sad, isn't it? Wasn't he the one who married that poor aristocrat, even though no one approved?"

"Sophie . . . yes. She was . . . was with him. And killed as well."

Her sorrow deepened, but it was still far too simple. "That *is* sad. Their poor children."

Peter shook his head. "More like the . . . the poor world."

She graced him with that lifted-brow look of hers that questioned his sanity. "Was he that good a leader? Or that good a man?"

"It's not that." Breath leaking out, he pulled out a chair and slumped into it. Maybe it was the writer in him who saw dominoes falling from this. Maybe it was nothing but imagination. Maybe, God willing, there would be a simple reckoning. "It was . . . was Bosnians. With the Black Hand."

Now her brows drew down in that way that said she was trying to remember when and where she'd heard the name. "I thought the Black Hand is . . . Serbian, isn't it? It was mentioned in one of these books somewhere . . ." She shuffled the tomes, her pages of notes.

He stilled her hand with his. "Yes. Serbian — the organization is. Austria has . . . has already issued a statement. That Serbia must . . . take responsibility."

The rest of her went still along with her fingers. "Do you think they will?"

Did he? No, though he would pray it would happen. Pray the Austrian demands were reasonable. Pray the Serbs could appease them. But he shook his head.

She reclaimed her hand and rubbed it over her temple. "What happens if they don't?"

"I can't . . . say with certainty." But he had his suspicions. The more powerful Serbia grew, the more impatient Austria-Hungary grew with her. Tensions had been rising in that region for decades. How much would it really take to set off a powder keg? "I fear . . . I fear Austria may declare war. On Serbia."

Rosemary winced. "But Austria-Hungary is allied now with Germany, aren't they? Would that mean, do you think . . . ?"

He nodded. "It could. But Serbia . . . Serbia is allied with . . . with Russia."

Now she saw the dominoes — the panic of them settled in her eyes. "And Russia has entered into an agreement with Britain. Britain with France."

"The T-Triple Entente." That was what they were calling it. Not a military pact by any means, but the whole purpose of it was to pledge support against Germany. Peter closed his eyes briefly against the headache ready to pound.

He needed to pray about all this. He needed to pray for wisdom, because he knew without a doubt that a letter would be arriving in the next few days from King George.

This one wouldn't be warning him about *his* potential lot — the king had already stepped out on a limb to do that. It wouldn't ask him for advice — he was no military or political counselor. But it would ask him for prayers. It would ask him if he had any spiritual insight.

Would that he'd have something to give beyond *I pray this isn't as bad as I fear it could be.*

He pushed back to his feet. "I need a . . . a walk. Interested?"

She sighed and surveyed the mess of books on her table. "I should really stay here and buckle down. The shelves are finished, and though I haven't found those journals, I could possibly piece something together from all this, as many pages as your father and grandfather have marked. Then there's the attic — the journals could be there. Or those documents you need, at least. I need to search the attic."

It would all be there still in an hour

though. "Please?"

She drew her bottom lip between her teeth, stared at the books a minute more. Then stood with a sigh. "All right. But remember you're the one who pulled me away from it, though by all accounts this research just got a bit more pressing, don't you think?"

He could manage only half a smile. Perhaps a quarter. Because while it was good to have a friend so dedicated to helping him protect his name, it was terrible that it needed such protection. "I'll . . . help you. Read."

"Oh?" She shot a glance toward his study door. Closed.

She had a point. He had a deadline. But there was no way he could write today. None. Perhaps, if he focused today on these fears and on giving them to the Lord, then creativity would whisper back tomorrow. He shrugged. "It'll . . . keep. A day."

Most days, she would have gotten that sly smile on her face, would have asked, *What will keep?* Today she apparently knew he was incapable of jesting. She simply nodded and reached for something on another chair. Her hat — she didn't usually wear it for the short walk to the house, but it was Monday after all. She'd go straight to the village after she was done.

She put it on as she followed him to the door. Once in the hall, when he offered his arm, she tucked her hand into its spot in the crook of his elbow.

A *sniff* echoed down the hall. He didn't have to turn to know Mrs. Teague was there, and she was glaring at them. Well, at Rosemary.

Rosemary didn't turn either. Just rolled her eyes and called over her shoulder, "And you have a lovely morning too, Mrs. Teague!"

Another day, he may have chuckled over it. Today he just led her toward the rear exit, into the garden. And through it, toward the trees. He needed towering trunks and limbs today, to remind him that there was Someone always over and above him. Then perhaps later, the wild expanse of ocean to remind him that he was just one small part of this world. That his country was just one small island. That all these men who thought they controlled the tides of nations were subject to the tides of nature, set in place by One far more powerful than any archduke or king.

"Have you . . . have you had *any* luck? With my family . . . history?"

She sighed. "I have established that both

your father and grandfather had more than a passing acquaintance with England's royal family. But the books don't tell me *why.* Or why your father returned to Germany for his bride. And they certainly don't mention Holstein citizenship."

And those were, of course, the crucial questions. "Their . . . journals. Have to be there . . . somewhere."

"Well, until we find them . . ." She looked up at him, her brow creased. "I did find your father's will, in the attic. Though I doubt it would suffice."

He doubted it too, so said nothing.

The breeze stirred as they put their feet to the wooded path. Peter pulled Rosemary to a halt. "Do you . . . do you smell that?" Cigarette smoke. Again.

She waved it away. "I often do. Rather unpleasant compared to the scents of nature, I grant you."

"It's not . . . not any of our people." At this time of day he knew exactly where all his employees were — he could in fact look over his shoulder and see all the men not employed in the house in the paddock, exercising the horses, or there in the garden with Mr. Teague.

It wasn't one of his people. But whoever it was, they were out here — *now.* And close

— the smell was a sharp sting rather than a faint brush.

Rosemary frowned. "That bloke you pointed out in the village, do you think? The one in the bowler? I looked for him last Monday, but I didn't see him. Does he smoke?"

"I don't . . . know." He removed Rosemary's hand from his arm. "Stay . . . stay here."

"Oh, don't be an idiot." Rather than move behind, she pushed in front, turning into the wind, into the smell.

A second later he heard a strange *twang*. And then her sharp, infuriated scream blistered him.

Eighteen

When she staggered back, Peter saw what had elicited the scream, though it took his befuddled brain a long moment to make sense of the lengthy, slender stick that seemed to have attached itself to her shoulder.

An arrow. He was seeing the shaft of an arrow. She'd been shot. "Rosemary!" He reached to catch her as she stumbled into him, but her feet tangled with the roots. The only thing he could do was break her fall, make sure she eased down rather than crashing upon the thing and making it worse.

She loosed another scream, but it didn't sound simply pained. It sounded absolutely furious. "Come out and face us like a man, you coward!" Her fingers curled around the shaft — it was only then he noticed the fluttering white rectangle the thing had pinned to her body — and pulled.

Pulled. As if she'd just yank the thing directly from her own shoulder. Which might be the right thing to do, but how were they to know? He'd never studied how to treat an arrow wound. It hadn't ever seemed relevant. "S-Stop." He covered her hand with his. The white crinkled under their hands.

Paper.

Crunch. Swish. They both looked up, but the figure beating a hasty retreat through the woods was nothing but dark pants and a white shirt and trees getting in the way. But dark hair — not the grey of Jasper's man. Why did that make terrible dread curl up in his belly?

Not Jasper's man. Just like the fire. A local then, most likely.

"Stop! Get back here, you blighted coward, and look me in the eye!" Rosemary struggled to stand.

Peter held her down. "Don't b-be an idiot!" And here he was calling a young woman, a friend, an idiot. His mother would box his ears. But it was a valid accusation just now.

Blood was seeping out, staining her once-white shirt. The white rectangle of paper. She didn't look down to see it. "I'm gonna find you! And you're gonna regret ever tangling with Rosemary Gresham, you cursed fool!"

The man's crashing through the underbrush faded into nothing. Peter thought that perhaps then she'd sag. Realize she was in pain.

Instead, she tried again to stand. "Of all the blighted, archaic things — a dashed *arrow*? Are you Robin Hood, you blazing coward?" This last she said at a yell again, aiming it at the now-silent trees.

And she did that thing again — pronouncing *archaic* with a *ch* sound instead of a *k*.

He wasn't about to correct her, not this time. Not when her blood seeped a little faster with every move she made. And why hadn't he ever researched how to deal with arrow wounds? He was a dashed adventure novelist, he should know these things. "Will you p-please be still? You're . . . you're making it worse."

"How in blazes can I make it worse? He *shot me.* With a blighted *arrow*!" She raised a hand again, probably to grab once more for the shaft. But her fingers shook.

He gripped them before she could grab the wood. "I daresay he . . . he wasn't aiming for you."

Only when she went still, her gaze latched upon him, did he realize she'd still been

429

straining against his arms, trying to rise. "Do you think he was aiming for *you*?"

He pressed her hand to her stomach and reached for the shaft. For the paper pinned to her shoulder. Carefully he tore it free. "I think . . . I think he was aiming for a . . . a tree."

"Well, he missed."

"Yes." And if ever he learned who did it, there would indeed be a reckoning. "Come. Carefully. I'll . . . I'll help you up." The arrow itself probably helped keep the blood from doing more than this trickle, but they had to get her home.

Mumbling and grumbling and growling words no lady should know — but which he could hardly begrudge her just now — they got to their feet. She swayed a bit once she stood upright, which only made the anger snap back into her eyes.

She snatched the paper out of his hands, no doubt to compensate. "Give me that. Let's see what message was so important that he had to shoot me to deliver it."

He didn't want to see. Not now, when she was standing there like a poor hedgehog, that long shaft her sole spine. Not knowing it would be some message against *him*. His fault, then, that she'd been injured.

Dear Lord, touch her. Keep her well.

She unfolded the paper with the arm opposite the arrow. " 'Someone should tell the Black Hand they missed one.' Oh, for the love of — you're not even Austrian!"

Their gazes met. He drew in a breath.

She spewed one out. "No. I don't even care if anyone's sending messages to him. We're not going to go rushing in like a bunch of blighted heroes to make sure that old man's all right."

Maybe *they* wouldn't — seeing to this wound was priority. But someone had to. Mr. Arnold had no one but his servants to make sure he was well, and what if someone had found him on one of *his* walks?

He slid an arm around her waist, on her uninjured side. Though she'd probably never admit in a century that she needed anyone to lean on, he wasn't taking any chances of her falling over and making the wound worse.

Her arm looped his neck, every bit as bony as it looked. And she glared at him. "You're too blasted good for your own good — you realize that, I hope."

"Ready?" He looked down the two inches into her eyes, trying to find the pain beneath the anger, so that he could measure it.

What he saw was the eyes of his friend, brown and as clear as jasper. Hurting because of him. He gripped her waist — too slender, too strong — and held that too-sparking gaze when he would usually have looked away. "Rosemary. I . . . I'm sorry."

Her bony fingers curled into his jacket. Into his shoulder. "It's not your fault, Peter. None of this is your fault."

He'd brought her into this, hadn't he? It had never occurred to him, when he'd hired the stranger from London with blades for shoulders, that she'd be injured because of her work for him. He should have sent her back to Town that first day.

He set his gaze on the path. Drew in a long breath. And was glad, despite it all, that she was here.

Rosemary marched into the village with fury enough to make up for the weakness she had denied feeling as she'd met Peter's concerned gaze and insisted that, yes, she would still go to the pub tonight. Her shoulder was bandaged, and though she'd changed her shirt — she'd been tempted not to, just to make a point of it — the bleeding hadn't quite stopped by the time she'd done so. New stains had soaked through the linen.

Good. The mood she was in, she needed to shock the whole blasted village, and this seemed a fine way of doing it. Summer's long light was still bathing the land in gold when she shoved open the door to the pub and stomped in.

A gasp, and a clatter. It came from the right, but she kept her eyes trained on the echoing gasp from the bar, where Eseld tossed down a towel and made to round the wooden counter. "Rosemary! What happened?"

"What happened?" It wasn't Eseld responsible, that she knew. But someone here was, or knew the someone who was, or could *find* the someone who was, and in a village this small, word traveled. Let it. "I'll tell you what happened. Some blighted idiot who thinks himself Robin Hood shot me with a blighted arrow!"

"*Shot* you?" Eseld froze at the end of the bar, then rushed forward. "Who would do that?"

"Now that's a good question, isn't it?" Stopping her friend with an outstretched arm — her bad one, just because she knew she couldn't contain the wince, and just because she wanted everyone to see it. "I don't know who in this supposedly God-fearing village decided it sounded like a fine idea to be medieval and shoot a stupid message at Peter Holstein, but he ought to have done more target practice before he tried it. Because now he's gone and made me angry — and you don't want to see Rosemary Gresham angry. Do you hear me?" This she shouted at the room at large. "You want Robin Hood, I can show you Robin Hood!"

"Rosie . . ." Eseld eased forward another step.

Rosemary's nostrils flared. Only her family called her Rosie — and much as she liked Eseld, she wasn't family. She hadn't earned that right. Shaking her head, she backed up a step. "No. I just took a blighted arrow in the shoulder, because some idiot thinks Peter Holstein is his enemy. Well, he's wrong. But he's earned *me* as one, and he's going to regret it. Because I'm not nearly as nice as Mr. Holstein is."

Footsteps, light and harried, and then Betty rushed to Eseld's side. Concern darkened the circles ever present under her eyes. "I'll help you! I'll help you find who did it — I owe Mr. Holstein everything."

Blast. She didn't want to go soft, not now — but Betty didn't need to be involved in this.

Someone else stood up from a booth in the corner. A man, though she couldn't remember his name just now. "We'll all help. He did right last week — he's not our

434

enemy. None of us thinks he is, not anymore."

Someone else snorted. "Well, *some* might still. But we'll talk to them, Miss Gresham. We will. If they did this, they'll pay. And if it's *not* one of ours, then we'll find out straightaway and run them out of Cornwall."

She had her doubts, when it came down to it, that any of these people would turn on their own — or that they really considered Peter one of their own, to stand for him against a stranger. *She* surely wasn't to be counted among them.

But she'd made her point. And she couldn't well afford to go tearing out of here and do what she wanted — get a name and then steal every blasted thing the idiot belonging to that name held dear. All that would accomplish would be to land her in the cell next to Tim's.

So she spun on her heel and marched back out the door, and she ignored the calls of Betty and Eseld as she went. She'd get back to Kensey, she'd go into her cottage, and she'd go to bed. She'd let the pain have its say. She'd take the aspirin Grammy had given her, but which Rosemary had only stuffed into a pocket.

Those men in the pub had a point though.

As she blinked away a haze edging toward dizziness and strode out of the village along that too-narrow road, she knew they did. Peter *had* won the hearts of plenty of villagers last Saturday night. The very ones she'd have thought most apt to hate him — the common people — now thought him a champion, if not a friend.

But for every ally he'd made, he'd made an enemy too. Those with a claim to gentle blood had been grumbling all the louder about him. Those like his adversary in London. For all she knew, that was Mr. Jasper's goal all along — to seed unrest against him even here. To send in men with shadowy purposes meant only to rouse the disquiet of the people.

Men like that stranger in the bowler. Or, if Jasper was linked to Mr. V, *her.*

Her stomach went wobbly. Mr. V had employed her as a thief — something everyone would label a lowlife. What *other* kinds of criminals would he employ? Thugs? Vandals?

Assassins?

Her blood chilled. Her breath felt heavy, made the distance between her and rest stretch into forever. What did she really know of her employer? What was he capable of? How deeply did his distrust of — or even hatred for — Peter Holstein go?

She rounded a bend in the road, her attention snatched by a woman on a bicycle. Or rather, a woman *not* on a bicycle who obviously wanted to be. The large basket on the front seemed to have come unattached and spilled her packages all over the road, and now the woman struggled to fasten it into place and hold up the bicycle as well.

Something she could help with easily enough. And frankly, a distraction from her current thoughts would be welcome indeed. So she called out, "Just a moment, I'll give you a hand!" and trotted in that direction.

Or perhaps *not* so welcome — Mrs. Teague looked up from her task, and the relief on her face changed to a sneer as fast as the wind could whip off the Atlantic. "I don't need any of *your* help."

"Oh, really? Evidence says otherwise." She ought to just leave her to fumble — it would serve her right. But then, it would irritate her more if she insisted on helping. Rosemary strode over to the wobbling bicycle and gripped the handles.

Mrs. Teague's glare would have been more biting had her hat not gone askew and were tendrils of grey hair not plastered to her face and neck in the late-June heat. The woman glanced once at Rosemary's blood-stained shoulder, but it didn't seem to soften her any. "I don't. Need. Help. Especially from someone bleeding all over herself."

Rosemary pasted a cheery smile onto her lips and ignored the way her shoulder throbbed down into her arm. "Looks like what you need is a screwdriver to get that basket to stay on. Do you have one?"

Mrs. Teague looked fit to snarl. "Does it *look* like I have one? Why would I have one?"

"Because a girl never knows when she might need something like that." Using a hip to hold up the bicycle, Rosemary opened the handbag she'd had looped over her good arm and fished about inside until she came up with the little screwdriver.

The lock picks she left securely in the bottom, wrapped in their scrap of muslin that matched the lining of her bag.

Mrs. Teague, of course, didn't take it. "I don't need your tool."

Was it possible to be in this woman's presence and not roll her eyes? "You know, I'm all for stubbornness. Really, I am. Until it just makes you look stupid, at which point you ought to say thanks and tighten your blighted screw back into place."

"Stupid now, am I?" Knuckles white around the handlebars, Mrs. Teague bared

438

her teeth. "Go back to Kensey. Better still, go back to London, you hussy. No one wants you here."

Her shoulder pulsed, sending pain all down her arm. And probably making her face go red — unless of course it had gone white with all that blood surging toward the aching limb. Rosemary gritted her teeth. Telling herself to just stomp away and leave the woman to her own devices. Telling herself to point out that Peter *did* want her here, so take *that.*

Telling herself that the burning in her eyes was from her dratted shoulder, not the words spoken by a woman she didn't even like.

No, she wouldn't be so weak. Not over the likes of Mrs. Teague. Holding her anger tight, Rosemary shook her head and dropped the screwdriver back into her handbag. "What the devil is the matter with you? You've hated me from the moment I showed up, though heaven knows why. What is it about me that you despise so, huh?"

"I don't *hate* you." Though her voice fair to dripped hatred. "I don't *despise* you. You're not worth it."

Rosemary was eight again, standing on a filthy street, her shoes stolen by older urchins, along with her coat. Shivering in the winter wind and looking up at the irate woman brandishing a broom, ready to smack her for going through the rubbish bins in the alley, looking for scraps. *"You don't deserve any,"* the woman had said. *"Get you gone, you worthless rat."*

Her fingers curled into her palm. Maybe she *was* worthless, by rights — but not anymore. What God and society hadn't seen fit to give, Rosemary had taken for herself. And she wouldn't let some self-righteous cow ruin it.

Sneer in place, Rosemary stepped away. "It must make Peter proud, seeing how loving his people are to a stranger."

Mrs. Teague's red face mottled. She lifted a finger, waved it. "I knew it! I knew what you were about, I saw it from the first! Calling him *Peter,* as if you've any right to do so."

"What in blazes are you talking about?" She didn't mean to shout it, it just came out that way.

"I know your kind. Nothing but a money-grubber, that's what. Thinking to come into the house of some wealthy gentleman who everyone knows is awkward in society and . . . and seduce him!"

Rosemary, mouth agape, just blinked. Blinked again. Then untangled her tongue.

"I beg your pardon?"

Mrs. Teague let the bicycle fall and came forward to poke that offending finger into Rosemary's chest. "I won't stand for it, do you hear me? That boy's like a son to me, and if his sainted mother were here, she'd say the same. Peter Holstein is too good for the likes of you!"

"You think I don't *know* that?" And where had *that* come from? Disgusted with herself as much as with the housekeeper, Rosemary shook her head and took a step away. "I'm not after his blighted money, nor to . . . to *seduce* him, or marry him, or whatever else you think I mean to do. I'm here to do a job. Nothing more, nothing less."

And she'd do well to remember that herself. She was here to do her job, not to make friends. Pivoting, she pointed herself in the direction of Kensey Manor again.

Mrs. Teague was on her heels, a dog growling over a bone. "Oh, and you expect me to believe that, do you? A job, she says. As if long walks to the cliffs are part of your *job.* Or trips to St. Michael's Mount. Or rides into the village. Or going to a *ball* with him —"

"You know what?" Her body felt strangely heavy. Or maybe light. Or perhaps just a bit wobbly, like Mrs. Teague's discarded bicycle. She lifted her good arm. Or meant to. Pointed. Maybe. "I don't care what you think. I don't need your approval. I just need you to stay out of my way so I can . . . so I can . . ."

The world went blurry around the edges. Tilted a bit. Or perhaps more than a bit. And what was the ground doing, rushing up like that to meet her?

She blinked, trying to clear away the fuzziness. Trying to figure why she felt so blasted heavy. Or light. Or wobbly.

"Rosemary?"

She blinked again — but it was the kitchen ceiling at Kensey staring back at her, not the evening sky. Peter's voice in her ear, Peter's fingers about hers, not the condemning tones of Mrs. Teague. She lifted a hand to her forehead. "What happened?"

Peter sighed. His hair was falling over his forehead, a golden wreck in need of a trim, and his shirtsleeves were rolled up. Blood — her blood — still dotted his waistcoat. "Did you . . . did you eat today?"

Eat? "Of course. I had . . ." But she hadn't had breakfast, not after last night's big dinner. She'd been waiting for luncheon.

But they'd gone out for that walk before luncheon. And then this blighted arrow, and the doctor had come, and Grammy had been fussing, and Rosemary had just wanted out of the house, away from all the bother, and . . . and she'd thought she'd eat in the pub, after she'd had her say, but stomping out had felt more dramatic. So . . . "I may have forgotten."

A bit of a smile teased the corners of his mouth. Just the corners. Just enough to, somehow, draw attention to that cleft in his chin that Elinor would love. He pushed a steaming cup her way, and then a plate full of sweets. "You . . . you fainted. On the road. Mrs. Teague . . . had to fetch us . . . to fetch you back."

It was the bleeding, that must be what had done it. She had no problem going without food for a day under normal circumstances. But her shoulder had leaked too much of her energy away, apparently. She reached for the cup but, given the shaking of her hand, thought better of it and lifted a fairing instead. The sweet ginger biscuit tasted like nothing to her tongue, felt too dry, even though she knew well Grammy was a master of fairings.

Blast it all. She swallowed the tasteless bite and sat forward until she could rest her forehead on the worn, smooth surface of the table. "My shoulder hurts."

"I know." His hand came to rest against

her hair.

Those stupid tears burned again. She could handle electro-magnetic alarms. Security dogs. Museum guards. She could handle disregard. Distrust. Outright hatred. But she wasn't at all sure she could handle him being so blasted *nice.*

NINETEEN

Rosemary breathed in one more long breath of the fresh air spilling through the window and then told herself to get back to work. She had only another hour in the day before she'd have to stop anyway and go dress for dinner. The Penroses were coming over to dine with them, and her mind was already going over the gown waiting in the cottage rather than the books still waiting in the library.

That wouldn't do. She turned from the window, straightened, and fastened her gaze on the shelves. They were ordered now, and she'd done a fine job of it, if she did say so herself. There was something rather alluring about that many books marching across the shelves in neat lines, their spines all ordered and even.

Mostly even. She frowned as she viewed the books in the middle shelf of the third case. From this angle, they looked as if they stuck out farther than the books above and below, though they were all part of the same set. Matching spines, identical dimensions. Why then were they out a full half-inch more?

Perhaps she'd left something behind them on the shelf? She pursed her lips and strode that direction. Pushed on the spines.

Flush with the back of the bookcase. So why . . . ?

It must be the back of the case itself that was uneven. But that made precious little sense. The whole unit was built as one, flush against the wall. Unless . . . unless.

Her hands shook as she pulled the books off the shelf — careful to keep them in the correct order — and then ran her hands over the wooden back. It lined up perfectly, as all the others did. It surely didn't have —

It did. Her fingernails could just catch under the edge of the wood, though by rights it shouldn't have been a separate panel back there. It should have been one with the rest of the backing. But it wasn't. And as she prodded at it, that piece of wood popped easily, smoothly out.

Her breath caught. She pulled the piece of wood away.

The small door of a safe stared back at her. It had no combination, just a key hole.

She would need the picks in the bottom of her bag — no, she wouldn't. No need to pick what she had a key for. Her breath coming fast, she dashed to that low shelf, the one on which she'd sat a few miscellaneous items. The book on library organization. A few slips of paper that she'd have to give to Peter to file away somewhere. And that small silver key.

A few seconds later, she found it to be a perfect fit. And a few seconds after that, she was staring at what Peter would call treasure. Two stacks of four journals, leather-bound and aging. Feeling a bit like Locryn James had when he pulled out that missing artifact from a hidden tomb in the Orient, Rosemary reached in and slid them out.

She held answers in her hands. Though flipping them open made her excitement turn to exasperation. It was written in that gibberish — the same as those notes she'd found. What was it? And how was she to read it?

She wasn't. But in this case, she had reason to ask Peter to explain. Two of the journals clasped to her chest, she dashed to the door connecting their rooms and pounded upon it.

When he didn't answer straightaway, she knocked again. And again. Then gave up for a while and went back to the journals. Surely some of it was in English or German. Surely. But much as she searched the tomes, she found precious little she could interpret herself. A few words or sentences here and there.

And time was ticking away. Back and forth she went, from door to table, until the clock on the mantel told her she had no more time to indulge him.

Rosemary gave in to the urge to tap her foot. Just once, before it occurred to her that it was something Mrs. Teague would have done. She shifted the stack of leather-bound books to her other arm — the one that had been shot was mostly healed after two weeks, but it couldn't quite hold the same weight as her good arm for long periods of time. And glanced at the clock.

The Penroses would be here for dinner in twenty minutes. If Peter didn't open that door soon . . .

Her fingers rapped on the wood again, pounding.

Still no blasted answer. Though there was no *click-clack-ding* coming from his study. Hadn't been for the past hour, but would the man answer her? No. She'd think him not in there, if she hadn't heard him sneeze two minutes ago.

This time she slapped the door with her palm. "Peter Holstein! Open the blighted door!"

Still no answer. Then a faint, "Quiet . . . please."

"Love to, but there's no time. And you'll want to see this." A moment. Two. *Tick. Tock.* She slapped the door again. "Peter!"

Nothing.

A growl formed in her throat. "Peter, I am coming in, so if you need to hide any treasure maps or stolen relics or whatnot, I suggest you do so now. Five . . . four . . . three . . . two . . . one." She opened the door, half-expecting a landmine to explode when she stepped inside. Or at the very least, for something to be thrown at her.

He didn't even look up. He was at his desk, hunched in a way that was sure to put a crick in his neck, bent over a page of cream-colored stationery on his desk. Tapping his pen against it. "I don't . . . I don't know w-what to . . . to tell him."

She frowned. Not just because he could have opened the blasted door a blasted hour ago if he'd just been staring at a sheet of quarter-filled paper the whole time. But also because she'd scarcely heard him stutter in recent weeks. She eased into the room and slipped the journals onto the corner of his desk. "Who?"

"King George." He said it on a sigh. Shook his head. And folded up the piece of paper he'd been writing upon, slipping it then into his pocket. Finally he looked up at her. And scowled. "Did you come . . . come in without knocking?"

"Do *you* exist on the same planet as the rest of mankind?" She motioned to the tall case clock in the corner. "I've been knocking for an *hour.* You're going to be late for dinner if you don't get up, and I have a surprise to show you before the Penroses arrive, if you can emerge from your own little world long enough to see it."

"Sorry." Scowl erased, he leaned back in his chair and rubbed a hand over his forehead. "What . . . is it?"

She waved a hand at the journals. "See for yourself."

His eyes went wide. "Ah!" He reached for one of the books. "The . . . journals?"

"The journals — though I can't read a one of them. They seem to be in some sort of shorthand."

His brow furrowed as he paged through them. "This will take . . . take forever to decode."

Her heart sank — it must *not* be the same gibberish. But it had looked it to her eyes.

His gaze latched on the clock. "Where did . . . the afternoon go? You should have . . . interrupted me sooner. We could . . . could be late."

Rosemary breathed a laugh. "Why didn't I think of that, I wonder, and start knocking an hour ago?"

He rounded the desk and paused beside her, resting the journal he'd picked up back on its brother. "Where were they?"

She smiled. "Hidden behind a false back to a shelf." She would have to put it to rights tomorrow.

He wore a smile in his eyes, though his lips remained neutral. He motioned to the door. "Good work. I can't . . . can't wait to study them, but . . . it must wait, I suppose. We'd . . . better hurry if we don't want . . . to be late. If you weren't so . . . so oblivious to the time . . ." A grin tugged at the corners of his mouth now.

Rosemary sent her gaze heavenward, exaggerated, and waved him on. "You go ahead. I need to make a quick note first." She hefted the books again and scurried back into the library. She set these few journals beside the stack of others on her table and then turned back to his study.

He'd gone already. But had left both his doors open, which generally meant that the

451

room was due for a cleaning. Which she should have known when she saw that his desk was tidier than usual.

Though he'd left the stack of stationery out upon it. Her gaze snagged on that, and her breath quickened. Messy as he was, he was always meticulous in the extreme about what he left out for eyes other than his own to see. She'd yet to catch any correspondence on his desk, or anything typewritten. Certainly she hadn't a clue what King George had written to him to require a response that stymied him so.

But he'd left the paper out. Or rather, hadn't thought to move the piece he was writing upon off the stack beneath it. There would be imprints from his pen. Perhaps not strong enough to discern every word, but there could be something of import there.

After glancing at the door to make sure neither Peter nor Kerensa nor the ever-scowling Mrs. Teague lurked in the hallway, she slunk over, lifted the blank sheet off the stack, and then slipped back into the library, silent as a cat, just as the housekeeper's heavy step entered the hallway.

She didn't dare do a rubbing here, where anyone could see her. But she had a pencil in the cottage. So she folded the sheet of paper and slid it into the novel she'd been carrying back and forth with her this week. She had only a chapter left and had thought to finish it today during a break, but hadn't felt like reading. Which worked well enough for her now.

No one so much as passed her as she rushed out of the manor house and nearly ran to the cottage, and no one would have thought anything of her hurry, given the time. To be sure, she had no idea how she would get ready before the Penroses arrived. But her primary purpose here wasn't to enjoy dinner with the neighbors. It was to do her job as outlined by Mr. V.

She told herself this every day. It didn't calm that wiggle inside.

The cottage was summer-warm and welcoming, the small kitchen smelling of the fruit Grammy must have sent over for her. Rosemary's lips twitched. She'd asked for some four days ago. Apparently the cook had just remembered.

Dumping *The Poison Belt* onto the table, Rosemary took the blank sheet from it and ran to the bedroom she'd been using as a makeshift study when doing any work over here. On the desk she had a variety of writing instruments, and she selected a pencil.

Held it as much to the side as possible and rubbed.

Words began to appear. Faint traces of white against the grey-black of the pencil. The date, the greeting. *Dear George . . .*

George. She still couldn't fathom simply writing to the king and using only his first name. She kept her strokes light and steady, and more words appeared.

I have been praying for a fortnight for wisdom. For myself, so that I might give you whatever words you need — and deal with my own troubles, of course. But mostly for you, as you wait and weigh your decisions, which are by all accounts far larger than anything I could face. I know how difficult this is for you. Kaiser Wilhelm is family. I know you wish, as I do, that enmity could simply be avoided.

But the world does not rotate around our wishes. In this world, there is always trouble. There is always war. There is always strife and tragedy and cruelty. You do not need me advising you on what political course to take, I know. And I would not know what to tell you on that score.

What I can tell you, after these weeks of prayer, is this.

Here the words ceased. Rosemary set down her pencil and frowned at the page. Apparently even after a fortnight of prayer, Peter hadn't the words. Not that she would have either, but he didn't usually suffer such a lack when it came to prayer. She highly doubted he agonized every night over what to write to her. But his prayers, scrawled in that familiar script, were always strangely right. And his insight, when he answered the questions she asked about this strange thing he called faith, always made perfect sense.

She picked up the page, carrying it with her to her bedchamber. It would have to be included in her packet for Mr. V. She stored it with the other notes she'd accrued, in a slender folder under her mattress. And then pulled out the evening dress she'd decided on — another of Jenny's old things, done over.

Peter had used it as an example in one of his notes this week. That giving one's life to God was very much like what she'd done with those dresses of Jenny's. It was still the same fabric — still the same basic person. But just as she'd changed the shape and the drape and the seams, God remade the old man into a new one. But unlike the dress, which had no say, people had to choose to put themselves in God's hands. He wouldn't start snipping and sewing against their will.

What he hadn't asked, but which she'd read between his words anyway, was the question underlying his explanation: Did she trust Him enough to be fabric in His hands?

She slipped the satin over her head and watched it drape her in the mirror. And was none too sure. "It's nothing personal, God," she whispered to the mysteries that lived beyond the looking glass. And then frowned at her reflection. "Maybe it is. If you're really there, what's your excuse, huh? What kind of Father leaves His children to the streets?"

She shook her head, shook the questions away, and went to the dressing table to re-pin her hair. She hadn't the time for any fancy arrangement. A simple chignon would have to suffice, though she added the beaded headband to dress it up a bit more.

And that would have to do. She slipped her evening shoes on, opted for leaving her handbag since she was only going to the big house, and was back out the door.

The Penrose automobile was already parked in the circle before the house, empty. And Peter was likely staring into that netherworld of his mind in his room upstairs, having forgotten again that his friends were coming, or perhaps he had given in to the allure of those journals and was poring over them instead of playing host. It would rest on her to entertain them until he shook himself from it, most likely. Not that the Penroses needed to be entertained, precisely. They were arguably more at home here than Rosemary would ever be.

She found them in the drawing room — along with a feeling of rather amused guilt for false assumptions. Peter was there already too, head bent over papers that Penrose still held. The lawyer was pointing to something or another.

Jenny stood at the window but wasn't looking out it. She was frowning at the men. Usually she would be chiding them for focusing on work when it was time for relaxation. And indeed, she opened her mouth. But only said, "Are you quite sure you mean to do this, Peter?"

Do this? Rosemary edged into the room, expecting to go unnoticed, so intent were they all upon whatever Penrose held.

Jenny half-smiled a greeting though, and the men looked up too. Briefly.

Peter's jaw was set in firm lines. "As . . . as sure as I was s-six months ago. M-More."

Rosemary's neck went tight. He was stuttering again. She wanted to ask what they were discussing, but it seemed unnecessary. So she just slid nearer to Jenny.

Jenny's face was pained. "It's only that I want you to have options, just as your parents always did. Not that we'd ever want to see you use them, but if the actions against you here don't let up . . ."

"You th— think it would . . . would be b-better there?" Peter shook his head and took the papers from Penrose's hand. "I am not . . . I am not German. I made my . . . my decision when I was eighteen. I am . . . English. I n-neither need nor . . . nor want this p-property. I just . . . I will not s-sell to just . . . anyone. My c-cousins are concerned. About potential . . . buyers."

Property. The *German* property? Rosemary sank onto a chair, scarcely even noting which one.

Penrose pursed his lips. "I understand, old boy. You know I do — but you must also entertain the notion that your cousins are only looking out for their own best interest, not yours. Certainly not England's. This other stockholder — AGD, apparently — has been up-front about their aims and has, you'll see there on page two, made a most generous offer for your share of the stocks."

Peter's nostrils flared. "That would give

them . . . more than a c-controlling share. It would give them nine . . . ninety percent. N-No one else would have any say. My cousins . . . They could be ousted."

Sighing, Penrose leaned back against his seat. "But your cousins cannot pay fair market price for your shares, Peter. I know you want to be rid of these ties, I know you want to handle it responsibly — but it's still business, and a business in high demand, as one of the only steel mills in Germany not already completely privately owned. You must make the decision based on numbers, not on emotion. Then you can do whatever you like with the money — give it all away, as you've been doing with the profits from it in any case. Fund another orphanage. Build another hospital. Whatever you like — but be smart."

Pushing to his feet, Peter flipped the papers in his hand. She expected him to just pace with them. But his steps were more focused than meandering. He headed straight for her and passed her the first sheet while he looked at the second. "What do . . . what do you think, Rosemary?"

For a moment she could only stare at it. He wasn't objecting to her presence during the discussion but actually inviting her into it? "Oh. Well . . . I don't really know what you're talking about."

Penrose hooked an ankle over the opposite knee and waved a hand. "Peter still owns the family property in Germany, including two houses — one on a rather large plot of ground — and the *pièce de résistance,* controlling shares of a steel mill."

"He has wanted to sell them ever since he realized he owned them, when Aksel died." Jenny's smile was that of an indulgent sister. "But couldn't find the paperwork."

At that Rosemary could hardly resist a snort of laughter. Or deny the relief that settled through her. "I am utterly shocked."

"Be nice." Leaning against the back of her chair, Peter shuffled another page. "I found . . . found them eventually. As I will find . . . the ones for Kensey. And the naturalization documents."

"And it only took him three and a half years." Penrose folded his arms over his chest. "At which point he asked me to assist him in divesting himself of the properties. But during the process, his cousins began telling him of another stockholder buying up shares, which they found quite concerning. Their fear, I believe, is that it's a group aligned with one of the other combined business concerns — the Krupp Company or GHH — that means to incorporate their mill into another in the region and replace all current management with their own. I maintain, however, that this is nothing Peter needs to worry over."

"They are . . . entirely dependent upon it. What . . . what would they do if I . . . sold it out from . . . from under them? If they were forced out?"

Gracious, but he was a good man. He had no business being so good — no one did. Did he never think of himself? Rosemary shook her head and read through the page he'd handed her, though it largely just summed up the situation. Then she answered Peter's question. "Work for someone else, I should say."

"Or." Penrose sat forward again. His face had gone hard. "I know it isn't your usual way, Pete, but you could use that mill for England's benefit. You could shut it down. Cut into the steel production, thereby stunting the outfitting of the German army."

Rosemary had to consciously tell her fingers not to grip the page. He could, of course he could — and England would thank him.

But German mill workers couldn't be so unlike English ones. They were just people trying to feed their families. Families that would go hungry if their work was suddenly taken from them.

"No." Peter didn't even hesitate to let that option sink in. "Much as I . . . as I would like to hinder war, that mill em— employs hundreds of . . . of families. I'll not . . . I'll not be responsible for hurting them."

She looked up and over at him. And found him looking down at her. "You agree with me . . . don't you?" he asked, quietly enough that she knew it was a question for her, not for his friends.

His *other* friends. She was one too. And she nodded decisively. "Entirely. And if war does come, that mill won't sit empty, no matter what you want. It would be seized, your efforts worthless, and who knows who would be in charge of it then? You're right to give it to your family."

"Look at the other offers before you decide that," Penrose advised.

Peter obligingly handed her another sheet of paper, then leaned down to look at it with her.

Her eyes slid over columns and figures and names. The first, from fellow Holsteins, was the lowest by half. Then came a handful of bids all in a similar range, their names nothing more to her than a collection of vowels and consonants.

Then a final one at the bottom, quite a bit

higher than the rest. Which made her scowl. "This AGD is the one that has been buying up stock?" She tapped a finger upon the name.

Gryff nodded. "I know you have questions about that. But for all my research, I cannot link them to the Krupp or GHH. If they are part of a competing firm, they've hidden it well. And so we have no reason to think they'll sack your cousins, Pete." Penrose pushed to his feet and wandered toward Jenny.

Peter stared at those numbers. "I don't . . . I don't like it. No one outbids . . . by so much. Without reason. And I . . . I daresay I wouldn't like . . . like the reason."

"So pick one of the middle offers. Pray over it, as I know you'll do anyway, and try to discern which will help the most people and hurt England the least. But don't just sell to your cousins when they cannot afford the asking price."

Peter took the papers from her hands and folded them up. "But I . . . know my cousins. They are good men. And if I . . . if I sell to someone else . . . *they* will likely just sell out to . . . to AGD."

Penrose sighed and took his wife's hand, tucked it around his arm. "Pete, you'll be the ruination of all your legacy if you continually refuse to think of the bottom line, of profit, of your own gain. So if you won't, I will. You'll take a week or two to consider this, whether you like it or not, because I refuse to communicate a decision until then. And if you try to send it yourself — well, the postmaster and telegraph clerk like me better than you. They'll hold it for me."

Had he said such a thing to Rosemary, she would have snapped at him. Peter, however, just chuckled. And held out a hand to her when Mrs. Teague cleared her throat from the doorway — all the signal they needed to know the meal was ready.

"A week won't . . . won't change my opinion," he said, helping her up and then setting her hand on his arm.

Rosemary rested her other hand there too, atop her first. Silent support.

Penrose grinned. "It might. You never know."

"Give it up, darling." Jenny nodded, somehow making it a dismissal. "And let's talk about something lighter over dinner, shall we? Rosemary, have you finished *The Poison Belt* yet?"

Peter was leading her into the hall as the question reached her. She shook her head but held off answering until they'd filed into the dining room. "I've a chapter left."

"You ought to have a definite opinion by now, then." Penrose and Jenny headed for their usual seats. Gryff's brows lifted. "What do you think of it? I know it isn't quite like Conan Doyle's other Professor Challenger story, but I rather enjoyed the change of pace. Doom looming, but from one's own home rather than some exotic locale." He shot a glance at Peter.

Peter pulled her chair out for her and loosed what sounded half like a laugh and half like that *chuff* he made sometimes.

Rosemary settled in with a shake of her head. "It's ridiculous, in my opinion."

"The premise may be . . . may be a bit farfetched, but . . ." Peter moved to his own chair and, once Jenny was situated, sat.

Rosemary sent him a glare — the comfortable kind she'd never had cause to send anyone but her family before. "I don't mean the premise — though granted, the idea of Earth passing through a belt of poison that will kill us all is absurd. I mean the fact that Challenger thought to warn and hopefully save all his rich little friends and yet he lets his servants pass out in the hallway without even a thought of concern for them."

Penrose frowned. "I hadn't even noticed that. He did, didn't he?"

Peter's expression mirrored his friend's. "I suppose . . . he did."

"Typical thinking from gentlemen, if you ask me." Rosemary opened her napkin half a second before Jenny did and smoothed it over her lap. She had gotten the hang of this fancy-dinner thing — but the minds of the so-called gentle class she would simply never understand. "And if Conan Doyle thinks anything like his character, happy I'll be never to meet the man."

Peter's lips turned up in a lopsided smile. "It's only . . . a story, Rosemary."

She answered by lifting one brow in a lopsided arch. "What happened to fiction being how man expresses his deepest heart?"

Penrose chuckled. It may have been the first time he'd chuckled over something she'd said. "Sounds like your words tossed back at you, old boy. I always knew I liked you, Miss Gresham."

A statement so obviously false that Rosemary couldn't help but laugh too. "To be sure you did, Mr. Penrose. About as much as Mrs. Teague does still."

Peter signaled for the silver domes to be removed from the food. "I only mean that . . . Conan Doyle needn't be . . . be judged based on his characters."

"Oh, you wouldn't judge him, would you? You're so *nice.*" And she smiled, even as she shook her head. "I say that a man's true thoughts likely come out in his stories. And if they do, then Conan Doyle is a snob."

"Rosemary." Jenny's voice may have carried a bit of horror, but it was overshadowed by a healthy dose of amusement. "Don't be rude."

"Why not? He was. And frankly, I find it disturbing that no one else seems to have even noticed this about him. I mean, I know well you three wouldn't treat your servants that way." Peter had dashed into a burning building for one, after all. "But you still don't recognize it."

She didn't really mean it to be an indictment. But silence followed her statement, and her three companions all sat for a long moment as their food was served, staring at their plates and then at each other. Rosemary suffered it while Kerensa slid a plate of fresh greens in front of her with a mute grin, but that was as much as she could take. "Somebody say *something.*"

Jenny opened her mouth.

But it was Peter who spoke first. Quietly and with a smile. "I'm glad you're . . . here, Rosemary. You . . . you make me see the world . . . differently."

It shouldn't have warmed her. Or maybe it should have, given the look Penrose and Jenny exchanged, proving his statement an unusual one. Still. It was a strange realization. And stranger still to realize that *she* was glad of it too. And not just because of Mr. V's pound notes. She was glad because . . . because otherwise she might never have known that a man like him existed. One with a full purse *and* a good heart.

She wondered, after Peter blessed the food, as she ate, what he would do with the money from the German steel mill when he sold it — some sort of charity work, apparently, given Penrose's statement about it. Had he really already done all those things Penrose had mentioned? Funding orphanages? Hospitals? He would do more charity work like that, she knew he would. Supporting missionaries, perhaps — that seemed like him. Spreading the gospel of Christ, as he would say.

Something noble. Something good. And, hours later as she stood with him on the front steps of the manor and waved farewell to the Penroses, she voiced the thought that followed every one of those musings. "Why don't you just tell people what you've done? With the money, I mean. From the steel mill. If you let them know how very good you are, they'll stop suspecting you of being so very bad."

"Will they?" With a shake of his head, Peter lowered the hand he'd been waving and started, for some reason, down the steps. He paused at the bottom and held out a hand. "Come on. It's . . . it's getting dark. I'll escort you home."

It wasn't *that* dark. But she wouldn't argue. Padding down the steps, she put her hand in his, expecting him to tuck it against his arm as he usually did.

He didn't. He just held it as he led her toward the garden path. And he sighed. "Broadcasting my . . . my good deeds . . . will only come off as . . . as trying to convince them. Like a Pharisee."

Two months ago, she wouldn't have had a clue what that meant. Today, she could argue with it. "No one thinks that of you. You are many things, Peter Holstein, but a hypocrite isn't one of them. I just don't understand why you're so secretive. I mean, you're the one who hired a lawyer for Tim, aren't you? Betty said a fancy one from London showed up the other day, offering to represent him at no charge."

Peter took to studying the sky.

She rolled her eyes. "Who else would have

done that? Penrose?"

"He . . . he may have."

"But he didn't. *You're* the one who championed that boy. And everyone in the village suspects you're the one paying for his defense now."

He went stiff beside her, and his fingers tightened around hers. "Do they?"

"It's a good thing, Peter, not a bad." She squeezed his fingers back. Something she would have done to Barclay or Georgie, to Retta or Willa. So why did it feel so different? "The villagers are softening toward you. You only need to keep fostering that. I still say you should write a few editorials for the newspaper or something. Put that typewriter you so love to good use."

His thoughtful hum blended with the trills of a nightingale.

Rosemary listened to the song for a moment, breathed in the riot of scents from the flowers that Mr. Teague tended so carefully. Fastened her gaze on the shadowy form of her cottage at the edge of the garden.

No. His cottage, not hers. His world, not hers. So why had she become so comfortable there? It couldn't be a good thing. It couldn't. Because in another week or month or two, she'd complete her research on the

Holstein family, she'd present her findings to Mr. V, and she'd be gone from this place. Back to London with its fire bells and bobbies' whistles in place of nightingales. With its sewage and unwashed bodies instead of fragrant flowers.

With her family, though. Which was what mattered.

"I do, you know."

She looked over, up at Peter, and had no idea what he did.

His smile said he knew well her mind had wandered. And he didn't mind. "Put my . . . my typewriter to good use."

"Ah." The sunlight had faded, the moon hadn't yet risen, but there was still light enough to see his face. To see that silent question in his eyes. The one that asked if she believed him, and if believing him was enough.

It shouldn't have been. It wouldn't be enough for Mr. V.

But it was enough for Rosemary. She nodded. "I'm sure you do."

"Are you going to ask again?"

The smile in his voice teased out a matching one on her lips. "Actually . . . no. Everyone is entitled to a few secrets, I think." And his couldn't be anything bad. They couldn't be. Because he was Peter.

"Intriguing. What are . . . what are yours?"

She laughed. And yet didn't feel like laughing. She felt — what was that she felt? Something heavy and dark and mournful. "If I told you, they wouldn't be secrets, would they?"

The path led them out of the flowers, to her door. She'd left a light burning in the kitchen — it probably cost him a pretty penny in electricity, but he'd told her she could, on these nights when she was likely to be home late because he knew how she disliked the dark.

They both came to a slow halt. His fingers still clasped hers. "We could trade. Our secrets."

The something inside started smoldering. Burning her from the inside, making her eyes want to tear up to put it out. She shook her head. "No, we can't."

His thumb stroked hers. "Why not?"

Because he was a gentleman. Because he was a good man. Because, more, he was what his Bible would call a *righteous man.* And she was . . .

She was a thief. Sent here to steal his good name.

Unable to meet his gaze, she focused hers on that cleft in his chin that Elinor would love. "Because if you learn mine, you won't like me anymore."

The lips above the cleft didn't quite smile. But they didn't quite not. "Impossible."

She was set to argue. But his other hand lifted and rested against her cheek, and she forgot what it was she'd meant to say. Just as she forgot that she couldn't look him in the eye. She did, and found those eyes, even in the twilight, to be what she'd come to expect — light.

He just looked at her for a long moment, and he leaned a little closer, and she wondered if he was going to kiss her and if she should let him and what it would feel like to have his lips on hers. Would it be sweet, like the strawberries he kept requesting once he learned how she loved them? Warm, like his fingers around hers? Comforting, like the tea he'd had sent in for her one rainy, cool afternoon last week?

Or perhaps blazing and exciting and . . . destructive, like a stable on fire.

Probably the last. And yet, even knowing it, she still wanted to feel it.

His lips settled on her cheek. Lingered in a way that made her pulse far too fast for something so very innocent. Barclay kissed her cheek all the time, as did Pauly and Georgie. But it wasn't like this. They didn't linger. And they certainly never then rested their forehead against hers and held her fingers tightly.

"Impossible," he said again.

It was. But not like he meant.

TWENTY

"Have you given so much as a lick of thought to what you mean to do once she leaves?" Gryff leaned back in his chair, front legs off the ground in a way that would have made Jenny scold him had she seen it.

Peter studied the sheet of paper in his hands and listened to the steady *tick . . . tock* of the clock in the corner of Gryff's office. "Is that . . . really all he knows? He couldn't . . . couldn't follow the money anywhere?"

"She isn't going to stay forever. She can't. She has to work to support her family, and unless you intend to make the librarian role a permanent one, she'll be gone in another few weeks." Flipping a pen between his fingers in a way that Peter never could master, Gryff drilled him with that lawyer-look of his. "You had better start preparing yourself for it. I know how you detest change."

And he hadn't expected to feel the nip of panic when he'd walked into the library and realized Rosemary had been so quick and efficient about it all. Surely he could find something else to add to her list of tasks, to keep her here until . . . until he came up with another way to keep her here.

He returned his gaze to the report from the London investigator. "So how do I . . . how do I know the money went where it should? What if it's not . . . helping Olivia at all?"

"Then you ask Miss Gresham outright and put it in her hands next time. Are you listening to me, old boy? I know you hear me, but are you *listening*?"

"She would refuse it." She was proud, was Rosemary. And stubborn and outspoken and bold and witty and clever, and she looked at things in a way no one else did. He needed her to stay. He needed to hear her opinions, her exasperations. He needed her to point out where his thinking wasn't deep enough, the things he'd forgotten to question.

He needed her.

Gryff sighed and let his chair land back on all fours again. "Listen, Pete. Tensions could erupt on the Continent any moment. You know they could, and who knows what shrapnel will fall this way for you when it does? And if she up and leaves in the middle of it all, which she inevitably will — are you going to be all right? I need to know you will be. I need to know that you'll still fight for your good name when she's gone."

That might depend upon what she discovered about his name, mightn't it? But after demanding a lesson in what was apparently family shorthand — he'd never really paused to realize that Petese had been learned from his father, but it must have been — she'd all but forced him from the library, saying she'd have something worth showing him tonight if he'd just let her work on the journals.

He let her work on the journals.

He tapped the sheet of paper. "This former boss — we're . . . we're sure he knew where to find her . . . her family?"

Gryff, when Peter glanced up again, looked ready to growl. It was from concern, he knew that. Still, Peter was rather glad when a tap upon the door interrupted them. Gryff's next appointment, no doubt.

And Gryff obviously knew Peter's relief — he pointed a finger at him. "We're going to finish this conversation."

"Sure." Peter grinned. "Dreckly." He stood, ready to show himself out.

Another tap on the door, and Gryff said through his blustery sigh, "Yes, Simmons?"

His aide poked his head in. "Mr. Arnold has dropped by, sir."

Peter rather wished the office had a back door. Mr. Arnold had been scowling at him every time their paths crossed since the Midsummer Ball.

Which was no doubt why Gryff said, "Show him in," where he usually would have said to show him in after just a moment, giving Peter time to escape.

As it was, his choice was either to run out and appear utterly devoid of manners, try to pass him in the narrow hall and likely knock the old man's cane from beneath him, or wait here until Mr. Arnold entered, and then take his leave after a polite greeting. "Tyrant."

Gryff gave him an unrepentant smile.

Folding up the sheet of paper from the investigator, Peter stood, ready to make his escape as soon as he reasonably could.

Gryff stood too. "How goes the deadline, by the way?"

Not that he could give much of an answer, what with Mr. Arnold's steady *tap-step* gait coming down the hall. But he nodded. "Nearly . . . finished." Though after Rosemary's observation about *The Poison Belt* last night, he'd lain awake wondering if there was anything he'd written that he oughtn't. Anything he'd never paused to consider. What assumptions he had been making. What she would say if she knew he was Branok Hollow.

What she would have done had he kissed her lips last night, rather than her cheek.

Mr. Arnold's hunched frame filled the doorway. He wore a smile on his wrinkled face today — perhaps he hadn't caught sight of Peter yet.

But no, the old gentleman looked directly at him after a nod to Gryff. "I am glad I caught you, Mr. Holstein. I was hoping I would when I saw you come in."

Peter shifted his weight from one foot to the other and prayed his smile was all it should be. "Nice t-to see . . . to see you, M-Mr. Arnold."

"You have been heavy on my heart." Mr. Arnold shuffled his way to the chair beside the one Peter had just vacated and eased himself to a seat upon it. "I thought I would catch you and see how you are. There have been no more incidents, have there, in the last fortnight?"

Peter shook his head. "All has b-been . . . quiet." His gaze strayed to the silver coin still sitting on the corner of Gryff's desk —

the one with the inverted triangle and concentric circles. All had been quiet, but the threat was still hovering. He cleared his throat. "And w-with you?"

Mr. Arnold glanced toward the desk as well and narrowed his eyes. But his sight wasn't very good, was it? He probably thought it only a florin. Gripping the head of his cane, he looked Peter's way again with his lips together. Peter could never quite find the words to describe the expression, much as he tried. One that managed to convey both hope and sorrow with its simple lines. "Still nothing. I daresay no one considers this old man to be any kind of threat." But his chuckle sounded sad and faded into a sigh. "Young Pomeroy said his father was grumbling in the pub the other day. Something about how you still have such firm ties to Germany."

Peter hadn't remembered that the trouble-maker had a son working for Mr. Arnold — perhaps that, too, contributed to the old gent's safety. If it were locals responsible for the vandalism, either on their own or at the bequest of Mr. Jasper, and if Pomeroy or one of his cronies were leading those efforts, they wouldn't want to risk his son's well-being — or livelihood.

Gryff aimed his smile at Peter. "Well, we

are in the process of —"

"Looking . . . into it." He didn't need Mr. Arnold's opinion. There was no room for debate. He was going to sell it to his cousins, and that was that. He edged toward the door. "I ought t-to go and . . . and r-review it all a . . . again. G-Good day . . . Mr. Arnold. Gryff."

He was out the door as their farewells echoed, and soon out of the building altogether. He really ought to get home. Not that he needed to review the offers again, but he *did* have to finish that letter to King George. And get back to work on his manuscript. Another week or two and it would be finished, ready to send to his publisher.

It wasn't going to end quite like his others had. It couldn't. Rosita wasn't just going to be arrested, as his other villains had been. No, that would never work, not given how Locryn had fallen for her. She was going to have to get away. And he would have to decide if he was chasing her to pursue justice . . . or to pursue his heart.

Peter headed for the open carriage he'd brought today, parked midway between Gryff's office and the hotel. It wouldn't be exactly a cliffhanger — the mystery would be solved, the adventure complete. But the ill-fated love story . . . that couldn't end so simply.

Hopefully readers would like that. Would like seeing deeper feeling in Locryn James than that which was inspired by his quest for adventure, for truth. Peter had certainly enjoyed delving into it, more than he'd thought he would. Had enjoyed digging deep into Rosita's motivations too, making her at once a villain and a heroine.

Mostly a villain. But a villain, he hoped, that people would almost want to root for, if she weren't directly opposed to their hero.

He reached his carriage and prepared to climb up. Then stopped, eyes narrowing. The train must have just arrived at the village station, given the dozen or so people making their way toward the hotel from that direction. And one of those people looked vaguely familiar.

A young woman, perhaps near Rosemary's age. Perfectly average-looking, the kind that struck one as pretty only after one had studied her for a minute and realized she wasn't *not* pretty, so she must be. Broader face than Rosemary's, flatter nose.

Where had he seen her before? Not here, he knew all the villagers. Not in London, no one so normal-looking would ever have stood out to him in London.

Miss Anonymous walked briskly, obviously knowing where she was going. Straight for the hotel. She had one small valise in her hand and a handbag looped over her shoulder. Its strap she clutched, as if afraid someone might try to steal the thing directly from her, just like Rosemary always did. It came, she said, of living in London.

Like Rosemary did. That was it. It was no wonder he cataloged this woman's features only as a contrast to Rosemary's — that was with whom he'd seen her the first time. Abandoning his carriage, he hurried toward the hotel. If Rosemary's sister were back in town, it was either very good news or very bad, concerning Olivia.

Willa, that was who this girl was. The sister closest to Rosemary in age.

He was twenty seconds later entering the hotel than she'd been, which was apparently just enough time for her to have approached the clerk at the counter. As Peter entered, he heard the clerk say, "Good to have you back, Miss Forsythe."

Peter's feet came to a halt. "For . . . Forsythe?" But that made no sense. Perhaps this wasn't Willa.

She turned, gripping both her bags now exactly as Rosemary always did. And when he saw recognition dawn in her eyes, he knew he wasn't wrong.

Though it still made no sense. He cleared his throat and stepped out of the way of the door. "P-Pardon me. You are . . . you are R-Rosemary Gresh . . . Gresham's sister. Are y-you not?"

They looked nothing alike, but the mannerisms were certainly the same, even down to the way she held herself. The lift of her chin as she declared, "That's right. You must be Mr. Holstein."

He nodded, but he couldn't quite wipe away the frown that had overtaken his brows. "But . . . Forsythe?" Was that why he'd had no luck finding Olivia? Was neither Gresham *nor* Parker the family name?

Willa's lips fluttered up in a smile. "Married name."

Oh. Of course, that made sense — she looked to be in her mid-twenties, so a husband was to be expected. Though Rosemary had talked as if all her siblings were still at home.

"Widowed," she added, shifting the bag in her hand. "And not sorry for it, so don't apologize. He was a nasty bloke."

The clerk was frowning too. "You said 'miss.' "

"You wouldn't claim him either, if you could help it." Unfazed, it seemed, by airing such laundry, she turned back to the desk and tapped a finger to the clerk's register book. "My room, if you please? Unless you've a policy against renting rooms to widows of blighters."

The clerk flushed. Peter cleared his throat. "It isn't . . . I-I mean . . . why not s-stay with . . . with Rosemary?" The cottage had plenty of rooms — though he could well imagine Rosemary not wanting to assume having a guest was allowed. She hadn't even wanted to leave the electric lights on to welcome herself home on those evenings she was at the house, even though she was only there at his request. He motioned toward the door. "I've a . . . a carriage. You c-can come . . . with me."

"Oh." For one second, two, her face was utterly blank, no thoughts betrayed in her eyes. Then she smiled and looked perfectly at ease. "All right. Thank you, sir. I appreciate the offer."

Peter nodded to the hotel clerk and held the door open for his new guest, who breezed by him. She still wore an expression on her face that declared herself unfazed by the change in plans, like the one Rosemary often donned. But hers, he'd eventually understood, was nothing but a mask. A cloak, as he'd observed during that first dinner at Gryff's house. Was her sister's the same?

And where did they learn such things? It was a shame their parents had died — he had a feeling he would have liked to meet the people who had shaped their children into such strong, determined individuals.

He motioned toward his carriage.

Miss — Missus — Forsythe . . . *Willa* — he couldn't help but think of her as such, since that was all Rosemary ever called her. Willa tilted her head. "Have you no automobile, sir?"

How had those things so taken over the world in such short order? A decade ago, he hardly knew anyone who had one. Now everyone looked at him as though he were a relic for not. "I d-don't . . . don't care f-for them."

Rosemary did, though. She loved getting to ride in the Penroses' with Jenny. Perhaps he would . . . A frown creased his brow. Where in the world had that thought been going? He could hardly buy an automobile just for the entertainment of a woman who wouldn't, as Gryff had helpfully pointed out, be here much longer.

He offered a hand to help her sister up. Maybe Gryff's off-the-cuff suggestion could work. Maybe he could simply make the librarian position a permanent one.

Willa settled on the seat, positioning her bag at her feet. When he vaulted up on the opposite side, she offered him a vague smile. "Well, thank you for the lift, Mr. Holstein. I promise I'll not impose long upon your hospitality."

He returned the vague smile and picked up the reins. And prayed her easy demeanor wasn't a cloak for bad news. "How is . . . how is Olivia? Improved?"

He waited for an old farm wagon to trundle past and then signaled his horse to join the street's fray.

Willa frowned. "She told you about Olivia?"

"Of c-course. She was . . . she was v-very distressed. She asked m-me to . . . to pray."

"Did she?" Willa tucked a strand of straight hair behind her ear. "Forgive me, but that's surprising. She doesn't usually air family concerns with strangers. Nor request prayers of them."

It had been a unique situation, he granted that. And through it, they'd emerged as something far different from strangers. But he wasn't going to get into all that with her sister — his tongue would never survive it. So he simply nodded, kept his eyes on the road, and said, "I . . . I know."

"Hmm." The hum didn't sound exactly pleased, but it didn't sound exactly anything. It was as vague as her smile. Then she said, "Well, she is much improved, is Liv. Thank you for inquiring."

They went over a bump as they left town, and her valise shifted, forcing her feet to do so as well. Peter glanced down to see if he could help in any way and glimpsed scuffed, worn half-boots under her fashionable skirt. Far worse-looking than the ones Rosemary wore. Leaps and bounds worse, as if they might fall apart at any moment. An odd contrast indeed to her clothes.

But then, Rosemary could make the clothes. Apparently none of the siblings had mastered the cobbler's art.

He had the sudden urge to ask Willa what she did for a living, since all of them must work. And the sudden certainty that she wouldn't answer him if ask he did. He cleared his throat. Best to focus on another subject. "Did . . . did C-Cressida pass a . . . a good birthday?" He glanced up to her nothing-like-Rosemary's face.

Said face had incredulity coloring its blank edges. "She told you that too?"

"Was it a . . . a s-secret?"

Another nothing-smile. "Of course not. Though I'm afraid the day was greatly overshadowed by Olivia's convalescence. We were none of us in the mood to celebrate."

Rosemary *had* secrets though, she'd said. Ones she thought would ruin his opinion of her. Peter had turned that statement over every which direction last night, but he kept coming back to the same certainty — unless she were a murderer, he didn't much care. And even if she were, he was certain she'd have had good reasons for it. She was too concerned with the plight of everyone to hurt anyone. Anyone undeserving, that is. Though had she been there when that villainous gent kicked Olivia into the street, he would have been surprised had she not delivered a blow to his jugular.

He never would have thought the prospect of violence would make him grin. But there was something alluring about that fierce light that lit her eyes when she spoke in defense of the downtrodden, or of her family.

"Is that amusing?"

"Hmm? Oh. P-Pardon me." What a dunce he was, grinning after she'd said they'd no reason to celebrate. "I was . . . I was j-just . . ." He cleared his throat, having a feeling she wouldn't much appreciate those thoughts of his. Or rather, she wouldn't like that he knew her sister well enough to think them. Apparently Rosemary hadn't written all that much in her letters home about the life she'd been living here.

Or . . . or just hadn't mentioned him and their friendship.

The summer air suddenly felt over-hot. Stifling. Heavy. He sighed. It promised to be a long two miles back to Kensey.

TWENTY-ONE

Rosemary wrote down another sentence, still not quite believing the words she penned. Not quite convinced she hadn't concocted the whole theory from her imagination.

But her imagination had never been very good — unless it was concocting monsters in the dark. This . . . this was something well beyond her abilities. From the books, she had pieced together the bare facts — that Wilhelm and Aksel Holstein had both been friends of England's royal family. Though all the mentions of them were vague, the photographic evidence was too great to be ignored. In an unfathomable number of pictures, they were there, somewhere in the background.

It was the journals that had provided the motivation. Assuming she had translated them correctly. She would have to ask Peter to double-check them. Perhaps he would take the day away from his typewriter tomorrow and look at them with her. And she fully intended to spend the evening in the attic — she'd find those documents he needed. They would be there; the journals said they would be. She had only to —

Knock, knock, knock.

She looked up, over to the door in the hallway. And frowned when she saw Peter there rather than Kerensa or Grammy or a scowling Mrs. Teague. Since when did he enter through the hall door? "Did you lock yourself out of your study?"

He smiled. "Let's . . . let's hope not. I brought you . . . I brought you something from town."

She grinned and pushed away from the table. It was just like him, though she couldn't think what he'd have brought. "Did you? You know you needn't . . ."

Still smiling, he stepped to the side. And a new figure stepped into the doorway. Rosemary leapt up and flew across the room, shrieking like an utter ninny. "Willa!"

Willa met her a few steps in, laughing as they shared a fierce embrace.

Then Rosemary pulled away and slapped her on the arm. "Why haven't you written? It's been ages, I was getting worried. How is Liv?" She stilled, searching her sister's face for news. "You wouldn't come unless she was well. Unless — unless she . . ." If the worst had happened, she wouldn't write it. She'd come.

But there were no lines of grief in Willa's face. Certainly not in her smile. "She's well, Rosie. I swear it. I wouldn't have come if she weren't well."

"Oh, thank God." That anxiety, so quick to pounce, unwound again, letting her shoulders sag.

Willa frowned. "Not sure what He has to do with it, but all right."

Rosemary breathed a laugh and looked over Willa's shoulder. Peter still hovered in the doorway, watching them with a little smile on his face. A bit of it, no doubt, because he'd apparently rubbed off on her more than she'd thought. Listen to her, casually thanking God as he was more apt to do. She glanced back to Willa. "Did you just arrive?"

"On the train. Mr. Holstein saw me going into the hotel and offered me a lift. And to stay in the cottage with you."

He'd recognized her — from that one glimpse he'd had of her when Rosemary first arrived? She arched a brow at him, impressed. "It really does astound me how you can notice and recall some details so perfectly yet never remember when it's time for a meal."

He chuckled and pushed off the doorway he'd been leaning on. "Speaking of . . . would you . . . would you like your s-sister to . . . to join us for luncheon and dinner, or . . . or shall I have Grammy s-send something to the cottage?"

It could be fun to have Willa in the big house for a meal — when else would they ever have a chance to eat together in such opulence? But when she glanced at Willa to verify that, she paused. Willa's face was carefully blank. And her eyes were absolutely raging.

Rosemary cleared her throat. "The cottage, I think. Thank you. I'll just show her the way now and then come back to —"

"Take the day." He nodded, his eyes soft, and backed up a step into the hall. "You . . . you deserve it. Have fun."

He vanished, his steps heading toward the kitchen. Otherwise the only sound was the ticking of the clock. And the simmering throb of Willa's temper.

Rosemary cleared her throat and trotted back to the table to grab her things. "Well then. Let's go, shall we? Do you need help with your bag?"

"I can carry a blighted valise, Rosie." And

smile sweetly while drilling her with visual daggers, as could they all.

Rosemary sighed and rolled her eyes. "All right, then. Let's go so you can say whatever it is that's burning you up."

"Rosie! Who's your friend?" Treeve's voice came from the open window. It was smiling, which meant *he* was, though she didn't turn right away to see it. Rather, she squeezed her eyes shut.

"Rosie, is it?" Willa hissed.

Rosemary cleared her throat and pivoted to send him a smile of her own. She hadn't invited him to use the nickname — but he'd taken to doing so, and she hadn't seen the point in objecting. "Hello, Treeve. This is my sister, Willa."

Treeve's eyes sparkled, and his grin was his most charming one, good teeth gleaming. "Pleasure to make your acquaintance, Miss Gresham."

Willa stood ramrod-straight, her smile surely cutting poor Treeve to shreds, it was so brutally sharp-edged. "It's Forsythe. Mrs. Forsythe — I'm a widow."

Rosemary barely kept from lifting her brows at that little tale. Until it hit her — Peter must have heard her last name. Leaving Willa to scramble for an explanation as to why they didn't share the same one.

Treeve didn't seem hindered by the false and finished nuptials. "Mrs. Forsythe, then. Will you be staying at Kensey for a while?"

Willa's smile was ice. "No, I daresay not. I must be back to London tomorrow."

"Oh, so soon?" Rosemary frowned. That would barely give them time to get through the fighting and on to the fun. And why would she have come all this way for so short a stay? "That hardly seems worth the price of the ticket."

Willa turned that slicing smile on her. "Well, a friend paid for it."

Mr. V.

Rosemary's stomach went tight. "How kind." She turned back to Treeve. "I'd better show Willa to the cottage, so she can rest for a bit."

"Aye, and Kenver'll be on me for wasting time. Just wanted to say hello." He nodded, his amusement still firmly in place, and took a step back, lifting his burned arm in farewell.

"What happened to him?" Willa asked in a low tone as he strode away. "His arm looks terrible."

Rosemary hadn't mentioned the fire in her letters home — it only would have worried everyone. "The stable caught fire, and a beam got him. But the arm's much better than it was — he's back to work, and he doesn't keep it bandaged all the time anymore."

"I saw the new construction — and the rubble of the old one. But I thought *surely* you would have mentioned something as noteworthy as that." Willa gripped her arm and tugged her toward the door. "But it seems you've neglected to mention any number of things, haven't you?"

"Well, it isn't as though *I* was in any danger from the fire, and I didn't want you to worry." Because she would have — Rosemary hated fire, but Willa feared it like Rosemary did darkness.

Willa snorted. "Oh you weren't, were you? Funny, I could have sworn that when I mentioned the rubble to your beloved Mr. Holstein, he said something about how you were in — invaluable in the effort to extinguish the b-b-blaze."

Rosemary pulled her arm free, barely restraining herself from slapping at Willa in earnest. "Don't make fun of him. Don't."

Willa stepped close. "Will you listen to yourself?"

This, the hallway of Kensey Manor, with Peter likely just around the corner, was not the place to get into it. Setting her face in a neutral expression, Rosemary yanked the valise from Willa's hand and strode through the passages she deemed it least likely to encounter anyone in, then out one of the side doors that put them into the garden.

Willa snorted. "Know your way around rather well, don't you?"

"Well, of course I do. When do we *not* know our way around a place we're working?" Her blood rose a bit more in temperature with every step. Willa had some nerve, showing up here and promptly judging her. Looking at her as if she'd committed some kind of crime.

Or, rather, that she hadn't, when she ought to have.

Mr. Teague's prized gladioli waved a greeting as she stormed through, but she didn't pause to greet them or admire the fragrance wafting on the breeze. She all but stomped to the cottage, the silent and simmering Willa a step behind.

She unlocked and opened the kitchen door of the cottage and dumped Willa's bag rather unceremoniously on the floor. Spun to face down her sister.

Willa was smirking on the threshold. "Well, at least you still lock your door. What, don't trust these people quite as much as all that?"

Rosemary shoved a chair away from the

table, though she didn't much feel like sitting in it. "What are you doing here, Willa? I appreciate knowing that Liv is doing better, but you could have just written or sent a wire."

"No. I couldn't." Willa tugged off her gloves and tossed them to the counter, her hat following a moment later. "Mr. V sent me for an update."

And Rosemary felt prickly as a hedgehog. "Why would he do that? He said I'd have as much time as I needed until war was declared, which it hasn't been. I don't need a . . . a nursemaid."

"Look." Willa edged half a step closer, face hard and one hip cocked out. "I came here fully expecting to have a nice chat, get an update on all the things you can't send along in the post, and go back to Mr. V ready to tell him that Rosie's got it all under control and will be home soon. Then I get off the blighted train and run into that man, who starts talking about our family like he knows them. Our *family*. Rosie, we don't talk about our family!"

Rosemary rolled her eyes. "I've been here for months, Will. What am I supposed to talk about?"

"The blighted weather! *His* family. Not ours!"

"What am I supposed to say, then, when I'm so exhausted with worry for Olivia? When I burst into tears at random moments for thinking of her? Do I just let him think me unhinged?" Not that she actually burst into tears in front of him, but she'd come close a time or two, and he would have noticed. He always noticed — when he wasn't in his other-world.

Willa shook her head. "This is what we do, Rosemary. We hide things. We find things. We don't . . . we don't let the marks *in*. We don't ask them to pray for our sisters."

"Well, why not? It worked, didn't it?" When a curl had the audacity to tickle her cheek, she shoved it back behind her ear. "God listens to him."

"Then I want nothing to do with Him, if He exists." Willa slashed a hand through the air. "Because I don't need the favors of a traitor."

"He's not though." She said it calmly. So calmly that it wasn't until that moment that she was absolutely, properly sure. Peter Holstein was many things. And he had his secrets. But he loved England. He would sooner cut off his own hand than betray his country.

Willa went still too, but the fire in her eyes

was only banked. Cautious. Not extinguished. "I beg your pardon?"

Rosemary leaned close and pitched her voice low. "Peter Holstein is not a traitor. And I can't prove he is — because he's *not.* All the evidence —"

"Evidence be hanged!" Willa's voice was naught but a hiss, low and throbbing. "You *have* to prove it, because that's what you're being paid to do." She charged past her, to the table, where a vase of flowers sat. Mr. Teague had clipped them for her himself yesterday. Willa motioned to them as if they were, somehow, the proof she needed. "The problem is that you've been blinded. By flowers and good food and —"

"I have *not* been blinded!"

"— and people thinking you're more than you are. You've let it go to your head."

"I have not. I know exactly what I am." Knew, perhaps, better than she ever had before. It kept wiggling and niggling and slithering around inside, when she least wanted it to.

"Then by people knowing your name. Greeting you warmly. By, I don't know, Holstein's handsome face — though I thought cleft chins were Ellie's thing, not yours."

"They are. Ellie's, I mean." She didn't

even like them, especially. Or hadn't. Much. "And I've scarcely noticed if he's handsome or not." Which was true. Perhaps he was — certainly he was, if one thought about it — but why would one? When it mattered so little next to the heart of him?

Willa growled and pivoted, marched to the far corner. "Let me remind you of facts, Rosie. You were hired to do a simple job."

"Yes, to find the truth."

"No. I don't recall the word *truth* coming up when you told me what was said." She spun back around but leaned against the wall over there, a room away, rather than stalk her way back. "You deliver what you were asked for, and you keep in mind that the stammering fool —"

"Stop it!" She didn't mean to shout. It was a bad idea to shout, she knew that. "So he stutters — that is not a crime, it is not a fault. It does not make him a fool. He is a wise man, a clever man, a good man, a kind man, a nice man — the best man I've ever known, and I won't suffer you or anyone else speaking ill of him just because he has difficulty expressing himself!"

For a second Willa just stared at her. Then she loosed a low curse and shook her head. "Blazes, Rosie. You're in love with him!"

"I am not! I'm not stupid enough to fall

in love with a gentleman, no matter how good and noble and handsome he is!"

"Not that you've even noticed if he's handsome or not."

"You're insufferable." She spun away, needing space from her sister before she strangled her. But one step toward the door and she growled too. "Ducky." Mrs. Teague stood just a few paces from the door, luncheon tray in her hand, and her expression . . . oh, who even cared what her expression was? Condemning, no doubt, as always.

Rosemary strode forward and jerked the tray from her hands. "Go ahead. Add it to my litany of sins and shortcomings and whatever else you're keeping track of day in and day out. I'm sure it is somehow a new fault in your eyes that I recognize the basic truth about him." She pivoted back through the door and sent it slamming with a well-placed heel.

The sound should have soothed her. It only made her angrier. She set the tray on the table with a clatter of fine china and motioned toward it. "Eat. Unless you think it'll blind you to some wisdom I can't even fathom."

Willa pulled out a chair with an arm as inflexible as the wood. "You're an idiot.

He's *not* a good man. He's a gentleman."

"Yes, well, apparently the two aren't as mutually exclusive as we assumed." She couldn't sit. She *couldn't.* So she leaned against the counter and folded her arms over her chest. "He's loyal. And he's good. And he's —"

"A gen—tle—man." Willa exaggerated the enunciation, punctuating each syllable with a gesture of her hand. Then she reached for a sandwich with a sad shake of her head. "You've always been the reasonable one, Rosie. I might have expected Ellie to fall in love with a rich bloke someday — star-crossed lovers and all that nonsense — but not you."

"I have not *fallen in love with* him." This she delivered from between clenched teeth. And spun to look out the window, so she could be sure Mrs. Teague wasn't still hovering.

She wasn't. She was sitting on a bench in her husband's garden, staring up at the sky. Curious — Rosemary had never seen her idle.

But she was too far away to listen, so what did it matter? So long as they could keep from yelling.

A challenge, that.

Willa had taken a bite, swallowed it. "It's

doomed, you know. Men of his station only have one use for women of ours."

Her hedgehog spines came back, all bristling out around her. "Hiring them to clear their libraries?"

Willa rolled her eyes. "Don't pretend to be naïve. If he cares for you at all, he'll just think it's reason to make you a mistress. Is that what you want?"

"He wouldn't. You don't know him, Willa. He's . . . he's godly. The real kind, the kind that reads his Bible every day and actually believes it. The kind that lives by it. He gives to the poor and visits people in prison and feeds the hungry and —"

"And puts on a good show, apparently, if you believe that." Willa poured some lemonade from the pitcher on the tray into a glass. "He's. A. Gentleman."

"I know what he is! And I know what *I* am." Now she had to sit. Her knees wouldn't hold her any longer. "He's a good man. And I'm a thief."

Willa's hand, as she set it upon the wrist that Rosemary let rest on the table as she sagged to a seat, wasn't exactly encouraging. It was more purposeful. "No, Rosie. You're a *good* thief. You're one of the best thieves in England, that's why Mr. V came to you for this. And you have to ask how he knew that. How he knew who we were, why he ever came to you last year for that first job. How he does the things he does. You have to ask, and you have to respect him. And fear him. Because if you don't give that man what he asked for . . ."

Rosemary pulled her arm away and used it to hold up her head. "I'll give him what I've found. I owe him that, I know it. But I can't help it if it's not what he wants. The truth is the truth."

"Rosie."

"I can't hurt Peter. I can't. He's done nothing wrong."

"And what will you gain by protecting him? He's still a gentleman. He's not going to . . . to marry you or whatever you're hoping."

"Of course he isn't. And I'm not hoping it. I'm not in love with him." She just wanted to make sure he was safe. That he was appreciated for being the amazing man he was, not lied about so slanderously. She just wanted to make sure of that, no matter what Mr. V demanded from her when she handed him proof of innocence instead of guilt.

"Peter Holstein will hang you out to dry if he learns what you are — don't think he won't. He will *especially* if he fancies himself a good man, a godly one. He'll say you're a thief and you deserve what's coming to you."

But that wasn't how he'd been about Tim and Betty, was it? Still. Rosemary drew in a long breath. "It doesn't matter what he does. I've got to do the right thing. I've got to do . . . Willa, I can't keep doing this."

The words hung there in the air, a mirror. Reflecting thoughts she hadn't even known she'd been thinking, much less contemplating enough to spew them out there like a firm decision.

Willa froze, her lemonade halfway to her lips. "Doing what, exactly?"

Rosemary sat up straight and splayed her hands out on the table. "I'm a thief. It's all I have to define me, and . . . and I don't want to be just a word like that. I can't be. I can't keep taking things from people, just assuming they're all selfish and cruel and have it coming. What if they're not? What if they're all like him? Good and kind and willing to give if you just ask?"

"They're not."

"But how do you know?" She looked up, over to those familiar eyes that were begging her to be quiet. Those familiar eyes that were shadowed with fear. Rosemary's nostrils flared. "We always hated it, didn't we, when people just assumed we were rubbish because we were poor? That we deserved all the ill to befall us? How are we better if we do the same in reverse? If we assume that *they're* rubbish because they're *not* poor? That they deserve to be cheated and robbed?"

"Rosie. You can't. You can't quit. It's what you are, what we all are. What makes us family."

"No." She traced a chipped nail along the wood grain in the table. "It's love that makes us family. Not the stealing."

"You don't know anything else! What could you possibly do?"

She sighed and flexed the fingers that would hate her for saying it. "I can sew. I've got some seamstress work while I've been here. I could make a business of it."

Willa snorted. "You hate sewing."

"But I'm good at it."

"You'd be miserable in half a day. And you'd never make a living like that in London, there are too many other seamstresses."

"So we leave London. Let the little ones breathe fresh air for a change."

A dry laugh blew past Willa's lips like a leaf in the wind. She stood. "I see where this is going. We can all just move down here, yeah? Set up house here in the neighborhood. Maybe Georgie and Barclay can work in your darling Mr. Holstein's burned-out stables. And what of us girls? Should I be a housemaid?"

Rosemary closed her eyes. "I don't have the answers. I just know that I can't. I can't keep doing what I've always done. It . . . it doesn't sit right anymore."

"Well, it sits just fine with me." Willa's footsteps moved behind her, toward the door. "I've delivered my message. And I'll tell Mr. V what you've said. Don't be surprised if he shows up himself here soon."

"Willa." She opened her eyes again and spun on her seat.

Willa had her bag and gloves in her hand, her hat on her head. And her other hand on the door. "I never thought I'd see the day when you chose a bloke over your own family, Rosie."

Her throat had gone so tight. "I haven't."

"You have. And it'll be your ruin." She pulled open the door. "Well, when he breaks your heart and kicks you to the curb, come home. We'll be there. And we'll still love you, even if you are a thief."

Rosemary's lips turned up, though it didn't feel much like a smile. "Will you love me if I'm not?"

"You will be. You always will be. We can't just change who we are."

She'd never thought so. But maybe they could. If they were willing to pay the price.

After Willa left, Rosemary padded back to the hall, to the bedroom with the desk and the paper and the books and the piles and piles of letters she'd stacked up. Unwilling to throw them away or burn them. Unwilling to even put them out of sight.

She pulled out the one she'd just reread yesterday and fell into the armchair while she flipped it open. While her gaze found so easily the words Peter had written for her after the Tim and Betty incident.

Sometimes the price of our faith is the loss of esteem. I've always known that — now, it seems, the world is proving it. Jesus tells us that if we follow Him, it may cost us our family. Our friends. Turn brothers and parents against us. But some things are worth the sacrifice. My Lord is one of those things.

Perhaps my neighbors will never like or respect me. But I'll do what He asks anyway. Because to do any less would mean I'm not really His follower. And if I'm not His follower . . . I'm nothing.

My father once told me that all a man

has is his name. I've been thinking about that a lot, as you can well imagine. And I've realized . . . I've realized there's only one name that matters. And it's Christian. Christ-follower. If I am that, then I am all I need to be. And if I'm not . . . then all the respect of all the men in all the world will avail me nothing.

She touched a finger to the words and let her gaze wander, unseeing, over the room. She didn't know Jesus like Peter did. She was no Christ-follower. But she knew He ate with sinners and hung on a cross beside a robber, and He promised that thief Paradise. She knew He forgave, if one asked Him to do so.

All He seemed to ask in return was that one repent. That one change. That one go and sin no more.

She let her eyes slide shut again. If Willa was right, that was an impossible request. And just now, it felt it.

TWENTY-TWO

Three days, by his estimation. Three more days of solid writing and Peter could finish his manuscript. It would need to be reread, parts of it no doubt retyped as he corrected and changed. But still. He was within sight of the finish line.

But he was looking now — not at his typewriter or his growing stack of completed pages or the dwindling stack of fresh sheets of paper — at the table in the library, completely covered with books, all opened to marked pages.

It was going to take all day. All day, and perhaps then some, to go through it all.

He chuffed. "Can't you just . . . just summarize it for me?"

Rosemary didn't even look over at him as she added one more book to the table. "If you like."

Come to think of it, she hadn't looked at him all morning. Not when she came in to the dining room for a cup of tea. Not when she'd asked him if today was good for him to look over her findings. Not when he'd entered.

She had that stiff look about her. And circles under her eyes again like he hadn't seen since that first week after Olivia's accident. She wore a dress in a green that usually put roses in her cheeks, the one with the lacy under-layer in a cream that perfectly set off her skin.

"I'm . . . only teasing. I want . . . I want to go through it all."

She still didn't look at him. "Very well. Sit down then, Mr. Holstein."

Mr. Holstein? She hadn't called him that in weeks, not since the arrow had struck her. He'd been *Peter,* just as she'd been *Rosemary.*

He reached out when she would have breezed past him for another book, and caught her hand. Mrs. Teague had told him that Willa had stormed off yesterday, valise in hand, but Rosemary hadn't returned to the house. He'd given her space, figured she'd tell him what had happened when she was ready.

But maybe he should have sought her out last evening. "Rosemary. Are you all right?"

For a moment she was a statue, still and

stony. Then she let out a breath, and her shoulders relaxed from their blades, and she almost, nearly, looked at him. "Just a bit of a squabble with Willa, that's all. Nothing unusual. We fight as often as we don't. Sisters, you know."

"Not . . . not really. Never had any. Just Gryff."

Her lips quirked up. "I'm going to tell him you likened him to a sister."

Peter chuckled and tugged her closer. "Sit. You look . . . tired."

"I spent most of the night searching the attic. For those documents you need." She let out a long, defeated breath. "Nothing, thus far. But they're there somewhere, the journals said they were. I'll find them for you."

She would, he had no doubt of that. Though they should have organized their efforts, for he'd been going through the attic as well. They could have been looking through all the same boxes, for all he knew.

Or . . . what if she'd found where he'd hidden the letters from his readers? Could that be why she wouldn't meet his eye?

He waited for the panic, the fear to strike — it didn't. Instead . . . instead he almost, strangely hoped she *had* found them. That his secret was secret no longer from her.

He cleared his throat. "Did you . . . did you find anything of interest?"

She offered a tired, halfhearted smile. "Only that you write to far too many people."

"Hmm." He nudged her into a chair. It was for the best. If he were ever to tell her who he really was, then *he* should tell her, not let a bunch of letters do it for him. "I'll get the . . . the rest of the books."

It took only a moment to grab the remaining volumes she'd had sitting before the neat stacks. Though when he turned back to the table with books in hand, she was poring over one already.

"We've already established the Holsteins have long had a firm connection to the Saxe-Coburgs — ever since, apparently, your grandfather came here with dire predictions about von Bismarck. He shared them with Queen Victoria, and that appears to have been the start of generations of friendship. I think today we need to begin with your mother's side. The von Roths had a few surprises up their sleeves."

He slid the books onto the edge of the table and took the chair beside hers. Maybe it was just the late night in his attic that had painted such circles under her eyes. Or maybe it was something more. "What did you . . . you and your sister squabble about?"

Usually he wouldn't have asked. But it was Rosemary, and she was obviously upset.

She tapped a finger to the book in front of her. "Your maternal grandfather wasn't so quiet in his life as your mother apparently made it seem. He was, in fact, often traveling with a rather interesting contingent of high-class blokes."

His lips twitched. *High-class* and *blokes* weren't usually put together. "Did I . . . did I offend her somehow?" He wouldn't put it past himself — he seemed able to offend half the country by merely existing.

Rosemary flipped the page. "You remember that I asked you whether your maternal grandfather's second wife — the Russian — knew the Duchess of Edinburgh?" She pulled another tome forward. This one was in English. "Well, she did, without question."

The Duke and Duchess of Edinburgh were part of the English royal family — the duke was a prince by birth, King George's uncle. The duchess, a Russian princess. Perhaps she had known Peter's own step-grandmother from school or some such? A strange coincidence. "Willa seemed . . . a bit put out that I knew about . . . about Olivia."

Rosemary cleared her throat. "Did you know that the duke spent much of his time in Malta and Coburg?"

Well, that only made sense. The Saxe-Coburg family obviously had ties to Coburg. "I'm sorry if . . . if I upset her. By asking after Olivia."

Sighing, Rosemary finally looked at him. "It isn't your fault, Peter. You were being you — thoughtful and considerate and all other things polite and good. We fought because we fight. Because she's afraid that I'm growing spoiled by your lovely house and unending generosity, and she wouldn't believe me when I assured her I'm not. But she'll see, won't she, when I go home. It's nothing."

Nothing? It felt like an arrow through his middle, with a white page fluttering from the shaft, proclaiming him alone.

Of course she would go home though. She had family. He, of all people, could appreciate that.

She turned back to the pages. "Right. Coburg. The thing with Coburg is . . ."

"Can't you stay?" Blast. That wasn't exactly an eloquent — nor thoughtful — request. He flushed when she looked over at him so quickly, as if hearing something in the words beyond the short ones he'd spoken. And why shouldn't she? A gentleman didn't just go making such requests. He cleared his throat. "I mean . . . ah, drat." He tried for a grin. "You know I . . . I detest change. I've only just got . . . got used to you."

Her smile was exactly like Rosita's. Slow and warm and charming. "Your library is neat as a pin now, Peter."

His grin went crooked. "I could mess it up again in . . . in a blink."

Now she laughed, tilting her head back with it, exposing her slender neck where it peeked from the cream lace. "That you could. In *half* a blink."

"It's . . . a talent."

"And you are the master of it. Even so." She leaned forward to rest her elbows on the table. "I've got your library organized. Found the journals for you. I'll find those documents before I go, I swear it. But that's all I can do."

"All right." It wasn't, but what was he supposed to do? Maybe . . . maybe he should have let her find those boxes of reader mail. Maybe, somehow, it would make him grow in her eyes. Make her want to stay a little longer to help him with his stories. Maybe she would decide she couldn't well let Jasper and his man and whatever villagers hated him ruin all he'd worked for.

Maybe he should just tell her. Tell her he needed her. Tell her why.

He leaned forward too and reached in front of her to tap her page. "Coburg."

"Coburg." She looked at him rather than at the book. "The von Roths had a house there."

He hadn't known that . . . had he? But they *had* taken that one trip to Malta and Coburg when he was a boy. To visit Mother's family. "Is this . . . significant?"

"Rather." She reached for another book, one in the center of the table, and pulled it forward, setting it on top of the others. It was open to a photograph.

Mother. He recognized her right away, though she was young in the photo — perhaps fourteen or fifteen. His gaze traced the familiar features, too long unseen. He could see a bit of himself in her, here and there. And he could see *her.* The gracious, loving woman one couldn't know without adoring.

It took him a minute to realize there were other figures of note in the picture as well, including a little girl on her knee who bore more of a resemblance to the dark-haired people in the photo than to Mother's fair family. He had to read the caption to identify those. And sucked in a breath when he did. "The Duke of Ed . . . Edinburgh."

"And his wife and children, 'on holiday with friends in Coburg.' "

"Friends." Through this second wife of his grandfather's, who had known the duchess. Mother's half-siblings — all a great deal younger than her — were in the photo too, and looked to be of similar ages to the children of the duke and duchess.

But studying the picture didn't answer the questions. "So M-Mother knew the . . . the royal family?"

"That branch of it, it seems. This is where it gets interesting. Where we answer a few of the real questions." She pulled forward one of Father's journals. "If I'm reading this right — and you'll want to double-check my translation of this gibberish — your father didn't go back to Germany for his wife at all. He met her in Scotland."

"Scotland." They'd never mentioned that, neither of them. They'd never mentioned anything about how they met. "How?"

She tapped the photo with the Edinburghs again. "The von Roths were on holiday with the duke's family. Your father was on holiday with King Edward's."

Peter had to sit back. Yes, he knew Father had an acquaintance with the late king — but enough of one to holiday with him? "To . . . to Scotland?"

"Exactly. They met there. In Scotland. With the royals."

Peter sat back in his chair, trying to remember anything Mother had said about her stepmother. They had gotten along well enough, he knew. But Mother had never felt particularly close to her. Perhaps because she was already eight when her father remarried, and her new stepmother was soon doting on her *own* children. And, apparently, still seeking the company of her old friends.

But why would Mother have always claimed the von Roths lived a quiet country life?

"That makes sense with all she said, doesn't it? It wasn't the von Roths with any connection to anyone, really. It was her stepmother." Rosemary sifted through her notes.

Peter pulled another book forward when another photograph caught his eye. "This is . . . is George."

"Mm." Apparently abandoning whatever search she'd been on, Rosemary tapped the photograph. "With Princess Marie — eldest daughter of the duke and duchess. Who happens to be the little one on your mother's knee in that other photo. All grown up."

Peter hummed as he studied the image of his friend. George was young in it, and in naval uniform. Peter hadn't known him in those days, of course, having been only a boy. But that was before George had married Mary, when Victoria was still queen and ruling with an iron fist.

"You probably know this history too, but I didn't. He wanted to marry her — George and Marie. He proposed even, the books say, and she turned him down. Because her mother told her she ought. The duchess always resented being below the Princess of Wales — George's mother — in status."

Politics, even within family. Peter shook his head. "It's . . . it's hard to imagine. George and Mary are . . . are completely devoted to each other."

"Well, according to this one" — she indicated another book — "George's mother was none too keen on that other match either, claiming, and I quote . . ." She picked up a sheet of paper and cleared her throat. " 'The Edinburgh family was too closely aligned with Germany.' "

"Interesting."

"Not as interesting as it's about to be."

She shuffled a few books and came up with another of Father's journals. But then went silent. So silent that he had to look up, had to meet her clear brown eyes, had to wonder why she said nothing.

For one moment dread possessed him. Until he remembered that she couldn't have found evidence of loyalty to Germany — she couldn't have found that, because they weren't loyal to Germany.

She moistened her lips and leaned just a bit closer. "There's more to this than their loyalty, Peter. Much more."

Silence had been walking with them for the last half a mile, and today Rosemary found she appreciated its company. Silence was a lot like a sibling, she'd decided — sometimes you didn't want it hanging about, getting in the way. And other times it was the best companion imaginable.

Her hand was warm in the crook of Peter's elbow, and the rest of her was warm simply because the summer sun beat down upon her. She glanced up at his noble-looking profile and wondered, not for the first time in the last half mile, what wheels were turning in that who-cared-if-it-was-handsome head of his.

They rounded a bend, and the village

came into view. With it came a long sigh from Peter. "No one would . . . would believe it."

It *was* a bit hard to believe, at that. But the evidence had all been there. Evidence that Peter was the third generation of Holstein men to claim a friendship with the British monarchy. That the relationship the Holsteins had forged with Victoria and then Edward to warn them of von Bismarck's politics had been what had introduced Aksel to his wife. And that *that* connection with the Edinburgh side of the family — the Edinburghs, who were far "too chummy" with the German rulers, as Aksel's journal had put it — had led the aging Queen Victoria to ask a strange favor of them.

It had been there, in detail. The records of his parents' trip to Malta. Receipts, even, from the hotel at which they'd stayed while there — the very same week that George had been there, proposing to his cousin, the daughter of the Edinburghs.

Peter had been there too, in Malta. While his mother called on the girl she'd once bounced upon her knee and read bedtime stories to, and set about convincing her to listen to her mother rather than her heart. To refuse to marry the cousin she loved.

To keep the man third in line to the English throne from a marriage that would have meant a stronger alliance with Germany.

Critics would scoff and ask why they went to such trouble, when George hadn't even been the heir at the time — his elder brother had yet lived. His father had yet lived, and Victoria still reigned. Why bother with him?

It was, Aksel had written, a matter of thoroughness. Neither Victoria nor her son wanted the royal house to enter into a stronger alliance with Germany. And if by chance George's older brother died — which he had — and left George the heir . . .

At the time, George's older brother had been betrothed to Mary. When he'd died of pneumonia in 1892, she and George had begun to write to each other, to try to get each other through the grief. They'd fallen in love. And *she* had already been fully approved by the queen. And had no ties to von Bismarck's Germany.

And now King George, who once looked up to Aksel — never realizing he and his wife had helped prevent the marriage to his first love — sought the advice of Peter. Even though Peter hadn't quite known why.

Peter sighed. "Do you think that . . . that's why he first in — invited me to tea? Because he . . . he expected me to be like Father?"

Rosemary looped her other hand around his arm too. "Probably. At first. But it's no reason for him to have continued to do so. You're his friend, Peter."

Peter sighed again. A chuff this time. "I'm no . . . no political advisor."

"No. Thank heavens." She laughed at the sharp look he sent her. "Well, that would be utterly boring, Peter Holstein. I know you *say* your father and grandfather were quite interesting, but I'm suddenly doubting you now. Knowing they *did* talk so much about politics."

His smile was fleeting, and his gaze was soon back on the ever-growing village. "But they . . . they didn't. Not t-to me."

She rubbed her hand over his arm. His father, she suspected, would chide himself if he knew he was making his son stutter. Even though in the final journal, Aksel's reasons for his silence were clear.

With politics comes power. And with power comes corruption. My father taught me that — a lesson he learned watching von Bismarck turn Germany into something it never should have been. I'll have no part in it. All these years we have hoped that Germany would see where it was headed and make amends. All these years we preserved our ties there in that hope, so Peter might know a different Germany than we did. But all these years have only made the division more clear — and our part in it all too. Our part is to use our ties for the good of our adopted homeland. In service to God and King.

She bumped her arm into his. "Is it such a bad secret to learn? That your family has been advising England's monarchs for sixty years?"

"No, but . . ." He shook his head. "No one will . . . will believe it."

"No one will believe you're actually taking a meal in the pub either, until they see it with their own eyes. But here we are, en route to do just that." Action, that was all they needed. It could work with the simple, and it could work with the complicated. "We'll make them believe it, all of it. I'm telling you, put that typewriter to good — or *more* good — use. Write your family's story up. Submit it to newspapers. It'll make a smashing good tale."

Peter sent her a look. But then he smiled again, a bit. "I can't. It's not . . . not just my story. It's George's."

Stubborn man. "Ask him first, then. I bet

527

he'd think it a fine idea." As if she had any idea what kings thought fine or not.

Maybe Willa was right. Maybe the good food had gone to her head.

"Maybe." For a moment, she thought perhaps he was agreeing with her thought. Then she realized he was still talking about talking to the king. "Or maybe — after we find those papers proving I'm English — maybe I just let . . . let it rest. I will prove I'm not German. But if . . . if people will h-hate me for my name anyway, then . . ." He shrugged. "Or I could ch— change it. Like George is . . . is considering."

"Change your name?" Women, she supposed, did it all the time — but it was different, somehow, to take another name when it was the name of a man whose history you were willing to weave your future into. Quite a different tale to just abandon one's family legacy altogether. "Well, you can't do that. And you obviously don't really think you should, either, given that you stutter when you suggest it."

He rolled his eyes. "You sound like . . . Gryff."

"Take it back!" She bumped into him again, a little harder this time.

He laughed. And then frowned. "Do you hear . . . something?"

They were at the edge of the village now, the first few houses just beyond a copse of trees. And now that she listened, she could indeed. The rather frantic cries of a woman just barely reached her ears on the summer breeze.

Peter, of course, was off at a lope before she'd even had a chance to process which direction the sound came from, tugging her along with him.

She moved to let go of his arm when she saw that it was Mrs. Gladstone bellowing. Except that he must have read her mind — he grabbed hold of her fingers before she could pivot on her heel and leave the woman to whatever horror had befallen her. Probably a squeaky stair. Or an insect that had the gall to land on one of her pretty little flowers.

"Mrs. G-Gladstone! What is it?"

An itch on her back she couldn't reach. A shoe pinching her toes.

Mrs. Gladstone flew at them, tears streaming down her face and arms waving in the air. "Help me! Mr. Holstein, help, you must! Little Marcus is in there, and I've done it again! I've locked myself out!"

Peter let go of Rosemary's hand to catch Mrs. Gladstone as she landed on his chest, sobbing. He patted her back. "There now.

We . . . we'll fetch a spare k-key. Does your . . . your brother have one? Or your son?"

"They're both away, that's why I've got Marcus. Oh, I'm a wretch! An absolute wretch."

Rosemary couldn't entirely disagree with that. But as the woman quieted, a new wail painted the air. Rosemary's brow wrinkled. She had assumed, she supposed, that this wasn't really a crisis — that Marcus was probably ten and perfectly capable of unlocking the door himself.

But that was the cry of a baby. Perhaps not a newborn, but a baby. And it wasn't the halfhearted cry of a child just waking, it was full-fledged wailing.

Rosemary vaulted onto the porch. "Have you a window open?" Surely she did, as hot as it was. They could simply climb inside.

"No! He was napping. You can't have fresh air on a baby when he sleeps, don't you know anything?"

Rosemary rolled her eyes at that rot and reached for a window, through which she saw the red-faced little boy, standing up in his crib and trying, it seemed, to climb out of it. "Unlocked, though, surely."

"Surely *not*. You never know what thieves and worse are lurking around." Mrs. Gladstone pushed past Rosemary and set to banging on the door again. As if the baby would come and unlock it for her.

Peter mounted the steps at a more reasonable pace. "We'll . . . we'll have to break a window."

The lady, naturally, went into a fit at that. But there was little help for it. Peter went off to look for a handy stone or brick or tool, and Rosemary debated whether it would be cruel to him to send the blubbering Mrs. Gladstone after him to help in the search.

Then a *crash* sounded from within, and the cries inside redoubled. There was something in them now — not just panic, but pain. Rosemary slid back to the window.

Mrs. Gladstone pushed her aside. "The crib!" Mrs. Gladstone, looking through the window, raised a fist to pound on it. "It's broken!" She pounded again.

Rosemary lunged at her, pulled her away. "Stop! You can't just break a window with your fist, you'll cut yourself to ribbons and spray glass on the babe besides. Just give me a moment." Heart galloping, she flipped open her handbag and reached for the roll of muslin at the bottom. The slender metal tools she kept there.

Her hands were steady as she pulled them

out and moved back to the door. She was used to adrenaline pumping while she had these out, used to distracting noises and panic nipping. It didn't slow her, didn't make her fumble. She inserted the pick into the lock, gave herself a moment to gauge where the tumblers were, and within a few seconds heard that beautiful *click*.

Mrs. Gladstone charged through the doorway the moment Rosemary turned the knob. She was crying as loudly as her grandson was, though a glance inside seemed to say the little one — probably about a year old — wasn't badly injured. He had a scrape on his chubby leg, but he was quieting, now that his grandmother's arms were about him.

Rosemary shook her head and slid her pick back into her bag. Turned.

And smacked directly into Peter's gaze. He stood there with a pry bar in hand, and with questions rioting over his face.

She couldn't quite manage a masking smile. Just a feeble clearing of her throat. "Many siblings . . . few keys."

He didn't believe her. His brows said as much when they lifted like that. But he didn't go screaming for the constable either. He just set down the pry bar and held out a hand. "Hungry?"

Why, to her ears, did it sound like *Guilty*?

TWENTY-THREE

She'd be leaving soon. Locryn could see it in the way she held her head. The way her shoulders were two blades again. The way she refused to meet his gaze. He rested a hand on the pistol that hung, as always, at his side.

He ought to do something. Say something. Grab her arm and haul her in to the authorities. He ought to

"Mr. Holstein!" The beckon came simultaneously with a knock, which may not have fazed him had the knock not also accompanied the distinct *whoosh* of his door opening.

Peter looked up, eyes wide, not quite believing Mrs. Teague actually stood in his doorway without waiting for permission to enter. "Is something else on . . . on fire?"

He stood, ready to run out the door.

But it wasn't panic on her face. Not *ex-*

actly, anyway. She shook her head, and her hands fluttered, and she stepped two inches into the room and then back into the doorway. "It's — you've a guest, Mr. Holstein."

"A guest." He wasn't sure if he should smile or frown. "An . . . an angel? A ghost?" He couldn't think of what else would put that particular look on his pragmatic housekeeper's face.

Her hands fluttered again. "It's . . ." She looked over her shoulder, out into the hall. Then back to him. "It's *the prince.*"

"Prince Edward?" Curious. But hardly cause for alarm. He pulled the sheet of paper from the typewriter, set it in the drawer, slid the drawer closed, and turned the key.

Not, apparently, that keys mattered in the world, so long as people could just carry small pointed tools in their handbags and open any doors they pleased.

He smiled at Mrs. Teague. "Is he in the . . . the drawing room?"

"The gardens." She sucked in a long breath and fanned herself with her hand. "He said they were beautiful. My Teague's gardens, complimented by the prince himself!"

Peter chuckled and slid the key into its

usual place in his pocket. "They are. Have I not . . . said so often enough?"

"Oh, you." Apparently regaining herself a bit, she stepped into the hall with a smile. "Forgive me for barging in, Mr. Holstein. But I couldn't very well let you keep *the prince* waiting, could I?"

"Of course not. It's . . . it's quite all right." He paused for a moment in the hall and looked toward the library door. Rosemary sat hunched over her table, not even looking up. She had carried a few boxes down from the attic this morning that seemed to have Father's legal papers in them. One could well have the deed. The naturalization records. And if so, then . . .

Then she'd leave.

He drew in a breath and took the quickest path toward the gardens, stepping out into the sunlight and having to shade his eyes to see where amid Teague's cultivated wilds the prince might be lurking.

It wasn't hard to spot him. He was pacing back and forth, his Grenadier Guard uniform a stark contrast against the flowers. He had his hat under his arm, leaving his fair hair to gleam in the sunlight.

Blast it, but he looked young. All the younger in a military uniform. Which made Peter feel disturbingly old. "Your Highness."

The prince spun, eyes alight, and hurried toward him. "There you are. You've got to talk sense to them, Peter. You *must.*"

His lips twitched. "And this 'them' is . . . ?"

"Father. And Kitchener." The young man motioned northeast, toward London more or less. "They won't listen to me. But they'll listen to you. Tell them that I'm not going to sit back and watch it all happen. I won't."

Kitchener? Peter felt cooler than he should have, out here in the July sun. "Slow . . . slow down, David."

Hearing his preferred nickname — the last of his many middle names, as it were — brought a measure of calm to the young man. He drew up, drew in a long breath, let it out.

Peter nodded. "Now. Kitchener?" He wasn't sure he wanted to know why Prince Edward would be in debates with the military commander.

The prince's nostrils flared. "Father said I might tell you — news just reached us last night. Austria has issued an ultimatum to Serbia and given them two days to comply."

Peter reached behind him to the stone bench. "What k-kind of . . . of ultimatum?"

"According to Churchill, the kind no country could actually agree to." The prince spun back to the path, pacing a few steps before pivoting. "They did it with Germany's approval. Everyone — the cabinet, Father, the prime minister — they all think Austria and Germany mean to make a quick strike. Take over Serbia, then back out before anyone else can be drawn into it. But Russia won't let that happen. They've already pledged their support of Serbia. War will be declared within a few days, Peter, and I must be *in* it. What kind of leader will I be if everyone in England knows I was safely behind the lines through the whole blasted thing? It would make a mockery of this uniform."

Dominoes. The dominoes were falling — he could hear them clicking together in his ear. He shook his head. "David, you're . . . you're the heir to the throne. You cannot . . . you cannot serve on the f-front lines."

"Of course I *can* — if they'll only agree." He stopped again and lifted a hand to his face. "You surely understand, you always understand everything. I want to help. I want to make a difference. I want . . . I want to be who I am."

Peter sighed. "I understand . . . perfectly. But your desires cannot . . . change facts. You are the heir. To the crown of Britain. If you were killed —"

"Then my brother will inherit. It isn't as though Father is without another heir. But if I *live* . . ." His blue eyes went brighter still, bright as the summer sky above them. "If I live, Peter, and I have fought, then I'll be the kind of king the people will rally around. And more, I'll . . . I'll be a man worth knowing. A hero, perhaps."

Had he sounded so idealistic at twenty? Peter stood again and motioned for his young friend to walk with him. "But what if . . . what if you're captured?"

Prince Edward gusted out a breath. "That's what *they* said. 'Think of the immense harm that would occur, Your Royal Highness,' " he said in a voice made deep and gruff, presumably in imitation of Kitchener, " 'should *you,* the very *heir* to the throne of Britain, fall into the hands of the enemy.' "

Peter smiled. "They have a . . . a point."

The prince didn't look inclined to grant it. He set his jaw in the very way King George did when he'd had enough of whatever poppycock someone was trying to feed him. "As have I. But they'll never grant it." And his eyes, when he shot a glance at Peter, were flinty. "But they cannot keep me under their thumb entirely. Perhaps they can order my regiment behind the front lines, but I'll find a way to get to them. I will."

He would. Of that Peter had no doubt. "Then I shall . . . I shall pray God's protection ever . . . around you."

They walked a few more steps in silence. Out of the garden proper and toward the back of the house.

Once past the kitchen — and the noses within it pressed to the glass — Prince Edward sighed. "Sometimes I just wish I could be *David*. That I could sign up like any other man. Serve like any other man."

As he wished he could just be *Peter*. He nodded. "We cannot . . . we cannot change who we are though. Even if we go by a diff . . . a different name."

Even if the world knew him as Hollow, he would still be Holstein. He would always be Holstein. And any who would forget it weren't the ones who would cause him trouble for it anyway.

"No. But the opposite is true too, isn't it? No matter our name, our title — we cannot be but who we are. Underneath."

Peter smiled. "You have a . . . a point."

"Good. Tell my father so, will you?"

His chuckle was picked up by the wind, echoed by the leaves. Died down again. "I will . . . write to him. Advise him that you must . . . you must stretch your wings. But, David — you must respect him too. His concerns. His wishes."

The prince sighed and flipped his hat around. "You're always so blasted measured. It can be annoying, you know."

They crossed the back path but kept heading around the rear of the house. "Yet you came . . . here."

"Because measured seems to work for you. And Father listens to you. Everyone listens to you."

Not everyone. If everyone listened, then he wouldn't be looking for a man in a bowler every time he stepped outside. Wondering which neighbors had turned so thoroughly against him. But perhaps Rosemary was right — perhaps enough would listen to him, if he spoke up. Or wrote something, as the case may be. "Do you listen?"

The young man grinned and positioned his hat back on his head. "We'll see, I suppose. I'll try, but really, Peter — no one can live like you do. It isn't possible."

"No?" Looking around at his world — the cliffs, the woods, the home, the friends — he didn't know why not. "I rather . . . like it."

"You've a beautiful home. I grant you

that, most readily." He made a show of looking around him as they rounded the far corner. And then he came to a halt, a boyish — yet not — smile on his lips. "I was about to say you were missing one rather vital piece of a happy life — a woman. But it seems you have one after all, you old dog."

"What?" But he had only to look forward to see Rosemary leaning out the window as she often did. Eyes closed, face tilted up for the sun's warmth. Looking . . . beautiful. Utterly beautiful. "No. That's . . . Rosemary. My librarian."

Prince Edward laughed. "I wish our librarians looked like that."

"David." He couldn't help the chiding, it just came out. Even though plenty of people would have been amazed — or horrified — that he dared to rebuke the heir apparent. Said heir's father, however, would fully approve.

Said heir just laughed again. "You mean to tell me you don't appreciate that she's a far sight prettier than Mr. Hall?"

Peter's lips twitched as he watched her roll a kink from her neck. "She is. Isn't she?"

"And you, good Mr. Holstein, can't seem to take your eyes off her." He slapped a hand to Peter's shoulder — none too gently — and jogged forward. "Hello there!"

Oh, blast. Rosemary would skin him alive for letting her meet the prince while hanging out a window. "David! Wait."

But the prince was already nearing the window, grinning up at Rosemary like Treeve always did. Saying, "Good day, lady fair. Had you a braid reaching down, I would think you Rapunzel."

Peter rolled his eyes as he neared. "That is a . . . a terrible line."

Rosemary, her hand currently being kissed by royal lips, looked over at Peter with a grin. But the kind that said, *What a sweet little boy* and not *What a dashing man.* Which, he had to admit, made it far more amusing. "Who's your friend, Peter?"

She wouldn't know, of course — he was in a military uniform, not his regalia. And the prince wasn't in the press all that much. Yet. Peter cleared his throat. "Your Highness, allow me to . . . to introduce to you Miss Rosemary . . . Gresham."

"Your *what*?" Pulling her hand back, Rosemary jerked away — and promptly smacked her head against the window frame above her.

"Oh!" Prince Edward leaned forward. But his concern was a bit tarnished by his laugh. "I'm so sorry. Are you all right?"

Rosemary had disappeared. But her voice

543

floated to them. "Yes, quite. Of course. Your Highness. An honor to . . . to meet you."

Well. Now *she* was stammering. Peter smiled, stood on tiptoe, and leaned through the window. She was on the floor, but he suspected it was mortification that kept her there, not pain. He tapped her on the head, albeit lightly. "Rosie?"

She peeked up at him. And mumbled, "If you won't do the merciful thing and kill me, at least *go away.*"

First he had to prod a bit. It was his duty as a friend. He hooked a thumb toward the outside. "Prince Edward."

Her glare ought by rights to have set him on fire, so hot was it. "I gathered."

He chuckled and leaned back into the outside.

The prince was grinning at him. "I like her," he declared as he took off for the front of the house. Loudly enough that she had to have heard. Then — more quietly, thankfully — he added, "Just your librarian, you say? Are you quite sure?"

Peter sighed. "And . . . my friend."

Shaking his head, Prince Edward picked up his pace. "Sometimes, man, you baffle me. A pretty girl you obviously fancy, and she's only your *friend*? And *librarian*?"

"I'm not . . . you know I'm not . . . the

type to . . . to . . ."

The prince laughed again. "You can't even talk about it without blushing. What of marriage, then? Aren't you the type for *that*?"

He slung his hands inside his pockets and focused his gaze on the new beams going up for the stable. "We're from . . . different worlds."

"I wouldn't let that stop me if I loved a woman."

At that, Peter had to send him a lifted brow.

Prince Edward grinned. "Or I like to think I wouldn't. I suppose it's possible I would cave in to the pressure of my parents. But you haven't that worry, have you? You've no one to answer to but yourself. Why shouldn't you marry whomever you please?"

He wasn't about to have this conversation with the twenty-year-old prince. Largely because he wasn't sure what his own position was — or what his heart wanted. He'd never been in love. He could write about it — hopefully well enough to be convincing — but he'd never experienced it, but for watching others.

And the last thing he needed was Prince Edward returning to the king and telling him that Peter Holstein had said that a man ought to marry whomever he wished, regardless of station. Perhaps it *was* possible for him, a man of some means but no title to worry with. It was certainly *not* the case for the prince.

They reached the drive, where an automobile gleamed black and silver and two armed guards stood beside it. Peter cleared his throat. "Stay for . . . for tea?"

"Better not. I want to be home when we get news of Serbia's answer. And then I'll have to report back to my commander."

War. War was coming. Was only days away, most likely. And this young man before him was determined to have a piece of it. He shook his head. "Go with God . . . David."

Prince Edward stuck out a hand. "Don't wait around for life to happen to you, Peter. Give it a good chase."

He shook his young friend's hand, smiled. "Perhaps . . . perhaps I will." As soon as he figured out what it was he wanted from it.

"You've got to be joking." Eseld stared at her with large, round eyes, her fork just hanging there in midair, forgotten. "The *prince*? Of *England*?"

Rosemary grinned. And rolled her eyes for good measure. "No, Seld, the prince of *Denmark* came by to speak with Peter. Of course of England."

The fork wobbled, and the bite of mushy peas fell from it and landed with a *plop* on the table. "And you *met* him? I don't believe it!"

"Well, do. I still have the knot to prove it." She touched her head where she'd struck the windowpane, giving an exaggerated wince. It didn't hurt anymore — hadn't for days — but if she were going to tell the tale, she might as well make it good.

And it was too good not to tell, even at her own expense. Just think — she, Rosemary Gresham, had met the crown prince of England! She leaned forward, toward her stupefied friend. "And he kissed my hand." Before she'd made an utter fool of herself, but that was entirely beside the point. She could hardly wait to get home to London and tell the family about it.

Funny, though, the pang that resonated through her at that thought. She wanted to see them all. Missed them terribly.

But she'd miss *these* people when she left. Eseld with her pretty curls, Jenny with her brilliant smile. Penrose with his abundant glowers. All right, not him quite as much. But little Elowyn, who still insisted on being called Wyn. Treeve and Kenver and Tamsyn.

And Peter. *Peter.*

"Let me see it." Eseld dropped the fork and reached over to take Rosemary's right hand, lifting it and holding it to her cheek.

Rosemary laughed.

Eseld closed her eyes and rubbed Rosemary's hand a bit against her face. "There. The closest I shall ever come to royal lips upon my flesh."

"You bet it is." Moody Colin Thorn stood there at their table, glowering at his wife. With a twinkle in his eye. Rosemary hadn't been able to spot that twinkle when she'd only looked at him from across the room, but once she'd actually bothered speaking to him, it had been apparent. Especially when he watched Eseld moving about with her tray.

He still wasn't quite as handsome as Treeve. Nor as basically good-natured, to her way of thinking. But hearts had their reasons, as someone or another had said.

She'd ask Peter who'd said it. He would know.

Eseld slanted a flirtatious look up at Colin and pressed her lips to Rosemary's hand. He narrowed his eyes at her and planted his hand on his hip. "Can't let you out of my sight for a minute, can I, my 'ansum?"

She wiggled her brows. " 'Ere, love — Rosemary actually met Prince Edward. He came to visit Mr. Holstein."

"Aye, I saw the car going by with its flags and guards and nonsense. Don't know what all the hullabaloo's about." He used the cloth tucked into his belt to wipe up the peas. And grinned. "Now when the *princess* comes, let me know."

Eseld smacked him, sending him off with a booming laugh.

Rosemary grinned and cradled her mug of tea, now that she had her hand back. Then froze. Movement in the corner caught her eye, though she didn't know why it should. Sure, the form looked familiar — but everyone in the village did, these days. The stranger in the bowler — Mr. Jasper's man from London — seemed to have vanished. So why should one particular shift catch her eye? Was the man back?

The slant of evening light through the window caught on silver-and-gold hair. The tea she'd just drunk turned to sludge in her stomach.

"Did I hear you say something about the prince?" Betty slid into the booth beside Rosemary, her eyes also wide, though guileless.

Rosemary let Eseld do the telling this time. She added a word here or there for clarification, but mostly she focused on keeping her glances to the corner discreet.

It was a full two minutes before the man moved enough that she caught sight of his profile.

Blast it to London and back — it *was* Mr. V.

Betty gave a happy sigh and stood again. "I can hardly believe I was within a mile of the prince. I'll have to tell Tim about it when I visit him tomorrow."

Rosemary dredged up a smile. "You're looking better, Betty. How have you been feeling?"

Betty nodded by way of answer and gave her a sweet little smile. "You want more tea, Rosie?"

It wouldn't settle, not now. So she shook her head and scooted to the end of the bench. "Actually, I'd better be going."

"Oh, not so soon!" Eseld had only just picked up her fork again but now put it back down. "I hate to eat alone, you know I do."

"You'll survive it somehow. I've faith in you." With a grin, Rosemary reached for her handbag.

She'd half-expected Mrs. Gladstone to have gone about town shouting about what she kept in her bag, warning everyone not to speak to her. More than half-expected, honestly. But the woman had, in an unprecedented display of self-restraint, remained mum about her little rescue.

No doubt because it would have made the matron look irresponsible with her grandson.

She could hear Peter in her head, telling her not to be uncharitable. Then she could see him in her mind's eye, looking at her again as he'd done that day.

In self-defense, she'd decided to avoid him after that, using the excuse of needing to find his family's documents. Which mostly worked. Except for the dozens of times she had to ask him to help with the translation of his father's bizarre writing as she sifted through the stash of his things she'd found in the attic. And those instances when he was suddenly there in the library when she looked up, holding another journal she might want to look at or to read her the latest article in the papers about the ultimatum. And perhaps, too, aside from those times when she wandered into the dining room for a cup of tea or coffee and ended up sharing a meal with him through no fault of her own.

But she was a realist. She knew those moments didn't mean he'd forgotten his suspicion — Peter wasn't the type to forget such a thing.

And it absolutely didn't mean she was in love with him. Which she would tell Willa again when she got home.

Which should be soon. Could, honestly, be any day. She'd found them that afternoon — the papers he so desperately needed. The deed and the naturalization documents for both Wilhelm and Aksel. Proving that, by default, Peter was English as well. Yes, they had done everything necessary to assure him dual citizenship during his childhood — he had been born in Germany, in fact, and they had spent the requisite number of months there with him throughout the years. All that was carefully documented as well.

But born to an English father. That made him an English subject. And when he gained his majority, he'd had to decide which citizenship he would keep. A choice he hadn't, she knew, really had to debate. Germany had not become again what Wilhelm had prayed it would. It had rather continued down the path that had sent him away from it to begin with.

She'd found the proof. And rather than rush in to show him, she'd stowed the papers behind that false-back to the shelf where the journals had been. Because finding them meant, in his eyes, that her work was done. She'd have to leave.

But she still had to figure out what to tell Mr. V. And apparently she'd better figure it out quickly.

Eseld gusted out a sigh. "Fine then, abandon me. Force me to go and eat with my surly ol' husband who's over there bemoaning that it wasn't pretty Princess Mary who came to the village."

Rosemary chuckled and forced herself not to look at that corner booth again. "Trying for you, I know. See you later. Good night, Betty. Tell Tim I said hello." *And I'm sorry.*

Betty smiled and moved off to take someone's empty plate.

Rosemary headed for the door. She didn't make it out, of course, without parrying three shouted greetings, including one that turned into recounting yet again the prince's visit to Kensey. She left out the reasons for it — everyone knew by now about the ultimatum, of course, but they didn't need to know that the prince had told Peter the news before any of the papers had gotten wind of it. And no one seemed to question the *why*. They were too awed by the *that*.

At last, she made it outside. A glance at her watch told her Mr. Trenholm would still be at Kensey for another hour at least. Usually she stayed in the village until she figured he was gone. The long summer evenings made it no great thing, with the light lasting so long, to walk back even at eight o'clock. But tonight she'd start in that direction. If Mr. V didn't find her, then she'd just slip into the cottage. Or, since it could well be her last Monday here, perhaps . . . perhaps she'd go in and say hello. Trenholm wasn't a bad sort.

She'd made it half a mile toward home before the car puttered up behind her and slowed. The passenger door opened.

With a sigh, Rosemary slid in. "Willa said you'd be coming."

Mr. V drove as he did everything else — as if it required no effort, as if he were merely sitting there reading a book. He didn't so much as glance at her. "And she told me you were having some difficulties."

She had the sudden urge to give Willa a good shaking. "No. I've found the answers for you — they're just not what I was expecting, is all. Peter Holstein isn't a traitor. He's as loyal to England as a man can be."

His hum didn't sound disbelieving. It sounded amused. "Is he."

Why did the man never ask questions? He just stated things, as if he'd known them all the time. But he couldn't have, not this time, or why would he have sent her here? She turned a bit on the seat to face him. "Look. You sent me here for answers, and I've found them. Peter Holstein has no great love for Germany. His family left because they hated the politics of von Bismarck, of which they advised the royal family for generations. He's trustworthy. He's loyal."

"What else is he?"

A question, but it still didn't sound like one. Didn't feel like one. Rosemary felt her spine go stiff. "What do you mean, what *else* is he? What does it matter? He's a loyal English subject. A good man."

Mr. V's chuckle sounded far less amused than his hum had. "You've found nothing, really, have you? What does he do all day, Miss Gresham?"

She dug her fingers into her handbag. "He reads, much of it. Have you seen his library?"

"Miss Gresham."

Blast it, he had no right to know when she lied. Was the man even human? "He types."

"Types. What?"

She could feel the pick on the bottom of her bag. Evidence of who she was. What she was. "I don't know. Nothing bad. All he ever speaks of is his faith — it's probably a treatise on it."

He took the big bend between the village and Kensey without even slowing down. "I don't deal in 'probably,' Miss Gresham. What of the mountains of correspondence?"

"It's nothing. He writes letters to everyone — authors, artists. Just letters. Friendly. Talking, again, of faith."

Mr. V lifted his brows. "He has whole boxes of it delivered, you know. Through his lawyer. What are *those*? I daresay not more of the same."

How? How could he know so much? Rosemary shook her head. "I've found nothing but those normal letters. And I've been all through the attic where he stores them." Mostly. Perhaps. She may have missed a box or two, somewhere or another.

"Then you're missing something." His hands didn't go tight on the wheel. The muscles didn't go tight at his jaw. But he was angry. She knew it in the same way that she knew when to duck, when to hide to avoid a bobby. "I need to know what he's writing all day."

"I've tried to find that out, but he's in there almost all the time. And he keeps everything locked up. Every time I've attempted to get in, I've been stopped."

Now he let up on the gas. And he looked

at her. And she wished, as those icy blue eyes drilled into her, that he hadn't. "Miss Gresham, why do you think I employed a thief for this task? The girl who could gain entrance into the British Museum in thirty seconds flat in order to steal a rare German manuscript ought to have no problem opening a German's study — nor his desk drawers."

Her mouth went dry. And she gripped her handbag as if it could save her.

Maybe it could. But she wasn't so sure she'd still be able to live with herself after it did. "How do you — ?"

"It is my business to know things. And to tell them only when needed. Thus far, I have had no great need to tell anyone about your exploits, as I knew they could someday serve me. But fail in this, Miss Gresham . . ."

And she'd go to prison, for that job she'd learned German for to begin with. He'd have evidence, no doubt. Scads of it. A man as careful as him, who knew as much as he did, knew to have carefully constructed evidence before he made a threat.

She would go to prison. She deserved to go to prison.

She didn't *want* to go to prison. What would her family do? And what would Mr. V do to them, if she didn't deliver what he wanted now? When she blinked, she saw little Olivia, her leg in a cast, held up by one of those odd contraptions to keep it raised. She saw Willa and Retta, Lucy and Elinor out on the streets, trying to steal enough to get by. She saw Barclay . . . in prison with her. Because they'd worked that museum job together, and if Mr. V had dirt on *her* for it, he had dirt on *him.*

The family would fall apart without Barclay.

The car slowed. Mr. V was still looking at her. "Get me evidence, Miss Gresham. Solid evidence of what he does all day. I need typed pages. Proof. Do you understand?"

She could only nod.

The car halted, and Mr. V leaned across her to open the door. He smelled of peppermint. Which was a deceptively friendly smell given the words he'd just spoken.

She turned to slide out, but then stopped. She couldn't just give up without a fight — it wasn't in her. "Are you working for Mr. Jasper? Or *are* you him?"

His eyes narrowed, though it was the only movement in his face. "What is that name to you?"

Her throat went tight, but it was more with anger than apprehension. "I know that he's trying to prove Mr. Holstein isn't an

English subject. Trying to cast suspicion of espionage his way. I'll not have a part in it — you need to know that now. Whatever it is he does all day, he's a good man, and I'll not be party to him being imprisoned or worse."

Mr. V lifted a brow. "I'm not paying you to make judgments, Miss Gresham. Just to deliver to me the information I requested. Now, if you've quite finished . . ."

Blast the man. She slid out, into the half-muddy road. "I'll only deliver the truth to you. Nothing more, nothing less."

Mr. V gave her a cool smile. "Friday, three o'clock. Meet me at the big tree on the corner of his property, the one with the heart carved into it."

He knew Peter's wood? She shivered, though the evening was hot and sticky. And she nodded.

The car door closed. "Have a good evening, Miss Gresham," he said through the open window. "And remember — with the greatest risks . . ."

Even that — even that he knew. She swallowed. ". . . come the greatest rewards."

But as he drove off, leaving her standing there at the base of Kensey's winding drive, she knew a thousand pounds wasn't worth it. It wasn't worth being in league with a man like that, who could deliver innocents to possible death, who could very well be behind the fire and the arrow. No amount of money was worth that.

Her family, though . . . how could she ever put a price on them?

TWENTY-FOUR

Peter stared at the page for a long moment. Reread the last few paragraphs. The *last* paragraphs. Or he thought they were. Endings . . . endings were work for him. Even when he knew exactly how he wanted them to happen, he had a tendency to rush through those closing pages, which meant having to ball them up and toss them in the grate and write the last chapter over.

Not this time. He hoped. He'd been deliberate. Careful. Largely because he wasn't entirely sure how the last scene would have to play out. Locryn and Thomas — should their friendship be back on solid ground, or would a bit of quaking make the next book better? Then Locryn and Rosita — he was letting her get away. Knowing well he shouldn't but doing it anyway. Because he loved her. And she . . . she was tossing that charming smile over her shoulder at him.

A promise for another match someday. Another game.

And Locryn, the fool, was looking forward to it.

Peter steepled his fingers and rested his lips against them, staring at that final sentence. Was it good enough, this story? This villainess-heroine? Or would his publisher declare it rubbish? His readers hate it?

He breathed out a prayer and breathed in peace. He'd spent a fair bit of time on his knees this morning, asking for God's guidance as he typed these last pages. He would trust that he'd written what he should have. And that if it could be better, his editor would tell him so.

Knock, knock, knock. "Pete? Can I come in, old boy?"

And Gryff. Gryff would tell him so too, if he had time in his schedule to read it before Peter had to ship it off next week to his publisher. He settled his fingers on the keys. "Come in." Typed those two most beautiful words: *The End.*

Gryff opened the door just enough to slide in, then closed it behind him. Rubbed his hands together. "Well? Have you finished it yet?"

"Just." In proof, he pulled the sheet from

the typewriter and set it, just so, facedown on the stack of its comrades.

"Cutting it rather close this time, aren't you?" But Gryff was smiling as he came over to peer into the drawer at the sheets that had multiplied several times over since he saw that meager stack with which Peter had come home from London.

Peter grinned. "Genius takes . . . time."

Gryff snorted and made himself comfortable in Father's leather chair by the unlit hearth. "Jenny sent me over. She said you need to join me and Santo at the pub tonight — talk's been of nothing but this ultimatum, and word of Serbia's response ought to be coming any minute. When it comes over the wire, someone will announce it there. You need to be there. With me, with us. With everyone."

Dominoes. Peter sighed and slid the drawer closed. Then opened it again. Drew out the thick pile of pages, straightened them, and put them back in their drawer right-side up. He'd read the thing tomorrow, into Thursday if it took that long. Correct. Tweak. "I had hoped . . . had prayed. But war — it will be here. Soon."

"I know." He did, his tone said as much. Said he felt the strain of it. "Santo wants to join the military once it's official. Officer training, he hopes."

Peter nodded, searching his friend's face. And didn't much like what he saw. Even as he admired it. And wondered if he should mirror it. "You will . . . too?"

Gryff sighed. "Jenny doesn't want me to, of course. And I doubt I will right away — let all the young pups eager for conflict get out of the way first, see if perhaps they can win it quickly. But if it lasts a year . . . I don't know how I could do otherwise. How I would look myself in the mirror if I didn't, when I am able."

Peter rubbed at his nose. He wasn't sure he was able. He'd probably be no good on the front lines — he wasn't like Prince Edward, full of the certainties of youth. But surely there was some role he could play. Some way he could serve. He had a decent brain, it ought to be put to use for England somehow. Preferably in a way that required little by way of verbal communication. Perhaps it would involve sitting in an office most of the day, alone.

He would pray for guidance there. And the Lord would give it, as He always did. "I'll come. To . . . tonight."

"Good." Though Gryff grinned, it was still tight around the edges. "Now. When can I read this book of yours?"

"Soon. I have to . . . have to correct it first." He looked again at the drawer. At the lock, with its key sticking out of it. From habit, he took it out and slid it into his pocket. And stared at that little metal hole that didn't mean all that much. "I'm going to tell her."

Silence greeted him, so he looked up to see that Gryff was just giving him that look. The one that said he hadn't enough information to make an educated response.

Peter leaned back in his chair. "Rosemary. I'm going to . . . to tell her about this. Who I . . . who I am." He would hand her the manuscript. Ask her to read it. To give him her honest opinion.

Gryff's breath wheezed out. "Are you sure that's wise? You've scarcely known her two months. She could go and blab it all about England. Ruin the secrecy you've gone to such great lengths to preserve."

She could. "She won't."

"Pete." Pushing to his feet, Gryff gestured, not unlike the way he did when delivering a final argument before a judge. "I like her. Jenny and Wyn adore her. The whole town is fond of her — but there's a difference between trusting her with your library and trusting her with your very identity."

Perhaps. But there seemed very little dif-

ference between trusting her with his identity and trusting her with his heart. And as
he'd written Locryn saying good-bye to
Rosita, felt his pain, he'd known he couldn't
just say good-bye to Rosemary. He couldn't.

He reached for the jacket draped over his
chair. "We had better . . . better get along.
Did you drive?"

"You're not just going to ignore me, old
boy. Not this time. It's too important. If
you tell her about this —"

"I wasn't . . . asking your opinion."

"Made up your mind, have you?" For a
moment, he wavered. Peter watched him as
he rocked a bit, his face alternating between
the desire to argue and the instinct to trust.
Trust won, with an exasperated sigh. "Stubborn as a mule. Just for that, I'm not sending your answer to your cousins until next
week."

He hadn't yet? Peter bit back the shout
that wanted to slip out. He'd told Gryff on
Friday to do it straightaway. Before war
could be declared and things would get
more complicated. It already ran the risk of
getting all fouled up. He let only a low,
frustrated "Gryff!" slip out.

Gryff, the jester, grinned. "Got you. I sent
it Friday night, as you requested. And also
as you requested, instructions on flushing

566

out who AGD is. Though I seriously doubt they're anyone to worry about."

He hoped so. But couldn't quite rid himself of that niggle at the base of his neck that said otherwise. Scooping up his hat from the corner of his desk, he then turned to the library door and pulled it open.

Rosemary was at the window again, which made him smile. "Any . . . princes out there?"

She ducked back in with a chuckle. "Not today. Though one never knows when King George himself might come strolling by, I suppose." She took in the jacket, the hat, and lifted her brows. "Going out?"

"With Gryff. To the . . . the pub."

"Ah." She nodded, and the sobriety in her gaze said she could guess at why. "That's a good idea. Want me to let Grammy know you'll not be here for dinner?"

"If you . . . if you would."

"Certainly." Though she screwed up her face a bit as she moved closer. "You've got your tie all askew. You can't go into the pub like that. May I?"

She was already reaching for him. His "Of course" was superfluous. And he could only pray she didn't notice the way his breath caught when her hands went to work there at his throat. She didn't even touch *him,* just his tie. And still his pulse kicked up. But then, she was standing close. And right in front of him, rather than at his side. He could just lean over and kiss her, if he were brave enough. Slip an arm around her waist and . . .

"There we are." She stepped back again with a satisfied nod and smiled up at him, clearly oblivious to how close she'd come to being kissed.

Or how close she'd come to him seriously considering it, at any rate.

He cleared his throat and stepped back. "Do you . . . need anything? F-From the . . . village?"

Now she frowned. Naturally, she never missed a stutter any more than Gryff did. "No. Are you all right?"

He sighed. "Just . . . anxious. For the news."

"Oh." Her fingers caught his, tangled with them, and made his breath tangle up again. "Don't be, Peter. Everyone who counts knows where you stand. What you stand for."

Before he could lay hold of a response, a cleared throat from the doorway to his study interrupted. Pointedly. Gryff, under his scowl, looked decidedly amused. "Better hurry, old boy. Santo will be there any minute." He nodded at Rosemary. "Evening, Miss Gresham."

"Mr. Penrose." She let go of Peter's hand, but not until after another squeeze. "Have a good evening. And bring me the news when you get back, if you would."

He could only nod. And turn. And follow Gryff back into and through his office, closing both his doors behind him.

Gryff was chuckling as they headed out the main hall toward the front doors. "Peter has a crush," he delivered in a singsong more suitable to his daughter.

"Stop it." Peter smacked him with his hat. And then put it on his head. "I do not."

Crush didn't begin to cover it.

Rosemary waited until she heard the telltale clamor in the kitchen. The laughter from Kerensa and Treeve, the deep voice of Mr. Teague, the sweet insistence of Grammy. Those who lived off the property had left. The rest were all gathered around the big wooden table, ready to share their meal.

Mrs. Teague had already delivered her a tray. It sat right where she'd left it.

Rosemary couldn't eat. Not now.

She waited until she was sure they were all settled. And then she slid on silent feet over to the door to the study and put her hand on the knob.

It didn't want to turn. Not the knob — her hand. It didn't — *she* didn't want to take this final step. It was different, somehow, than looking through his library. His boxes in the attic. He'd given her permission for those — eventually.

But she'd done it all with the intention of betraying him. The damage was already done. She had to see it through.

Still, she had to squeeze her eyes shut. "Forgive me." That whisper may have been aimed at Peter . . . or perhaps at his God.

She sucked in a breath, turned the knob, and followed the swing of the door into his study.

It looked as it always did — an utter ruin. Books and paper everywhere, cups with tea dregs and plates with crumbs. As always, the only clear spot on the desk was the typewriter, where she'd left that first note her first day.

She owed him another. But how could she write to him, asking him all the questions on her heart, when she was about to intrude upon his sanctum?

"To help him," she told the typewriter. "To prove him innocent."

The typewriter just stared at her.

So long as it didn't tattle on her. After

taking note of the position of the chair, she sat down in it and surveyed the drawers. Reached for the one on her right. It slid easily open, despite the lock on its front.

Paper inside, to be sure. Familiar paper, many of the edges ragged from where she'd torn it from her notebook. She reached in and pulled out the stack. Seventy sheets of it — one for each day she'd been here. He'd kept them, all of them.

Of course he did — Peter never threw out a letter, that was why his attic was so full of them it was a wonder the floor didn't cave in.

But he'd not relegated them to a box, like the rest. What did that mean? Anything?

She bent back over the drawer, but the only other thing within it was some unused paper. The drawer beneath had an assortment of paper clips and rubber bands. The bottom had a mish-mosh of pages scribbled all over in Peter's hand, in that gibberish that had stymied her so until she'd found the journals.

Her lips quirked up. She could read it now, but her glances told her that it was nothing beyond what she'd come to expect from him — notes on things he didn't want to forget, or on history he had apparently found interesting for one reason or another.

The middle drawer, long and slender, under the typewriter had two new ribbons for that machine, and an assortment of pens.

She reached for the top left drawer, tugged. It stayed resolutely closed.

Her breath leaked out. She'd known he locked up something in here — she'd heard him with the key. Obviously she'd found it. And obviously she would have to open it. But first she went through the other drawers, neither of which offered anything other than what one would expect to find in a desk. Back to that top one.

She stared at it, stared until she stopped seeing the drawer and saw her family instead. Then she drew out the pick she'd slid from handbag to pocket this morning and bent down.

It only took a few seconds — it wasn't much of a lock. A few seconds, a soft *click,* and then one tug.

Paper, in a stack so neat it didn't seem to belong here amid all the chaos. Paper, with a page on top nearly blank, but for a few centered words.

The Deepest Darkness
A Novel
by Branok Hollow

For a second — one second — she thought

572

he must know Hollow after all. He'd written to him, he'd gotten a response, made friends as he so easily did through pen and paper, and Hollow had sent him something to read.

One second. Then she realized what an idiotic thought that was.

She reached in with the utmost care and pulled out the stack. The manuscript. That was what they called them, wasn't it? For lack of other space, she put it on her lap and lifted that first page off. Saw *Chapter One* in the center, and then *Argentina* below it.

Her eyes went further, unable to help themselves. *Locryn James stood outside the tavern and wondered that the Amazonian night didn't swallow it whole.*

She puffed out a breath and leaned back. Squeezed her eyes shut. Of course. It made complete sense. That other world he lived in — a fictional one. One he crafted carefully so he could transport readers away. With Locryn James, the stalwart adventurer.

Written by Peter Holstein, the recluse.

Everything fell into place. The subtle teases from Penrose when he complimented another writer. The papers they would occasionally pass between them without a word. Peter's eloquence, especially on matters of fiction. The way he took such joy in talking about "hypothetical situations," as he called them.

"Oh, blast." The things she'd said about his villain that day on the way to Marazion! She groaned and squeezed her eyes all the tighter. She never would have said such things if she'd known she was talking to the author!

Well, perhaps she would have. But she wouldn't have been so glib about it.

Probably.

Shaking her head at herself, she forced her eyes back open — but returned that cover sheet to its place. She wouldn't read any more. She wouldn't. It was enough that she knew. Enough that she could report to Mr. V that . . .

But she couldn't tell Mr. V, could she? Peter had obviously gone to the utmost trouble to keep his pen name a secret. How could she betray that? It would destroy him. And could destroy his career, if the wrong someone got hold of it first and spun it the wrong way.

And Mr. V, she knew, was the wrongest of someones.

She reached back into the drawer for an envelope on the bottom. It was addressed to Penrose, to his office in town. From a publishing company in London.

This she pulled out, sending her eyes over the letter within. Or perhaps a contract. It was for the sixth novel of Branok Hollow, to be delivered no later than August 15, 1914.

Two weeks. Was that even time enough for it to get safely there? What would happen if it were late?

She slid the letter back into the envelope. The envelope back into the drawer. The manuscript back in overtop it. For a moment, she just stared at it, hearing Barclay in her head. *Take it now. Go and find Mr. V. Deliver it and get out. Get home.*

And Willa. *One thousand pounds, Rosie. One. Thousand. Pounds.*

She closed the drawer. With the greatest risks came the greatest rewards — but this wasn't about risk. This was about causing someone injury. And she couldn't.

She *wouldn't*. It was probably his only copy of it, and if it vanished . . . he didn't have time enough to write it again. Not before his deadline.

Mr. V would just have to take her word for it. She raised her pick again, worked it in the lock until she heard another *click*.

Her assurance would just have to be good enough. And if it weren't . . .

She wondered if prisons had electric lights.

TWENTY-FIVE

Peter hadn't been to the pub so many times in a week . . . ever. But on Thursday night he entered again, behind Rosemary, and nodded at Kenver and Tamsyn, Treeve, and Cadan, who sat in the corner booth.

People looked up when he entered. But no one seemed particularly surprised to see him. Everyone, it seemed, was here, packed in like so many sardines. Under normal circumstances, this was the last place he would want to be.

But he was here for the same reason everyone else was — to hear whatever news came in over the wire.

Rosemary had his hand in hers and tugged him through the crowd, toward the bar. Where he would have found a corner to lean into, she sidled directly up to the barkeeper and said, "Anything new, Colin?"

This was Colin? Peter tried not to study him too closely, though he had wondered what kind of man had inspired Eseld to toss over Treeve. He knew the Thorns, of course — more or less — but hadn't been sure which brother Colin was.

The tall one, apparently, who could whip one pint along the bar even as he drew another from the tap. And he regarded Rosemary as everyone here seemed to — like a friend. "Have you heard about the Austrian bombardment of Belgrade, across the Danube?"

Rosemary nodded. "Yesterday. It wasn't successful, right?"

"Nah." Colin set the new pint on the counter too and wiped up a spill. "Nor have been their continued attempts to scare Russia away from the border. They're still mobilizing."

Someone bumped into Peter, sending him into Rosemary, all but pinning her to the bar.

He probably should have minded more than he did. But then, she was smiling too as she shouted, "Watch it, William! There are delicate ladies here!"

William — an Ellis, wasn't he? — grinned over his shoulder. "Where? I only see you, Rosie."

Rosemary laughed. And ordered, "Slap him for me, Eseld."

Eseld, maneuvering through with a tray held high in one hand, obligingly delivered a friendly cuff to the back of William's head with the other.

Peter eased away. A bit. But stayed closer to her back than he usually would have. For safety's sake, of course.

Rosemary nodded to Eseld. *"Meur ras."*

"Heb grev."

His brows moved up. "You're learning . . . Cornish?"

"Not on purpose, but you can't help but pick up a few things here and there." She rested her forearms on the bar and drummed her hands upon it. "Have you got the *Telegraph* back there? Peter isn't a subscriber."

Peter rolled his eyes. "I get . . . four newspapers. And you n-never read . . . any of them."

"Because you don't have the right ones, luv." She reached out for the newspaper Colin liberated from another man farther down the bar and then spread it open before her.

Peter scanned the headlines over her shoulder. They all looked the same as the ones he'd already read — which left his mind free to wander to the lemon scent that clung to her hair. And to that *luv*. It meant nothing, he knew that. Like the Cornish *an-sum* or *dearovim*. But he was tempted to pretend it did.

She tapped a finger to the page. "Did you catch this?"

"Hmm?" He blinked to clear his mind of lemon and *luv* and focused upon the words beneath her finger. He read a paragraph, unsure of whether to smile or frown. Kaiser Wilhelm, according to one source anyway, had been against the attacks, maintaining there were still diplomatic solutions. "King George will . . . will be g-glad of that . . . anyway."

"That's about enough."

A man two stools down turned toward them, his face mottled. It took Peter a long moment to recognize him as Pomeroy. He looked not quite sober. And more than a little angry as he stood and shoved a finger in Peter's direction, though it didn't reach him. "Who do you think you are, talking of the king that way, huh? You being a blighted *German.* You think you know what His Majesty thinks?"

Colin slapped his cloth to the bar. "Sit down, Pomeroy, or get out. You'll not be starting a row here."

Pomeroy staggered a step into what would usually have been an aisle. "No. I'll have my say. Bad enough that we've got a traitor here — worse that he thinks he's some kind of friend to the king."

He heard shifting and scooting from behind him, from the corner of the room. Kenver and Treeve and Cadan, he'd bet. But there were also men behind Pomeroy — his cronies. FitzSimmons. Foote.

Peter sighed. "Listen, M-Mr. Pomeroy, I'm not —"

"You're not much of anything, are you? Nothing but a coward who thinks he's too good for us. A traitor. From a long line of traitors."

Peter shifted. One foot a bit in front of the other, weight balanced. Arms limber, at the ready. Facing him down. "Say what you want . . . about me. But you w-will not . . . insult my f-family."

Pomeroy's sneer was an ugly thing. Not because of the brown teeth or the red nose. Because of the hate in his eyes. "I'll insult whomever I p-p-please."

The scent of lemon hit his nose a second before her curls appeared in front of him. Rosemary charged at Pomeroy like a battering ram, knocking him back a full step — likely because the man hadn't been expecting that.

No one had been expecting that. A hush

580

fell over the pub, except for the scraping of chairs as everyone stood to better see.

Peter reached to pull her back before Pomeroy could recover and lash out at her. "Rosemary."

She shrugged away from his hand. "No. It's time someone stands up for *you,* and if no one else has the guts, I'll do it."

He could stand up for himself. And he would now. When it was the entire Holstein name, the Holstein honor, at stake. He reached for her again.

Pomeroy leered. "That's right, Holstein. Get your London hussy under control before *I* do."

Peter, standing even with Rosemary now, dropped his hand before he could be shrugged away again. He'd never seen that particular set to her jaw before, but she had the look of a steam engine ready to blow to pieces.

She stepped closer to the old drunk. "You think you can control me, Pomeroy? If anyone's a coward here, it's you and yours. Only cowards resort to vandalism. Or to stupid insults. Does it make you feel big and powerful to spout off like you do? Or maybe you need to hit a girl to achieve that? Prove yerself a man."

Pomeroy's face went red, and his hands

went into fists. Peter saw his lunge as he coiled for it, prepared his own.

Needn't have. Rosemary had already ducked the swing, had already stepped aside and landed her own in the sot's drunken face. And now jerked a knee into his groin that doubled him over in half a second.

A chorus of cheers — and grunts of sympathetic pain from a few of the men — filled the pub.

Rosemary shook out her hand. "Lesson number one for you, Pom. Don't mess with a London girl. You don't hold a candle to the thugs I'm used to." She spun, her face still a fury. But it was hidden now behind that mask she wore so often. Peter saw it only in the snap of her eyes, the curl of her fingers. Her gaze met his. "I think I've had my fill of news, if you have, Mr. Holstein."

The *mister* was for them, he knew. A sign of respect. He inclined his head. "As you . . . wish. Miss Gresham."

There was something else beneath the fury in her eyes too. Something he couldn't see quite clearly enough to name.

She nodded and turned toward the door. Peter glanced down to make sure Pomeroy was still on the floor — he was, and Colin had emerged from behind the bar to grip FitzSimmons by the scruff of the neck. But

Foote hadn't been restrained.

"Rosie, watch out!"

Betty's cry filled Peter's ears even as he saw the man charge forward.

Peter moved before he could think, Father's training taking over. A jump into his path, a block of the raised hand. Another block when Foote swung his other — this one he grabbed, since some neighbor or another had surged forward to take hold of Foote's other arm.

What made a man turn into this? Full of hate ready to spill out on whoever was handy? Peter, just because of his name. And Rosemary, just because she stood up for Peter.

He shook his head and forced Foote's arm down. "If you hurt her, you'll . . . regret it."

"Aye, that he will," said the man who'd grabbed him from behind.

Peter let go of him when someone else moved forward. Turned to Rosemary.

He rather liked the smile that played at her lips. It was small and mischievous and exactly like the one Rosita had given Locryn just before she'd abandoned him to the natives halfway through the book. Except Rosemary didn't run away. She held out her hand. "My hero."

He breathed a laugh and took it. "I

d-daresay we're . . . even."

"Even better."

They strode together out of the pub, into the familiar little street. His carriage was there, waiting for him, his horse snorting a greeting. He helped Rosemary up.

She was, by the time he rounded the curricle and climbed up, sputtering. "I hate bullies. Hate them. Men like that — they're the kind that would take the bread right from a baby's hand, even when he's all but starved and they're fat and spoiled. The kind that would step on a person just to hear him scream. I detest men like that!"

He gathered the reins, clucked to the horse. "I never . . . would have guessed."

"And don't you laugh at me, Peter Holstein, or I'll let loose my Cockney fury on *you*."

"I'm not . . . laughing." Except that he was, even as he said it. "Wouldn't dare. I'm . . . afraid of you."

"You should be." She curled her fingers again, uncurled them. Held them up. "That blighter's got a hard head."

"Ooh." One of her knuckles had a cut, and the others were red. "We'll . . . tend it. When we get home."

Her shoulders sagged as they drove out of the village. "It wasn't one of them though.

In the woods that day. That blighted Robin Hood was younger than any of them. Leaner."

He was. Peter sighed. "They all have . . . have sons. In their twenties."

"I know, I've asked around. Young Fitz-Simmons is a nasty piece of work too, it's said. His wife's often sporting bruises." Her hand fisted. "Like to get ahold of him some-time."

Peter shook his head. "Pomeroy's . . . he's more solid. Works for . . . for Mr. Arnold."

"And never goes about spewing hate against Germans, I know. What of Foote's son?"

Another shake of his head, but this time because he hadn't any idea. "I don't . . . don't know him."

"We'll ask Kenver or Treeve. They will."

They would. And perhaps they'd know, too, if any of them were chain smokers. Maybe that information would lead them to their answers.

For a few minutes, Rosemary said nothing more. Until their drive came into view, at which point she said, "We'll figure it out. Before I leave."

Funny how that spoiled the evening more than the barroom brawl. Peter turned the horse toward Kensey. And sighed. "You don't . . . have to."

"I won't be able to rest easy until I know that whoever's been wreaking such havoc is behind bars."

That wasn't what he'd meant. He'd meant she didn't have to leave. But he'd already said that once. Just saying it didn't make any difference, not if he couldn't give her a reason to stay.

Benny was jogging out of the house to meet them and take the horses. Peter said nothing as he drove the last little distance, nor as he climbed down and reached to help her do the same. He took her hand — her left one — and tugged her toward the house.

She tugged back. "I think I'll just go home. Anger's tiring."

He didn't let go. "Your knuckles."

"I can tend to them."

"But you . . . won't." She'd just go in and make herself a cup of tea and fall asleep in that chair by the window with a book, her lights all ablaze. As she did eight nights out of ten.

Her lips twitched. "All right, you can be my hero again. Tend my battle scars."

"That's better." He led the way through Kensey's main doors, through the halls, to the kitchen.

It was empty. Grammy would be abed

already, what with getting up so early each day. The Teagues were likely outside on the bench the mister had made for his missus years ago, enjoying the evening.

The quiet suited Peter well. He fetched the jar of honey and lavender, and a slender bandage.

Rosemary was leaning against the table, her gaze on the dried herbs hanging above the sink. When he drew near, she focused on him instead, produced a smile, and held up her hand. "Be gentle. I'm a delicate lady."

He chuckled and dipped his finger in the honey, spreading it gently over the cut. "Delicate when . . . when it suits you. Strong . . . always."

She laughed too, a soft version that tied a knot right in the middle of his chest as he reached for the bandage. "Careful," she said, "or you'll turn my head with such flattery."

He wound the cloth around her injured knuckle. Then let the knot inside him have its way. He lifted her hand and pressed his lips to the bandage. Looked into her eyes, clear as a jewel. "Maybe I . . . mean to."

She went still. Breathed his name. But she didn't pull her hand away or make a run for it.

So he eased a little closer. Lifted his other

hand to cradle her face. And kissed her.

It was fire. Definitely fire. That force that could take and destroy. That could rage and consume. It was fire, and Rosemary wrapped her arms tight around the flame and held on.

It *shouldn't* be fire. How could it be, when Peter was all cool reactions and self-control? He'd never sent her a smoldering look. Never flirted, not until just that moment. He'd never been anything but a friend.

A gentleman, in the real sense. The *true* sense.

It was fire — but it wasn't the fire that destroyed lives and homes and stables. She dug her fingers into his shoulders and tilted her head a bit so he could kiss her more deeply. More fully. *More.* It was a hearth ablaze on a winter's night. A torch lighting the darkness.

It was life, and she couldn't get enough. Didn't want to. Because as long as he was kissing her, she could think of nothing but him and her and this nebulous *them* that hadn't existed until a minute ago. That would flicker out of being again when he pulled away.

He pulled away. Dragged in a breath. And his eyes were the sea, blue and green and swirling, which everyone knew extinguished a flame without a thought.

And she was an idiot, because he was a gentleman — no matter how true a one — and she had no business standing here in his pretty kitchen and kissing him when she'd be gone tomorrow. When she'd leave him with his lovely secrets and his welcoming home and his mostly friendly staff, who would all wag their heads while Mrs. Teague proclaimed, *"I told you that girl was no good."*

"Oh blast," she said on a breath. He still held her between him and the table. And his arms still felt so strong, so perfect around her. And his lips were on her cheek. Her jaw. Her ear. "Mrs. Teague will have a fit. She's convinced . . ." Her jaw again, in a slow, slow move toward her mouth. "She's convinced I only came to seduce you. Which you had better know isn't true, because if you think I'm kissing you now because of some plot on my part —"

"Rosemary." He was smiling, blast him, even as he traced his nose along her cheek.

She couldn't breathe. Maybe he *was* that other kind of fire. The kind that sucked the air right out of a room. "What?"

He hovered there, a whisper away. "Stop talking. Please."

Her laugh only had a moment to escape

before he was kissing her again. She let him, though she shouldn't. And kissed him back, though she ought to have better sense.

She'd be gone tomorrow, whether she could figure out who Robin Hood was or not — she'd have to be, or she'd end up in jail. She'd be gone tomorrow. But she'd miss him every day for the rest of her life. He'd stolen her heart right out of her chest when she wasn't looking, and she hadn't the foggiest idea how to get it back. And didn't much want to. He'd take better care of it than she ever could anyway.

At some point, his lips left hers and settled on her head. Which had nestled, somehow, against his shoulder. His fingers were trailing up and down her back. And because she was an idiot, tears were stinging her eyes.

She wasn't who he thought she was. And he was so much more than she deserved. "Peter."

"Don't. Not yet. Don't . . . don't tell me how you must . . . must leave. I haven't the words yet to . . . to argue."

He'd find them — likely with a pen and paper tonight. He'd write her some heart-stoppingly beautiful letter that would make her want to stay — even more than she already did.

But it wouldn't be real. Because it would

be to Rosemary Gresham, librarian. And she wouldn't be that anymore after tomorrow.

She pulled away, careful to keep her gaze just below his. Careful to keep her muscles loose, relaxed, or he'd know something was wrong. And if he knew something was wrong, he'd try to put it to rights. And she couldn't bear that right now.

So she cleared her throat and hoped he'd chalk it up to a belated bashfulness, or awkwardness, or whatever he wanted to call it. "I found your documents," she said. "Last week. I just . . . they were my last reason for staying. They're in the library, behind that false shelf back."

"I don't . . . I don't care about that. Not now."

But he should. They were what mattered — his proof of who he was. Those papers meant he would be fine, he would be safe.

She'd managed that, at least. And she'd leave him a letter of her own, one warning about Mr. V. One, perhaps, that confessed how much he meant to her.

No. She couldn't do that or he'd come after her, because it was the noble thing. Which wouldn't do. She'd have to tell him it had all been a lie. That she was just a thief.

She turned away when those burning tears

turned to falling tears. She hurried toward the door.

"Rosemary!"

She *was* just a thief. But it hadn't been a lie. She loved him. God help her, she loved him. *God, help me!*

Somehow she managed to get the kitchen door latched behind her, managed to stifle the first sob with a hand over her mouth. Not yet, she couldn't let it loose yet. Not so close to where he was, where he could hear. He couldn't hear, couldn't know how she ached, or he would try to soothe her.

The second sob rose in the garden, and this one wouldn't be repressed. She tried, and it choked her, made her stumble over one of the stones of the path. The tears were rolling down her cheeks, and her nose felt pinched, and then the heaving cries came in waves.

She barely made it to the cottage, all but falling through the door, and she didn't care. She sank to the floor and curled up into a ball and let the tears come.

It was dark. With her eyes closed and the crying surrounding her and with this gaping hole inside. It was so *dark.* It had always been dark, but she'd never known it fully. Because she'd never seen that light shining just out of reach.

Now she did. She saw it. It was partly Peter, with all his goodness. His nobility and his quiet strength and his silly quirks and his utter *niceness*. It was partly Peter, shining there. But it was mostly what shone through him.

She'd seen bits of it before — in Pauly, who took in a bunch of street rats as best he could. In the motley assortment of desperate children who had declared themselves her brothers, her sisters. A little splinter of light here and there, reflecting back slivers of love.

But this — this was the sun. And it made her feel small and dark and cold in comparison. Because she was nothing. Worthless. Rubbish. A thief. A rat scurrying along the world's underbelly. Just someone who took, who took and destroyed and laughed about it.

It hurt. It hurt so much she felt sure she would break open, and it would all come spilling out, all those gallons of darkness filling her up. And it would consume her, and there'd be nothing left but an empty shell.

"There now." The words intruded, soft and gentle. A small, soft hand smoothed hair away from her face. "It can't be as bad as all that. Come here. Tell me what's wrong."

Grammy? She couldn't open her eyes to see — and the kindness only made it worse. Made the tears clog her throat so that she thought she'd never be able to breathe past them. She couldn't fight as those soft hands urged her head into a soft lap. She could only cry.

She'd been light once. Light with innocence. She'd cried in her mother's lap over foolish things she couldn't even name now, and she'd known, as she did, that she could. Because Mumma was there, was always there, and Daddy would be home soon too. He'd swing her up and tickle her and declare her his little rose, and she would laugh and forget why she'd been crying.

Then they'd gone. Died. And . . . how had it happened? When? When had that darkness she so feared crept inside her and taken hold?

"All right, then." The words were like Mumma's humming, soft and gentle and meaningless. "Let it out. Just let it out." The hand rubbed a circle on her back. "How long's it been since you had a good cry, hmm? Too long, I'm betting."

Ages. Decades. A century, perhaps. Because tears like this were weak, were *for* the weak, and she couldn't be that. That was death or starvation or worse. That was letting the bullies win. That was admitting that life had gotten the best of you.

But she was weak. And she was starved, not for food but for something deeper. Something that whispered, *Rise and sin no more.*

But she couldn't. She was too heavy. She was too dark. It hurt too much.

She ran out of tears though. And the sobs just turned into gasping. Shaking.

Those small, soft hands kept up their soothing circles. That familiar voice kept up its crooning.

It was Mrs. Teague, not Grammy. As she caught half a breath, Rosemary recognized the voice. And was too spent to care. She closed her eyes. And waited for the gasps to calm enough to say, "You were right. Not about the why. But I'm — no good."

"Shh." The circles didn't halt. Didn't even falter. "We're all no good, Rosemary, at the core of it. Every one of us."

She shook her head against Mrs. Teague's soft lap, and the gasps quickened again. "No. Not him. He's — he's perfect."

A soft chuckle, warm as tea. "No, child. Master Peter's no better than the rest of us. Not on his own."

But he was. He was everything, and she was nothing. And she couldn't make any words come out, just a high keening and a nod of her head.

"No." The hand left her back and took to smoothing her hair away instead. Soft, gentle strokes over the curls, luring them away from her tear-encrusted cheeks back where they belonged. "You know it too. He's been writing to you, so he'll have explained it. He can't write without explaining it — that it isn't him. The faults, the absentmindedness — those are him. The goodness . . . that's the love of Christ."

Jesus — that name Peter always penned so carefully. Lord — the title he used most often for Him. His Savior, as he called Him, who would remake her into a new garment, if only she'd let Him. Who would send her His Spirit to guide her, if only she'd listen.

But she wasn't one of Jenny's dresses, old but still whole. She was rags. Filthy, threadbare rags. There wasn't anything left to remake. "I'm not — I'm not worth — saving."

"Oh, now." Mrs. Teague shifted, urged her to move, to roll, until her head was facing the opposite way. Until she was staring at that crisp white apron. And then, when she nudged her chin, those condemning eyes.

But they weren't condemning. They were shining with tears of her own. "You listen to me, Rosemary Gresham. If Jesus could save tax collectors and harlots, thieves and hypocrites, who are you to say you're too far gone, hmm? Our God is bigger than our sins. And if there's something saying otherwise into your ear, know it's a lie straight from the devil."

She closed her eyes. *Thieves.* He'd forgiven them before. "But — how?"

Mrs. Teague pulled a few more strands of hair free from her cheek and smoothed them back. "You believe, child. That's all. You look to Him. And you ask Him to help you. You tell Him you know where you've done wrong and ask Him to forgive it. He does, every time. That's why He gave himself up on that cross. And it's why He rose again — to show us we can too. Always, from anything. To Him."

The gasps eased. She ran her tongue over her salty lips and let the words sink in, rooting their way through the fog of tears and the exhaustion of life.

"Do you believe that, child?"

Did she? She wasn't sure. She had to look inside for the answer, look at where the darkness had long ago extinguished hope for anything but what her own hands could take.

But it didn't look so dark. It looked . . . it looked a bit like Peter — shining. And mostly like whatever it was that shone through him.

Light. The light of Christ.

She sniffed. "I do."

"Well then. Welcome to the family. And forgive me, if you can, for treating you as I've done — it was fear, you see. Fear you'd hurt that precious boy."

"I will hurt him." She dragged in a breath and didn't dare look up again. "I don't want to. But I will. I can't . . . I can't undo things. Even if — if God forgives me for them."

"Then we'll get through it." Mrs. Teague patted her cheek and then moved her legs. "Time to get up now, Rosemary. I'll draw you a bath."

She let herself be helped up and winced at the way her head pounded when she rose. "Shouldn't I feel — different? Good?" Or at least stop gasping?

Mrs. Teague chuckled. "When you come in out of the cold and sidle up next to a fire, you don't feel warm all at once, do you? Your hands thaw, and then your nose. Your toes. It'll come. In bits and pieces, or in a flood, but it'll come if you seek it. If you stay there by the fire. And then one day you'll realize you're warm all over, and have been for ages."

Rosemary sighed and rubbed at her crusted face. She must look a sight.

Mrs. Teague shooed her out of the kitchen, toward her bedroom. "To the bath. You'll feel better after a bath. And what did you do to your finger?"

"Oh." The bandage was coming undone — Peter hadn't done much to secure it, just tucked in the end. Then kissed it. Her cheeks felt hot under the grime. "I punched Pomeroy."

Mrs. Teague barked a laugh. "Did you really? I would have liked to see that. What did he do?"

"Made fun of Peter." She frowned as she moved into her room and looked over her shoulder at the housekeeper. "Was that wrong of me? Should I have turned the other cheek or something?"

Mrs. Teague was still smiling — an expression Rosemary hadn't seen on her face much these last few months, unless she entered a room unnoticed. "You'll have to learn to listen to the Lord's guidance on that — when to turn away and when to take up your sword. Though when it's in defense of another, I tend to say 'let him have it.' "

She paused, her smile going self-deprecating. "Even when I oughtn't to do. I still need to learn to listen too."

Perhaps it shouldn't make her feel better. But it did. And she felt better still as Mrs. Teague hummed her way into the bathroom and turned on the tap — for her. As she poured in something that smelled divine that Rosemary hadn't even known was in the cabinet, then patted her cheek on the way out and said she'd have a cup of tea waiting for her when she was done.

She took a bath. She had a cup of tea. She let the housekeeper, still fluttering about, urge her into bed as the sun went down.

She looked out her window into the new night. Tomorrow would be a bad day — it was bound to be. And yet . . . it didn't look so dark.

TWENTY-SIX

Peter peered out the window toward the cottage, knowing well he was driving both Grammy and Mrs. Teague to madness but not quite able to help it. "Are you . . . are you sure she is all right?"

The first time he'd asked it this morning, Mrs. Teague had been full of assurances. The second time, she'd been amused. From there, it had been a slippery slope down to the exasperated sigh she gave him this time. "Do you think if she weren't, she'd be made the better by your standing there and staring at her window? She's *fine,* Mr. Holstein. I told you that. And told it to you again. And again. And again."

Grammy, hands full of vegetables, cleared her throat.

Peter backed up to let her pass. But couldn't tear himself away from the window with the best view of the cottage. He'd made it as far as the garden last night when he'd heard her sobbing, would have gone after her then and there — but Teague had intercepted him and assured him that the missus would see to her. He'd brooked no argument. Had threatened, even, to carry him bodily back into the house if he didn't "give the girl some room to cry freely."

Perhaps he'd been hovering right here the whole time Mrs. Teague was in there — which was half an eternity — and perhaps he'd pounced on her the moment she'd come back in to demand what the matter had been.

But he'd been appeased at the soft light in her eyes. At the soft smile on her lips. At the soft whisper that Rosemary Gresham was now a child of God.

But blast it all, he needed to see her for himself. So why wouldn't she come out of her cottage and see *him*?

He turned to pace the path that he'd already — so said Grammy — worn down across her kitchen. It couldn't be a coincidence that she'd fallen apart like that right after he'd kissed her. And while he couldn't possibly be happier about that spark of new faith inside her, he hadn't meant to drive her to it in quite such a way. Inspire her, perhaps. He'd been praying, of course. Night and day. But she'd literally fallen into her house in tears.

What did that mean? That she loved him and feared it couldn't work? That she hated him and wished he hadn't kissed her? That she wanted only to be his friend, and he'd ruined it, and now she had to figure out how to get away?

He reached the far wall and pivoted.

Sweet-tempered Grammy set down her knife with a clatter. "Will you just go and check on her again, Millie? Before I'm forced to make him into soup just to get a little peace in my kitchen?"

Part of him wanted to smile. And part of him wanted to dog Mrs. Teague's heels as she spun for the door with an *I give up!* lift of her hands. She wouldn't let him if he tried it though — she hadn't last time, saying Rosemary wasn't dressed to receive callers.

He pulled out a chair at the table and sat. *"Drog yw genev."*

Grammy took the knife to the vegetables. "I don't need your apology, Mr. Holstein. I just need my kitchen."

"I'll get . . . get out of your way. I p-promise. Just as soon as . . . as Mrs. Teague returns."

Grammy shook her head. "I haven't seen you like this since your mother lay on her deathbed, God rest her soul. You care for her that much, do you?"

He put his elbows on the table. His head in his hands. He wasn't very well going to confess his heart to Grammy. It was Rosemary who had a right to hear it first.

He should have written her a letter. Something long and sweet and full of the words of love he had absolutely no experience with.

But he couldn't. Baring his heart, for him, meant giving promises. And he couldn't give her promises. Not then, not last night. Promises couldn't coexist with secrets.

So he'd sat up in his bedroom reading his manuscript most of the night. Then he'd wrapped it up and bound it with a few rubber bands. He'd give her that first. The truth of who he was. Show her his secrets.

Then . . . if she accepted it, and if she would reveal hers to him . . .

He'd ask her, if he must. Ask her why she kept a lock pick in her handbag. Why she didn't know how to pronounce words she should have. Could fight the village bully without breaking a sweat. He'd ask her, if she wouldn't volunteer it, and he'd pray she would trust him with the answers. Pray that, having them, they could move on. Forward.

Mrs. Teague bustled back inside. "Alive

and well, as I promised. Reading one of the Bibles you've left in there, is all. And deciding, she says."

"Deciding?" Grammy turned from her vegetables to frown at him. "What did you do, propose?"

"No." He pushed up from the table. And then frowned right back. "Do you . . . do you think I sh . . . should have?"

The sisters exchanged one of those looks they'd been exchanging over him all his life. The one that was half *Isn't he precious?* and half *What are we going to do with that boy?*

"It'll all work out," Mrs. Teague predicted in her omniscient voice. "So long as Grammy doesn't turn you into dinner. Get out of the house for a while, Master Peter. Walk to the Penroses, or to the village."

It would give him time to pray, he supposed. And perhaps spare his life. With a nod — and the relieved sigh of his cook — he left the kitchen.

He couldn't help but step into the library on his way by. Too neat, too tidy, too organized. Too loud a claim that she'd done her job and had no reason left to stay. Unless he could give her one.

For now, he settled on grabbing his hat and heading outside. Toward Gryff's, even though he would be at his office in town, it being Friday. Because it would take him by the cottage.

He glanced down at his watch as he gained the out-of-doors. Two o'clock. Surely by the time he walked there, said hello to Elowyn and Jenny, and came back, she'd be out and about. And ready to see him.

Surely.

Rosemary watched him stride past, careful to stay cloaked behind the heavy curtains. Wise, on her part, as Peter kept looking toward the cottage. His face, the longing look upon it, made an ache thrum to life in her chest.

She pressed a hand to it. She couldn't face him. Not today — which meant not ever. But she could help him. She could refuse to turn over any evidence to Mr. V. Refuse to give him anything to use against Peter — even the truth.

She chafed her hands over her wrists. Mr. V would likely grab her right then and not let her go. She'd be in jail within hours — perhaps in the cell next to Tim's, or perhaps he'd ship her straight-away back to London.

Imprisoned . . . but freer, on the inside, than she'd ever felt in her life.

Once Peter had vanished into the wood and she'd counted to three hundred to be sure he wasn't coming right back again, Rosemary turned to shrug out of the dressing gown she'd had on over her evergreen dress. She checked her room again to make sure everything was packed, put her valise by the door — if she *did* get away from Mr. V, she'd have to make a quick escape. And then she grabbed the letter from the desk. The one that told him she loved him and she'd done all she could to protect him. She'd had to say it.

The one that begged him to send a wire to Barclay posthaste, warning him to go into hiding. *He* couldn't be arrested. The rest of the family needed him far too much. She would take the blame, she alone. One last gift to her brothers and sisters.

She slid outside through the back door, the one they wouldn't see from the manor's kitchen. Sneaking to the house itself would be hard, given the open expanses of lawn and garden between them. But no one looked her way as she darted to the front of the house and went in that way. No one was in the hall as she slipped into the library.

It took her only a minute to stride to that middle bookcase, move the books aside, and then move the false back to the shelf. She took the small silver key from its place and had the safe open in minutes. She drew out the documents from the government verifying that the Holsteins belonged in England. And the deed to the manor in which she stood even now.

She traced its edge with a finger. A lifetime ago, with anyone but Peter, she might have been tempted to destroy the first and steal the second. Deliver that deed to Barclay and declare herself the best thief in London.

Today she felt only a bone-deep sorrow that she had to say good-bye.

And hadn't time to waste on such sentiment. Shaking herself, she replaced the shelf's back and the books in front of it and hurried into his study.

It was clean — he must have left the door open last night. She rather missed the mess. This wasn't the way she wanted to remember it. It wasn't its usual state.

But she had no time for that regret either. It would take her half an hour to walk to that tree on the corner of the property, and she meant to be there before Mr. V.

She set the documents on his desk, the letter on the typewriter. And then paused, fingers hovering over the handle to the drawer. A tug. And there they were. All the letters she'd written to him. With a sigh, she shut it again and fingered the opposite handle. It would, of course, be locked. As it should be.

Except it wasn't. One little tug, meant only to assure herself of its semi-security, and the drawer slid open easily. Revealing a gaping emptiness within.

"No. No, no no." He could have taken it out. He *could* have. Or . . .

She flew from the room, out the nearest door, and ran toward the wood. Of course Mr. V hadn't trusted her to get it — why would he? He had made it quite clear that he believed in spying on his thieves, so why wouldn't he just send in another to do the job if he thought she'd gone soft?

The woods had never seemed so vast, nor the roots so gnarled and grasping. She tripped half a dozen times as she ran deeper into the trees, away from the cliffs. But she couldn't pause, could only keep running through the stitch in her side, toward the far side of the property.

By the time she reached that ancient oak with the heart scored in its bark, she was gasping for breath. The August heat pressed down upon her, making those long, layered sleeves feel more ridiculous than pretty. Making her wish she had chosen some other dress, given the high lacy collar trying to choke her.

Mr. V was already there.

For a moment, he wavered before her eyes. She'd forgotten to eat again today. Or rather, couldn't, despite the tray Mrs. Teague had brought over. Just now she regretted it. "You." She dragged in what air she could through her splitting side. "What have you done? He's a good man!"

Mr. V's countenance, cool as ever, wobbled before her. She shook it away, reached out to steady herself on a tree, and blinked her eyes back into focus.

He was closer now, and not looking so collected. "Miss Gresham, easy. What in the world's the matter with you? I meant to light a fire under you, not send you into a fit."

"I'm fine." Or would be, if she could reconcile this tenor of concern in his voice with the harsh words he'd said to her on Monday. "Where is it?" she demanded. "What've you done with it?"

Now his expression shifted again, to something that on a normal man would have looked like excitement. He gripped her by the shoulders and pulled her upright. "Have you found something? You have. A manuscript? Tell me it's a manuscript."

"Tell you . . ." He didn't have it. Wherever it was, it wasn't here with him, or he wouldn't be in this state. Which meant she could yet salvage this. She drew in another long breath. "Look, sir, I don't know who you are or what your purpose here is. But I can tell you that Peter Holstein is a good —"

"Yes, I know, a good man. Get on with it." His hands pressed her shoulders, then retreated entirely and, just like that, he was calm again. "Forgive me. And again forgive me. I have put you under a false assumption, and I did so deliberately."

She backed up a step, leaning again on a tree. "You're not Mr. Jasper, are you? Or working for him."

He breathed a laugh. "That war-monger? No. I assure you."

That was something, then. If she could believe him. Which she rather did. "Good. Then . . . then let me take this time to thank you. For helping with Olivia's bills." Another something that didn't quite reconcile — the kind man with the one who threatened prison.

He lifted his brows. "Miss Gresham, I only delivered that money. As I told your sister, it came anonymously."

"But that makes no sense. Who else would —" She paused. Of course. And where else could he send it but to one of the addresses she'd provided in reference?

Mr. V loosed a dry, soft chuckle. "That was my guess as well. He *is* a good man — I've known that for years. What I need to know now, Miss Gresham — what the king needs to know — is if he's Branok Hollow."

"The king?" She leaned her head on the tree, letting the rough bark bite her. "*Which* king?"

He still looked amused as he clasped his hands behind his back. "*Your* king. Though I mean his government more than the man himself."

Unbelievable. And not. "Who exactly are you, Mr. V?"

"Someone who knows how to get things — in most cases, information."

"For the *government*?"

His lips twitched. "Often. Which of course means that *you* have been working for them too this past year."

She turned against the tree trunk, away from him. It should make her feel better. And would, likely, once she stopped being so angry she could spit in his face. "You told me I was here to prove him a traitor."

"Because if you were looking for proof against him, I'd know I could trust what you found in his favor. Now . . ." He stepped into her view again. Cool and calm, except for his eyes. "I need to know. Not to harm him, but to entreat him for help — are Peter Holstein and Branok Hollow the same man?"

Her instinct still said to play dumb, stay mum. But something else, something from that place inside that wasn't dark anymore, gave a funny little pulse. And she nodded.

His eyes lit still more. "You're certain? You've seen a manuscript?"

Another nod against the tree.

Mr. V breathed a small, victorious laugh. "Well done, Miss Gresham. Well done indeed. Your government thanks you, your pay will be waiting for you in London, and you can be sure I shall call on you again soon when I've another task that needs your particular expertise."

"Don't." The world was still a bit wobbly around the edges, but not so much that she'd forgotten that decision that had settled so sure last night. "I'm finished. With stealing, I mean."

That light in his eyes flickered. "You can't be serious — you've more talent for it than anyone in England. It took me years to track you down after the museum job."

A few days ago, the compliment would have warmed her. Today it left her cool. "Will you arrest me for it?"

His eyes were amused. "Don't be foolish

— I destroyed all the evidence a year ago, before I hired you. I couldn't have one of my agents arrested for such a crime."

"Your agent." Her eyes slid shut. "I can't be that either. I can't, not now. But . . ." But the income from Mr. V, if it continued, could mean life to her family. And if Willa's reaction were any indication, *they* wouldn't all be turning over new leaves just because *she* was. She opened her eyes again. "I didn't do it alone, you know. The museum job."

Mr. V regarded her, unblinking. "Someone in your so-called family, I presume."

"Perhaps."

He smiled. "Then I'll go to *them,* shall I, when I need a thief?"

She said nothing. Until he nodded and spun away. "Wait. Where are you going now?"

He didn't turn back. Instead, he took off at a run — a sight she wouldn't have believed possible for such a dignified personage if she hadn't seen it with her own eyes. Though he did yell over his shoulder, "To speak with Mr. Holstein, of course. I've a proposition for him."

"No, wait!" But he was already disappearing among the trees, and she was none too sure she could handle another sprint on an empty stomach. Instead, she granted herself the respite of bending in half to stretch her side and prayed that he wouldn't mention her in whatever this proposition was. Not until she'd had a chance to tell Peter first what she really was. Or had been.

She coughed, then coughed again. *Smoke.* Dread in her stomach, she came upright.

A man stood before her, lit cigarette dangling from his lips. Dark hair, lean figure. *Blast.* She folded her arms over her chest. "Let me guess — Robin Hood."

The man grinned a wicked little grin as another bloke stepped from behind a tree. This one had grey hair, a bowler hat. And flipped a silver coin into the air, letting it fall to the forest floor. "And his merry men."

Something came down over her head. And all was darkness.

TWENTY-SEVEN

Peter's pace increased the closer he got to home. If he were making excuses, he could blame it on any number of things — the dark clouds knuckling the horizon, the idea for a Locryn James short story he needed to jot down before he forgot it, the fact that no Penroses had been at home, so there'd been no reason to linger.

But he knew well it was because he hoped Rosemary had emerged from the cottage.

He was nearly jogging by the time he came out of the woods and onto the expanse of lawn that went by her cottage. Then he came to an abrupt halt when he spotted the man leaning against her back door. Average height, slender, in a grey suit of clothes at once impeccable and unremarkable. A bowler over silver-gold hair.

Peter drew in a breath and let his brows draw a frown. Not the bowler or hair he'd grown accustomed to seeing dogging his steps. So who was he, to stand so calmly outside Rosemary's cottage? To look over at him without the slightest hint of surprise?

To come a step forward with a hand outstretched? "Good day, Mr. Holstein."

"Good . . . good day." Peter shook the hand, knowing his question must be on his face. "And y-you are?"

The man offered a smile as nondescript as his suit. "They call me V."

Peter blinked. "Like the . . . letter?"

"Precisely."

This was going to be an odd meeting, he suspected. "Succinct."

V chuckled and motioned with an arm. "Would you walk with me, Mr. Holstein?"

He had no reason to refuse. Exactly. Though his gaze darted of its own will to Rosemary's windows.

"Ah." V adjusted his jacket and stepped away from the house. "You'll find Miss Gresham isn't within at the moment, I'm afraid. Though I daresay she'll have followed me back and will burst upon us at any moment. I'm rather surprised she hasn't stormed up already, in all honesty. Though she was a bit winded — did she forget to eat again today?"

Suspicion crouched on Peter's shoulders.

"Who . . . who are you? Her uncle — Pauly?"

V's lips twitched. "Do I look like a Cockney barkeeper, Mr. Holstein?"

Not exactly. But Rosemary didn't look like a Cockney barkeeper's niece either. Nor, usually, did she sound like one. Until she did. And this man . . . he had that flat non-accent that spoke of a careful education meant to cover one's native cadence.

Peter made no reply.

V chuckled and, hands clasped behind his back, led the way around the cottage. "I am not her uncle. I am her employer."

That crouching suspicion dug claws into his shoulders. He had rather thought *he* was her employer. Currently, anyway. "P-Previously . . . you mean?"

"No. I mean I am the one who sent her to Cornwall, to Kensey Manor. To get me the answers I needed about you."

Peter's feet had brought him to the front edge of the cottage, but there they stopped. And grew roots. "I beg your p-pardon?"

V looked around him, as if expecting someone to come leaping out of the shrubbery. "You needn't be put out about it, Mr. Holstein. She thought she was here to find evidence that you were disloyal to England and instead ended up — as I rather expected she would — your most strident defender. But I had to be certain, you understand. About your loyalties, and about your pastimes."

She had . . . Peter's breath seeped out. Not a chuff, but that tired *hiss* of the last of the steam escaping. Blast it, Gryff had been right.

Peter shook his head. "Why?"

V's face creased into a perfectly pleasant, meaningless smile. "And there is the crux of the matter. England needs you, Mr. Holstein. Or rather — Mr. Hollow. I had to be sure you were he, and you've left such a convoluted trail of barristers that I couldn't be certain I'd traced you properly back to *you*."

It should have shocked him, to hear someone other than Gryff address him with his *nom de plume.* It should have appalled him.

But he could feel nothing. Not just now. Not about that. "England . . . has me. Already."

V scanned the gardens again. And beyond. "One more minute, I think. So I'll make this quick. Austria and Germany have declared war on Serbia — it will be in the papers tomorrow, I expect. Russia will declare war on them. From there, dominoes.

Every major power in Europe will be at odds. This will be a war far different from those we've seen in the past. We'll need to fight it differently as well."

Dominoes. Peter put his hands in his pockets, not knowing what else to do with them.

Where was she? Why was she not here, butting in with her own explanation?

"The weapons are one thing — and they will be frightening enough. But this kind of war . . . it's going to require more than new guns and ammunition, Mr. Holstein. It's going to require changing the basic way our people think about it, and — ah, there he is." V straightened, though Peter hadn't thought him slouching before, and nodded toward the front of Kensey, where . . .

Mr. Arnold was emerging? Peter frowned.

V sighed. "I could not forestall this small interruption, much as I tried — your own fault, really, for sending that message to his company. But don't be alarmed. The authorities are waiting even now in your outbuildings. Though do stay out of swinging range of that cane of his — he's a blade within it, you know."

"He — what?" And what message had Peter sent to his company? Peter hadn't even known Mr. Arnold *had* a company. Unless . . . "Wait. You m-mean *he* is . . . is AGD?"

That made no sense at all. Why would Mr. Arnold, who was the most vocal man he'd ever heard against Germany, be buying up stock in a German steel mill? In *his* German steel mill?

The old man strode toward him far faster than he'd seen him move in a decade, his hand gripping the shaft of his cane but not using it for support. "Mr. Holstein!" he bellowed. "What is the meaning of this?"

He'd rather like to know the same. Uprooting his stubborn feet, Peter strode over the lawn between them. He didn't know what he meant to say.

And needn't have worried. The red-faced old man was at no loss for words. "I knew it! I always knew your family was still loyal to Germany, and this proves it! That you would sell to the Krupp concern — your steel will be used to make German battleships, is that what you want? You are worse than your grandfather!"

When Mr. Arnold pointed his cane at him, Peter halted a good ten paces away. Not because of the threat of a blade within — because it was the first time he really remembered seeing the handle. Usually Mr. Arnold held it so tightly. Or, when sitting, had the top angled toward himself. He had surely glimpsed it at some point over the years, but if so, he had never noted the design embossed in the gold.

The inverted triangle. The concentric circles. "You . . . d-did Mr. Jasper come . . . to you?"

Mr. Arnold shook. Not his outstretched arm, but all of him. "I went to *him*. I always knew your family was too loyal to Germany — making sure you were born there, preserving your citizenship. And then when you began visiting the king! You are a traitor. A weak, cowardly traitor. But I will not let you get away with it. You will sell that mill to me, so that I may at least mitigate the damage it does. Keep its steel from harming Britain. Perhaps arrange for sabotage, if I can. You will not sell to Krupp."

Peter shook his head. Sabotage? Was he daft? If he tried to implement something like that, he would likely get people killed. "I am not . . . not selling to Krupp." Or to GHH — though he'd had Gryff send messages out to all the bidders with both bits of false information, to flush out who AGD really was, whether they were part of one of those dominant concerns.

He certainly hadn't expected *this*.

"You certainly are not." Puffing out his

chest, Mr. Arnold pointed with the cane again. "You will sell to *me*. Do you understand? Or my associate will tear your precious librarian limb from limb."

"What?" V charged past Peter, gripped Mr. Arnold by the shirtfront. "My amusement with you has reached an end, old man."

Policemen spilled from the woodwork, led by Constable Newth himself.

Peter sucked in a long breath. It was only a threat. He didn't actually have her. He couldn't actually have Rosemary; there was no way she'd let herself be caught by a couple of country boys whom Mr. Arnold had likely employed to do his dirty work.

The old man lifted his cane again, aiming it at V's head.

His captor knocked it out of his hand with minimal effort and tossed the old man backward, into one of the bobbies, who steadied him — and gripped his arm to hold him still.

Arnold looked shocked at their audacity. "What are you doing? I am a loyal subject! I am trying to help England!"

V growled. "You are a criminal and a warmonger, along with your entire ridiculous brotherhood. Did you tell them that this so-called Ancient Order was of the old Austrian realm? Founded by your grandfather?

Founded solely on the idea of hating Germany?"

The old man sneered. "A sentiment shared by plenty in London. People were *begging* to join. As anyone would, were they not a traitor like this coward. I should have told young Pomeroy to aim for him instead of a tree!"

Newth stepped forward, his face in hard lines. "You're under arrest, Mr. Arnold. For arson, attempted murder —"

"Add charges of espionage to the list, Constable." V narrowed his eyes at them.

The old man's face mottled. "I would never!"

"Really? But you seem to care only for how things *look*. And you *look* ever so suspicious, Mr. Arnold. Trying to buy a German steel mill. Threatening a known friend of the king of England. And you *are* Austrian."

"An *old* Austrian — I *hate* Germany!"

"Yes, well. Austria and Germany are one and the same these days. How do you think that will look to the courts?" V turned his gaze on the constable. "Jasper and his man — did you track them?"

Jasper was *here*? Peter's blood went cold.

Newth nodded. "They went toward where Mr. Holstein's property meets Mr. Arnold's. I dispatched two men to follow."

It was probably technically laughter that came from Arnold's throat. But it sounded far more like venom would, if it were audible. "They'll have her by now. And if I don't come soon to tell them I've got the deed to the mill, they'll kill her."

No. It couldn't be — but Peter's feet didn't agree. They leapt into motion even as his mind denied the possibility, speeding him over the lawn like the ever-gusting wind, through the wood full of elms and oaks and the occasional cabbage tree that had baffled her so. Toward that corner of the property where his land met Mr. Arnold's — where the oak with the heart took up residence on the Holstein side. Where, a few minutes' walk away, one would find the plum orchard he and Gryff had so disastrously robbed as boys.

Toward the woman who could apparently rob much more seriously. Much more successfully. The woman who had entered his life solely to steal his secrets.

He would have given them all to her had she but asked.

But there was no one at the tree. No indication of where she could be. Were he Locryn, he would be able to look at the ground and see intent in the scattering of leaves. Direction in the placement of twigs.

He would take a glance and know exactly where she had gone from here.

Peter saw only leaves. Twigs. And the gleam of silver amid the litter.

Silver? He leapt toward it, snatched it up. It was the size and shape of a florin — but of course, not one. No, it was another of those blasted tokens of Mr. Arnold's Ancient Order.

Footsteps pounded up behind him. Peter swallowed. "They . . . they have her. They really d-do."

"She can handle herself, Mr. Holstein, I assure you. They may have grabbed her in a moment of weakness, but she'll make them wish they hadn't."

But they *had* her — because of *him*.

V was barely breathing hard after his sprint. And he looked around exactly as Locryn would have done, as if he could see something beyond the obvious. Who knew there were really men who could do so?

He nodded to the north. Toward Mr. Arnold's property. "What lies that direction? Anything that would aid them?"

"An . . . an orchard. A small shed."

"A likely place to begin, then. But do tread carefully, Mr. Holstein — Jasper is likely livid."

He started toward the property line —

more slowly for the sake of quiet. "You know him?"

"*Of* him. He is ambitious, which is always dangerous. And a war-monger long before Arnold sank his claws in. You are not the only man of German heritage he has targeted — nor the only family's records he had stolen from the Archives." V's lips, when Peter looked over at him, were twitching. "He will answer for that too. He thinks he got away with it, but he hired amateurs."

Peter shook his head and faced the path before him again. "Unlike . . . unlike you?"

Rather than answer, V held up a hand, motioned ahead. A racket reached them, muted by distance and the whistle of the wind but quite obviously the sound of someone pounding upon wood. Rosemary, he'd bet, in the shed.

Two policemen came into view within another few steps, hunkered down behind a mass of scrub. They turned their heads when they heard them, and Peter recognized both — local men, though they lived in the next village. They weren't likely to know the property all that well.

The younger of the two, with ginger hair peeking from his cap, nodded. "Four men, all armed with pistols. The sons of Pomeroy and Foote, that chap the constable said he'd been keeping an eye on, and one we've never seen. Well dressed."

"Mr. Jasper." V crouched down beside them.

"We saw them put the young lady in a shed. We hoped Newth would send reinforcements soon. Two guns to four didn't seem good odds."

"Three to four is doable though." V drew a pistol from under his jacket and glanced at Peter. "I don't suppose you have one?"

Locryn was never without his sidearm and machete — Peter could boast only a pencil in his pocket and a folded sheet of paper already half-scribbled upon. Unplanned inspiration was the only emergency he usually faced. "I don't . . . don't need one. I'll be the . . . the distraction." He met the gaze of the ginger-haired bobby. "You two can . . . can sneak around behind. I'll . . . confront them. V will . . . cover me."

The second officer peeked over the scrub. "Is there cover in that direction? We hesitated to venture beyond this point, not knowing what is past that rock outcropping."

He could tell them, but it would be just as simple to show them. And so he motioned for them to follow him and led them at ninety degrees from the shed, through the bit of woods stretching from his land and then into the plum orchard.

Here the trees were neat and orderly, their golden fruit hanging a week or two from ripeness. Thanks to the slope of it, they could easily remain out of sight of the shed and make their way around, then head to the path that led up the hill from the Arnold house, toward the shed.

Rosemary's banging was louder here, and punctuated with a stream of Cockney-flavored threats more creative than crude. Male curses stained the air too as Cornish voices told her to quiet down.

Peter motioned toward the path. "Give me . . . a few minutes. To get their atten . . . attention."

They nodded and proceeded toward the shed, careful to stay out of sight. Peter turned back the way he'd come. And paused at the last tree in the orchard. When he'd been six, the limbs had seemed impossibly high. He'd had to climb up on Gryff's shoulders to steal those unripe plums.

Today he had only to lift his arm and pluck one. He hadn't known as a child that he'd no need to steal them — Mr. Arnold had told his family they could have whatever they wanted. Had always, always made himself seem to be such a good friend to the Holsteins.

And why? When all this time he suspected the worst of them? Hated them because of the country from which they hailed?

The plum he pulled off was beautiful, its flesh golden and dappled with red. But it was hard yet. It would be as sour as those stolen ones. He slipped it into his pocket along with the silver coin and hurried back to V.

He was greeted with a lifted brow. "What exactly is your plan, Mr. Holstein?"

Peter didn't bother hunkering down again. He rather stepped past the scrub, back on the deer trail that would lead more or less to the shed. "Simple. Let them . . . think they've won."

V drew in a long breath. "Be careful. England can't afford to lose you."

When this was over, he needed more of an explanation than *that* from the man. But for now, he had to free Rosemary from that dark little prison. He started forward with a whispered prayer, stepping on every twig and leaf he saw to warn them of his approach. Still, he doubted they could hear him over the din she was making.

They spotted him, though, the moment he cleared the rock outcropping and came into view. He held up his arms, away from his sides — even so, two of the four men promptly pointed their weapons at him. Jasper and his grey-haired lackey. The two local boys were occupied holding closed the door that shook with every pound from within.

Months had passed since Peter had last seen Jasper's sneering face, and he'd rather hoped a few more would go by before he saw it again. The fine suit of clothes, the expensive hat that couldn't cover the darkness in the man's eyes. "Stop right there, Holstein!"

Peter could barely hear him over Rosemary, but he made it out well enough to obey.

Jasper turned his head just a bit, toward Foote. "Get her out of there so she'll shut up!"

"But —"

"You heard me."

Exchanging a wary look, Foote and Pomeroy obeyed. Slowly. They let off the door, flipped the latch. Rosemary came hurtling out, obviously not expecting the door to have moved. The men caught her by the arms, holding her so tightly it would no doubt bruise her arms.

Though to be fair, both men had a nice collection of scratches on their faces, proving Rosemary had not gone into the shed without a fight. He would bet their shins were sporting bruises as well, and any other place she'd managed to land a kick.

But she went silent and still when she spotted him. And perhaps the weapons aimed at him. Proof that she cared? Or that, like her *employer,* she thought him valuable to the country somehow?

His nostrils flared. "You have what you . . . what you want, J-Jasper. I gave . . . gave Arnold the deed. To the mill."

Jasper snorted and shifted from one foot to the other. The pistol, gleaming silver and deadly, looked out of place in his hands. He was, despite his behavior just now, a gentleman, city-bred. His shoes weren't built for tromping through the countryside, and perspiration darkened his jacket. He was a man with money, with power enough to make Peter's life miserable in London. Why had he decided to focus it where he had?

"That's what Mr. Arnold wanted — but not me. I won't be happy until you're out of England, Holstein, where you can't fill the king's ear with your peace nonsense anymore." He relaxed his arm for a moment — or seemed to. But then he simply swung the gun around and pressed it to Rosemary's temple.

Peter lunged forward a step, then stopped when the grey-haired man chuckled. As if inviting him to come farther, to test them.

Jasper's lips twitched. "Here's what you're going to do. My man Fisher here is going to accompany you back to your house, where you will have ten minutes to pack a bag. He's going to see you to a train, and then to a boat. I don't much care where you go, but it's going to be away from England — and there will be no point in your coming back. With the documentation I have against you, you'd be shuttled off to an internment camp, at the best. Imprisoned for espionage at the worst. So you will send me a wire as soon as you arrive in your new home. Knowing that each and every day you don't, beginning tomorrow, this little woman here is going to lose a finger. And then we'll move on to her toes. And if we run out of those —"

"Idiot." Rosemary stood tall, straight, not struggling against the ruffians nor flinching away from the barrel of the gun. She managed to look defiant, proud as she turned his sneer back on him. "Do you really think he'll give up his home to save *me*?"

Jasper pressed harder, forcing her head to angle. "I think he'd give it up to save anyone, even that stupid pickpocket in the village jail. Isn't that right, Mr. Holstein?"

He wanted to glance past Jasper, to assure himself that the bobbies were as close as he thought they were. He caught only a glimpse of uniform, but surely he wouldn't have seen even that if they weren't in position. "Of . . . of course I would. A life . . . is worth more . . . than a house."

"A noble sentiment that I'm afraid you won't have the opportunity to prove." V's voice came from a good ways behind Peter — no doubt he'd just stepped out from behind the boulder.

Fisher's aim shifted to V, Jasper's to Peter.

The two policemen stole along the sides of the shed.

Peter met Rosemary's gaze. He didn't have the time to read anything within it. Only to widen his own, to yell, "Down!"

Then it was a blur. A shot from Fisher. Another from behind Peter. The policemen charged forward, tackling the local boys to the ground. Rosemary dived away.

And then Jasper moved again, swinging that arm back toward her. Pointing his gun at her again, and this time Peter knew he meant to fire. To hurt him however he could before he went down, and no doubt knowing it would hurt worse to shoot Rosemary than Peter.

He had no time to think, just to act. To pull the plum from his pocket and lob the unlikely missile at Jasper. It couldn't do much damage — but it hit him squarely, hard, and made him flinch.

His shot went wild. And then in the next second Peter's feet carried him forward, shoulder down much like young Tim's had been when he'd rammed him in Mr. Arnold's front hall.

Perhaps Jasper hadn't brothers — or friends — to wrestle with as a boy. He *oomphed* at the collision, stumbled back, fell. The pistol went sliding out of his hand, and then slid farther still with the help of Rosemary's half-boot.

"I suggest you stay right where you are." V edged into Peter's periphery, his pistol extended.

Though his lip curled, Jasper obeyed. "Defending him is futile. Even if he stays in England, he'll end up relocated. He is a German."

V's lips curled up in a mean little smile. "You are as ignorant as you are amateur, Mr. Jasper. This man is a more loyal subject than you could ever hope to be."

Footsteps pounded their way from the direction of Peter's property — Newth must have dispatched more men to come and help them. Peter spared only a glance over his shoulder to verify and then straightened.

His gaze snagged on Rosemary again. Her hair was more down than up, the green linen of her dress stained brown by dirt and struggle, and shadows ringed her eyes.

Should he be angry with her? Disappointed, betrayed? He could feel none of that just now. Only profound relief that she was well. And so when she flew at him, his arms opened and then closed around her.

He held her close. Breathed in the lemon scent of her hair. "Are you . . . are you all right?"

She clung to him. "Thanks to you. Did you really save me with a plum?"

He chuckled, holding her tight and wishing this moment could last forever. Even as part of him knew it was a fool's wish. "It's . . . it's all I had handy."

"Locryn would be proud."

And that was what made him a fool. She knew — had to have known, to have told Mr. V. And that couldn't go unanswered. He set her back, stepped away.

And the light in her eyes went dim. "Right." Her arms slipped back down to her sides, and she looked over his shoulder, toward where the sound of feet crunching over last year's leaves filled the air.

The bobbies taking the thugs away. It took them a long moment to do so, to haul up the bleeding Fisher, the growling Jasper, the silent local boys who were no doubt wishing they'd chosen their side with more care. But eventually they were all tromping away, into the wind and over the leaves.

Except for one set of footsteps that came nearer instead. Peter didn't have to look to know who it was. He kept his gaze leveled on Rosemary.

She lowered her chin and rubbed her hands against her soiled skirt. "What did you tell him, sir?"

V stopped somewhere behind Peter. "The truth, Miss Gresham. That you were here at my behest. For the good of England."

The good of England. He said that so easily. "What is it . . . exactly . . . that you want me t-to do, V?"

"What you've been doing, Mr. Holstein. Write novels."

Now he *had* to turn, to look the stranger in the eye and try to make sense of that. "I . . . planned to."

V's lips curved, just slightly, toward a smile. "Unless you decided you must sign up in some way or another. But we can't allow that. The country — the *world* is going to need your words. Your stories and novels

637

and novellas. They need Locryn James to show them the way to be a hero."

Peter shook his head. "But —"

"You're not the only one we'll be asking. We'll be approaching Wells, Conan Doyle — all the popular novelists, especially those with a strong readership in America." The curve turned up a bit more. "We're likely to need them, before this is all over. We've got to make them think now that it's a cause worth dying for."

Peter shifted from one foot to the other. "You mean t-to . . . to tell me what to write?"

V chuckled. "No, nothing so restrictive. We just may ask you, from time to time, to include a certain theme. The nobility of fighting for one's country, for instance. Or, in the case of the females who cannot, of sending off their men to do it. If you are willing."

Peter looked at this near-stranger opposite him. Glanced at the bedraggled woman who had become so much more. Listened to the ever-fading sounds of policemen advising villains to behave themselves and many footsteps leading them away.

And he sighed. "I would have . . . would have done . . . it anyway. With . . . without all this."

V took a step back, hands clasped again behind him. "Well, we had to be sure of that, didn't we? And now we are." He took one more step back and pivoted halfway away. "Someone will be in touch, Mr. Holstein. And Miss Gresham — if you rethink your stance, do let me know. I hate to lose you."

Lose her? Peter waited until he had vanished, until the sounds of everyone's departure faded away entirely. Then, only then, did he turn to face her. "I believe . . . I believe you have something to tell me."

Rosemary walked beside him, a foot away. She had thought perhaps it would be easier if they were moving.

She was wrong. Sighing, she rubbed her hands on her skirt again and fastened her gaze on the long, spiky leaves of the Cornish palm. She would miss this place when she was gone. "I don't know where to begin."

"I have f-found the . . . the beginning is often a g-good place."

He was stuttering. Because of *her*. Rosemary turned her face away, not daring to look at his. Not now. "The beginning. I suppose that's when I was eight. When my parents died and left me an orphan."

How could he make one little exhale

sound so . . . disappointed? "What ab—bout . . . all those siblings?"

She snapped off a twig as they walked by it, just to give her fingers something to worry. "I found Pauly first. Or he found me, rooting through his rubbish when I was nine. His wife wouldn't let him take me in. So he left me a meal every day, when someone else didn't steal it first. Then he found Barclay. Willa. We decided to stick together."

He made no response, not that she could hear. Just kept walking beside her with steady, measured steps.

She might have cried again had she any tears left in her. "He helped us get a flat. It worked, for a while, until the building burned down. Lucy and Retta were both orphaned that night. So they joined us. Then the others over the years, as we found them. They *are* my family. Just . . . not by blood."

"How did you . . . survive?"

She let the twig fall again. "The only way we could. We stole."

A chuff. "That is . . . that is n-never the only . . . way."

"You've never lived on the streets. You don't know what it's like." She shouldn't be so defensive about it — but it was one of those toes that was still cold. Beginning to tingle from the warmth, as Mrs. Teague would say, but not quite there yet. She huffed back at him and rubbed at her nose. "It was all we knew. And . . . and we were good at it. Good enough that it attracted some attention, apparently."

From her periphery, she saw him shove his hands into his pockets. "V."

Which led them to the heart of the matter as they emerged from the trees and into the heather and gorse that led the way to the cliffs in one direction, the house in the other. He stopped, and stopped her with a hand on her arm, and then she had to look up at him. To look and see the blue-green eyes that matched the sea where it crashed against the rocks, and the storms in them that matched the clouds rolling over it. "How m-much . . . how much was a . . . lie?"

She wanted to walk into his arms and hold him tight. She wanted to run down that path to the house, and past it, to where she wouldn't ever have to face him again. She wanted . . . she wanted the words to be something other than what they were.

She lifted her arms away from her body. Let them fall. "I'm right-handed. I don't wear spectacles. My name is really Rosemary Gresham, but I've never had a day's proper education in my life. I'm not a librarian. I thought I might suffocate when I walked into that room of yours."

His hands were still in his pockets. And the storm clouds were still swirling in his eyes.

She sniffed. "Mr. V told me I was here to find evidence against you — but I couldn't. Because you really are the . . . the best man in the world. That's the truth." Maybe she *did* have a few tears left, because they burned, and she had to sniff again to restrain them. "I'm a thief — but I couldn't steal your good name. That's the truth too."

His nostrils flared. "Is that . . . all?"

"No." She couldn't do this, she'd fall to pieces. Sucking in a deep breath that did nothing to help, she said, "I broke into your office the other day. Well, the door was unlocked. I didn't break into the room — just your desk. I saw the manuscript. But I didn't take it, I swear to you I didn't. It isn't there now, but that wasn't me — and I only know it's gone because I was making sure it was still secure, when I left you the note and your documents."

Silence, but only for a beat. "I . . . I took it all out. So I c-could . . . give everything to you. Tell you. Who I am." Another beat.

"I didn't . . . didn't realize y-you already . . ."

And he made her feel more a villain than ever. She backed up a step, kept her gaze focused on the slope behind him, toward his house. "I'm sorry. That's more the truth than anything. That and . . . and I wrote it all in the note. You can just read it."

He didn't move. "I d-don't . . . don't want to r-read it."

She edged another step toward the path. Felt the return of last night's gasps, even without last night's sobbing. "Well then. It was — mostly just what I already said. And — and a bit about Barclay at the end — you can ignore that. Mr. V won't really be going after him after all, not to arrest him. He apparently didn't even know he worked the museum job with me."

"The *what*?"

Much as she wanted to turn and run away, he deserved the chance to look her in the eye and tell her what he thought of her. "British Museum, four years ago. We . . . may have liberated an old German manuscript. Some religious text Luther had written. I had to learn German, a bit of it, to make sure I lifted the right one, and . . . Why are you looking at me like that?" Like she was a specter. Or a monster.

"That was . . . was you? My father . . . he took me to see it. When I was a b-boy. I remember when it . . . went missing."

"Right, well . . ." She shrugged. "That was me. And Barclay. Mr. V threatened to send me to jail for it if I didn't give him the information he wanted about you, and I couldn't do that, so . . . so that's what was in the note. That I couldn't, and I was likely already arrested by the time you'd be reading it, and if you would just send a wire to Barclay — but you needn't. Obviously."

He just looked at her. And looked at her. And finally said, "Anything . . . else? In th—the . . . the note?"

He could read it when he got down there. Likely would, eventually. He'd know, eventually.

But he deserved this too. To know the truth, even if he despised her for it. "Just that . . . it wasn't a lie. Anything else. All the things I wrote to you, all the . . . and last night. That definitely wasn't a lie. That I've fallen in love with you, and that I've changed, and that I don't want to be the person I was anymore. And . . ." And still he just stood there. "And won't you say *something*?"

His Adam's apple bobbed as he swallowed, and he took his hands out of his pockets. "I . . ." He gestured, though he didn't move any closer. "Y-You . . ." And then he shook his head, and he lifted one finger in that way he'd done her first days here. And he dashed off, like he hadn't had to do in months, with that look on his face that said his tongue was in knots.

She followed, part of her wanting to yell at him that he'd forced *her* to just say what was in the note, so he ought to do the same, rather than writing one.

But that wasn't fair. Writing was who he was, how he best communicated. If he had to write his response, write the words that would send her out of his life, then . . . then she would let him.

He was charging into Kensey while she was still picking her way over the flat granite stones marking the path, and she sighed and debated. She couldn't go back in there, where she'd have to face Mrs. Teague and Grammy. And there were all those bobbies milling about the front. She couldn't see much of what was going on, but it looked like Mr. V was shaking the hand of one.

She headed for the cottage, where her valise waited by the door. She'd wait with it. She'd let him write his say, and then she'd leave.

The cottage welcomed her, warm and

cozy and not hers. It smelled of the tea Mrs. Teague had made, of the fairings Grammy had sent over.

She picked up one. The thought of eating it still made her stomach turn, but she'd need something for the road.

She'd go back to London — she had nowhere else. Home to her family and their tiny little flat and then . . . She'd try to find work. Honest work. With a seamstress, she supposed, even if she *would* be miserable in half a day. Jenny would give her a recommendation, she was sure, and . . .

Footsteps hurried along the garden path.

She set the biscuit down again and turned. Stepped back outside.

Peter stopped an arm's width away. Held out one of those folded rectangles of white.

It looked like a snake, ready to bite her. But she made herself reach out and take it. Drew in a long breath. Let it out. And opened it.

I love you, Rosemary Gresham. And I can think of no greater honor than to have you as my wife.

"Oh!" She lowered the note, pressing a hand to her lips.

He was on a knee before her, reaching for her hand. She gave it to him. And told that ridiculous sob trying to escape that she had no more tears left, so it had better go away. "How can you? How can you want me, knowing what I am?"

He kissed the knuckle where Mrs. Teague had retied the bandage. "That's not . . . not who you are. It's just . . . something you did."

"But — but I'm not the right kind of girl for you, even so. I'm a street rat. I know nothing of your world."

And yet his eyes gleamed. At her, for her. "And I . . . I love that about you."

Blast, but her nose felt all stuffy again. She gripped his hand and sniffed. "But I'll change things — you have to know that too. If you make me mistress of a place like this, I can't just let things run as they've always done."

And now the corners of his lips turned up. "I'm counting on it."

She tugged on his hand. "Get up, you idiot. How in the world am I supposed to kiss you if you're all the way down there?"

He got up, grinning, and stepped close.

She framed his face. But didn't kiss him quite yet. First she had to look deep into those eyes. "Are you quite serious? Even though I'm the least suitable woman you could possibly choose?"

He pulled her closer. Swallowed. "You're

the . . . the *only* woman I would . . . I would ever choose. If you'll . . . have me. Holstein is . . . is not exactly a popular name . . . just now."

She ran her fingers over his cheek, along his jaw. Over that cleft in his chin. "It's the noblest name in the world. I'd be honored to take it."

He rested his forehead against hers, but still she saw his smile. "Then it's yours."

Twenty-Eight

London
13 August 1914

Peter paced to the window. Again. And looked out at the view, such as it was, of London. The townhouse his father had chosen was in a good part of town, had a decent view of the park across the street. Neighbors who thought themselves worth knowing.

He just wanted to get done here and to go back to Cornwall. It wouldn't get him away from all the unfathomable news pouring in — Germany invading Belgium, refugees flooding England, campaigns being mounted in France. Suspected spies being rounded up even now all over Britain and imprisoned . . . and the announcement had already gone out that all German- and Austrian-born men between the ages of eighteen and fifty were to be relocated to camps on the Isle of Man.

His documents would protect him — but barely. V may have called the Archives thieves amateurs, but they had destroyed the original paperwork. Had Rosemary not found his copies, he would have been one of those relocated. Already he'd had to present his proof to the magistrate, to prove he was an English subject.

Even so. It would be better to be home again, out of the hustle and noise of London. Though he'd promised they'd spend a week or two here, at least.

He turned away from the window. Again. And back to where Rosemary sat on the couch, his manuscript in her lap. "Aren't you . . . finished yet?"

She didn't look up at him, just twirled a curl around her finger. And read, he was sure, all the more slowly. Just to spite him. "Perhaps I would be, luv, if there weren't so many interruptions."

He very nearly growled. This was why he liked the idea of the *nom de plume.* He detested knowing when someone was reading his books. Wondering what they thought. "You've had it . . . for a week. You don't . . . you don't read that slowly. I know you don't."

She sent him a look that was one part amusement and two parts exasperation. She had learned it, he was sure, from Mrs. Teague and Grammy. Which just proved how quick she was at *some* things. "I had a *few* other things to tend to in that week, don't you think?"

Back to the window. "You can . . . you can tell me if you hate it. I won't . . . cry or anything. Much. Just . . . just whimper. And pout. Make you regret ever . . . ever agreeing to be my wife."

"Peter."

"What?" He turned, though she *still* had pages in her lap, waiting to be read. *"What?"*

She gave him that little grin that did funny things to his heart. "Stop talking. Please."

He returned the grin. And strode to the couch to lean down and press a kiss to her lips.

She kissed him back — then pushed him away. "My favorite distraction, but we're short on time just now, and this thing is due to your publisher tomorrow, so why don't you just go to your study? Write something."

Write something. As if he could write something when she was sitting there reading the *last* thing he'd written.

But he left the drawing room — with a few loud grumbles about being booted out of it — and made his way to the study.

It wasn't like the one at home. Not so

large and roomy, not so filled with all the things he loved. But his typewriter was there on the desk he hadn't had a chance to clutter yet, so he sat at it. And since he did have that idea for a Locryn James short story swirling about in his head, he supposed he might as well get a start on it. It might not be any good, but he could always restart it later. Once they were home.

A sentence turned into a paragraph, and a paragraph turned into a page, and after three pages arms encircled his neck and he almost — *almost* — regretted the interruption.

Though not quite. He rubbed a hand over her wrist. "*Now* are you . . . finished?"

She chuckled in his ear. "Now I'm finished."

He stood from his chair and, since she didn't move her arms, put his around her. "Well? Did you . . . did you hate it?"

He would never tire of looking at that smile. Never. Nor of hearing her laugh. "How could I possibly hate it? It's the best thing you've ever written, Mr. Hollow."

A bit of tension slid right out of his shoulders. "Are you sure you're . . . you're not just saying that? Because you love me?"

Her fingers moved up into his hair. "They are both facts. Independent of one another."

His lips twitched up. Then down. "Even though I . . . I made you a villain?"

Laughing again, she leaned up to smack a kiss onto his lips. "You didn't make me a villain, luv. You made me an *excellent* villain." Then she leaned back, stretching against his arms. "I do believe Rosita is now my favorite character. I think I like her even better than I do Locryn."

He leaned down for another kiss. "I think I . . . I might too."

She lingered there for a moment, her fingers smoothing down the hair she'd mussed, resting her head against his shoulder. "Are you sure about all this?"

He didn't know if she meant his plan to deliver the manuscript in person tomorrow . . . or their plans for tonight. But either way, the answer was the same. "Very sure."

She nodded. Straightened. Smoothed his tie. "Then I suppose we'd better go."

Rosemary rounded the corner, her hand tucked securely around Peter's arm, and led him down the familiar street, toward the glowing light from the pub. Night clung to the buildings, to the hollows between the streetlights. But her step was light. And her heart was light.

And she had to smile at how out of place

Peter looked in this neighborhood — though to his credit, he didn't look around him as if expecting someone to mug him at any moment.

Though he probably should have. Rosemary saw the shadow slip out of the deeper shadows by the building, slide up to him, and reach for his pocket.

With reflexes born of necessity, she jerked him out of the way and prepared a hand for the would-be mugger's jugular.

Laughter stopped her, and she growled out, "Georgie! What have I *told* you about that?"

Her little brother stepped into the light and gathered her into a tight squeeze. "To wait for a rich bloke — and have you seen that one's shoes?"

Beside her, where she'd shoved him, Peter laughed.

Rosemary gave Georgie a fierce hug. And then slapped him on the arm as she pulled away, which only served to draw her attention to the olive cloth covering it. Her chest went tight. "Look at you. You've enlisted." Only officially at war for ten days and already England had one of her brothers.

"Gotta champion poor little Belgium. Besides . . ." He smoothed down his uniform. "They promised three squares a day

— can't beat that, can you?"

"No." Gracious, he still looked like a baby. Made her feel so blasted old. "You cut a handsome figure in it too. Though you do know you're going to have to behave yourself, right? Pick the wrong pockets there and —"

"I know, I know." Still grinning like a boy, he stuck out a hand toward Peter. "You must be Pete. I just came from the flat — had to check on Liv — and Ellie said I'd just missed you. Had to run to catch up, it's a wonder you didn't hear me."

Peter shook Georgie's hand, nodding. "Good to . . . to meet you."

Georgie grinned. "Come on then, this is going to be a good show." He spun toward Pauly's. And tossed over his shoulder, "Better watch those cufflinks, Pete."

Peter tugged on the sleeves of his jacket.

Rosemary chuckled. "He's only teasing. They don't steal from family." Except for a joke. In which case they'd give them back. Probably.

They hurried to catch up to Georgie, who was already pushing open the door to the pub. Light spilled out, along with the smell of meat pies, and music.

She bounced a bit and grinned at Peter. "Willa's playing."

Beautiful cacophony met them as they entered. Georgie was already sidling through the usual crowd, on his way to the back table where the family sat. All of them but the little ones, who would have already been here to eat and then gone home, and Elinor, who was looking after them. She'd been the one to inform Rosemary and Peter, when they'd dropped by Rosemary's flat, that everyone was here.

Then had leaned close, eyes still on Peter as he made friends with Olivia, and said, "His *chin,* Rosie! His *chin.*"

Hopefully they would all agree to come to Cornwall, for a visit if not forever. At least the little ones, though she could hardly imagine Willa and Barclay ever agreeing to leave their own turf. She couldn't imagine them accepting help that they didn't earn — or take — with their own hands.

But she would try.

Willa's back was to the door, her arms flying as her violin sang out some fast, feverish song that made her hair slip from its bun. The others, in the back, hadn't noticed anyone but Georgie. She tugged Peter toward the bar and slapped a hand to the counter. "Hey, barkeep!"

Pauly turned, eyes wide, and came at her with a laugh. "Rosie! You're back!"

She stretched across the bar to kiss his cheek. "What are you doing serving meat pies on a Thursday?"

"Hey now, missy — you disappear for months on end and there's no telling what might change." He gave her a wink. "Want one?"

"Two. But one's for him." She hooked a thumb at Peter and grinned. "Look after this one for me for a minute, will you, Pauly?"

Curiosity lit his eyes, but he only said, "Sure thing."

Peter smiled. "I know my . . . my cue."

Well then. Showtime. And perfectly timed — Willa was just finishing up her song, and the pub erupted in applause. Rosemary added a whistle to the mix, which nabbed her sister's attention, and shouted out, "Irish, right?"

Eyes wide, Willa lunged for her. "Rosie! You're home!" They held each other tight, Willa's violin thumping Rosemary's back, digging in.

She didn't care. "Of course I'm home."

"I'm sorry we fought."

"Well." They pulled away, and Rosemary smiled. "You were right — a bit. And wrong a bit."

Willa set the violin on her stool on the

657

little stage. "Care to explain that one?"

Rosemary just motioned for her to follow her toward their table.

Retta was the first to spot her, then Lucy. Soon they were all there, clamoring for a hug, talking over each other, shouting out questions and answers and laughter. She hugged them all and laughed along with them, then leaned against the table when Barclay told them all to sit down and let her get a word in.

He, naturally, sat in his usual place in the center and gave her that grin that bordered on too-handsome. "Well, I'd ask how the job went, Rosie-Posy, but given all those crisp pound notes Mr. V delivered a week ago, we already know that. And we've been waiting to spend it until you got home, I'll have you know. Thought you deserve a say."

She laughed. "Winter coats for everyone. Decent shoes. And, I think, a bottle of champagne. To celebrate."

Barclay nodded his approval. "I am all for celebrating a job well done — and you certainly did it."

"Oh, we're not just celebrating the *job*. We're celebrating the bet, Barclay Pearce."

Beside her, Willa grabbed her arm. "You didn't. You couldn't have."

"Oh, I did. I could." Rosemary reached

into her ever-present handbag, fished around for the metal, and dropped it onto the table in front of Barclay. The key ring fell with a happy clatter. "The keys to Kensey Manor, Penzance, Cornwall, sir. My new home."

Barclay rolled his eyes. "Good try, Rosie, but those could be keys to an old steamer trunk, for all I know."

"Hence why I didn't just come with keys. I came with paperwork." She pulled out the local Cornwall rag, already open to its society pages, and slapped it down in front of him.

Barclay's brows knit. "Marriage announcements?"

"Because I didn't just steal the manor, Barclay. I stole the master of the house too."

For a moment, there was only silence within the pub's din. Then . . . then, *not* silence.

"He *married* you?" Willa's shrill squeal was in tandem with her jerking Rosemary's hand from the table, nearly sending her sprawling. Her eyes went wide at the diamond and gold that sparkled in the light. "He married you!"

"He married me." She may stop grinning about it eventually. Perhaps.

Retta leaned across the table to have a

look too. "That was awfully fast, wasn't it?"

"Well, I had to act before he changed his mind, you know." Her eyes went to the bar, where Peter was straightening, and straightening the satchel on his shoulder. "He's all the time changing his mind. Moving to the next new thing. Never can stick with a thing, can Peter Holstein, as Willa can attest to, having ridden in his vehicle of choice."

Willa snorted a laugh. "His ancient horse and carriage, you mean? Oh yes. Obviously very fickle, that man."

His eyes were smiling at her as he made his way through the crowd toward them. Rosemary settled on the edge of the table. "Then there was the other woman I had to contend with. Elowyn — pretty as you please but no match for my wiles, of course. And when we told her Peter and I were getting married, she cried for thirty . . . whole . . . seconds."

He was only a few steps away now, his lips grinning along with his eyes. "Until she . . . she realized she got to keep . . . *you* around."

"And you promised her a new dolly while you were in London." She lifted a finger, pressed it to his chest. "You spoil that girl."

He just chuckled.

Willa gave him a friendly punch in the arm. "You married her."

"Now wait just a minute." Barclay stood again, pushing his chair back with a clatter. "First of all, it's not stealing a manor if he *gives* it to you."

"I think it's even better," Georgie declared from his seat. "Takes far more skill, if you ask me."

"Hear, hear!" Retta lifted her coffee mug.

Barclay just glared at them. "And *moreover* . . ." He turned that glare on Rosemary. "You can't just go off marrying a man we've never even met. How am I supposed to know if he's good enough for you?"

She glanced to Peter, who smiled and said, "You must be . . . be Barclay."

"Yes, I am, and as the head of this family, it's my responsibility to . . ." He frowned as Peter opened his satchel and started emptying it onto the table. "What are you doing?"

Peter didn't look up. "B-Bribing you."

"With books? You can't appease me with books." Though he reached for one and ran a hand along the smooth, crisp edge. The uncreased binding. "Even my *favorite* books."

Rosemary tried, and failed, to bite back a smile. "Open it, you idiot. Read the inscription."

"Inscription?" He flipped open the cover, tilted his head. " 'To Barclay, a new brother

I cannot wait to get to know. Branok Hollow.' " For a moment he just stared at it. Then stared at her. "You . . ." At Peter. "He . . . ? You married Branok Hollow?"

At her nod, he slapped down the book and yelled out, "Pauly, champagne! We need champagne!"

Laughter sounded again, and chaos, and the scraping of more chairs. Peter was pushed into one, and Rosemary to the one beside him, and Pauly emerged with a dusty bottle just waiting to pop its cork. He hadn't the right glasses for it, and no one got more than a few bubbles poured in their mugs, but that hardly mattered.

Barclay stood, his mug raised. "A toast! To Rosemary, one of my eight favorite sisters, and to our new brother, Branok."

"Peter." Rosemary grinned. "His real name is Peter."

"I don't care what his real name is, the book says Branok, I'm calling him Branok. Now, as I was saying —" Barclay waited for the laughter to die down before lifting his mug another few inches. "To Rosemary and her new husband. May you enjoy many happy years together. May you never forget to invite your family down for the holidays, nor fail to pay for their tickets."

More laughter. Rosemary reached for

Peter's hand, found it, and squeezed. Maybe they *would* let them help. At least a little.

Barclay met her gaze. Smiled. "May you never forget that with the greatest risks come the greatest rewards. Cheers!"

"Cheers!" She drank her sip of bubbly, held her husband's fingers tight in hers, and looked up when a familiar hand came to rest on her shoulder.

Pauly stood there, smiling down at her. Accepting her, as he always had done, however she was. "Been a good girl, Rosie?"

She leaned her cheek against his hand. "I have, actually. And you know what?" She surveyed this world, this family, these people who were hers, no matter their faults. And she smiled. "It's not so bad."

A NOTE FROM THE AUTHOR

Sometimes I can trace a book back to one discovery or question — and that's the case here. In my research for my previous series, I ran across the information that, during World War I, King George V had his last name legally changed from the German-sounding Saxe-Coburg to the more English-sounding Windsor. That stuck in my mind, and as I was exploring options for a new series, I started there. Which promptly led me to the question of, "What if someone else contemplated doing the same thing?" A little more reading, and I also discovered that some of England's most popular novelists were recruited by the government during the war to include propaganda messages in their novels — many specifically targeting American readers. Within a few hours, I had my stuttering novelist of German descent, and a thief trying to steal his good name. And I was thoroughly enamored with them both.

I loved learning about the beautiful region of Cornwall and describing for you some of the breathtaking scenery to be found there, which I had the pleasure of seeing for myself while still editing this book. I loved giving you a glimpse of Prince Edward, who did indeed manage to visit the front lines during the war, earning himself a medal in the process — he was a prince who was sung as a hero, loved by his people . . . and was king only for a year, after which he abdicated the crown to his younger brother so that he could marry the woman he loved (a divorcée, which wasn't sanctioned by the Church).

But most of all, I loved exploring the hearts and minds of these characters from two very different worlds and finding where they'd have common ground.

I can't, of course, speak to the thought processes of all novelists, but I will tell you that Peter's lapses into thinking about his novel are very much the way I go through my days when I'm actively involved in a story. You just never know what fleeting glimpse or random statement might trigger something for me. And though I don't keep my office door shut (wouldn't even if I had one), my family does know that they might have to ask for something two or three (or five) times before I actually hear what they're saying and get up to respond. I once even shushed my children because my characters were trying to avoid detection. The mind of a writer can be a crazy thing — I hope you enjoyed diving a bit into Peter's.

And I hope you join me for the rest of the series! Rosemary's family is in for a lot of adventure during the war years, thanks to Mr. V.

And remember — with the greatest risks come the greatest rewards.

ABOUT THE AUTHOR

Roseanna M. White pens her novels beneath her Betsy Ross flag, with her Jane Austen action figure watching over her. When not writing fiction, she's homeschooling her two children, editing and designing, and pretending her house will clean itself. Roseanna is the author of over a dozen historical novels and novellas, ranging from biblical fiction to American-set romances to her series set in Britain. She makes her home in the breathtaking mountains of West Virginia. You can learn more about her and her stories at www.roseanna white.com.

The employees of Thorndike Press hope you have enjoyed this Large Print book. All our Thorndike, Wheeler, and Kennebec Large Print titles are designed for easy reading, and all our books are made to last. Other Thorndike Press Large Print books are available at your library, through selected bookstores, or directly from us.

For information about titles, please call:
    (800) 223-1244

or visit our website at:
    gale.com/thorndike

To share your comments, please write:
    Publisher
    Thorndike Press
    10 Water St., Suite 310
    Waterville, ME 04901

BROOK IROQ WASHINGTON PUBLIC LIBRARY
P.O. BOX 155, 100 W. MAIN ST.
BROOK, IN 47922

DATE DUE